P9-CFQ-870

Secret of the Moon Conch

SECRET OF THE MOON CONCH

DAVID BOWLES
GUADALUPE GARCIA McCALL

BLOOMSBURY
NEW YORK LONDON OXFORD NEW DELHI SYDNEY

BLOOMSBURY YA
Bloomsbury Publishing Inc., part of Bloomsbury Publishing Plc
1385 Broadway, New York, NY 10018

BLOOMSBURY and the Diana logo are trademarks of Bloomsbury Publishing Plc

First published in the United States of America in June 2023 by Bloomsbury YA

Bloomsbury books may be purchased for business or promotional use.
For information on bulk purchases please contact Macmillan Corporate and Premium Sales Department at specialmarkets@macmillan.com

Library of Congress Cataloging-in-Publication Data
available upon request
ISBN 978-1-5476-0989-5 (hardcover) • ISBN 978-1-5476-0990-1 (e-book)

Book design by Jeanette Levy
Typeset by Westchester Publishing Services
Printed and bound in the U.S.A.
2 4 6 8 10 9 7 5 3 1

To find out more about our authors and books
visit www.bloomsbury.com and sign up for our newsletters.

Para Angélica:
Que sigan nuestros seres entrelazados dondequiera o cuandoquiera nos encontremos
—DB

To my beloved,
my warrior, Jim McCall,
because your love transcends time
—GGM

When what was broken is healed
and she who is destined to wield
and he who is commanded to shield
hold the conch in their hands
in two different lands
and each other in their hearts
though leagues and eons apart—
then will I reveal to the staunch
the secret of the moon conch.

In quin in tlapactli moyectlaliz
in quin occan intlalpan in tecciztli
immac quitzitzquizqueh
inyollohpan motzitzquizqueh
in cihuatlapitzcatzin, in oquichtli
in nahuatiloc in quimalhuiz
intlanel nehuan huehueca yezqueh—
in ihcuac nehhuatl niquinextiliz
in ichtacayoh in metztecciztli.

Historical Figures from Tenochtitlan, Capital of the Aztec Empire, 1521

Mexica Nobles and Military Personnel

Acacihtzin. Commander of the Otontin Knights.

Axoquentzin. A captain in the army of Tenochtitlan.

Cemiquiz. Calizto's page.

Cuauhtemoc (24). Last emperor of the Triple Alliance of Anahuac (the Aztec Empire).

Ehcatzin. A captain of the Otontin Knights. Head of Calizto's unit.

Moteuczoma. Tecuichpo's father, former emperor. Died a Spanish prisoner at age 54.

Poloc. Calizto's squad leader in the Otontin Knights.

Tecuichpo (16). Cuauhtemoc's wife, the empress.

Tlacotzin. Prime minister of the Triple Alliance of Anahuac (the Aztec Empire).

Spanish Invaders, Their Allies, and Their Support Staff

Pedro de Alvarado (36). Second-in-command for Hernán Cortés.

Chichimecatl. Commander of the Tlaxcaltecah forces during the siege.

Hernán Cortés (36). Leader of the Spanish invasion of Anahuac.

Malinalli / Marina (17). Indigenous translator who helped Cortés ally with Tlaxcallan.

Alonso de Ojeda. A lieutenant of Hernán Cortés.

Cristóbal de Olea (31). Spanish soldier.

Miguel de Palomares (21). Spanish priest.

Gonzalo de Sandoval (23). A lieutenant of Hernán Cortés.

Andrés de Tapia (24). A lieutenant of Hernán Cortés.

Gods and Legendary Figures

Centzonhuitznahuah. The Four Hundred gods of the Southern Stars.

Cihuacoatl. Goddess of childbirth. She and Quetzalcoatl created humanity.

Coyolxauhqui. Goddess of the moon.

Huehueteotl. God of fire.

Huitzilopochtli. God of war who protects the sun. Patron of the Mexica.

Iztaccihuatl. A Nahua princess who became a dormant volcano after her death.

Mayahuel. Goddess of the maguey plant.

Popocatepetl. An active volcano that was once a Nahua warrior.

Quetzalcoatl. God of order and creation.

Tecciztecatl. God who tends to and protects the moon.

Teteoh Innan. Mother of the gods.

Tezcatlipoca. God of chaos and destruction.

Tlaloc. God of rain.

Tocih. "Our grandmother," a title of Teteoh Innan.

Tonantzin. A divine title meaning "our beloved mother." Also used for the Virgin Mary.

Tonatiuh. God of the sun.

Xochipilli. God of art, games, dance, flowers, and song. Patron of LGBTQ+ folks.

Nahuatl Terms

Calmecac. An elite school for children of the nobility.

Calpoleh. Leader of a calpolli.

Calpolli. A neighborhood or clan.

Caxtiltecah. Spaniards.

Chinampa. A floating garden.

Coatepetl. The Great Pyramid at the center of Tenochtitlan.

Cuauhpilli. An honorary knight, whose military record has won him nobility.

Macana. A wooden sword with a shape like a cricket bat or an oar.

Maccuahuitl. A macana with obsidian blades imbedded along its edges.

Mexica. Nahua people from the isle of Mexico. They control the empire.

Otontin. "Otomi warriors," an elite order of Aztec knights.

Tenochcah. The residents of Tenochtitlan.

Tlatelolcah. The residents of Tlatelolco, the sister city of Tenochtitlan.

Telpochcalli. A neighborhood school for working-class teens.

Telpochtlahtoh. "School master," one of the principal teachers.

Temillotl. A topknot worn by seasoned warriors.

Tepoztopilli. A weapon like a spear or halberd.

Tiachcauh. Head boy, an older student put in charge of younger ones.

Tlaxcaltecah. The main enemy of the Mexica. Allied with the Spanish.

SITLALI'S AND CALIZTO'S JOURNEYS

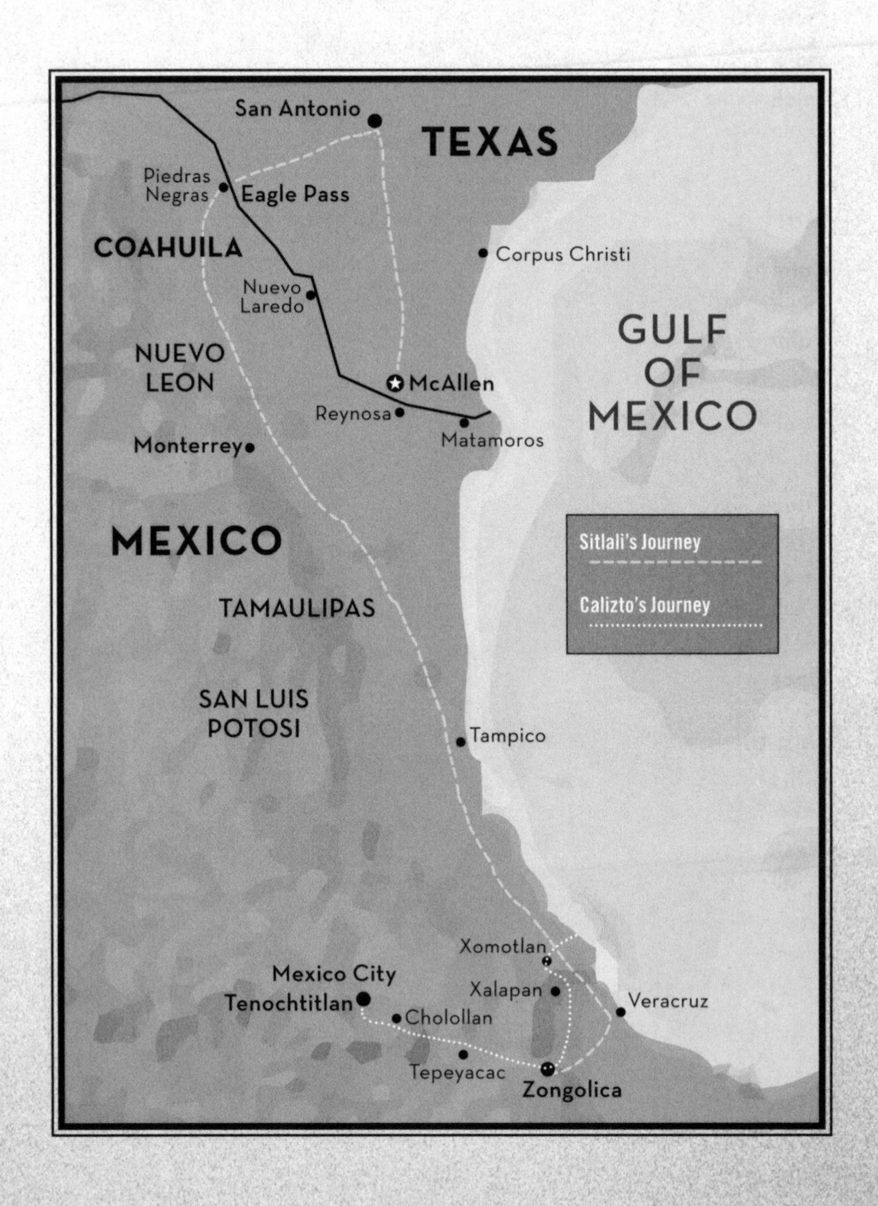

THE ISLE OF MEXICO

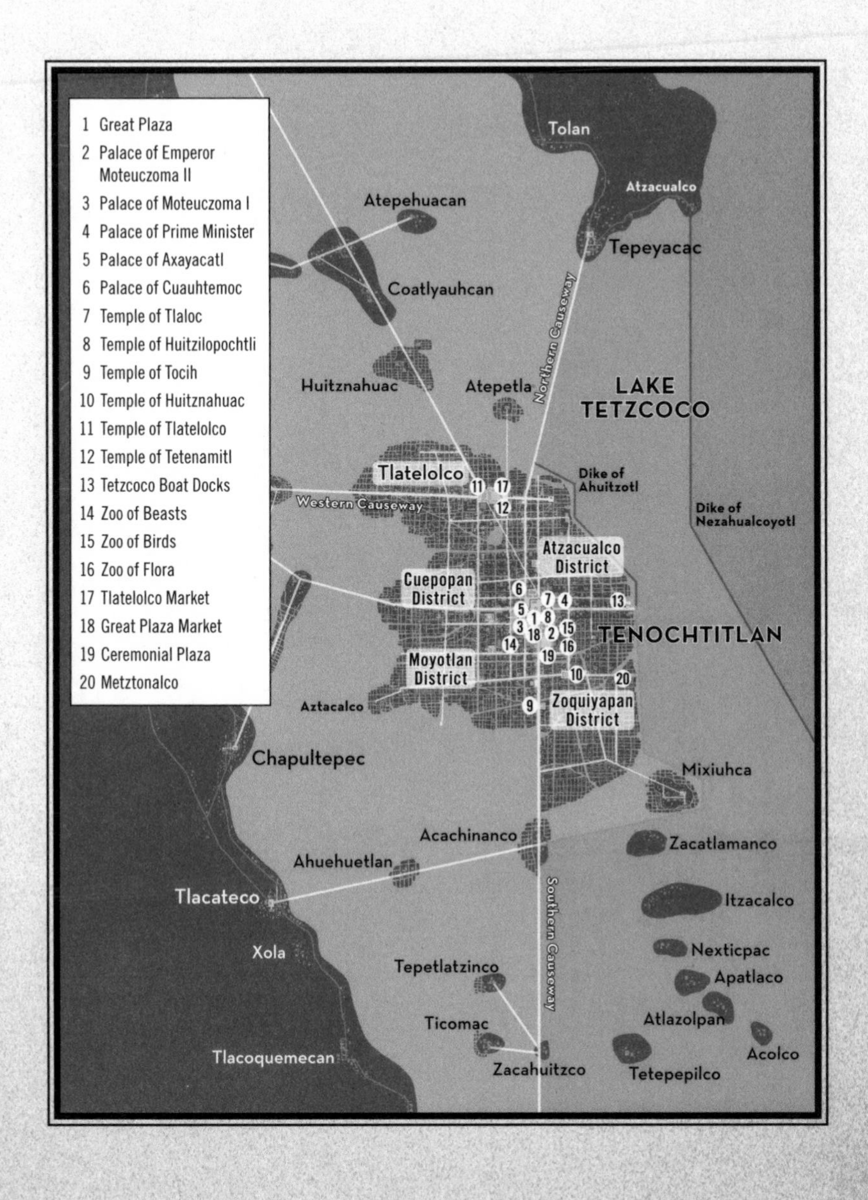

Secret of the Moon Conch

PROLOGUE

CALIZTO

I crest the low bluff, and the vast ocean spreads out before me, jade green and sparkling. I have never seen so much water, though I have dreamed of the ever-flowing skirt of Mother Sea, twining itself around the world, swaddling us in her watery embrace.

I would stare like this for hours, but the Spanish are still on my heels, reinforcements converging from the city they established at the mouth of the Huitzilpan River.

Gripping the moon conch against my chest, I begin my descent toward the beach, feet slipping clumsily on the tricky sand.

I am a child of the highlands, son of mountains, born to live and die close to our Father the Sun. But she needs me. She must receive this sacred shell, this tenuous thread of magic that connects her heart to mine across expanses of space and time.

Clinging to rock and root, I make my way down. A rod or so from the bottom, I let go and drop to the sand, resting for the briefest of moments.

Movement catches my eye, and I glance up the strand.

A hundred Spanish soldiers are rushing at me, some mounted on horseback. At their head stands the priest, his eyes wide as he sees the conch in my hands.

There is no time to lose. I cannot fail her. She must find it.

Without it, she will despair.

Without it, she will not have helped me.

Both of us will be lost.

Both of us will die.

"Goddess, give me strength!" I cry as I burst into motion, my feet pounding the beach, driving me toward the sea.

Their harquebuses spit lead balls into the sand around me. An arrow grazes my stomach, leaving a long and bloody groove.

I do not stop. Ignoring enemy fire, I plunge into the foaming waves, the conch held high.

"Take it, Mother Sea! Take this sacred shell and place it in her hands!"

And with all my strength, I fling the pink spiral into the swells.

Moments later, unexpected hands haul me from the water.

PART ONE

WAXING MOON

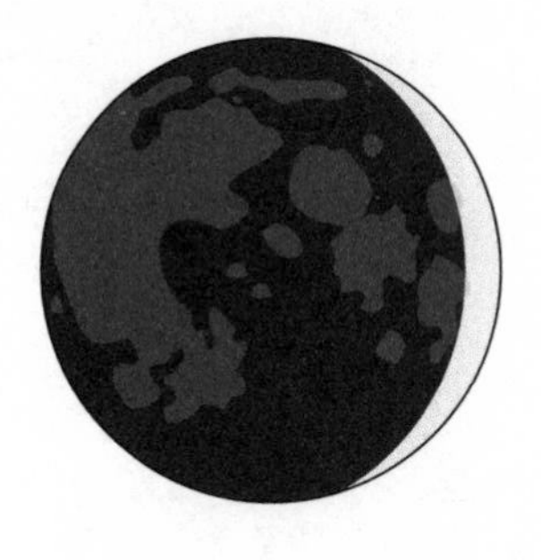

CHAPTER ONE

Sitlali

June 1, 2019

The crescent moon wavers and fades upon the black mirror of the darkest sea. Away from the city lights, the calm water looks black as tar and just as thick. I am afraid to think of what might happen if I should dive into it. Nothing good could come of that.

I've never been to Boca del Río at night. When I was very small, before my father left, I was afraid of the ocean. Mami used to try to make me strong. *Always challenge the darkness. Ask the ancients to help you stay strong!* she used to say.

But Mami has been gone for almost seven years. She died the summer after I turned ten. Her broken heart couldn't keep her alive anymore, not when she refused to nourish herself to spite Don Nicolás, the drug lord who wanted her to marry him and let him take my father's place in her heart. At her funeral, the women of Zongolica said Nora Morales was like a cardinal, the red bird that would rather perish than be taken captive.

I saw a red bird die in my father's hands when I was five years old.

The poor thing had flown into our house by mistake, a frightened, confused flurry of fiery feathers. It flittered from floor to ceiling, looking for a way out until my father lifted a bedsheet high over his head and flung the cloth over it. Carefully, he took it from under the sheet and held it in his left hand.

Mami begged him to let it go before it tensed up and died. But my father was hell-bent on keeping it. "I caught it for you," he said. "To remind you of my love while I am away."

I think the bird died because it knew my father would not return. Maybe it knew his love was untrue. I want to say I miss my mother, but how can I? When my father left, it was like she left with him. I tried getting close to her. I hugged her and kissed her and told her I loved her. But I was too late, her heart had seized up, and there was nothing I could do to save her.

I shake off all thoughts of my mother and sit on the sparse, sandy grass off the shore, away from the laughter of my school friends. They are too young and self-absorbed to understand what I must do. This is how they decided to spend our last night together before I depart. But, while they came here to ask the moon to find them new boyfriends, I came to get away from the predators taking over our neighborhood.

Like carrion birds, gangs of angry young men congregate in our streets. Veracruz is infested with them. And now that they are moving up into the mountains, Zongolica is not as safe as it used to be. If my father were still here, if he had not gone to the States . . . but that is not worth considering. With his strong character, he might have already met with violence. And then I would be a true orphan.

Before she passed away, my maternal grandmother, Lucía, who's been my caregiver all these years, prepared me for this journey. "Repeat her information, full name, address, and phone number again," she asked, quizzing me daily.

"Tomasa Ruiz, 1847 Prairie View." I repeated the address she had me memorize. "Von Ormy, Texas. I know it by heart, Abuela. Don't worry."

"She will take good care of you," Abuela Lucía said every time I repeated the foreign words. "Tomasita is your madrina, your mother's best friend in the world. It is her job to take care of you when I am gone."

For months after the gangs made it necessary for me to quit my job at the bodega, Abuela Lucía and I lived on the calditos I made from the vegetables I cultivate in our garden. After a while, though, she stopped taking nourishment. I took her to a doctor. He said it wasn't the meager diet or our poor living conditions that were taking a toll on her.

"She is old," he told me. "It is just her time."

I know we all have to die, but my wounded heart twists in my chest when I think of her now. Without my grandmother, I have no one to run to, no one to guide me, no one to love.

Looking back, I see Abuela Lucía was right; it's time for me to leave this place. Because even if I were to get a job in Zongolica, I wouldn't be safe living alone. I have no other choice. I have to go to los Estados. Maybe, with her knowledge of that foreign country, my madrina Tomasa can help me find my father. Because I don't know how to begin looking for a man I haven't seen in over twelve years.

"Sitlali!" Esmeralda calls out to me from the beach, where the girls are all dancing around and chanting an ancient song to the moon. I can barely make out their words as they move rhythmically over the sand.

I pick up my sandals and run down the incline to join them.

"Sing." Matilde grabs my hand and pulls me into their dance. I look up at the moon as I chant half-heartedly, because love is not a priority for me. I want the moon to see me safely out of Zongolica. A gust of wind hits us. My long black hair swirls and wraps itself around my face and neck.

"Sing!" Esmeralda cries over the roar of waves. "Come on! It's no good if you don't mean it!"

So, I sing.

"Nochan. Nochan. Home." I let go of Matilde's hand and walk toward the moon's reflection in the water. "I just want to feel safe again." I wipe roughly at my cheek because I don't like to cry. That's not the strong woman my grandmother raised.

That's when I see it; an iridescent, crescent-shaped sliver of moonlight rolls in with the tide. Slowly it comes to rest before me, gleaming softly at my feet. I squat, pick it up, and shake the water out of it, marveling at its luminescence.

"What's that?" Esmeralda looks over my shoulder.

"A conch."

"It's beautiful." Matilde squats beside me and tests the thorny horns with her fingertips.

"It's got some kind of markings," I say. "Can you read that?"

"Nahuatl?" she asks. "No."

"My grandmother could have," I tell her, turning the conch over in my hands and tracing the glyphs. "I only know enough to get by."

"Well, if it is Nahuatl, that makes it valuable," Matilde says. "We should wait for the tourist shops to open so you can sell it."

Esmeralda turns away from us. "We have to get going. We don't have time to waste trying to sell that trinket."

I examine the conch again. "It's not a trinket," I say, weighing it in my hands. "It's old. I can tell by the wear on the hieroglyphs."

"Chale. I know dozens of people who could make marks like that." Esmeralda rests her fists on her hips.

"You know people who can carve the old language into seashells? Seriously? Because I don't," I say. "Most people I know can't even write. And they're never going to learn because they can't walk to school safely!"

Esmeralda's face tightens. Then her lips soften, and she reaches out to touch my shoulder. "And you think selling this thing is the answer?"

"I do." I hold the conch tightly within the circle of my arms.

Esmeralda's eyes glisten in the dark. "Life doesn't work that way, Sitlali," she says. "Things like long-lost treasures and ancient relics don't magically appear for people like us. We have to fight for everything we have."

I caress the curved lip of the conch in my hands. "I don't care what you say. I'm taking it to the museo de arte today. I need to collect as much money as I can. It's my only way out."

"You don't have to go." Esmeralda's eyes glisten as she appeals to me. "My brother can protect you. He has connections now."

I shake my head and look away, because I don't want to tell her that her brother's connections are the reason I have to go.

"Whatever." Esmeralda turns away. "I'm catching the first bus back to Zongolica."

"Hey!" Matilde calls. She is running down the beach, getting farther away from us. Behind her, the sky is beginning to lighten. "Let's finish our song! Before the sun comes out and chases the moon away."

Esmeralda rushes after her.

I look at the conch in my hand. In the dawning light, its surface is radiant, almost magical. Then, for no reason at all, I put the shell up to my face, press it against my cheek, and ask, "When will this darkness end?"

Then, because there is no use waiting for an answer, I run to the incline, tuck the conch into my backpack, and turn back to chase after Esmeralda, who is gazing at the moon and chanting along with the girls.

"Will you wait for me?" I ask her. "When I go sell the conch?"

"What conch?" Esmeralda asks.

I sigh, because I was really hoping she would support my efforts.

"Never mind," I tell her, "I'll catch up with you after I make the sale."

"You're nuts—you know that? But I love you anyway." Esmeralda gives me a quick hug and then rushes off to join our group.

The girls start dancing and singing again.

Before me, sunlight torches the heavens, singeing the sky with red-and-pink strokes that shift and swirl until they fuse together. Then the sun breaks through the horizon. A newly formed day is born, and I run down to the shoreline.

"Come on! It's time to go!" Esmeralda calls to me from the incline.

I dig my heels into the sand and shake my head, because no matter how much I try to pretend it isn't so, it really is time for me to move on.

CHAPTER TWO

Calizto

Day 9-Eagle of the Year 3-House (June 4, 1521)

Once the younger students have finished whitewashing the telpochcalli, we make them drill with lances. Only one dares complain, muttering about his parched tongue. Ce Mazatl strikes him with a switch.

We're all thirsty. Nine days ago, our enemies destroyed the aqueduct that has for a century brought fresh water from distant Chapoltepec Hill to Tenochtitlan, the once mighty city in the midst of brackish Moon Lake. The well of this school has gone dry. Lines at the only spring on the island of Mexico, despite its bitter water, stretch up and down the canals.

Thirty thousand people. Trapped. Under siege, with little food or water.

Haunted by the loss of fifty thousand friends and family.

The sky glows golden at this late hour. A few clouds rush westward, desperate to plunge after the sun into the Underworld.

Tlaloc, I whisper in my heart. *Lord of Rain. Let the Green Time come early.*

Masking despair, I correct the stance of a few students. Maximum thrust is needed to pierce the armor of the enemy. There's no doubt in my mind. We'll all be called upon to fight soon, even this minor telpochcalli in a muddy neighborhood on the lakeshore.

Our telpochtlahtoh emerges from the school, looking grim.

"Fall in!" I shout. Like Ce Mazatl and Ayotochtli, I serve as a tiachcauh. At seventeen years each, we are the oldest students at our humble commoner school, watching over and training the newer boys. They obey us without question.

"Yes, Older Brother Calizto!" they shout as they line up, lances resting on their shoulders. We three older brothers turn and stand in front of them.

Master Miquiztin adjusts his white cape.

"Men of Metztonalco," he begins, using the name of our calpolli, the minor house to which we all belong, "word has come from our calpoleh. Chief Itzcoyotl instructs us to take up a position upon the southern causeway at first light."

The air becomes tense. Cortés has taken Acachinanco, the landing site and staging area just a few dozen rods south of the city. From the fortress there, he keeps us from leaving and goods from arriving.

And for the past two days, he has attempted to force his way up the causeway. Our warriors have repelled his army, but at a great cost.

"Earlier today," Miquiztin continues, "the enemy blew open a breach in the causeway south of Acachinanco. Four ships moved through it to the west side of the lake. Then the fleet advanced on each side of the embankment as the mounted Caxtiltecah and their filthy allies pushed toward the city, forcing our soldiers back."

The master of our school pauses, eyes red with emotion.

"Those bastards set houses alight. Fierce Mexica indignation rose in our heroes, who pushed them back on the causeway and in the water.

Tomorrow they'll come again. But we'll be waiting. Our school will erect breastworks and dig pits, removing wooden bridges so the enemy cannot enter the city again. There will be no dancing or singing today, little brothers. Go home. Eat supper with your families, if they yet live. Return here to sleep. We need you nourished and rested in the morning. Dismissed!"

The students stow their weapons and disperse. Once they're gone, I walk along the hard-packed dirt street beside my two friends.

Ce Mazatl is the first to bid us goodbye.

"Coming back after dinner?" Ayotochtli asks with a wry smile.

Ce Mazatl laughs despite the gloom that hangs over us. "You already know the answer, Brother. I've a rendezvous planned with the lovely Quetzpal. We have needs, and this may be the last night of my life."

As he walks away, his words bore into my heart. *I cannot die tomorrow. Someone depends on me.* The thought is cowardly, shameful. But my father made me swear an oath. I am honor bound.

"And you?" Ayotochtli asks.

I have much to consider, much to do. I may not be able to sleep at the telpochcalli tonight, no matter the rules. So I claim the one unspoken exception.

"I'm also meeting someone," I mutter.

"What?" he demands, grinning. "You? The most pious and self-restrained of us all? Who is she?"

I tell a lie he can't investigate. "A Huitznahuac girl. Saw her in the marketplace on Seven Reed. We agreed to meet in an empty house in her neighborhood tonight."

Ayotochtli slaps my back. "Lucky bastard. Why didn't you say anything? Ah, foolish question. Well, good to see you're human after all."

He laughs and heads for his uncle's home. Though the smallpox has orphaned him, he has some family left.

All of mine are dead. Yet I'm still responsible for one living soul, kin to no one, enemy of all I hold dear. It's my duty to sustain him.

I walk through my neighborhood of Metztonalco. Twilight deepens into night. A new moon. Only stars emerge, first Venus, celestial protector, and then the rest, constellations glittering in the canals as I pass over rickety bridges.

My father's house stands silent at the lip of the city, lake water just a stone's throw from the courtyard. Crouching at the edge of the canal, I scour our bedraggled chinampa garden for any vegetable I may have missed this morning. I breathe a sigh of relief when my hand finds a stunted yellow squash. We'll stave off hunger one more day.

If I survive tomorrow, I'll try the marketplace. But I have little left to trade, and while Emperor Cuauhtemoc filled this city with warriors and weapons, he neglected to stockpile food.

The thought of escape rises in some craven corner of my mind. I shrug it off and climb the ladder to the platform built by my grandfather and uncles.

All of them dead, though their footsteps and voices echo in my heart like lingering ghosts. A sob wrenches free from my clenched jaw as I stand before our once teeming, happy home. Now as silent as a tomb.

Punching my chest to keep from weeping, I enter.

"Finally!" a voice cries out in the foreign tongue I have been learning for nearly a year. "I've been sitting here in the dark, Calizto, worried for you."

His stomach grumbles.

"Hunger," I replied, the alien sounds twisting my lips. "Not worry."

At the center of the living space rest the hearthstones, lifted by a statue of Huehueteotl, the old god of fire. I stir the ashes, find a single glowing ember. In moments, flames illuminate the adobe walls and the features of my guest.

He is darker than me, resembling the Chontals who sometimes visit from their seashore kingdom. His hair is tightly curled, however, like none I've ever seen.

Though two years older than me, he's often impish, immature, and needy. Like my little brothers Ixconan and Huitztecol once were.

I squeeze my mind shut against those memories and focus on my charge.

"Hello, Ofirin," I say in the language of his former masters. "Is there water?"

He picks up a clay container, sloshes its contents. "A little, yes."

"Good." I take it from him, set it on the fire. With a sliver of obsidian, I slice the squash. The pieces make satisfying plops. I add a handful of chili peppers.

He looks at me expectantly, starved for conversation, but I wait. As he spoons the meager chayóhmolli into his mouth, I consider our situation.

When we drove the Caxtiltecah—the Spaniards—from our city last summer, raging at the death of Emperor Moteuczoma, hundreds died, many drowning in the canals, weighted down by their ridiculous armor and the gold they covet.

The following day my father, Omaca, helped to dredge the waterways and remove the dead.

He discovered Ofirin, clinging to a chinampa garden, near death. In secret he brought the strange young man into our home, where Mother nursed him back to health after consulting her astrological charts.

By fall, we were learning Spanish as Father prepared to sneak Ofirin to freedom.

Then the plague came.

For sixty days it ravaged the island of Mexico, reaping life after life throughout the sister cities of Tenochtitlan and Tlatelolco. Ofirin was impervious. He took care of us as we suffered, unable to rise from our beds, covered with boils that thrust hot shards of pain into our nerves with the slightest of movements. At night he picked vegetables from the chinampa and prepared us food.

All around, the screams fell silent as our neighbors, our friends and family, began to die.

In this house, my younger brothers succumbed, first Ixconan, then Huitztecol. A day later Mother passed, but not before wheezing out a command with her last breath: "Maintain the shrine, my precious Calizto. It contains a tool of great worth."

A week later I had nearly recovered, pustules fading to scars on my chest and arms, when my father called me to his side and commanded me as well: "I leave our guest in your care, beloved son. Perhaps the blessed Moon will light you a path out of this city. Perhaps you will be executed as a traitor. But our enemy enslaved this man, stole him from his distant homeland. Treat him with honor and dignity."

There could be no burials. Tens of thousands were dead. The city itself would have become a graveyard. No, my dead would meet the afterlife like nobles. They had earned that right.

I bundled them all. Brothers. Parents. Grandparents. Uncles. Cousins. Sisters. Brothers-in-law. Nephews. Nieces. Trembling with emotions no words can describe, I prepared the pyre.

I was not the only one. The sky above Tenochtitlan was thick with the smoke from thousands of funerals. No family member remained to say the old words. I didn't bother to look for an elder of my calpolli. My mother was a priestess of Coyolxauhqui, goddess of the moon. I knew the prayers.

In one single mighty blaze, everything that mattered to me was effaced from the world.

Ofirin can see the turmoil in my eyes. I've barely eaten.

"They're coming, aren't they? Cortés and his men?"

"And their thousands of allies. Yes. Along every causeway. In their water houses as well, their boats. Tomorrow I join my fellow soldiers in repelling them. I can't guarantee that I'll return in the evening. If I don't, you have to swim out to them."

Ofirin sets down his wooden bowl. "Are you mad? I've told you—they took Narváez prisoner. There's no one to advocate for me. I'm a dead man. A runaway. Colluding with the Indians."

"Mexica," I correct, my voice cold. "This is Mexico, not the . . . Indies or wherever you fools thought you were going. And if you think the Spaniards will treat you badly, trust me, you don't want *my* people to discover you here in the heat of battle."

Emotions play across his face. He is worse at hiding what he feels. "Then I'll pray that some god—my people's, yours, theirs—will keep you safe, that your warriors drive those bastards out again."

Prayer. Ofirin's words ring true. All that I have left is prayer.

"I'll return shortly," I announce.

He stares at the crucifix still hanging around his neck, running the beads through his doubting fingers. The Spanish forced their resurrected god on him, making him abandon his own. But I still have mine.

The shrine is not far. Always open to passers-by. Three walls of volcanic stone. A thatched roof. Inside, the altar, carved with conch glyphs. I bow to the stone head of Coyolxauhqui, the copper bells on her cheeks glowing as I light copal incense.

A broom stands in one corner. I sweep the flagstones till they gleam as white as the absent moon, white as a spiraling shell upon a starlit strand.

No hope. Every avenue despair.

I set aside the broom, kneeling. Once more, as I have done nightly since my parents' deaths, I whisper a prayer.

"Ah, Coyolxauhqui, Mother Moon, broken and then made whole again. And you, Tecciztecatl, son of Tlaloc, Lord of the Shell, immolated to protect her. I cannot see a way forward. My eyes perceive only destruction, only grief. Grant me some solace, I beg you. Send me aid in this my darkest moment."

Something tells me prayer won't suffice.

A rustling sound draws my attention to the altar. Quick as lightning, a white-flanked jackrabbit bolts away along the nearby canal. I examine its hiding place beneath the altar.

A wooden box sits nestled inside, out of view. My mind tingling with intuition, I reach in and draw it out, setting it atop the altar and lifting the lid.

Inside, cushioned by cloth, rests a large mollusk shell, pink and spiraled. I take its pale and ancient curves into my hand, and its name springs to my memory.

The moon conch. My mother's priestly trumpet.

Hundreds of stars have been carved into the shell. Glyphs from the time of giants glimmer inscrutable in the dim.

A dangerous impulse seizes me. My limbs tremble at the notion. As I hesitate, my breath quickens. What I would do is forbidden to anyone but a lunar priestess.

Yet these are desperate times, when courage must push custom aside and seize at destiny, no matter the cost.

I lift the moon conch to my lips and blow.

The sound. Oh, gods above, the sound. It blasts through the moonless night, echoing along the canals, shaking the withering chinampas. Surely it can be heard in the ceremonial center, atop the Great Pyramid itself.

And I remember.

My mother standing before a gathered throng, blowing a haunting melody through the pink-tinged spirals. All of us entranced at the touch of the goddess.

How could I forget that tune, the instrument from which it arose?

Why can I remember *now*?

A shudder underfoot. I grip the shell to my chest.

Standing, I turn to look out across the water. The white sails of Spanish brigantines flutter in the night breeze. Beyond them, in the eastern mountains, the rim of the volcano glows red with fury.

Popocatepetl is answering me. A warrior transformed by the gods into that mighty, smoking peak.

"Yes," I whisper. "Your will be done. I place myself in your hands."

CHAPTER THREE

Sitlali

June 4, 2019

Abuela Lucía's spirit sits in a corner, watching me as I light a fire in the hearth.

"I found a conch," I say, pointing to my mochila, which I haven't used since I left school last year. It has hung in the corner of the room from the head of a rusty nail for months, empty and sad as a dry corn-husk until today, when I filled it with the bulk of my clothes and the pink shell. "I was going to sell it to the museo de arte. But they were closed."

I throw one last log on the fire, put my hand on my knee, and push myself up.

"I'm leaving tonight," I tell her. "Don Efrain's nephew, Martín, is going to drive me up to the border in Coahuila."

Unlike my mother, who claimed she could perceive her family on the other side, Abuela Lucía is the first spirit I've ever seen. At first, I was scared of her, but then I got used to her sitting around with me. Her presence in this house breaks my heart because I don't know what she wants. She's come every night since her death.

On the day of her own funeral, she sat in the same corner and watched me cry. I don't know if the dead can talk. Maybe they do, just not in a way we can hear. But there are so many things I want to ask her. So many things I need to know.

"Have you found my mother yet?" I've asked her this question every night, and, as usual, she shakes her head.

Something stirs outside. The shrubbery rustles a warning, and I jump away from the window. Every muscle in my body tenses, and I pat the small bulge under the cloth at my waistline, where I keep my mother's knife.

There is no knock, only a hard bang and the door flies open. It hits the bench where my grandmother is sitting. She opens her mouth to scream at the intruder, but nothing comes out.

Esmeralda's brother, Jorge, steps into the kitchen. The light of the fire throws dark shadows across his face, and his silhouette wavers long and lean on the wall to the left of him, like a tall praying mantis.

"What the hell?" I ask. "I know your mother taught you to knock!"

"Esme says you're leaving." He pushes a strand of dark hair out of his eyes.

I inch my fingers past the cloth waistband. I know what he wants, and I tell myself he doesn't stand a chance. The reality is that he can disarm me, perhaps even hurt me with my own mother's weapon. But I can't think like that. I can't let him scare me. So, I wrap my hand around the hilt of my mother's dagger. The slim, wooden handle is warm against my palm, ready to slice through flesh and muscle, pierce to the bone if need be.

"Well?" he asks.

When I don't answer, Jorge walks toward the hearth. He reaches over and grabs my mochila off the wall.

"Stop!" I rush around the table, but I am too late. He's

disemboweling my bag, spilling its contents onto the packed dirt floor. Hairbrush, toothbrush, and a framed picture of my mother scatter all around. I lunge at him, but he moves away, turns to the chimenea, and throws several articles of clothing in. The fire spits and snarls as it licks at my shirt and pants lying over the bright red logs.

I pick up my mother's picture and set it on the table.

"Come here," he says.

I move toward him and, before he knows what's happening, I swing at his face. His arm snakes out and grabs my arm. The mochila dangles in the fingers of his left hand and he squeezes my wrist. His grip tightens as he looks into my eyes.

"I didn't come here to fight," he says.

I pull myself free and step away from him.

"What's this?" he asks, reaching into my mochila to pull out the conch I've wrapped in a shawl.

"Nothing," I say, and I put my hand out to him.

Instead of giving it to me, Jorge throws the mochila aside and examines the conch. "Esme said you were going to sell something. She couldn't remember what. Is this it?" he said. "What happened? Changed your mind?"

"I'm keeping it," I say. "As a memento, something to remind me of Zongolica."

My grandmother's spirit glides across the room until she is standing in front of Jorge.

"No te hagas pendeja," he says. "I know you're not that attached to this place. You wouldn't be leaving if you were."

"There's no reason for me to stay," I say. "Not anymore."

"Marry me."

He holds the conch under his arm, like a warrior's trumpet. Only he's no warrior. He's just a kid trying to act like a grown-up.

Abuela Lucía turns to me and shakes her head.

"I can't," I say, and I reach for the conch.

"Why not?" Jorge asks, pulling his chin up.

I take a deep breath. "Because you're too young for me. I used to take care of you when you were little, remember? You used to cry because you wet the bed and you didn't want your mother to find out. So, I used to sneak you out and bathe you while Esme washed the linens."

"Don't fuck with me!" Jorge throws the conch down. It hits the floor with a thud and rolls away from us.

I move to retrieve it, but Jorge puts his arms around me and pins me against his chest. Three dark figures rush into the room.

"You brought your thugs?" I ask.

"You okay?" one of them asks. I recognize his voice. His name is Pedro, but they call him La Mano now, because he's Jorge's second-in-command. I've seen him lift his hand to make everyone stop and listen. It's pathetic, how they've gotten the whole neighborhood afraid to do anything because they're tethered to the bigger monster, the narcotraficantes who've taken over Zongolica.

Jorge leans over and buries his face against my neck. He presses a kiss right under my jawline. "Well?" he asks. "What do you say?"

My mother died because the wrong man touched her. She turned into a little red bird and flew to heaven. But I am not my mother. I won't let a man's hand send me into a fright.

"You're a pig," I tell Jorge, wrestling against him as he tightens his arms around me.

La Mano steps forward.

Abuela Lucía lifts her arms and a strong gust of wind rushes into the room. It slaps the door back and forth against its frame and rips the threadbare curtains off the window. The cloth lands over the fire, smothering it for a second before the flames begin to eat through the fabric.

The room fills with a dark, blustering smoke that makes Jorge's men cough and flail their arms.

"Come on, Jorge," La Mano yells. "We've got more important things to do than mess with this bitch."

"Shut up!" Jorge yells at La Mano. "Get out of here."

La Mano turns to the others. "Let's go," he says.

When they leave, I twist out of Jorge's embrace, take my mother's knife out of my belt, and raise it over my head.

"Really?" Jorge laughs, but I am not afraid of him. He's a mocoso. When he first told me I was to be his girlfriend, the day before my grandmother died, I ignored him. The second time, I was gathering quelites in the backyard and he came up and tried putting his hand on my hip. I slapped it away and told him I was not interested. He didn't believe me then, but I hope the knife shows him I'm serious now.

"Don't do this," he says. "I can take care of you. You would be my queen. I would worship you."

His vulnerability takes me by surprise. I want to tell him I could never marry him because we are too much like family, that he is a little brother to me. But Jorge is different now. Hunger and poverty have changed him. He wants to protect his family, to provide for them.

"You need to go," I say. "Go on. Get out of here."

"You'll be back," he says, and he wipes at the tears gathering on the rims of his eyes. "Broken, hopeless, penniless, but you'll be back. I won't marry you then. I'll let my men have you—when I'm done with you."

I look at my grandmother floating beside me. Every wrinkle on her face is furrowed, and she has that glint in her eyes that says, *Don't let him treat you like that!*

I step forward and slice the air between me and Jorge in one swift motion. He jumps back, barely avoiding my blade.

"Go!" I scream. "Before I gut you and roast you in this fireplace!"

Jorge kicks a chair aside and walks out of the room. Abuela Lucía lifts her hand, waves it sideways, and the door slams closed behind him.

"Thank you," I say, and she floats forward and puts her hands over the roaring fire, tempering it until it is a warm flicker of light casting soft shadows between us.

I sit on the floor and pick up the conch.

"It's ruined." My voice trembles because the pretty shell is chipped at the tip. The broken piece is under the upturned chair, and I wipe at the tears burning at the corner of my eyes before I pick it up.

Abuela Lucía floats over to my cot and pats the thin mattress. With the conch in hand, I lie down for bed, cover up, and close my eyes. As I drift off, just as I am about to fall asleep, I think I hear Abuela Lucía humming a quiet, ancient lullaby. In my dream, the conch in my arms vibrates and hums, echoing my grandmother's soft, susurrous song. The sound of ocean waves lulls me to sleep, takes me to a different place, a different time.

Rest, a voice whispers in my dreams. *Your journey will be long and arduous.*

CHAPTER FOUR

Calizto

Day 11-Movement of the Year 3-House (June 6, 1521)

I wish to linger in this dream. A young woman's voice whispers, slipping between Nahuatl and Spanish. Her voice is like moonlight: insubstantial, silver, intoxicating.

Nicitlalin. The word makes me shudder. *I am a star. I am Sitlali.*

But I cannot cling to her fading murmur. Duty and training wrench my eyes open.

I sit up with a groan. My muscles ache from digging trenches and flinging spears and loosing arrows. Still, I'm alive despite breaking tradition and sounding the very moon conch I had forgotten.

I stand and stretch, wincing at the popping of my joints.

In the ashes of the fire, a clay pot still contains a bit of the hominy I brought home last night.

As I crouch and spoon the cold, nixtamalized corn into my mouth, Ofirin clears his throat from the corner where he has been sleeping.

"How did it go? You were too tired to speak last night."

I swallow. "We pushed him back to the fortress. He'll be at it again today."

"Any news of the empress?" His foolish gaze and trembling lip almost make me laugh. I'm reminded of lovesick youths inquiring about their first crush.

I'm curious about this reaction, so I feign indignation. "Why should you care about Lord Cuauhtemoc's young wife?"

He rubs sleep from his eyes, silent.

"Ofirin? Come, I deserve an answer."

He stutters, looking away. "I-I met her when sh-she was a captive of the Spaniards. Before your people expelled them. Very sweet."

I nod, understanding. During the Night of Victory, when we routed the Spaniards and Tlaxcaltecah, we also rescued Princess Tecuichpotzin, now our empress.

Of course, the two have met. Our empress is indeed noble of spirit. And beautiful. I cannot blame Ofirin for obsessing over her.

"As far as I know," I answer, "she is well."

His sigh of relief is almost comical.

I'm tempted to tease him, but I have dawdled too long. I stand, pulling my hair into a temillotl, tying it in place with a strip of red fabric. Then I slip on my quilted vest.

"That won't stop a Spanish bullet. Or cannonball."

Grimacing, I stare at him. "It's not meant to, Ofirin. Where's my maccuahuitl?"

"Your what?"

"My sword. Wooden macana, razor-sharp obsidian blades all along its edges, able to slice through Spanish armor like an oar through water?"

He gives a wry chuckle. "Oh, you're trying to make a point."

"Your former masters have horses and cannon and steel. But they're nonetheless outmatched. The Mexica are the chosen people of Huitzilopochtli, god of battle."

Ofirin laughs weakly. "Everyone thinks there's a god on their side. My people did, too. I suspect we're all wrong, Calizto. But there's your sword right there, leaning against the wall behind you. Your shield's strapped to it. I wish you luck. That's all it is, my friend. Chance."

I sling the shield and sheathed maccuahuitl upon my back as I leave.

The light of dawn is smeared across the eastern sky, pink reddened by the volcano's angry glow. The sun approaches with his retinue of fallen warriors, transformed into birds and butterflies. I breathe a quick prayer to him, despite Ofirin's doubts about the gods.

Others are exiting their houses. We make our way in silence along the biggest canal—Xoloco—trying not to look down at the abandoned chinampas snarling with weeds. There is no more time for gardens. No one can be spared to tend them. Emperor Cuauhtemoc has made clear our singular goal.

"Women," he cried out to a crowd two days ago, "when your men fall, pick up their swords, take up their spears, notch their arrows, and fight to your last breath!"

We reach the first canal running north to south. At the wooden bridge, everyone nods at the guards and crosses.

Waiting for me on the other side are Ce Mazatl and Ayotochtli, along with a handful of our students.

"You're almost late," Ce Mazatl remarks with a knowing grin. "Did a certain girl rob you of sleep?"

I laugh. He is more right than he knows. "I can hear her still, whispering to me."

Ayotochtli grabs my shoulder. "You crafty son of a bitch. Who would have figured you for a ladies' man? So serious all the time. Tell me . . . does she have a sister?"

"One that doesn't mind ugly young men of low birth?" Ce Mazatl adds jokingly.

A few students snicker. I shut them up with a glance.

The last of our group soon crosses the bridge with Master Miquiztin, fierce in his elite eagle battle helmet and uniform. He signals the three of us older brothers.

"Fall out! The Caxtiltecah won't just sit in that fortress waiting for us to get our carcasses in place, boys!"

At his gesture, I take the lead, trotting double-time to weave through the last block of buildings and cross the final bridge onto the broad causeway.

The sun is emerging from behind the eastern mountains. To my right, northward, I see the Eagle Gate and beyond it the towering pyramids and temples of the Sacred Precinct, to be protected at all costs.

To my left, southward, over the heads of several hundred men and women already fortifying our position upon the causeway, two stone buildings loom: the Fortress of Xoloc, teeming with Spaniards and their allies the Tlaxcaltecah.

Our sworn enemies.

The Tlaxcaltecah have resisted conquest by the Mexica for a century. Now, with Spanish weaponry on their side, they have tipped the scales. If they reach the center of Tenochtitlan, the city will surely fall.

Determined to stop them, our canoes ply the waters on either side of the causeway, heavy with warriors and arrows.

Closing on them are the Spanish brigantines, cannons already trained.

I find a place for our school. We dig in, sharpening stakes and carving a trench into the heavily packed earth of the causeway.

Then the Shorn Ones come running up from behind us, screaming, swords drawn. Their faces—painted blue on one side, red on the other—twist in snarls of rage as they rush to the vanguard. Already the enemy is approaching, having spent the night filling in the great pit we dug yesterday to keep them away. But these elite warriors of ours—banners and quetzal feathers fluttering majestic from poles on their backs—feel no fear. Defying musket and cannon blast, they berserk preemptively against the Tlaxcaltecah.

Chaos explodes.

All around me is the sound of battle. The hiss of arrows, the grunts and shouts of warriors hurling spears, the explosions of Spanish guns and artillery.

Our school is at the back, but we do not shirk our duty. Should the enemy make it this far, we must be ready.

So we dig. We sink sharpened sticks into the earth at an angle, creating a defensive palisade. At some point a group of children brings us water and hard tortillas. We eat quickly and continue our work.

Though I resist, the phantom voice of my dreams comes whispering into my thoughts.

North, I manage to make out. *Father. Coahuila.*

I must be going mad. Coahuila? I don't recognize the word. Could it be "coahuilani"? Who is it that "crawls like a snake"?

My eyes are drawn to the water of Moon Lake, upon which legendary chieftain Tenoch established this city generations ago. Some say the goddess Cihuacoatl—Serpent Woman—dwells in its depths. It was not even two years ago, in fact, that my younger cousins, *all of them now dead*, rushed to me when I came home from my first day at the school, whimpering that the goddess was walking the streets of our city each night, crying out in a spectral voice, "Oh, my children! What will become of you! Your doom is at hand!"

Signs. Could this lovely voice be a sign? Could it be the goddess herself, stirred to anger at my violation of sacred law? Is she snake-crawling her way across the lake bottom, coming to exact vengeance on me?

My hands begin to shake, but there is no time for fear. Not two rods ahead of me, a group of Tlaxcaltecah leap over a gaping pit and begin hacking at our warriors, screaming.

"Now, boys!" bellows Miquiztin, unstrapping his shield.

Without another thought, I unsheathe the sword my father left me upon his death.

Coahuila. The voice is louder, distinct.

"I do not know what you ask of me, goddess, but I will defend your city with my life today!"

I have spoken aloud. Ce Mazatl looks up, surprised.

An arrow slams into his chest. He tumbles into the trench, dead.

The Tlaxcaltecah who killed him are upon us, slashing through the palisades.

Howling, I leap to meet them.

I swing my father's sword. It bites flesh, passes through cartilage, nicks bone.

The world goes red as rage and horror and oh so much sorrow overwhelm me, and I fling myself headlong into the fray.

Long moments of chaos.

Cacophonous cries: "Castilla! Castilla! Tlaxcallan! Tlaxcallan!"

Then her voice again.

The conch. Broken. Worthless?

"No!" I scream. "Not broken! Not worthless!"

Her shock fills my mind, makes me recoil from the beast rearing above my head.

My eyes clear just in time. A mounted Spaniard swings his sword. I lift my shield, fire-hardened wood and salt-soaked leather in layers.

His steel shatters it.

I wheel aside. I could cut the legs of his horse out from under him. A blow of last resort.

A horse? Kill a horse? No!

Though the goddess is now shouting in Spanish, I cannot bring myself to disobey her. Instead, I slice upward, ripping through the

Spaniard's leather armor, opening the skin and muscle of his arm in a spray of blood. He drops his sword and screams.

Then the horse's hooves smash against me, and I go tumbling off the causeway.

Midair, I lose consciousness.

CHAPTER FIVE

Sitlali

June 5–6, 2019

Hidden behind limb and leaf, I wait in darkness. The scent of damp loam with its snails and earthworms, its fetid fungi and rotting roots, lives in the air. I take that mal aire into my lungs, force it to nourish my blood.

"With every breath, I am born again," I whisper to the sliver of moon in the darkened sky. Then, reaching into my bag and touching the conch, I gain the courage to say, "I am Sitlali, strong in spirit, a shooting star, propelling myself across your sky to a new horizon. Help me find my way, Moon Goddess. Help me reach Coahuila without incident."

All around me, the jungle shivers, and I say a quick prayer to the Virgen de la Candelaria. I listen to the sound of vehicles as they make their way down the mountain. Don Efrain's nephew, Martín, is supposed to be driving a small Chevy truck. However, it is two dirt bikes that come crashing through the shrubbery.

I push a branch aside carefully, watch the drivers stop and look around.

Pedro—Jorge's right-hand man! And he's not alone. What are Jorge's boys doing here? They couldn't . . . they wouldn't . . .

I tell myself I am being paranoid. Jorge wouldn't dare order an attack on Don Efrain's nephew. Would he? There is a third person among them, sitting behind La Mano, but I cannot tell who it is until he dismounts and then I see his face.

Jorge!

I consider confronting them, asking them what they want with Martín. But before I can gather the courage to do it, the lush jungle shivers again. This time, a pair of headlights come crashing through the shrubbery, and I know it is Martín's truck coming down the mountainside. I let out a huge sigh of relief when I know my ride is finally here. I had not realized it, but I'd been holding my breath.

I wait in the shadow until the truck slows down and comes to a complete stop beside Jorge and his goons. Did Martín know they would be here? What business could they possibly have with one another? As far as I know, Martín is a good boy. Don Efrain wouldn't lie to me about that, would he?

Although I have only seen Martín a couple of times, I recognize him as he steps out of his truck. He is thin and wiry as a fox, built like Don Efrain. La Mano and his companion dismount. I watch them shake hands, and I strain to listen to them, but I can't make out what they are saying.

Their easy manner around one another makes the tiny hairs on my forearms rise, and I shiver. For the first time since I decided to make this journey, I am afraid. I hear a voice, far and whispery, speak to me in the darkness.

I will defend your . . . , the young man's voice says, and, spooked, I let go of the branch. He is speaking the language of my antepasados, like the whispered prayers of some mountain shaman. Is this another ghost? An elder I didn't get to know in this lifetime? Could it be Tata Tapachtle, my mother's father, who died before I was born? But how are these ghosts suddenly in my periphery? And why?

The rustle of leaves makes the men turn around. My heart races. If they are talking about criminal activity, I could be in danger. I consider running down the mountain, getting back to my grandmother's house and locking myself in, but I can't afford to have them think I am doing anything else other than showing up to catch a ride from Martín. To flee, to hide, would intimate that I have knowledge of something more than what I am supposed to be here for. So, I do the only logical thing.

I make a show of pushing aside branches, tugging at my bag to disentangle it from the grasp of twigs and leaflets as I go. I push the straps of my mochila over my shoulder and pretend to only now see the lot of them standing there when I emerge.

"Martín?" I call out, feigning poor sight in the darkness. "Is that you?"

"Sitlali?" Martín calls back. His grin in the moonlight says I am not in danger. But still, my body shakes. I stand motionless for a moment, waiting for my limbs to stop shivering, before I continue.

With my life . . ., the same young man's voice from a moment before whispers in the silence, and I stop. The wind moves through the jungle like a quiet spirit, and I glance over at the others.

"Jorge. Pedro." I try to act casual, but every cell in my body is trembling. These boys are more dangerous than Jorge. They have no love for me. No memories of childhood kinship. If Jorge weren't their boss, they would slaughter me like a goat if they thought I had witnessed something I shouldn't have.

"Come," Martín says. "We don't have time to waste. Do you have the fare?"

"Yes," I say. Then I turn sideways and lean over so they can't see my skin when I reach inside my undershirt, to the secret pocket I've sewn there.

"Here," Jorge says, stepping out of the shadows to stand beside me.

I gasp as he reaches for something behind him. There is no telling where this is going, but I am afraid. *What if he has a gun?*

I quake and shiver as Jorge walks over to Martín and hands him a wad of cash.

"No!" I exclaim. Martín and Jorge turn to look at me. I step up to Martín and rip the wad of money from his hand. "I can pay my own way."

I push the money back into Jorge's hand. He takes advantage of the situation, grabs my arm, and pulls me close to kiss me full on the lips.

"Don't do that!" I shove him away and wipe at my mouth with the sleeve of my shirt. "Desgraciado . . ."

Jorge laughs at my disgust. Then he gives the wad of money back to Martín. "Take it," he says. "That's enough for two."

"Two?" I ask. "You're not . . . You can't . . ."

"Severo is going with you. He'll look after you." Jorge points at the third man on his crew with his thumb. His laughing eyes glisten in the darkness, and I tremble again. "What? You didn't think I was going to let you go alone, did you?"

Martín counts the thick bundle of money in his hand. He stops half-way through the bulk of it. "This is more than I charge," he says to Jorge. "It's enough to take all of you along."

"Keep it," Jorge says. "For anything else you might need when you bring her back."

"No!" I say, shoving my wad of money toward Martín. "This is my journey. I'm paying for it."

Martín looks at the wad in my hand. "I don't care who lays down the cash," he says. "I'll take your money too if you want to pay me twice!"

"Don't be stupid," Jorge says, pushing my hand away. "I'm trying to take care of you. Why can't you see that? You've won, Sitlali. You're getting your way."

"For now." La Mano snickers.

A gust of wind rushes in, sending the tops of trees swaying in the darkness, and I step back. "This doesn't change anything," I tell Jorge. "I won't listen to anything your goon says. He's invisible to me. He doesn't exist."

Jorge's body tenses, and he takes a breath. "You'll be back." He repeats the ominous prophecy from the night before, but I don't care. I refuse to be intimidated by him.

"Well, then," Martín says, shoving the money into his pocket and turning around to open the door of the truck for me. "Let's go."

When Severo tries to get in the truck, Jorge grabs the back of his shirt and pulls him out. "You go in the back," he says. "Keep your distance. Observe. Protect. But don't lay a hand on her. Me entiendes?"

"Come on, Sitlali," Martín says, holding the door open. "We have to go. I want to get out of Veracruz before the sun rises."

I want to turn away and walk back into the dense jungle. But then the breeze swirls up, and I hear the distant voice again. *I will defend . . . maltepeuh . . . with my life today!*

It's the same young man. I try to make sense of his words, but it's hard. *Maltepeuh? Your . . . home?* Is he saying he will defend *my home* with his life today? What does he mean? Where is he that I can hear him so clearly in my head?

"I'm losing my mind." I say it out loud and instantly regret it. This is the last thing I need Martín to think, that I can't take care of myself, that I need this goon, Severo, to speak for me.

I will defend maltepeuh *with my life today!*

I am walking toward the truck when the image comes, flooding my mind, striking me head-on, like a derailed train. It is so vivid, so real, I have to put a hand up against the tailgate, to steady myself.

A horse, rearing up on hind legs. An ancient sword ready to strike, gripped by strong, brown hands. My mind reels. My head spins. With all my heart, I push back against the carnage flooding my inner world, the vision is like a violent movie sequence in my head.

Kill a horse? No!

The young man's voice remains silent.

Martín, Jorge, and Severo are all staring. I hold myself together and climb into the truck's cabin. Committed. Silent. Awake.

CHAPTER SIX

Calizto

Day 12-Flint of the Year 3-House (June 7, 1521)

Trees flow past in streams of green. I'm jostled, as if riding rapids in a canoe. A monster moans at my feet, wrapped in steel.

Where are you?

A question in Spanish. Then the clear tongue of my people.

Here, I think. *Always and ever here, in your city.*

In my home?

Yes, Goddess. Your home. Your people. Your water, your mountain.

Her realization floods me. *Oh, I understand now! Ciudad! You mean city!*

"Calizto."

I open my eyes. I'm in the telpochcalli, on a mat. Ayotochtli kneels beside me. I pull myself up. My head aches.

"What happened?"

Ayotochtli gives a weak laugh. "You attacked a Spaniard riding one of their massive hornless deer. Made the rest of us look bad—until the creature knocked you into the canal. Luckily one of our canoes was close by. Warriors pulled you from the water, and then we brought your, ah, valiant carcass back. All night you thrashed about, talking to a goddess. Or perhaps a lovely maiden?"

Bruises mottle my skin, but nothing seems broken. I raise my hand to my head, find a sutured cut.

"Miquiztin patched you up," Ayotochtli says. "He's with the other wounded. A day of rest, but tomorrow we go back."

For a moment, I forget yesterday's tragedy. "And Ce Mazatl?"

Ayotochtli closes his eyes. "His uncle came this morning to retrieve his body. He'll be bundled and burned like a warrior."

The loss hits like the arrow that pierced Ce Mazatl's heart. I grit my teeth against despair.

"He—" My voice hitches. "That greedy bastard gets the glory first. He'll ascend with the sun soon, with all the great fallen warriors."

Ayotochtli opens his eyes, rests his hand on mine. "Always a show-off. Perhaps we'll see him soon. Perhaps we'll guard the sun together before the summer's done."

He helps me to my feet. My stomach growls.

Ayotochtli snorts at the sound. "There's food in the main chamber."

Students from the female wing are serving bowls of a stew that is more chili peppers than beans, along with tortillas made from stale corn. I devour half before spooning the remainder into a bit of cooling flatbread.

"I have to go," I say, stopping Ayotochtli's barrage of news. "I didn't . . . get to see the Huitznahuac girl last night, so . . ."

"Sitlali," he interrupts.

"What?" I'm dumbfounded.

"That's her name, yes? You kept repeating it last night. She must be an incredible beauty to have you in such a state, Calizto."

I say nothing, just grip the food tighter and head home.

Ofirin is frantic when I arrive.

"I thought you were dead. And I'm starving. By the Holy Host, Calizto!"

I scoff at the curse. Unlike our tasty effigies, the Spaniards eat tasteless wafers in remembrance of their god.

Ofirin devours the food I've brought.

"I'll find more. It means scavenging where I shouldn't, but I can't let you die."

His hand shoots out, but I twist away. He seizes empty air, tears dribbling onto his cheeks. They cry easily, these foreigners. Like children. I didn't even weep over my parents' graves, dug by my own hands.

"Don't leave yet. I'm going crazy from boredom and loneliness."

I narrow my eyes at him. "Endure it. I'll be back soon."

I grab a netted bag and step outside. Distant cannon fire makes me wince. Smoke billows from the northern boroughs.

I should just slip away.

The voice is louder. I look around in hopes of seeing her. But the young woman's words are just in my head.

Have to keep the conch safe—a secret.

At this second mention of a conch, I hurry to the shrine. Leaves and debris litter the stone floor again, but I ignore them. Drawing forth the wooden box, I remove its lid.

The ancient glyphs on the moon conch catch the midday sun, glittering. As I wrap my fingers around it, the world goes white, swirling mist and snowy feathers beating air that smells of salt and pine. I catch a glimpse of blue and green beneath my feet, a vast wood-ringed lake, and then I am pulled upward among stars that pulse and glow, racing toward one whose light resolves itself into the contours of a woman.

Sitlali?

What's happening? Keep calm. They might notice.

The vision shatters. I'm standing in my mother's shrine, blood thundering. Sitlali's voice becomes a river of words and feelings that make me shudder, as if some spectral wind is blowing through my soul.

I feel her worry. Her desire to reach someone she loves.

Grandfather. Nokoltsin. Is this your heartbeat I hear, Tata Tapachtle? Your strength and determination I feel coursing through me? Your . . . fear?

I'm not afraid, Sitlali. My goddess.

I'm not a goddess. I'm just a girl.

And I am not your grandfather. Only seventeen years have passed since my birth. I must wait three more before marrying and having children.

There comes a rush of emotions: mirth, mixed with confusion and doubt.

You use so many words I don't understand. Do you know Spanish? ¿Hablas español?

Yes. I've learned that barbarous tongue.

Her laugh is like joyful bells. *What's your name?*

Calizto.

Where do you live?

In Tenochtitlan.

The swirl of emotions deepens.

Oh, Virgen querida. I'm going crazy, no? Hearing voices?

I stare out at Moon Lake for a moment, then close my eyes to focus.

The moon conch. I have it. You wanted me to keep it secret, didn't you?

What do you mean? she asks. *How do you know I have a conch in my mochila?*

No. Impossible. It's in my hands. One of Coyolxauhqui's bells has been carved right into the mouthpiece.

How can you have the same conch as . . . ? Sitlali's voice trails off. *Tenochtitlan? Calizto, what year is it—where you are?*

A peculiar question, but I answer.

Three House. First year of the reign of Emperor Cuauhtemoc.

What would you call it . . . if you were a Spaniard?

I struggle to recall Ofirin's explanations of the invaders' calendar.

I believe this is . . . 1521.

Sitlali says nothing at first, but I can feel doubt and fear welling. *No,* she whispers. *That can't be . . .*

Before I understand why, a barrage of cannon fire makes the ground rumble, and distant screams ring out.

I place the conch back in the box, but then drop the whole thing into the netted bag and strap it over my chest.

Sitlali's voice returns, fainter but still clear as my own thoughts.

Calizto? What's wrong? Where did you go?

Hold, Sitlali.

I run toward the screams. Before long, I'm stopped by a flood of women and children, fleeing, some of them badly burned.

I stop an adolescent girl with a baby in her arms.

"What happened?"

"The Caxtiltecah forced one of their ships up the canal and set our homes on fire! Their warriors are slaughtering men and boys and hurling their corpses into the flames!"

Oh my God! Help them, Calizto!

I obey Sitlali, though my instinct is to head toward the fray. "All of you, follow me! The telpochcalli of Metztonalco has room enough!"

I lead them away from danger, wending a path through neighborhoods emptied by the plague, crossing rickety bridges over canals whose gardens have been picked clean. Musket fire has scored the tall willows and mud-daubed homes, most raided for supplies. These reminders of death keep the heads of my charges down, as if by focusing their eyes on the feet of the person in front of them, they'll avoid the same fate.

I keep my head high. I have faced death again and again. I won't bow before it.

Soon we reach the handful of buildings that make up our school—dormitories, kitchen, classrooms, shrine.

Sitlali must be conversing with someone. She composes her responses mentally, in Spanish, so I cannot help but overhear, though her voice is softer and more distant than when I had the conch in my hands. Might she be a witch of the enemy, attempting to cloud my mind? No. She holds the sacred trumpet. The goddess would never allow such sacrilege.

I'll trust her. For now.

The man she addresses is named Martín. He is taking her somewhere in some sort of . . . land-ship. *Camioneta.* Ofirin has not taught me this word.

The strange world growing in my head must wait. Master Miquiztin and the head of the girls' wing rush out to meet us, and the oldest students help the refugees find a place to rest while burns and wounds are attended to.

"Well done, Calizto," my telpochtlahtoh tells me at last. "As the Caxtiltecah push deeper into the city, more people will seek shelter. Word just came that the causeway to Tepayacac has been taken by Spaniards."

"But that was our last open route," I protest. "Wasn't Emperor Cuauhtemoc using it to smuggle in supplies?"

Miquiztin places a hand on my shoulder. "Now our resources will be stretched even thinner. But we are Tenochcah. Mexica. We will prevail, or we'll die in the attempt. Now go, help your fellow tiachcauh train the cadets. Tomorrow we face the invaders once more."

As I head to the training field, Sitlali shudders.

I can't believe I'm dreaming about the fall of Tenochtitlan.

Fall? Who said the city was going to fall?

It did, she says quietly, like she is afraid of giving me horrible news.

When? I ask. *When will it fall?*

Five hundred years ago. Everyone knows the story. It's in our history books, our museums. Our coins.

Five hundred years?

Yes. Today is June 7, 2019. Here. In my world.

She doesn't sound like a goddess. She sounds insane. I feel her pull away as the man named Martín begins to ask about their destination.

Anger wells as I approach Ayotochtli, who is sparring with a cadet named Epcoatl while a half dozen other boys between the ages of eleven and fifteen stand in a line, repeating basic offensive and defensive moves with practice macanas.

Epcoatl takes a misstep and Ayotochtli swats him hard in the stomach with the flat of the weapon. The boy drops to the dirt, clutching at himself and groaning.

"Get up," I say, unstrapping the netted bag from my chest and pulling a macana from the nearby rack. "Your enemies won't stand by while you catch your breath. They will slice your throat open. Yesterday, your brother fell in battle. Tomorrow, I may fall as well. No one will defend you but yourself, boy. Raise your guard!"

I move quickly, crossing the ground between us and swinging my wooden blade toward him. He barely lifts his own in time to parry. In seconds he has regained his feet. He's angry. But he's alive.

After the evening meal, Ayotochtli points to a group of whimpering boys. The encroaching darkness drives home the fact that they're now homeless orphans.

"We need to get them bedded down," my friend says. "They need structure and guidance."

I nod and call out. "Little Brothers, you'll be sleeping in the telpochcalli tonight as true cadets. Find a mat—there are plenty rolled up against the wall."

We spread them in pairs among the older boys. There's an unspoken agreement. Tonight, we remain with the refugees. They need us, their new big brothers.

I feel guilt about Ofirin, but these are my people. My obligation to them is greater. He'll survive another night.

Taking up my netted bag again, I feel Sitlali's presence return.

Hard choices, she murmurs. *I'm not sure what you are, Calizto. My imagination? My conscience? Some ancestral spirit? Regardless, thank you. You're a good person, trying to do the right thing. And that helps.*

I'm intrigued.

Helps what?

Me. I'm trying to decide. Should I stay with the caravan, continue to travel with these two men I don't trust—Martín and Severo—or should I flee, run off on my own?

I consider the dilemma. *What is the purpose of your trek?*

I'm searching for my father. He lives in los Estados.

I don't ask where that might be. It's clearly a distant land. *How old are you?*

Seventeen, like you.

It's difficult for a woman to travel alone. But if you don't trust those men, the dangers of a solitary trek may be preferable.

I think I can trust Martín. But Severo works for Jorge, this dangerous boy who's obsessed with me. I don't like Severo, and I don't like the idea that Jorge knows where I am through him.

I can feel the distaste that Jorge produces in her, the defiance that surges despite her fear, the determination to keep him from having her, no matter the cost.

I admire her. She hasn't let setbacks and tragedy overcome her, hasn't succumbed to the demands of an unworthy man. No, Sitlali is daring some long crossing—through deserts and over rivers—to find her father.

Escape, I say without thinking, almost urging her. *Wait until they're asleep and then slip into the night. You can make the voyage alone.*

There was a pause, then, *Not so alone. You're with me now. We're connected, somehow. Will you help? If I should need you?*

A strange warmth blossoms in my stomach, a blend of nerves and excitement.

I don't know why the gods have put your voice in my head. It may be madness. But yes, Sitlali. As far as I can, I will help you.

CHAPTER SEVEN

Sitlali

June 8–9, 2019

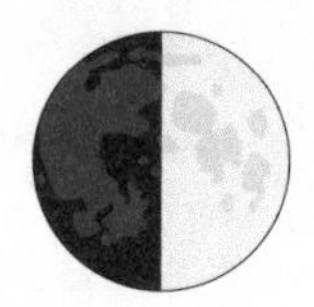

My mother laughs as she watches me paddle around in the water, suspended by my father's hands under my belly. Her eyes are bright stars, and her smile is resplendent against her sun-kissed skin. She is beautiful and young, the way she used to look before my father abandoned us.

"You're going to miss this," she says, when she looks up at him.

"I'll send for you," my father promises. Then he puts his arms around me and lifts me out of the water in one fell swoop. "Both of you."

I turn to look at my mother, but she is no longer happy, and we are no longer in the ocean on a bright beautiful day. My mother is a wailing ghost now, trapped in some shadowy place I do not recognize. "I'm sorry," she cries. "I'm sorry!"

Startled, I open my eyes and look around the truck's cabin.

"You okay?" Martín asks.

I nod, straighten up, and wipe the sleep out of my eyes. It has been a strange couple of days—sleeping beside strangers, hearing voices in my head telling me to escape, to run, to flee for my life. Surreal.

I've grabbed at my bag in my lap at every stop, while Martín shoves wads of money into the pockets lining his vest before bringing down the tailgate of his truck to let yet another passenger join us. With the conch secure in my bag, I've closed my eyes to the sight of his transactions and begged the moon to help us as more of us put our lives in Martín's hands.

The afternoon sun blazes everything in the road ahead, and I watch its rays glint off the belly of a water tower suspended on spindly legs to the right of us. Except for that structure, there is little else out here. The desert stretches for miles and miles.

As I sit between the two men, I worry that Martín might be just as dangerous as Jorge. How good could he be? He's eager to turn a profit from the desperation of people escaping their tormentors. Only I am not as lucky. My tormentor has sent a shadow to follow me.

"Are you sure you don't want to eat something? This is our last stop today," Martín says, pulling into a deserted-looking gas station.

"I'm just going to stretch my legs." I climb out of the truck and Martín and Severo walk into the convenience store and head for the restroom. While I wait, an old man comes out of the store carrying a feed bag. He tilts his bent cowboy hat and walks past me. As I watch him making his way to the side of the building, panic races through me. This is it. I have to do something, if I'm going to get away from Severo.

Glancing once more into the store, to make sure I am not being watched, I follow the old man around the corner.

"Excuse me, but can you give me a lift?" I ask. "Not far, just to the water tower up the road."

The old man hesitates. He looks me up and down and thinks.

"Just to the tower," he says, and then he opens the truck door. I climb in quickly.

He tries to make conversation during our short trip, but I only smile and agree, "Yes. It is a hot day."

A few minutes later, when he drops me off a quarter of a mile down the dusty dirt road off the highway, I give him a few pesos and he gives me two bottles of water and an old-fashioned compass he digs out of his glove box.

"Thank you," I say, moved by his generosity.

"I never saw you," he says before he drives away.

The unmerciful sun beats down on me, as I climb up to the water tower. Keeping an eye on the road, I shimmy along the catwalk until I am on the other side of the structure. When I'm sure I can't be seen, I lie flat on the hot, rusty metal, and wait for the darkness of night to make me invisible.

Severo and Martín look for me longer than I thought they would. Martín drives up and down the road for over an hour, stopping at intervals to let Severo scan the deserted landscape with his binoculars. But I am imperceptible, hidden in the shadows of the creaky catwalk.

When night comes, I climb off the tower and run—bolting into the desert like a newborn fawn when it's found its legs. The cool night breeze pulls the hair behind me, and the bright half-faced moon lights my way. I run so long and hard every muscle in my body aches. But it is a good pain. A safe distance away from the road, I find a little ridge and lie under it with the conch cradled in my hands because I think he can hear me better when I hold it.

Calizto? I call out in my mind. *Are you there? I did it. I escaped.*

When he doesn't answer, I roll over on my side and think about my grandmother again. As a ghost, she is lost to me. I left her back there, sitting on my cot, watching from the window as I walked away. The thought makes my chest tighten, and I rub at the spot where my heart aches. I miss her so much.

I am proud of you, Calizto's voice whispers in my head.

You heard me? I ask him.

Yes, he says. *You must rest now. Regain your strength.*

Yes, I whisper, and I close my eyes and thank the Moon Goddess for keeping us connected.

I must have fallen asleep right away because, when I open my eyes again, the sun is bursting through the horizon, lighting up the sky. Squinting, I stretch my arms and legs, push against the pain lingering there, and reach for my mochila. I open the hidden compartment inside my bag and lay out the marked map Jorge didn't find when he was going through my things. I'm pretty sure I'm fifteen, maybe twenty, miles north of Matehuala.

If I keep traveling north, following the sounds of the road, I should be in Coahuila by tomorrow night. Once I reach Saltillo, I can hire a private taxi, someone willing to drive me up to Piedras Negras. For now, I must concentrate on getting to Monclova. I don't want to spend another night in the desert. There is not much left to eat in my bag. I want to save the last packet of peanuts and the dried fruit for when I really need them. I tread through the dry grass, scanning the landscape for edible plants.

I push down brown brambles and desiccated chancaquillas with my shoes, making a path for myself as I go. The sun lashes at my back as I lean over a cactus with my mother's knife in my hand. The prickly pears at the top are ripe, big and purple, ready to be picked.

You have arisen early this morning.

I must be getting used to Calizto's voice coming into my mind when I least expect it, because he sounds like he's right here—walking beside me.

Yes, I admit. *I got hungry.*

We are doing the same thing, he says.

Starving? I ask.

He laughs low in his throat. *Scavenging.*

I laugh to myself too, as I press against a cactus pad. *There is always something you can eat in the desert if you know where to look.*

Same in a fallen city.

Fallen? Wait . . . what?

These dwellings are torched. The Spanish burned through this entire neighborhood at the water's edge.

Oh my God, what happened to the homeowners, their families?

Calizto's anger hits me, a wave of nausea in the pit of my stomach, and I know he's pushing against the rage he must feel at seeing such destruction. My eyes burn, and I will the tears away. I don't want to overwhelm him. I can get pretty emotional if I don't contain my feelings.

Most of them perished. Survivors will not be returning to this ruined place. But not all houses burned down. So, I am . . . pilfering death, like a wild musk hog. I do not need much. A few husks of corn. A bag of beans. Anything I can take back to my school.

As I think about what Calizto has said, I push a tuna away from me and slice at the anchored flesh. The fruit drops to the ground with a thud, and I kick it aside while I cut down three more. My mouth waters as I roll it around the rough pebbles and stones. When I am certain the prickly pears are free of spines, I use a hairpin and knife to peel them.

The work goes slow. Calizto has become silent. Our connection has cut off, and I am alone in the desert again. But I am exhilarated by the burst of sweet juice as I bite into the tender, red flesh of the prickly pear.

Refreshed, I get up and go, taking long strides to keep a good pace, but not so long that I wear myself out. One step at a time. One dry breath at a time. One bead of sweat at a time, I trek the desolate landscape.

A few hours later, I spot a low, flat rock in the shade of a huisache, and I ease myself down on it. My compass rattles when I shake it, and I wonder if it's working. I hear a loud bird's cry, and a dark-winged shadow swerves, dips, and then disappears. Squinting, I see it high up in the sky—an eagle, I think.

"Well, aren't you special?"

The eagle ignores me. Concentrates on the dip of its wings, flies off, and circles back. I watch it glide effortlessly. Oh, to fly, to soar, to drift beyond rivers and lakes—beyond borders—that would be spectacular. Life changing, I think.

A rivulet of sweat trickles down my forehead and pools inside the corner of my eye. I pull my shirt up and wipe my face. The eagle lets out a loud cry.

"What do you want?" I ask.

My answer comes quickly. A snake slithers on the dirt and coils before me. Its dusty body is perfectly wound together, ready to strike. While I hold my breath, the rattler sticks out its tongue and tastes the temperature.

Frozen, I press my bag against my chest. Consider throwing it at the snake. But I doubt it would do anything more than anger it.

Calizto!

I don't know why I call out to him in my mind. Am I crazy for hoping there is something magical, something otherworldly, at play with this conch? Maybe the sun has affected me and I'm losing my wits. Or maybe I call out to him because there is nobody else out here except for this seventeen-year-old boy fighting for his own life five hundred years away from me.

What is it? Is something wrong?

My heart beats hard in my chest, but I can feel Calizto's fear too; his concern for me pulsates like an echo at my temples.

Snake! I cry out in my mind.

What kind?

Diamondback!

I don't know that species . . .

Tzitzilika in kowatl! I shout in Nahuatl. *The snake that makes a rattling noise!*

Oh, tectli. Stay still, he advises in a calm voice. *She is more afraid of you than you are of her. She will not attack if you do not move,* he says. *She is curious. That is all.*

As if to defy his words, the rattlesnake zigzags sideways. *It's getting closer.*

Are you near a rock or tree limb? Something big you can throw at her?

I'm sitting on a rock, I tell him. *But it's too big to lift.*

Then you are sitting on her house.

What?!

Snakes burrow under rock formations. Do not move. Give her time to leave. She will come back when you are gone. Just breathe regularly. In. Out. In. Out. Concentrate on the rhythm of my voice.

I sit very still and breathe as Calizto guides me.

After an eternity, the rattlesnake shifts. I want to close my eyes, to escape this terrible moment, but I am too scared to do anything but watch the snake slide in beside me.

What is she doing now?

I'm about to tell him that it's trying to figure out where to bite me, when the eagle above me shrieks. In a heartbeat, the bird of prey descends on the snake, rips it off the ground, and flies off with it.

I must have screamed, because Calizto calls out to me. His voice is startled, panicked. I can sense his urgency, feel his despair coursing through my veins.

Sitlali? What is it? Did the tectli bite you?

No, no. It didn't. I'm all right, I assure him. *An eagle came down and grabbed it.*

Ah. The nagual of Huitzilopochtli, he says. *You are blessed, Sitlali. To be rescued by such a great god means you are protected.*

I hear a loud sound akin to thunder, and I know something is happening in that other lifetime where Calizto exists.

What's going on?

The Spanish, he says. *They are back. I must go.*

I sit still for a moment, waiting, but it's no use. The connection between us is broken again. I stand up and check my compass, wondering how far off course I am. Hoisting my bag over my shoulder, I start walking north.

I take a few swigs of water along the way. I want to drink so much more, but I have to be smart and ration it out. The heat of the sun is already burning invisible holes through my ball cap and the thin cotton of my white shirt.

I put the water back in the bag, and my fingers caress the conch. That's when it happens again—distant sights and sounds swirl inside my head, as blinding as the blazing sun above.

A crowded street.

Horses whinnying. Men shouting.

High-pitched screams. Metal crashing. Grunting.

Hooves. Swords. Metal. Obsidian blades. Horsemen. Feathers. Bright light.

A thousand rays of sunlight, sparking off silver swords, flashing from buckles and chest plates on beasts and men. And blood. So much blood. Blood dripping off steel. Blood splattered on the walkway. Blood on hands and forearms.

My heart thrums in my ears, a red bird trapped inside my chest, beating against me so hard I fear I might fall to my knees and faint.

Please, I beg the sun god, *don't let anything happen to Calizto. He is my lifeline on this journey. My heartbeat. My salvation.*

Help him.

CHAPTER EIGHT

Calizto

Day 2-Crocodile of the Year 3-House (June 10, 1521)

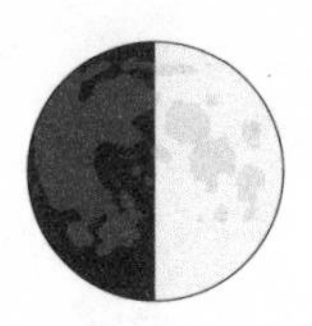

Cortés leads two hundred Spaniards and thousands of Tlaxcaltecah from the south. His commanders bear down on us as well: Alvarado advances from the west while Sandoval burns his way through our sister city of Tlatelolco.

If they converge at the heart of Tenochtitlan, we may be destroyed.

The emperor orders everyone to fight. Women take up the weapons of their fallen husbands and sons. Children are upon rooftops, ready to hurl stones.

Rage and fear keep despair from overwhelming my fellow Mexica.

"Dig!" I shout at the students. Ce Mazatl is gone. There is no one left to lighten this desperate moment. No black humor to soften the fierceness of my orders. "Dig or watch your families die!"

I squint into the distance. Cortés has brigantines on either side of the causeway. They fire cannonballs as they draw closer.

When they come to a gap carved into the causeway, they wedge a warship in place and cross defiantly. They are met by obsidian blades and clubs.

I turn from the glinting of the midday sun on bloodied armor, thrust my stick into the mud, and dig beside the others. I have the wooden box strapped to my back in my netted bag so I can perceive Sitlali—her voice fades the farther I get from the conch.

I don't want to lose that connection. I find myself eager to hear her impossible voice.

Today the girl doesn't speak, but sings to herself. From time to time comes a grunt of effort, a sigh of exhaustion.

She marches through the desert, undaunted.

We reach the waterline. Soon we are up to our waists in muck.

My muscles ache, as does my heart. The work feels futile.

The vanguard retreats. We clamber up, lay sturdy beams across the gap.

"Lift the bridge!" shouts Master Miquiztin. "And fall back at once!"

Sitlali squeals with pain or joy. I'm too exhausted to tell.

What?

A shallow creek! I'm going to follow it to its source.

"Calizto, move!" Ayotochtli shoves me. "Those bastards are coming fast!"

I shake free of the girl's troubles to focus on my own. I rush up the causeway. It becomes a broad street, edged by shattered, burning homes.

A glance over my shoulder: the Spaniards wedge another brigantine into the gap we spent hours creating.

At best, we have slowed them. Stopping them seems impossible.

We reach an earthwork of adobe and stone, right before the final canal. Squeezing between a gap, we pass through single file and then cross the bridge.

The gap is filled, the bridge lifted. Beyond stand the botanical gardens on the east side of the street, beside the abode of the king's councilmen. On the west side stretches the ceremonial plaza.

"Over the aqueduct!" commands Master Miquiztin. "Gather in the main plaza!"

Crossing that bridge makes my tongue swell in my parched mouth. No fresh water flows anymore.

Sitlali shouts. *A waterhole, nice and deep.*

For a moment, I feel she's mocking me. But she cannot see me, doesn't know of our shortages. She's simply relieved. I find some measure of joy in that relief.

We cross the aqueduct, spill into the main plaza on our left. Several hundred warriors wait, weapons in hand.

No one raises the bridge. No one believes Cortés will make it that far.

I'm less certain.

Ah! So refreshing.

Sitlali sounds happy. Scraping dried mud from my shins, I laugh despite my thirst, despite the odds.

I wish I could slake my thirst like that. Then I'd jump into the water and wash away all this mud.

Ooh, a bath! Sounds nice.

A nudge. Ayotochtli gestures south with his chin. "The enemy's reached the barrier."

I grit my teeth. "They'll use their *cañones.*"

He narrows his eyes. "Their *what*?"

A blast of cannon fire. An explosion of stone and dust, blossoming upward.

"Those things. Tlequiquiztli. Fire tubes."

When we can finally see, they're filling the canal with rubble from our own earthworks.

"Shit!" Ayotochtli grunts. "Those sons of bitches won't stop."

Across the street, Moteuczoma's palace looms mockingly. Our

former emperor did all he could to keep the Spaniards from marching into the heart of the empire. But once Cortés arrived with thousands of our enemies, Moteuczoma invited him into the city. A terrible mistake. The foreign invaders ignored all civil protocols, trampling on the truce and taking control of Tenochtitlan.

For months Cortés and his men held Moteuczoma captive within the walls of his own palace. There his will was broken, my father told me. There he offered up the imperial treasury and his own daughters to slake the enemies' greed. There his own people took his life in rage before running the Spaniards out of our city.

Now they've returned to finish the destruction they began.

"Fall back!" someone cries.

Men rush toward the southern gateway. We follow. The nahual of Huitzilopochtli, a massive stone eagle, looks down at warriors as they pass beneath him. To the left and right of the gate snarl a huge jaguar and wolf.

Master Miquiztin leads us to the gap between the temples of Lord Sun and Lord Wind.

Standing nearby is a massive sculpture: a ceremonial conch, carved from volcanic rock, painted bright red and blue.

A sign. Mother Moon is watching over me.

"We wait," the old warrior growls. "And if those dogs breach the gate, we ambush them on the priests' signal."

Thousands of warriors have spread throughout the ceremonial space, where a year ago, during the festival of Toxcatl, the Spaniards massacred hundreds of my fellow Mexica, including my mother's brother, Ceolin.

I hope to avenge my uncle's death.

Ah, this feels so good!

A bit of Sitlali's relief and enjoyment of her unexpected dip seems to spill from her mind into mine. My muscles loosen. The heat on my skin is soothed.

I wonder what she looks like, resting naked in that water, in the midst of a desert, far from everyone and everything she knows.

Hey! Our minds are connected. Stop trying to picture me. And I'm not naked!

My features twist with embarrassment. *Apologies. I'm in dire straits, so my mind seeks escape.*

Well, I'm not your entertainment.

Of course not.

But 'dire straits'? Her voice is full of worry. *Are you okay? I had a vision. Horses and armor. Fighting. Blood.*

How can you see the battles we're fighting? Why can't I see your desert?

I'm not sure. But . . . for a while now, I've been able to perceive certain spirits. Family members who have died. Maybe that gives me an advantage here.

I nod as if she can see me. *It seems proximity to the conch is necessary for us to communicate.*

Right, she agrees. *Too far away, and we can't perceive each other. But if we're kind of close, we can hear our voices.*

It requires effort, I remind her. *It strains the mind. But if one of us is touching the sacred trumpet, the connection is strengthened. If we both hold it, it's as if we are in each other's minds.*

And in that case, I can see what you see, for whatever reason, she surmises. *That seems clear. But you haven't answered my question. Are you okay?*

I'm fine. The Spanish keep trying to get in. We keep fending them off. But I need some distraction. Tell me about the waterhole. Are there animal tracks nearby? Something you might catch?

Actually, there's a bunch of crayfish moving in the mud. I'm keeping my feet away.

Cook them. Who knows when you'll find food again?

Good idea, Calizto. But in a bit. Right now, this cool water is all I care about.

From where I am crouched, I can see the Serpent Wall that surrounds the Sacred Precinct, its crenellations revealing the street beyond. The enemy cross over the bridge we left in place over the aqueduct. They pull a cannon into place, right in front of the barred wooden gates.

"Get ready," I mutter.

Reaching over my shoulder, I pull my maccuahuitl from its wooden sheath.

The cannon booms, and the wood of Eagle Gate explodes in a million splinters, leaving just the stone structure in place.

Enemy troops pour in.

I found enough firewood, Sitlali suddenly says. *Mamá taught me this trick. I start a fire, let it die down. Then cook the crayfish on the embers, nice and slow, till they're soft and juicy.*

Sitlali, I'm about to go into battle. Could you set aside the conch? It's best if you cannot hear my thoughts for a while.

And if you get hurt?

The gods' will be done.

A thunderous beating fills the air. I flick my gaze to Coatepetl, the pyramid that rises above the city. There, before the red-and-blue shrines upon its summit, the priests of Tlaloc and Huitzilopochtli pound out a signal rhythm.

Protect the temples, the drumbeats declare. *Keep safe the images of the gods.*

From everywhere, our forces emerge, howling. Muskets and cannon open fire.

The sky goes dark with smoke and falling arrows.

"Attack!" screams Master Miquiztin.

I lift my shield and rush headlong at the bastards.

Two Spanish soldiers dash up the steps to the temple platform. The priests keep striking their drums until steel swords run them through. Then, mocking our rituals, the armored dogs pitch them down the slope like sacrificial victims.

I slam into a Spaniard. He raises his blade, but I am faster. With a tremendous downward blow, I hack his arm off at the elbow.

He's still screaming as I wheel to slice the throat of a Tlaxcaltecatl behind me.

"Die!" I howl. "Die, you motherless monsters!"

Sitlali's cry sinks into my soul. *Don't be like them!*

But there is no other way to be, except dead.

Not understanding how, I reach into my mind and . . .

push

her

out.

Chaos reigns for half a watch. The Spaniards may have their guns and steel and horses, but in such close quarters, weighted down with armor and weapons, they're no match for us. Nor are the Tlaxcaltecah, as generations of flower wars have shown.

At last, the enemy retreat. We run them from the heart of Tenochtitlan, hacking at their backs, flinging arrows in their wake. In their haste, they leave their cannon sitting on the street. Master Miquiztin signals a halt to the handful of us who remain.

"Let the others give chase. We must do something about their large weapon."

Working to calm my labored breathing, I crouch beside the cannon. Ofirin has explained the basics of its workings.

"Look for bags full of black powder," I say.

Ayotochtli leans over the barrel. "We have none of the big metal balls."

"We can shove stones inside instead," I counter.

Unfortunately, the enemy has taken his gunpowder with him. The weapon is useless.

"Drag it to the canal," Master Miquiztin says. "Dump it in."

After meeting with other captains, Miquiztin speaks with Ayotochtli and me.

"Thank the gods, neither Alvarado nor Sandoval got close to the ceremonial center. As it stands, Cortés met with further losses as he retreated: women and children dropped heavy stones on passing enemy soldiers, and many arrows winged their way into their pale and putrid flesh." He wipes blood from his lips. Not his own. "So the cowards set fire to the buildings. Many innocents died."

We disperse as night falls. When I arrive, Ofirin is asleep, but he has prepared a meal using what I scavenged yesterday.

After eating a little, I unroll my mat and pick up the conch.

Sitlali. Are you there? A moment passes with no response. Perhaps it's over, the conch's magic only so powerful across such a distance.

Sitlali? It's for the best.

How could you just shove me away? I was so worried, and I didn't know . . . What if we'd been cut off forever?

Relief steals my breath. *I apologize. It wasn't pleasant, what I had to do. But I'm back in my parents' home now. Safe. Unharmed.*

Thank the Virgencita.

The little virgin?

You know . . . wait, no, you wouldn't. The Virgin Mary. Mother of God.

Ah. Teteoh Innan. Tonantzin.

Yes, Tonantzin! Exactly. She—wait.

There is nervous stillness.

What? I ask.

I'm not alone. There's something . . . Oh no!

I sit up, my body tense, as if I could leap into that desert and keep her safe.

A coyote! It's standing on the other side of the fire, snarling at me!

I take a deep breath.

Tezcatlipoca. The trickster god. Sower of chaos. The coyote is one of his faithful lieutenants. But it fears fire.

Mine is dying! Just a few flames left.

Is there a branch nearby? Take it up; set it alight. Keep it between you and the coyote.

Okay. I'm— Shit!

All I can sense is fear, the pumping of her heart, the darkness looming all around as she runs.

Sitlali! Sitlali, what has happened?

The agony of those few seconds is almost worse than hours of battle. In all this devastation, her voice is the only surcease. It can't be silenced. I can't bear more loss.

Okay. I'm

—wince—

okay. Had to clamber up a mesquite super fast to get away from it. Cut myself a little on the thorns. But I'm safe now. Nice forking branch makes a perfect bed up here.

Oh, thank the Moon.

I wish she were shining brighter. I could see better. Feel calmer. And the stupid creature is staying put, watching me from the fringes of camp. For now.

If only I could help, I mutter.

Maybe you can, she says, after a few moments. *Tell me something about yourself. Distract me a little.*

Unsure of what to say, I start with where I am.

This is my parents' house. It belonged to my great-grandparents once. Their parents came to Tenochtitlan from the kingdom of Cuitlahuac, an island where Lake Xochimilco joins Lake Chalco, to the south. When Emperor Itzcoatl—who created the Triple Alliance of Anahuac—conquered Cuitlahuac, he took farmers back with him. My ancestors.

What's the "Triple Alliance of Anahuac"?

You know, the three seats of power. Tenochtitlan, Tetzcohco, Tlacopan.

Oh, the Aztec Empire.

What?

That's what we call it nowadays.

We aren't Aztecah. Our ancestors were, long ago. But they left Aztlan.

Sorry. Didn't know. What happened when the farmers came to Tenochtitlan from Cuitlahuac?

The emperor settled them in the Zoquiyapan borough. Where this house stands, on the southeast edge of the city. The farmers intermarried with Huitznahuac folks, Tenochcah from southern neighborhoods. And a new calpolli arose.

I'm not one for talking. Yet my heart seems to open, and the story of our minor house comes spilling out. Metztonalco, small but proud. Its role in important moments. How the drought and famine nearly killed my great-grandparents. How they built this home, raised their children, spread their green chinampas along the canal.

Rage and fear drain from me as I relate the long history. By the time I realize Sitlali has fallen asleep, I feel more at peace than I have in months.

Holding the conch tight against my chest, I lie back and slip into dreams.

In them, a beautiful girl sleeps in the arms of a mesquite.

The stars glitter above her, silent and watchful.

CHAPTER NINE

Sitlali

June 11, 2019

Wake up, Sitlali . . . , the voice whispers my name softly, like a feather tracing the side of my cheek, and I smile in recognition.

Calizto.

I lie still, refusing to relinquish my dream, because I know when I open my eyes, he will not be here with me, and I wish he was.

I wish I were there too, he says. His sweet voice is so intimate, so in tune with my thoughts, that my cheeks warm.

I'm awake, I tell him, a bit startled. Because now that my eyes are open, I remember I am up in a tree.

I shift slightly to the left and see that this ancient tree is sturdy and strong. I can see the dawning of a milky cerulean sky peeking through a canopy of branches with sparse fernlike leaves.

I can feel the mirth as it enters Calizto's heart and mind. *What's so funny?* I ask.

I have slept in many strange places, but never in the arms of Mother Mesquite.

You can also see me now? I ask.

Only in my imagination. But I can hear and feel your thoughts. Can you feel . . . my presence?

Like you're right here, lying beside me on this tree branch, I admit, and my cheeks warm again.

"Oh shit!"

What is it?

The coyote's back! He's after my mochila. I must have dropped it in the middle of the night, I say.

Be careful, Little Star, Calizto warns. *Coyotl is the eternal trickster. He will not give up easily.*

The coyote digs with his narrow nose through my bag, attempting to get its flap open.

"Hey!" I yell. "Get away from there!"

The coyote snarls up at me; his long canines glisten in the sunlight.

Do not turn your back on him, Calizto warns. *He's not averse to attacking humans. Break off a long tree limb. Beat him away.*

I watch the coyote shake and toss my mochila around.

I'll do more than beat him, I say, pushing Calizto out of my mind so I can think straight.

Focusing on the coyote, I find a long, lean limb and pull at it. Wasting no time, I cut it off the branch with my mother's knife.

The coyote tears my mochila open and chomps on the packets of peanuts and dried fruit he's stolen from me.

"Euph! You're going to pay for that," I tell the scrawny beast, and I fasten the knife to the end of my javelin with the sweaty bandana I was wearing around my neck.

When I am done, I ease myself off the mesquite. Wielding my weapon, I scream—a loud, warrior-like roar that echoes in the distance.

"Ah! Ah!" I shout, making fierce, stabbing motions in the coyote's direction.

The scavenger bares its teeth and snarls at me.

"Go away!" I yell. "Go on! Get out of here!"

Not ready to let me win, the coyote barks and snaps at the end of my weapon. Instinctively, I jab his cheek. But it is a weak jab, and I can see my mistake as soon as the coyote jumps back and then jumps forward quickly.

I see the blood before I feel the pain. But when it comes, the agony is a quick tearing of nerves and flesh. It rushes up my forearm and explodes like a bullet in my left shoulder blade, and I am momentarily thrown back against the mesquite's trunk.

As if stunned by my high-pitched scream, the coyote jumps back and lopes away, watching me peripherally as it walks sideways, thinking about his next move. Then, because he sees me writhing, he dashes forward, intent on claiming my mochila.

I don't second-guess myself. This time, I lift my javelin high up in the air and stab him hard, using both hands and putting all my weight into it. The weapon pushes through the coyote's shoulder. The scraggly beast cries and yips as he runs off, intent on getting as far away from me as possible.

I look at my wounded forearm. It is a deep cut. His teeth did more than tear the skin. They sliced through muscle. Cradling my arm, I pick up my mochila and swing it over my right arm. Then I walk back to the creek, where I wash my wound in earnest. It is a painful process, but eventually my forearm stops bleeding and I wrap it with strips I rip off my nicest cotton shirt.

The sun in the sky is a merciless god, oblivious to my misery as I trek north for a few more hours. Because my arm hurts so much, I walk at a slower pace, my makeshift lance in hand. A rivulet of sweat rushes down my forehead and sneaks past my eyebrow. I close my eyes and listen, but it is not the mice in the underbrush I hear.

Instead, it is a young man's prayers that come into my mind. I catch only words and phrases. At first, I am not sure if I am seeing things. But it is there, about twenty yards in front of me, a wavering, ghostly apparition—a young man holding a luminous conch.

The wind whips his long, black hair all around him, but he is focused. His lean, wiry body is naked, save for a white loincloth wrapped around his slim waist and doubled over the front. His bare feet are planted firmly on the ground shoulder width apart.

Perplexed, I stop, listen to the murmur of his voice.

Mother Moon, shining silver,
bells dark upon your cheek—
at the vanguard you went marching,
all Four Hundred Southern Stars
glittering in your wake.

Calizto! I cry, because I recognize his voice. The soft, low timbre is unmistakable. But how is he *here* in my time? Did he cross over?

Calizto! I call again, as I rush toward him, but no matter how far or fast I walk or run, Calizto is never more than a ghostly outline, surreal as sandstorms and sunlight, always standing the same distance away from me as when I first spotted him.

Calizto! It's me, Sitlali! Can you see me? I cry, but he cannot hear me. He is in the middle of some kind of ceremonial ritual.

I listen. Mesmerized.

At Serpent Hill the sun arose,
and snuffed out all the stars.

He broke you into glowing bits
and hurled you from the heights—
your hummingbird brother.

Yet piece by piece you healed yourself
and rose once more into the sky
to light the night for broken souls.
An orphan, I call you mother.
Come make me whole as well.

He is beautiful. Eyes dark and glassy as obsidian rocks. Skin smooth and lambent as ancient copper. He is handsomer than any boy I've ever met before. His physical beauty is . . . distracting. And my thoughts feel out of place—out of time. I close my eyes and remember the last night I spent with my childhood girlfriends on the Veracruz shoreline.

My friends had begged the moon to find them boyfriends. But this is not what I asked for—not what I need. As Calizto continues praying, I look at his long, lean muscles, his strong thighs, and wonder what ancient god has brought him here to me? And to what end?

Sitlali?

I look up.

Calizto is standing before me, close enough to touch.

You can see me? I ask.

The conch held securely under his left arm, Calizto extends his right hand and reaches out for me. It passes through me without making contact.

Vaguely, he explains. *As in a vision.*

You could only hear me before. I could only catch glimpses of what you saw. What's changed?

Calizto frowns. *We hold the sacred trumpet of the moon goddess,* he says. *I know very little about its timeless, potent magic. Those who did are . . . dead.*

And why me? I ask. *Why did the sea leave it there for me to find?*

There is a pause. *You must have called it to yourself, the way we call all things into our lives. Your desire must have been strong. The conch had no other choice but to come into your hands.*

My arm is throbbing, so I pull it up and hold it against my stomach.

You are hurt! Calizto reaches out again. *What happened? Was it the coyotl?*

He took a good chunk out of me, I admit. *But I taught him a lesson.*

You must be careful, especially now, when you are wounded, he says. *Sit down. Rest.*

Calizto descends slowly to the ground. I watch his lithe actions. He is melody in motion, built for movement, for song, for love. The thought makes me blush.

It's nothing. It will heal, I say, fussing with my bandage.

His handsome face is scrunched with concern, and my heart beats a little bit faster at the sight of him. I try to ignore my body's physical reaction to his proximity, but my attraction to him is palpable.

Shocked, I push the feeling away.

I think it's Tonantzin, the Virgen de Guadalupe, using this conch to bring us together, I tell Calizto. *Though I have to wonder what it means.*

Calizto considers my words.

No, he finally says. *Why would Mother Goddess call us together now? This is not her domain.*

Oh, Calizto, it's all her domain now.

What do you mean?

Tonantzin is our Great Mother in Heaven, the one who came to offer us love and peace. We adore her in our time. Many temples have been erected in her name.

What about Coyolxauhqui? Is she as widely adored?

I'm sorry, Calizto. I think Tonantzin is the only deity you would recognize today.

He scoffs. *One goddess cannot do everything for mankind. You have clearly misunderstood your priestess. My mother explained the mystery to me. Tell me, Sitlali—are there images of Tonantzin in your temples?*

Yes.

And are they all identical?

Well, yes, and no. I can see where he's going with this line of questioning. *We know them by different names, Virgen de la Candelaria, Our Lady of Fatima. But they're still all Mary, Queen of Heaven. In Mexico we call her Guadalupe, but she identified herself as Tonantzin when she first appeared on the hill of Tepeyac, just a few decades from your time. She is the mother of our mestizo nation, worshipped for centuries by Indigenous and Spanish and their children as our cultures intermarried.*

Intermarried? You mean, the Spanish do not retreat?

I consider shifting the conversation to something else, but that would be too much like deception. *I am sorry,* I whisper. *But, no, they do not retreat.*

Calizto inhales deeply. I feel him fighting his emotions.

I understand, he says. *There are no images of my people's gods because the Spanish have gathered them into their coateocalli, the serpent temple where foreign deities are guarded with honor.*

More like in their museums . . . but sort of. Yes.

I knew it! We are subject to the Spanish. But our ways endure, do they not?

Yes. The Mexica ways are very much alive, I tell him. *Everywhere. Traditions, foods, language, and especially my people's religion, which is a mixture of both cultures.*

Calizto is silent. I can feel his confusion and sadness.

Are you all right? I ask, after a moment.

Calizto puts the conch down, carefully placing it beside him on the dirt floor. *I am weary,* he admits. *I have been putting out fires throughout the city all day. My heart is heavy for the loss. And I wonder . . .* He rubs his face, presses his fingertips against the bridge of his long, straight nose, and sighs. *I wonder if perhaps the Spanish priests and sorcerers have bewitched me, if they are readying me.*

Readying you for what?

Surrender.

My heart lurches in my chest. *No, no,* I say. *That's not . . . You can't give up, Calizto. Promise me you won't give up.*

He nods, and, when he looks at me again, his eyes are obsidian gemstones, dark and full of mystery. But the corners of his full lips are slightly lifted, and there is a gentleness in the way he says, *I promise.*

When Calizto moves away from the conch and disappears into thin air, I take a deep breath. Then I get up and start moving again, slowly but purposely through the sparse thicket. After a while, my face begins to feel hot. I touch my fevered forehead and laugh. Out loud. To myself.

When I finally look at it, my watch tells me I've been walking five hours. I've had to stop so many times to catch my breath, assuage my thirst, and pull my scattered, rambling thoughts together I worry my disorientation might have thrown me off course.

By sunset, I am in a state of despair.

Thirsty. Tired. Timeworn.

My arm is on fire. When I look down at it, I know I must be delusional because the dark, bloodstained dressing has shrunk. It has shriveled up and transformed itself into a huge, spindly spider, a giant brown recluse that's wrapped its eight steely legs around my forearm in a vicious vise. I tear at its skeletal thorax, but then the spindly spider turns to cotton again, and my fingernails get caught in the fabric.

I tear it off, exposing the angry, red wound beneath it to the elements.

Exhausted, I close my eyes, and I pray that my spider-infested arm might be saved—that the baby spiders pulsating under the skin, feeding off my wounded flesh might be figments of a festering, fevered mind.

Looking down at the parched earth under my feet, I wonder if my blood and my organs will slip into the crevices of this desolate land. Will the best parts of me give birth to red-and-orange cactus blossoms? Will my restless spirit fade and blow away with time, sending seedlings of my soul adrift, like the feathered dandelions?

I look at the desolate landscape stretching for miles around me and cry.

I am afraid of never reaching my madrina Tomasa's house, afraid of not finding my father and handing him my mother's picture—of not ever being able to remind him of what he left behind. But, more important, I am afraid of never reuniting with him, because that is what I want most of all. My heart wants what every wounded heart wants.

Reconciliation.

CHAPTER TEN

Calizto

Day 4-House of the Year 3-House (June 12, 1521)

Sitlali's hair, cascading in waves, night reflected upon the ocean. Her eyes, wide and mischievous. That inviting smile, teeth impossibly white, stars and moon glimpsed through parting lips.

And her skin. Glistening gold, like honey or amber. I lean in, eager to be trapped.

Her eyes close, long lashes around my soul.

Then I sit up with a start. I'm in my parents' house. My heart is pounding. My palms ache.

But as the dream fades, there's a lightness in my heart. I set aside the yearning of my flesh as dawn awakens.

Coyolxauhqui sent me Sitlali. The conch must have a greater purpose. Perhaps we can use it to defeat the Spanish.

I won't accept the future Sitlali has described. I refuse to see Mexico bound to Spain as a vassal state, paying tribute, our gods held hostage across the sea.

"Are you well? And what is that conch you hold?"

Ofirin has risen on one elbow. His once boyish face is now thin and drawn. Hunger has added years to his features.

"Just a dream. The conch I've already told you about. My mother's trumpet."

I stand, pour water into a basin, rub sweat from my face and chest.

"Are you sure? I don't think I've ever seen it before."

"I'm not in the mood for games."

"All worn out from your dream, eh?" he says with a low laugh. "I don't know who Sitlali is, but you kept calling her name. No wonder you're gone more often."

Ignoring his goading, I dry myself. "Need anything? I'll scavenge this afternoon."

He taps the Spanish book and papers beside him. "Any reading or writing material. I'm penning an account of my year in Mexico."

The strange glyphs capture the sounds of Spanish speech, as well as the Nahua tongue, Ofirin asserts, and Yoruba, the language of his homeland.

"I'll see whether the Spanish left anything else."

Ofirin clears his throat. "And, of course, food."

I nod, take up sword and shield and conch. Then I leave him to his hungry solitude.

Walking to the telpochcalli, I grip the conch and *look*. Her ghostly outline stumbles a few rods ahead.

Sitlali! I call. *How does the morning find you?*

She doesn't answer. Doesn't turn to look at me. Have I offended her? She can see things others cannot. Perhaps she's peered into my dreams.

No matter how fast I run, her specter remains distant.

When my feet slap against the last wooden bridge, she turns. Her face is pinched in pain. She clutches her wounded arm.

When she speaks, it's as if we're in the same physical space, our voices borne on the air.

"Calizto. Is it you? Am I hallucinating?"

Something unseen squeezes my chest.

"I'm here," I tell her, speaking aloud. "What's wrong?"

"My arm feels like it's going to fall off."

Anger and concern bite into my gut. "You need to rest."

"No," she mutters, shaking her curls. "I've got to find help. A town. A house. Something. If I rest anymore, I might never get up again."

"Calizto!"

I glance beyond Sitlali. Ayotochtli is running toward me. I wave my arms for him to stop, but he keeps coming.

Runs into Sitlali.

No.

Runs *through her.*

In a shudder of lunar magic, she disappears.

"What?" I demand, furious.

"Not enough rest, you lusty rascal? Wipe the sleep from your eyes. The master got everyone up before dawn. Something's about to happen."

There are fewer refugees at the telpochcalli, now that the healers have set up a field hospital in the Great Plaza. But some of the older orphans remain, training to fight.

"Calizto, Ayotochtli," Miquiztin calls. The students and refugee boys are seated in the courtyard, facing our teacher. We soon stand between them. "Long have you both battled. Many enemies have you slain. In other times, a general would have offered you the greatest glory. But even I can confer titles. Harken, all: I have nothing further to teach these two. Today, I declare them telpochtlahtohqueh. No longer my students, but masters of the school. My colleagues, your instructors."

Overwhelmed, I drop to one knee. With my index finger, I scrape dust from the stones before his feet. Then, relishing the tang of humility, I place the earth on my tongue and swallow, as my father taught me to do.

Ayotochtli performs the same obeisance, and we rise.

"The Caxtiltecah have a blockade in the north," Miquiztin says, "keeping food from the city. Rations will be even further reduced. Calizto, you've shown an uncanny knack for scavenging. But today, a simpler task. The emperor has ordered the Palace of Moteuczoma abandoned. Its contents and remaining residents are moving to the military headquarters in the borough of Atzacualco. Take a canoe and bring us whatever food you can. Ayotochtli and I will attempt to impose some discipline on these pups."

I set off at once, making my way along the canals of Zoquiyapan, giving wide berth to the men and women tasked with pulling corpses from the water. A few gardens sprawl on rooftops here and there, vegetables for noble families that remain in their white houses.

I paddle past the Temple of the Centzonhuitznahuah, the Four Hundred Southern Stars that once followed their sister, silvered Coyolxauhqui, into battle against their mother. In other times, I would meet with patrols and royal guards. Today, however, the air is still, and no one walks the shady paths along the edge of the canal. I squint my eyes against the rising sun, but Sitlali never reappears.

The canal opens up into a small lagoon. A raucous chattering comes from the royal aviary as I round the bend. At last the Palace of Moteuczoma looms before me, still majestic. Though its front façade is scorched and pitted, its main entrance shattered by cannonballs, the rear gate rises pristine and white above glittering green water. A series of statues atop the gateway make my heart skip a beat: the curling speech glyph, again and again. Heralding the home of the Hueyi Tlahtoani, the Great Speaker. Emperor, Ofirin would say.

I'm reminded of Sitlali's hair, forming the same symbol over and over as it spills down her shapely back.

Enough. I dock beside a few larger canoes that are being loaded. Nodding at workers as if I belong, I climb the steps.

A guard gestures. "You are?"

"Calizto. Telpochtlahtoh of Metztonalco, in Zoquiyapan. Two dozen boys, in need of rations."

He gestures inward with his spear. "Look for the giant."

I have no idea what he means, but I touch my heart in salute and obey. Ignoring the empty gardens and bustling administrative offices to my left and right, I head west along the broad corridor that leads to the living area.

From the shadows along one of the walls steps a giant.

A man, of course, but half again as tall as me.

"Here for food, are you?" the giant rumbles.

I nod.

"Follow me." He turns toward a staircase leading downward. As I follow, he continues to speak. "Not up. That's the royal dwellings. Down, into the servants' quarters."

We descend into semidarkness. Then high windows spill light onto a hall lined with scores of rooms. More than two thousand people once lived here, a small army to meet the needs of an emperor and his court.

We move past the maze of living quarters and emerge near the palace kitchens. A half dozen people are busy organizing, measuring, filling baskets.

Seated at a table is a beautiful noble, making calculations upon a strip of paper. As we move closer, I realize from the ceremonial clothing they're not a woman but a xochihuah from the temple of Xochipilli.

They raise their head and smile. "What a handsome fellow. How can we help you?"

"I am Calizto, telpochtlahtoh of Metztonalco in . . ."

"Yes, in Zoquiyapan. Calizto." They glance at the engraved box hanging at my side in its netted bag. "By the Divine Blossom! I know those markings. You're Meyalli's son."

Surprised to hear my mother's name, I can only blink and swallow. The xochihuah's mascaraed eyes narrow below their elaborate, ribboned hair.

"She's gone?"

My voice hitches as I reply. "All of them are gone."

They take my hand. "I'm truly sorry. Your mother was a wise and holy priestess. Your loss is ours as well."

The giant clears his throat. "Noble Quechol, he's come for rations."

Smiling, Quechol releases me. "Of course. Number of students?"

"Two dozen, including orphaned boys. Another five in the girls' wing."

Quechol makes a note on their ledger. "Friends, two baskets for young Calizto."

"Thank you," I say.

"You're welcome. The state coffers have already been transported away, but the royal larders still burgeon. Lord Cuauhtemoc, understanding his duty to give each citizen a role in such difficult times, recruited me to oversee the distribution."

I cannot help but glance about, hoping to see Sitlali again. The absence of her voice troubles me. I call her name in my mind, but there's only silence.

"Are you well?" Quechol asks.

I should say nothing. Madness has likely seized me, not divine visions or the actual voice and form of a girl from the future. But Quechol is an acolyte of Xochipilli, adept in piercing the veil and seeing creation with unhindered eyes.

"Noble Quechol," I begin, pulling my mother's trumpet from its box. "For some days now, I've had a continuous vision. A voice I believe Mother Moon sent me, a figure I can see when I hold this holy conch. But something has happened. The voice is gone, the apparition absent. Can you . . . help me?"

They stare at the moon conch, entranced. Then they begin to recite in a whisper.

"Up from the depths of the sea, a conch that glowed pink arose on roaring waves, drifting slow into a bay."

Something stirs deep in my mind. A memory, struggling to surface.

"Eyacatl?"

"Yes, Noble Quechol?" the giant replies.

"Please take Calizto's baskets. Wait for him above."

"Of course."

With a single hand, he scoops up both loads.

Quechol stands. "Come. The temple is a smoking ruin, thanks to the godless Caxtiltecah, but there may be an option in this palace."

I follow them, eyes fixed on the flowers embroidered onto their long huipil, shimmering threads from shoulders to knees. We climb stairs and then descend again, twisting and turning through the sprawling innards of the royal complex.

At last, we reach a door. Quechol opens it to reveal a windowless room. Floor and walls and ceiling are slabs of black basalt.

A single mat, unrolled at the center. A low table against one wall, replete with jars and bowls and other utensils.

"This was Moteuczoma's meditation chamber," Quechol explains, approaching the table in the light that filters through the open door. They begin to grind ingredients in a stone mortar. "Here he could block out the waking world and explore the Divine Dream."

They hand me the mortar. It smells of honey, of magnolias, and of something earthy, musky, fungal.

"Xochinanacatl," Quechol explains. "Nectar of the Sovereign Flower. When you drink it, hold Coyolxauhqui's conch tight against your chest. Your vision will return."

They guide me out of the palatial maze to where Eyacatl awaits with the baskets.

"Be well." I bow my head as I take my leave. Quechol kisses my forehead.

"And you, Calizto. May your heart and eyes remain ever open."

The giant carries the baskets to my canoe. As I board, he pushes the boat from the dock with a massive hand.

Not knowing what to say, I incline my head. He does the same before disappearing into the royal complex.

I paddle out of sight, then let the canoe slide under its own momentum along the sun-dappled water of the canal. I drink the potion Quechol has given me, taking the conch in my hands and hugging it to my heart.

"Sitlali," I murmur. For the first time since childhood, my tears well. "Where are you?"

The sun is slanting toward the western horizon. I think of the cihuateteoh, fearsome protectors of the sun, women who died in childbirth and were transformed into goddesses that streak through the evening sky, howling.

What if she's dead? What if she's succumbed to the coyote's bite or some other peril of that desert? Can I survive another loss?

Gradually, these concerns fade. I'm filled with a sense of peace. The scorched and shattered buildings I float past seem a cheap illusion, a painted façade atop reality. My eyes and mind adjust to the truth. Tenochtitlan is not real. Neither is this body.

Beyond the surface, I see the glowing knot of my identity—three souls bound into one—and the tether that anchors me to the conch.

And flowing from the conch, a silver-bangled stream that arcs through the air . . .

. . . and binds me to Sitlali, who has fallen to her knees not far from my canoe.

She is weeping and begging, staring at the sky.

"Please!" she calls. "God of the Sun. Show mercy! Don't let me die."

"Sitlali!" I cry with my whole being.

With a shudder, she lowers her eyes. They are sunken, full of fever and madness. Her arm is red, dark threads of poison twisting under her skin toward her shoulder.

Then she sees me.

"Calizto! Oh, I thought I'd lost you forever."

It takes every ounce of will in my unmasked heart not to leap from the canoe and try to cross the centuries to her side.

"I found a way back to you. But you must get up now. You need help. You're dying. Yet you cannot die. Do you hear me?"

Sadness and despair and rage shatter the peace in my heart.

"I won't let you die! On your feet, woman! Keep walking!"

Startled, she pushes against the sand and stands. Takes a wobbly step. Another.

Then she stops.

"I said . . ."

"Wait, Calizto. There's something on the horizon. I think it's a house."

She takes another few steps. The glow of her knotted souls burns brighter.

Sitlali starts to run.

I row after her with all my might.

"Ay, mamá! Abuela! Virgencita! Don't let this be a mirage. Let me find shelter and help."

She stumbles along, running as best she can. I follow in my canoe, heedless of my route or surroundings.

"It's a farmhouse, Calizto! I see fields, horses. I'm going to be . . ."

Sitlali suddenly falls, face-first. She appears to hit the surface of the water, disappearing into its depths.

"No!" I scream. "Sitlali!"

Then the explosions begin. I rip my eyes from the water. I've paddled into my neighborhood in Zoquiyapan, the eastern edge of the city.

There's my parents' house, just down the canal.

And beyond, anchored near Nezahualcoyotl's Dike, is a Spanish brigantine.

It fires a volley. I see the smoke before the sound reaches my ears.

All around me, houses are smashed into kindling by cannonballs.

"Oh, shit!" I exclaim. "Ofirin!"

Reaching the nearest pier, I leap from the canoe and rush toward the humble abode where I was born and raised.

Before I can reach that final remaining heritage of my family, it explodes.

CHAPTER ELEVEN

Sitlali

June 13, 2019

In the dream, I am six years old. My father twirls me around on the beach at Heroica. He tosses me high up in the air, into the misty coolness of clouds and sky, and, for a moment, I am weightless. My hair waves and bends like dry beach grass around me. But soon, I am falling, descending, helpless. I inhale a lungful of salty air and scream. My father catches me in his strong arms, pulls me against his chest, and laughs.

I laugh too.

"What? Did you think you could fly away?" he asks as he dips me. "Never. You're mine. My little seagull. My tiny osprey."

Then he nuzzles my neck, like a shaggy dog. I scrunch my face and push him away.

Somewhere behind him, my mother giggles and says, "No! She's mine!"

In a heartbeat, she grabs me and steals me away from my father. I bounce on her shoulder as she runs down the beach, laughing. Then, breathless, she stops and says, "You're my little sparrow. My little partridge."

I laugh and laugh as she smothers me with kisses, but when I open my eyes, it is not my mother I see. A white, floppy-eared goat is nuzzling my earlobes. I try to push it away, but she is too strong for me.

Two small boys are sitting on their haunches, hands on their knees, giggling as they watch me try to shoo the goat away.

I try to sit, but my vision spins and swirls. I need help, but I can't open my lips wide enough to say anything. I try to lick my parched lips, but my tongue feels swollen.

Speak, I tell myself. I know what I want to say, but the muscles of my face won't respond. I feel helpless.

I squint as the barn door opens. An older boy pushes his dark hair out of his eyes and frowns. Without saying a word to us, he turns sideways and screams, "Dad!"

The younger boys stand up and rush off. They squeeze past the older boy and run into the bright wash of sunlight outside the door. The older boy comes over and pulls the goat off me.

"What happened to you?" he asks.

When I don't say anything, just close my eyes to keep the world from spinning out of control again, he puts the back of his hand against my forehead. The dark figure of a man stands in the doorway, blocking out the radiant sun. His shadow looms long and lean before him. It creeps toward us, getting closer and closer, until I can see a pair of dusty, worn work boots.

"She not talking?"

"I don't think she can," the boy says. "She has a fever."

The father crouches, puts a knee on the ground, and looks at me.

He takes my chin in his hands and moves my head. The world spins again, and I shut my eyes. "We need to take her inside. Bring her mochila."

Then he puts one arm around my back and the other under my knees and starts to pull me up. A hot, angry pain shoots up my wounded arm, and I pull it against my rib cage.

"Something bit her."

"I'm sorry," the father says. Then he hauls me up and carries me out of the barn, like a ragdoll. The green trees, the white clouds, the bright, azure sky swirl around me, blurring and blending together. I pray for the spinning to stop.

"Water," I beg weakly.

"She's trying to say something," the boy tells a woman who I assume is his mother when we are on the porch and she is opening the door, her brows knitted tightly together over her bright, dark eyes.

The father carries me inside and sets me down on a cot, and the boy places my bag beside me. A moment later, the mother presses a glass of water against my lips. The coolness of the glass startles me, and a splash of water falls into my mouth and trickles down my chin.

I drink greedily. The woman lets me have a few more sips, and then she pulls the glass away. "That's enough for now."

But I am not worried anymore, because when I close my eyes and everything stops spinning, I see Calizto in my mind. I know I am not asleep. Yet I can see him in that other time. He is searching for something. Through rubble and blackened ruin, he rummages, urgently looking for something.

Ofirin! Calizto calls out. His voice is quiet, but urgent—desperate. *Ofirin! Can you hear me?*

"Ofirin." The name escapes my cracked lips.

Yes. Yes. I understand now. It is a friend he looks for in the remnants of his home in Tenochtitlan. Calizto stops rummaging. He lifts his head and listens. But when he doesn't hear his friend's response, he goes back to pushing a long wooden stick through the piles of burned rubbish. *If he is dead, I must bury him. To leave his body here would be my ruin.*

"Calizto," I call out again, only this time, I know I have said his name aloud.

"She has a fever," the boy tells his mother.

"She's delirious," the mother says.

"Is that a wolf bite?" one of the little ones asks. "Is she going to turn when the moon gets full?"

"Coyote," the father corrects. "You two need to go now. She'll be okay. Your mother will take care of her."

I open my eyes. The mother smiles down at me.

"There you are," she whispers. She picks up the glass of water and presses it against my lips again. I cough when it goes down the wrong pipe.

"Thank you," I whisper because it hurts to talk.

"See?" the father says. "I told you she was all right. Now get back to your chores."

When I sip more water, the mother looks pleased. She goes into the kitchen and comes back with a little brown bag. She sits beside me and inspects my forearm.

"My name is Zaragoza," she says. When I nod, she takes a bottle of iodine and some cotton balls and begins to clean my wound.

I scream, once, instinctively, when she first touches the red, angry lacerations.

"Relax," Doña Zaragoza says.

I hold my mochila tightly against my chest and try not to scream again. But I shift, writhing in silence, because the pain is excruciating.

"Are you allergic to penicillin?" the father asks from the doorway, where he is leaning against the frame.

"No."

"Good," he says.

Then he is gone, and I am left alone with Doña Zaragoza, who gives me some aspirin for my fever. "Sleep," she says and leaves the room.

As I lie still and close my eyes, I can think of nothing more seductive than the possibility of disappearing, of leaving this temporal plane and finding my way into another time—a time where a young Mexica warrior looks at me with gentle eyes.

I wake up to the smells of food, something light and delicate. Doña Zaragoza walks into the room holding a wooden tray. When she sets it down on the little table beside the cot, I can see that it's a nice, brothy soup, and it smells heavenly. My mouth waters, but only for a moment, because I notice the medical supplies sitting beside it, a new syringe and a small, round bottle of clear liquid.

"A little lentil soup to fortify the blood," Doña Zaragoza says, picking up the syringe and taking it out of its wrapper. "But first, we take care of that arm."

She injects the long needle with precision. I squeeze my eyes shut and breathe deeply while the penicillin moves through the muscle, welcoming its curative power into my system.

"You never told me your name," Doña Zaragoza says, while she changes the dressing on my wound.

I smile, a nervous little smile that pinches my sunburnt face.

"Maria," I whisper, silently begging the Virgen de Guadalupe to forgive me for lying to this kind woman. It's just not wise to give her my real name. "Maria Rodriguez."

Doña Zaragoza fastens the gauze with a tiny, metal clasp. "Maria from . . ."

"Veracruz," I tell her. It's not a lie, but it's not specific either. "I'm on my way to the States."

"Hmm. Lots of people doing that these days," Doña Zaragoza says. "It's hard."

"It is—it has been," I admit. "Lots of predators out there, waiting to take advantage of people. That's why I travel alone."

"I know," Doña Zaragoza says, taking the old dressing and putting it on the tray. "But why were you in the desert? Wouldn't a bus make more sense?"

I think of the money hidden in my mochila, and, though the bag has been sitting beside me all this time, I've been in and out of delirium for most of the day. There was opportunity for anyone in the family to go through it. If I lie about having the money for bus fare, and she catches me, would that make her mad? Would she distrust anything else I have to say? Would she worry about her family?

"There is a boy in my hometown who says he loves me. He doesn't. He's just . . . confused. I am sure of it. But he wants me back." As I confess my plight, my eyes burn, but I force myself to be strong—to disclose everything.

When I am done, Doña Zaragoza sighs. Her eyes glisten. Then she touches my shoulder and says, "You are safe here."

After a quick trip to the restroom, where I sigh at the sight of my crackled lips and sunburnt face, I return to the cot. The second bowl of lentil soup Doña Zaragoza brings me is like a sedative, and I find myself nodding off while she crochets a delicate white doily.

I dream of my mother, but not the happy, joyful mother of my younger years. No. In this dream, my mother is sullen and somber. Her sunken eyes and sallow skin cause me great worry. But it is her glassy-eyed silence that torments me. "Mami?" I call out to her from my cot in our house in Zongolica. She looks at the forest outside our weathered window and wails. I reach out to her, but she is not there. She is dead. And the dead don't speak to me.

"Sitlali."

I jump, startled by the sound of my name, a soft, seductive entreaty that perforates my dreams. The silvery face of the waxing moon outside my window is hidden by dark clouds. I see the outline of a shadowy figure in the corner, crouched low to the floor. As my eyes adjust, I realize it is the otherworldly visage of Calizto, alone in the darkness, holding the conch, staring off into space.

I get up and go sit with him. His eyes are wide. Luminous.

"Calizto," I whisper, and I reach out to touch him. My hand goes right through him, but the action startles him out of his trance.

"Sitlali. I was just . . . thinking of you."

Something about the way he hesitates, almost stumbles, on his words makes my cheeks warm, and I am glad we are sitting in the dark.

"Did you find your friend?" I ask.

His smile changes. It shifts wryly over his face, an expression that barely keeps the corners of his lips turned up. "Ofirin was lucky. He ran out of the house as soon as he heard the shelling. He was hurled halfway across the canal by the cannonball's impact. I found him, stunned but alive, clinging to the foliage of a chinampa garden."

"Where is he now?"

"I hid him in our shrine. The house is in ruin. No one will discover him there."

He is not saying it, but I can hear the sadness in his voice. His spirit is overburdened. I want to reach out and put my arms around him. I want to hold him close. I want to kiss his cheeks, his temples, his eyelids, and tell him he's going to be okay, but I can't.

"Where will you go now?" I ask him.

A fierceness enters his eyes, and they become obsidian gemstones again, bright and full of life—and something else, something dangerous.

"I cannot linger here," he says. "I must forage and scavenge to keep my schoolmates alive. It is my duty."

CHAPTER TWELVE

Calizto

Day 6-Snake of the Year 3-House (June 14, 1521)

I awaken before dawn. The others breathe softly or snore in the gloom.

I sense another person. An intruder. I turn my head, my body tense.

Sitlali lies beside me, on her side. Her eyes are closed, eyelashes nearly long enough to reach her full cheeks, lips parted just enough to show her perfect teeth.

I remain motionless, drinking in the sight. My mind quiet, I stand and head outside.

The mother of one of our students is preparing steaming atolli from rations I brought yesterday. Though I expected a rebuke from Master Miquiztin, he received me with tears of relief. Many had died in the shelling of Metztonalco.

"Young Master Calizto," she greets me. "Are there any dried squash seeds in the school's stores? The boys would love some sprinkled atop their breakfast."

"Let me go check."

I feel Sitlali stir in my mind as I walk. A sidewise glance shows me that she has sat up and is speaking with someone.

Her hunger reaches me, doubling my own.

Good morning, Little Star. I speak into her mind since I'm not alone. *Breakfast invitation? I recommend getting up.*

Good morning, Calizto. I could use a bath, but let me get something in my stomach first.

I take the seeds back, and then I check on my charges. Ayotochtli has already roused them, and they stumble into the morning chill to grab a bowl and thick tortilla. Everyone takes a seat on the ground.

Sitlali goes through some morning routine, splashing water on her face, scrubbing her teeth for an inordinate amount of time, and brushing her hair.

Ah, better. I feel almost human.

But a very hungry human. You had no dinner. Please eat.

As I scoop corn gruel into my mouth with my tortilla, she sits and consumes what seems an ample breakfast.

She laughs.

What's so amusing?

To me it looks like you're sitting here, in their kitchen. On the floor, with your back to the wall. It's weird . . . but also comforting.

You also seem to be here with us, eating off an invisible table. But . . . you seem less invisible today.

You too! What's happening?

Let's think. I sounded the conch on a moonless night.

And I found it right before the new moon.

As the moon has grown larger each night, we've first begun to hear and then see each other.

As long as the conch is nearby. Especially if we touch it.

Yes. And we perceive each other more clearly with each passing day, as if we're getting closer.

To what? Each other? Some important event? I don't know why, but this feels very fortuitous, almost . . .

Predestined?

Yes! Like this is part of a bigger plan . . . something divine. But what could the gods want from us?

I cannot fathom the will of the Moon Goddess. But I have noticed the progression.

I wonder what will happen when the moon is full? Hearing, sight . . . maybe . . . touch?

I feel her imagination go wild, and I repress the anticipation rising in me. The mere thought of ever placing my hands on that honeyed skin, of pressing my lips against hers . . .

Sitlali's face goes cold and indignant. For a moment I think I've angered her, but she's replying to someone in her time. Then her features relax and she bows her head slightly.

"Calizto and Ayotochtli," calls Master Miquiztin. After setting our empty bowls near the washing basin, we join him. "Orders have come. The Eagle Knights need you to oversee a team today, clearing rubble from the causeway south of the ceremonial plaza. Take five older boys with you."

As we lead the students, Ayotochtli raves about some girl he met when bringing fresh water, but I cannot focus on his conquests.

What happened?

Nothing. Don Ramón, the husband, asked if the money in my bag was stolen.

Money?

It's what we use to exchange for things we want when we can't barter.

Did you steal this "money"?

No! And that's what I told him. I was upset, but I calmed down and thanked the family for everything they've done. Then Don Ramón offered to drive me into town when I feel like I can continue.

He wants you gone.

Maybe. But Doña Zaragoza told him she'll *decide when I'm ready. Since I'm not harming them, there's no need to send me away. God has provided them with the means to help me, and she intends to do so.*

"Did you hear a word I said?"

Ayotochtli shoves me.

"Not really."

"You're the worst friend ever," he scoffs.

Then he points at the netted bag strapped to my back beside my sheathed sword. I've left the box at home, letting the shell touch my skin so my connection with Sitlali is unsevered.

"What's that, a conch horn? Do you intend to make music with it? Is it a war bugle?"

The death of Ce Mazatl has left him bitter, curdling his humor into something cruel.

I narrow my eyes. "I've told you twice. It was my mother's. It's all I have left of my family."

He shakes his head. "I'm sorry, friend. I don't mean to piss you off, but I've never seen it before. Still, I understand why you're keeping it close."

Argument with Ayotochtli? Sitlali asks.

Something strange. Both he and Ofirin . . . appear to forget about the moon conch each day, as if sleep erases it from their memories.

Weird. But you also told me that you *had forgotten about it until you found it in the shrine, until you blew it and the memories returned. Hrm. Let me see if people can remember it in my time.*

Ayotochtli and I reach our assigned spot after a ten-minute walk. A motley crew of some thirteen women and children await us, standing beside a pile of rubble that was once a row of homes.

"Incredible," Ayotochtli groans. "If the Caxtiltecah come marching up with their Tlaxcaltecah dogs, we'll surely fend them off with this impressive squadron."

The oldest woman, well past her fifty-second year, gives a wry laugh. "Those bastards would be eating pozolli in the Sacred Precinct were it not for us widows and orphans, Young Master. We've been unfilling the gaps each night, making the enemy waste vital time refilling them."

I nod. "You perform a crucial task, Aunt."

She waves away that term of respect for older women. "Call me Eyolin. You're my superior today."

"Then, Eyolin, let's make it even harder. In teams of three, we'll drag this rubble away so Cortés cannot easily use it to fill in the gaps."

As I show them how to secure a hempen rope to a large chunk of debris and drag it to the north–south canal one block west of us, I notice Sitlali standing, clutching something.

What's that? I ask.

Doña Zaragoza gave me a dress. Belonged to her daughter, who has moved away. I'm going to bathe and change.

Sitlali appears to shut a door behind her. She's more solid than before. Only the slightest glow of light flickers through her strange warrior garb, those pants that cling to her legs, that cotton shirt that hugs her every curve . . .

"I'm getting some weird vibes from you, Calizto." She speaks aloud since she's alone.

Apologies. I try to calm the rush of my blood.

"Listen," she continues. She's flustered, though hiding it with sternness. "I've got to take my clothes off now, and I can't do that while you're still here."

Oh! Yes, I understand.

"Just—put the conch somewhere. Don't carry it. And don't focus on me. For a little while so I can have some privacy. I'd rather not push you away. I'm not sure if the connection will break, and I don't want to wait to speak to you until the moon is out again."

Though I long to touch her, lay eyes and fingers along her cinnamon skin, I agree.

Of course.

"Thank you. I'll reach out to you later, when I'm done."

I ask Eyolin—who along with a young boy named Ceyozomah is working with me—to keep the conch safe.

"Certainly!" she says, taking the bag and peering at its precious contents. "It's a moon conch, yes?"

"Correct. It belonged to my mother, who was a priestess at our calpolli's shrine."

She nods, slinging the bag over her shoulder. "Coyolxauhqui may be a minor goddess, but you do well to keep her aegis close. Before the epidemic and the siege, I was a tonalpohuani. As I prepared people's horoscopes, I learned to respect the power of the moon."

I cannot help but be intrigued. After we dump our next load of rubble into the water, I ask her about the conch.

"One finds them at all of Coyolxauhqui's shrines, of course," she explains. "But I've heard they are all replicas. Apparently, your people possess the original, a shell carved by Tecciztecatl himself at the beginning of this age, a tool for drawing down the power of the moon."

My pulse quickens. "What else have you heard?"

Eyolin closes her eyes, as if remembering. "Snatches of a song. Old Toltec melody."

The world seems to go completely still as she chants in a wavering voice:

On the world's very first night
the moon lifted itself to the sky
and over the world shone bright

till up from the depths of the sea
a conch that glowed pink
arose on roaring waves,
drifting slow into a bay
and onto the bone-white strand
of sacred Tecciztlan.

A rushing like the sea, a memory floods my mind.

My sisters at the shrine, holding the conch with my mother, singing.

I fall to my knees as if someone has punched me in the gut.

But their voices, oh those beloved voices I've tried to forget, echo down the years:

From on high, She of the Bells
called out to He of the Shells,
as he emerged from the swells:
"On those spirals you shall carve
the Four Hundred Southern Stars
and nine inscrutable glyphs
so all who look away forget
save those I choose to spark
through paradox to fight the dark.

"When what was broken is healed
and She who is destined to wield
and He who is commanded to shield
hold the conch in their hands
in two different lands
and each other in their hearts

though leagues and eons apart—
then will I reveal to the staunch
the secret of the moon conch."

Startled, I realize I've been chanting the words in a hoarse whisper. And just like that, the spell is broken.

"There's more," I rasp, looking up at Eyolin, "but my memory fails me."

She helps me to my feet as I wipe away tears.

"As does mine. But yes," the old woman assures me, "there is more. Perhaps it will come to you when you least expect it . . . as all good memories do."

After we transport another load, Ceyozomah begins to complain. "Can we take a break, Master Calizto? This work is hard."

I gesture toward the shade of trees beside the canal. "Though you should count yourself lucky. Other teams first drag corpses away from the rubble. Ours is the easier task."

"Might the enemy attack while we are here?" he asks timidly.

Eyolin shakes her head. "From what I understand, no forces are amassing near the Fortress of Xoloc today. We are doubly fortunate because the Eagle and Jaguar Knights have gone north."

I lean forward. "Truly?"

"Rumors claim our emperor is negotiating with the leaders of Tlatelolco. They are willing to help Tenochtitlan, as long as Cuauhtemoc gives up the title of Hueyi Tlahtoani."

"What?" Ceyozomah is shocked. "He'll never agree."

"It does seem unlikely," I concur. "Tlatelolco has had no king in more than forty years. It's no more than a larger borough of

Tenochtitlan. How could it control the Triple Alliance? Why would Cuauhtemoc even permit the attempt?"

Eyolin clicks her tongue. "The emperor's mother is the daughter of the last king of Tlatelolco. And Cuauhtemoc was governor there for five years, until the Caxtiltecah arrived. He has no problem with Tlatelolco's ascendance."

Ceyozomah spits at the canal. "We Tenochcah are finished, no matter who wins."

I shake my head, then put my hand on his shoulder. "This news is a cause for hope. The Tlatelolcah people are Mexica. Though we have been separate cities for nearly two hundred years, we are a single people."

Eyolin stands. "Not to mention its greater tactical advantage."

"Indeed. It's harder to access than Tenochtitlan. Its canals are wider; its neighborhoods aren't laid out on a grid. The generals of Cortés haven't been able to make significant inroads into Tlatelolco. You'd be safer there, boy."

Calizto?

Just a moment.

I gesture back at the rubble. "Eyolin, hand me my netted bag and accompany Ceyozomah back to the rubble. See about food. I'll catch up."

As they leave, I take the conch and cross a wooden bridge to a series of shattered warehouses.

"Okay," I call out as I enter the semi-gloom of the most intact building. "I'm alone now."

Stepping out of the shadows, Sitlali appears.

My breath catches.

I see her fully for the first time, as if she were standing before me in the flesh.

She is wearing the sun-yellow "dress" the Zaragoza woman gave her, a sort of long huipil that reaches just above her knees. Sleeveless, the dress drapes from her elegant shoulders by thin straps. Her curls are pulled back in a cascading tail, revealing her beautiful neck and shoulder blades. Her toned, smooth legs draw my eyes down to her shapely feet, cushioned by a pair of white sandals. Tecpilcatli. Worn only by nobility. Fitting.

"Do you like it? It's beautiful, isn't it? I've never had such a fine dress."

I shake my head, unable to find the words. I stare at her bandaged arm and babble like an idiot.

"Your bandage."

"It's ugly, isn't it? Does it ruin it? I can't take it off."

Her eyes narrow, and I notice that she has applied a hint of makeup to her lips and eyes, just enough to enhance their natural appeal.

I lose control, let it all come rushing out.

"You are breathtaking, Little Star. All that is beautiful about my people, blended with the imperious dazzle of our enemy. A perfect balance. Divine. Incomparable."

My face burns, and I close my lips. I want to tell her so much more. I want to say that I'll never understand why the gods chose me to meet her, that I'll spend whatever is left of my life proving myself worthy of their wisdom. But I don't, because I've yet to understand this magic, and it wouldn't be fair to promise more than what I'm sure we can have.

She moves close. I cannot hear her steps upon the stone or inhale her scent, but the whirling of her souls is as clear to me as my own thoughts.

"Thank you," she says. Then her cheeks bloom as pink as acocoxochitl, and she looks down at her hands.

It is agonizing to stand so near to her and yet so impossibly far away.

Straining against the distance, I reach out with my heart itself, aching to touch her blooming cheeks.

She shivers, an unexpected reaction.

"What did you do?" she asks, her eyes bright, full of wonder. "I felt that. It was like a ghostly whisper, just barely grazing my skin. Look," she says, showing me her bare forearm and rubbing at it. "I have goose bumps."

"No idea. I just . . ."

"Just what?"

"I just . . . I yearned to touch you." I stop myself, before I say that I yearned to touch her with every atom of my being.

"Calizto! Where in shit are you, lazy bastard?"

It is Ayotochtli. His heavy footsteps slap across the wood of the bridge.

"I am needed. There is much work yet to be done. What will you do?"

"Rest. Watch television with the doña. Catch up on my novelas."

"I understood nothing but 'rest.' And that is what I hope you do. Until tonight, Sitlali."

She smiles at me, lifting her hand, palm up.

I lift my own, holding it as close as I can to hers. The illusion of our touch nearly breaks my heart.

"Until tonight, Calizto."

CHAPTER THIRTEEN

Sitlali

June 15, 2019

Because Doña Zaragoza didn't let me help her last night, I take it upon myself to dry and put away the morning dishes as she washes them. I am holding the last plate in my hands, reaching up to put it in her little cupboard above the stove, when Don Ramón comes into the kitchen with a couple of fresh eggs in his hand.

"What are you wearing?" he asks when he catches sight of me.

"I gave it to her." Doña Zaragoza takes the eggs out of Don Ramón's hands.

"But it's her favorite." Don Ramón's eyes redden, as if he's about to cry.

"I know. So, what now? Are you going to make her take it off?" Doña Zaragoza puts the eggs on the hanging wire basket and turns back to stare at her husband, her hand on her hip. The awkward moment extends itself, and I can feel the tension growing between them before he turns away from us.

"God damnit," he curses under his breath as he slams the screen door behind himself on the way out.

When he's gone, Doña Zaragoza and I straighten up the living room and sit down to watch the morning variety show. I take a moment during that down time to detach my knife from the spear the father set by my cot and put it back in my bag. "You'll have to excuse my husband," she says when she's settled in. "He didn't mean to be rude. It's just that he loved her. She was our first child—our first love. I miss her. But he . . . Well, I think he's expecting her to walk in that door any day now."

When Doña Zaragoza casts her eyes down, a tear falls from her nose. She puts her doily aside, lifts her apron, and weeps into it. I rush to put my arms around her and rock her softly as she sobs onto my shoulder.

"I'm sorry," she finally says. "I didn't mean to . . . burden you with this. It's such a beautiful dress. It shouldn't be tucked away in the back of a closet, waiting for the moths to get to it."

"It's okay," I say. "You don't have to explain anything to me."

"Her name was Mónica, but everyone called her Mona, because she loved dressing up." Doña Zaragoza wipes her nose with a tissue she digs out of her pocket. "She used to work in that big factory in Monclova, as a secretary to the manager. She needed to look good, you see. So, she made herself up and floated into that place looking like a summer breeze every day. Pretty hair pins. Pretty dresses. Pretty shoes."

"I would dress up too," I say. "If I had that kind of job."

"One day, she didn't come home after work. Everyone went looking for her, but nobody ever found her. The police couldn't do anything. She was just gone."

Gone. The word reminds me. I take out the conch again and set it on the coffee table.

"Oh, that's pretty!" Doña Zaragoza exclaims. "Where did you get it?"

It's confirmed. I did exactly the same thing yesterday, telling her the whole story.

She remembers nothing.

Somehow, the moon conch makes people forget it exists, just like in the song.

After changing back into jeans and a T-shirt, I spend the day resting or sitting at the table, studying my map, trying to figure out the best route to take when I get on the road again. Doña Zaragoza sweeps her porch and putts around in the garden.

At dinnertime, the older boy, Josué, comes running into the kitchen. He takes off his cap before he joins us at the table, head hung low and eyes downcast.

"Where were you?" Don Ramón asks as Josué tears into a tortilla. "Not with those hoodlums, Miguel and Rafael, I hope."

"I was looking for work," Josué says.

Don Ramón nods. "Find anything of significance?"

Josué looks at me sideways as he chews and swallows his food. He wipes his fingers on a paper napkin. Then he reaches into his back pocket, pulls out a piece of paper, and hands it to his father. Don Ramón opens it and stares at it. His eyebrows furrow, and he takes a deep breath.

"What is it?" Doña Zaragoza asks.

"It's a missing persons flyer," he tells her. "With Maria's photo."

"They were everywhere. Grocery stores. Shopping centers. Everywhere. It's you, isn't it?" Josué asks me. "Your real name is Sitlali?"

Don Ramón hands me the flyer. It's a close-up of me, in profile, standing beside Martín's truck. The flyer quotes a ridiculously high reward for information leading to my "rescue." I feel nauseated.

"Who would pay so much money?" Don Ramón's question interrupts my panicked thoughts. "What have you brought into our home?"

My eyes start watering, but I push the tears away. I don't want Don Ramón to think I am playing the victim here, but it is clear that Doña Zaragoza did not share with her husband what I confessed to her.

"This picture was taken by a thug," I say, explaining everything to him as quickly as I can.

When I am done, Don Ramón looks over at his son. "Did anyone see you take this? You didn't tell those good-for-nothing friends of yours about it, did you?"

Josué shakes his head. His eyes are red, brimming with unshed tears, and he wipes a clear line of snot off his nose with his knuckles. My heart aches for him. He is obviously humiliated.

"I should go," I say, pushing back my chair.

Don Ramón raises his hand, palm up.

"Hold on," he says. "Let's not panic. Let me see that map."

I grab my map off the counter behind me and put it on the table. Don Ramón takes a small pencil and traces a few lines on the map.

"See these," he says. "These are the back roads around Piedras Negras. I can drop you there at dawn, but you'll need to keep to these country roads if you want to stay alive. Understand?"

I nod. "Thank you."

"Who's that?" Doña Zaragoza asks, getting up to look out the window.

Standing behind her, I see a familiar truck coming down the long, dusty driveway.

"Martín," I whisper.

"Who's Martín?" Doña Zaragoza asks.

"He was driving us to the border," I explain. My heart is beating so fast I feel breathless.

Don Ramón turns and grabs Josué by the scruff of his shirt.

"What did you do?" Don Ramón asks. "Why would you call them?"

"I didn't know the whole story," Josué says. "I thought it was her family looking for her."

Before I can run, Severo kicks the front door in and rushes into the house with Martín behind him.

I freeze. *My mind swirls, and somewhere far away from this terrible moment, a sword slashes downward, barely misses Calizto, and hits the ground. Spears whirl past him, and he crouches. The sun blinds him. He squints.*

"There you are," Severo says, waving a gun at us.

"Listen, I don't know what this is about. But my boy made a mistake." Don Ramón tries to talk to him.

Standing in the middle of the living room, Severo looks over at me, and then, without saying a word, he points the gun at Don Ramón and shoots. The sound reverberates in the room as it hits its mark.

Doña Zaragoza screams.

Don Ramón falls to the floor and lies immobile, curled up in a fetal position, his hands clutched at his chest. Blood begins to flow from him, a crimson puddle that grows slowly around his torso.

My beating heart echoes the sound of distant hooves pounding across a causeway.

Doña Zaragoza howls. Her two young sons fall to their knees beside Don Ramón and shake his body in earnest.

"Papá! Papá!" they cry.

Martín stands in the doorway, behind Severo.

"What're you doing?" he asks Severo. "You said there wouldn't be any trouble."

As Doña Zaragoza reaches for the rifle lying on a wall mount, Severo moves his arm and points the gun at her.

In another world, Calizto swings his obsidian sword, slashing a Spaniard's neck.

Instinctively, I take my knife out of my bag and rush at Severo from behind. I jump on his back. Wrap my arm and legs around his waist and stick the side of his neck. The knife pierces the thick skin, and I shove it deeper, putting the full force of my rage into the plunge.

Severo screams and drops the gun. He grabs my arm and tosses me off his back in one violent thrust.

I fall. Slide on my side. Sit up. And scuttle across the floor.

Quickly, I seize Severo's gun and scramble to stand up. My trembling right hand is bright red, covered in Severo's blood. The silky velvet feel of it is all over the handle of the gun. As I consider this, Severo pulls my mother's knife out of his neck and roars.

"Shit!" I curse under my breath, because now he has my knife.

"You bitch!" Severo says as he comes at me, my mother's knife held high.

I shoot him once. In the leg.

The gunshot rings in my ears. My heart thrums. My legs weaken. My hands shake.

Severo drops the knife, falls, clutches at his leg with both hands, and screams for Martín. "Kill her," he says. "Kill the bitch!"

I shake my head, pointing the gun at Martín as I kick the knife away from Severo's reach. Martín raises his hands and steps back. I move sideways, pick up the knife, wipe it against my jeans, and dump it into the mouth of my open bag on the sofa.

I point the gun at Martín. "Keys," I say. "Now!"

Martín sighs and pulls the keys from his pants. A small wad of money pokes out of his front pocket, and he stares at it. "I guess you'll want this too," he says.

I nod. "Your phone, too."

Martín shakes his head. "Oh, come on," he says. "You can't use it. It's locked."

"I said now!" I yell. Martín pulls out his phone. "His too. Out of his pocket." Martín does as I ask. "Set everything on the ground. Kick it to me. Now lie down. Crawl over to the wall. Shove your hands in your pockets. All the way!"

"I'm going to kill you," Severo swears weakly, because he's losing a lot of blood. "When this is all over, I am going to find you and kill you."

"You should leave now," Doña Zaragoza says, aiming her husband's rifle at the back of Severo's head. "Take Ramón's truck."

I wipe my hands clean on my T-shirt and quickly throw their phones and keys into my bag. Then I grab the keys to the family vehicle and run out of the house. In the driveway, I look into Martín's truck and grab his duffel bag from behind the driver's seat before I blow out his tires.

When I hear shots inside the house, I jump in Don Ramón's truck and drive off. At the gate, I turn north. By the time I jump on the highway, my hands are not the only thing trembling. I am shaking all over.

About thirty minutes after I pass Monclova, I find a secluded dirt road, drive into it, stop, and look around. When I don't see anyone, I step out of the truck, take the cell phones and gun out of my bag, wipe them down with a clean shirt, crush them with a rock, and fling them into the brush as far away from the road as I can get them. I scrub my hands quickly with a handful of dry dirt and use a bottle of water to rinse them clean. Then I change out of my bloodstained T-shirt and bury it under a cactus.

When I get back out on the highway, I keep my mochila close by and go as fast as I can without exceeding the speed limit because I don't want to get stopped. I look at myself in the rearview mirror. I don't look like I've just committed a crime, but I know I can't explain the large amounts of cash in Martín's duffel bag.

And then, as if I had called on him, Calizto appears, sitting beside me in the cab.

I tell him what happened, and he shakes his head.

"We have survived much today, Little Star. But don't be remorseful. A warrior feels nothing but pride in the aftermath of a well-executed defense."

"I'm not sorry," I tell him. "I'm just upset that I couldn't help Doña Zaragoza. I hate that I'm not free to live my life like everyone else."

"I am likewise trapped. I have been hiding in a temple with Ayotochtli and other warriors while the enemy swarmed the ceremonial center. The Eagle and Jaguar Knights are now pushing them out through the Southern Gate, blocking my escape route."

"I still don't understand why you need to go back," I say, exasperated. "Why can't you leave through some other route? You need to trust me when I say you must get out of Tenochtitlan."

"I made a vow to my father. I am bound by honor to protect Ofirin," Calizto explains. "He knows but a few words in our language and looks nothing like us, so he cannot pass unnoticed. I must go back for him."

I think of Doña Zaragoza, her two small children, and Don Ramón. My blood boils at their circumstances. Frustrated, I focus on Calizto and his situation.

"You need to escape—before it's you who gets killed," I say, gripping the wheel and facing the road ahead. "You can't protect your friend if you're dead."

Calizto is so close. I reach out to touch him. My hand doesn't make contact, but Calizto shudders. Startled, he looks at my hand. I know he felt something, a ghostly caress against his smooth skin. I know because I felt it too.

I smile and put my hand back on the wheel.

"Your counsel is wise, Sitlali. Cortés is at the Southern Gate, but I can circumvent them and then head back tonight. Say a prayer for me, to your Virgencita Guadalupe. That I make it to safety."

And with a sad smile, he fades away.

CHAPTER FOURTEEN

Calizto

Day 8-Deer of the Year 3-House (June 16, 1521)

It is the deepest hour of the night. Warriors sprawl asleep throughout the ceremonial center. After traveling for hours, Sitlali has hidden the "truck" behind an abandoned warehouse, where she now tosses and turns with unseen dreams. Such bravery. Truly she's descended from the formidable Nahua peoples of Anahuac.

Ayotochtli and I are about to slip out through the Northern Gate when messengers arrive.

"Halt!" one of them calls. "Where are you sneaking off to?"

"We're returning to our telpochcalli," I answer. "We got separated from the other students."

"Change of plans. We need every cadet we can gather to carry out the emperor's command."

Ayotochtli smirks. "And what does Lord Cuauhtemoc require?"

Another officer snarls. "The military headquarters are being moved to the Yacacolco complex in Tlatelolco. The emperor wants the image of Huitzilopochtli to be transported there. You buggers, having risen so early, are the first volunteers for the task. Wait at the base of Coatepetl until we send a supervisor and other sleepless rogues."

The pyramid rises like a mountain above the plaza. We approach the massive slab that serves as its base. A squadron of Jaguar and Eagle Knights slumbers there, so we sit on the steps, leaning against a carved serpent head as we wait.

We are nodding off when a handful of warriors about our age approaches, led by a broad-shouldered, scarred captain.

"Okay, boys," he says. "My name is Axoquentzin, and I have the dubious pleasure of supervising you greenhorns. Sunrise is still an hour or so away, but the moon's nearly full. Should be enough light. We need to lower the divine effigy down that stairway." He gestures at the slanting face of the pyramid, looming over us, another 120 steps beyond the platform.

"Lovely," mutters Ayotochtli. "I thought only priests and victims could ascend Coatepetl."

Axoquentzin grunts. "The emperor's given us a special dispensation."

"Once we've gotten it down," I point out, "we have to transport it to Tlatelolco."

"Exactly. Where are you two clever, talkative boys from?"

"Metztonalco. In Zoquiyapan."

The captain gives a strained grimace. "Well, you'll be traveling far from home, if yours is still standing after all that shelling. Come on, step lively."

We climb onto the base platform. While Axoquentzin explains our duties to a pair of grumpy knights, I wander over to the massive stone at the base of the southern stairway, a circular disk twice my height in diameter.

Upon it, painted blue and gold, spattered with blood, is the image of Coyolxauhqui, shattered in pieces. The pyramid symbolizes the mountain from which Huitzilopochtli hurled her body.

Ayotochtli comes to stand beside me. He sucks in a startled breath at the sight.

Soon the captain leads the other boys over.

"What are you two do—ah. Moon worshippers, yes? Hard to see the goddess like this, I suppose."

I glance at him. There is no mockery on his face, just compassion.

"All must be broken to be made whole," I say, repeating the ancient phrase.

Axoquentzin raises an eyebrow. "Indeed. Did Quetzalcoatl and Cihuacoatl not break and grind up the old bones to make our ancestors? But enough philosophizing. Climb."

The ascent is steep. Several times I reach out to steady myself on the steps above, trying not to imagine meeting my fate this way: chosen, blessed, but near death.

When we finally reach the summit, chests heaving, a priest is waiting. He says nothing, just peers at us with cool eyes, his long black hair, split earlobes, and stained robes making him an awe-inspiring figure. He leads us past the offering stone and eagle basin to the Temple of Huitzilopochtli, its red walls almost black in the moonlight.

Following the captain's example, each of us drops to our knees, lowering our faces and kissing the flagstones before entering. The priest has lit torches that flicker upon the stone walls to either side and upon a stretch of heavy fabric draped before us.

"You are about to behold the Xoxouhqui Ilhuicatl, the earthly representation of that fold in the heavens where Huitzilopochtli dwells, meting out justice from on high. None but priests and the most noble of warriors is permitted herein. Count yourselves blessed beyond measure."

He pulls the curtain aside, exposing a green chamber. In its center, on a blue litter, sits the effigy of Huitzilopochtli, carved from pine, painted and inlaid with jewels. Cotinga feathers hang from his ears, a blue netted sash crosses his chest, and his legs are bound with war bells. Above his headdress rises a crown of reeds and plumes, supported by a frame at his back: the Aneucyotl, which he stripped from his brothers the Southern Stars after he slew them. In his hands lie both shield and fire serpent staff.

Standing near him is another figure I recognize: Tlacahuepan Cuexcochtzin, companion and protector of the sun god. As a boy, I used to love attending the festival of Panquetzaliztli, when the whole city would break and eat sweet figures of the two friends, baked from amaranth dough and honey.

The captain arranges us: Ayotochtli and I take one side of the litter, while two of the cadets take the other. The remaining cadets steady the effigy at the front and back.

Cautiously, we emerge to make our slow way down the 120 steps. As if summoned by Huitzilopochtli's form, the sun begins to lighten the eastern sky, and I see Sitlali stir. She sits up and looks at me.

Where are you? What're you doing?

I'm still in the ceremonial center. I've been recruited to take the statue of Huitzilopochtli to Yacacolco, a neighborhood in our sister city of Tlatelolco. The emperor's moving his headquarters.

So you're going north, right?

Yes.

Good. I'm on the outskirts of Piedras Negras. I'm going to leave the truck here and walk into town. I need supplies and a change of clothes.

I see worry cloud her features. Her trek has been perilous, but the most difficult stretch still lies ahead of her.

Are you ready? For whatever lies north there, in your time?

As ready as anyone could ever be, heading into the unknown.

Indeed. Be safe, Sitlali.

You too, Calizto.

At the base of the pyramid, we take a break. A minor priest brings us a basket of totopochtli and a sloshing jug. I devour two toasted tortillas and take a great swig of the freshest water I've tasted in weeks.

Axoquentzin, after consulting with several officers, returns to guide us.

"The emperor's given the word. Citizens should make their way north, into Tlatelolco. Tenochtitlan is a battlefield."

Taking up the litter, we leave through the Northern Gate, traveling up the Tepeyacac Causeway. As we cross the canals and streets of the Atzacualco district, we rotate roles: four god-bearers, three guardians, weapons at the ready.

The sun rises, and we see homes being abandoned. A flood of living souls heads north. A great leader is a cypress, my father always said. His people take refuge in the shade of his branches, which block sun and rain from their heads.

But Cuauhtemoc's shadow doesn't reach this far, to this stretch of road a block from the Great Canal that separates the two cities. A group of women and children have just reached the bridge, but musket fire makes them scatter. Behind us, families duck between houses.

Coming down the waterway from the east are a dozen canoes, burgeoning with fierce Tlaxcaltecah and Spaniards wielding rifles and crossbows. The lead canoe pulls to the bank, and our enemies leap onto land.

"Back up!" shouts Axoquentzin, lifting his obsidian sword. "Protect the god at all costs!"

Then I witness the bravest, most breathtaking fighting of my entire life.

Our captain rushes the Tlaxcaltecah. Leaping into the air, he brings his maccuahuitl slashing down, killing two warriors instantly. He hits the ground, tumbling forward and rising into a crouch from which he severs the legs of three more invaders. Wrenching another sword from one of their hands, he begins whirling around, using *two* maccuahuitl as he plows through the Tlaxcaltecah, an obsidian tornado, reaping red blood and screams of pain.

A handful of Spaniards run past, giving him a wide berth. The two cadet guards hurry to intercept, but the bearded foreigners drop to a knee and fire their harquebuses, piercing the gut of one boy and shattering the face of the other.

A Spaniard with only a sword sheathed at his side has continued running, pursuing women and children across the bridge. He seizes a young girl and starts dragging her back toward Tenochtitlan. His companions regain their feet and go after other victims.

"Captain!" I scream, desperate to drop the effigy and help.

Axoquentzin strides away from the twitching bodies of the Tlaxcaltecah. He lifts his obsidian sword, but a blast from a Spanish gun smashes it to splinters.

In a rage, the captain hurls himself at the bridge, howling a war cry. He grabs the Spaniard with the little girl in his arms. Spinning the foreigner about, Axoquentzin forces him to release his prey. Then our captain slams the soldier to the ground, yanking the steel sword from its scabbard and stabbing the man through the neck.

"Come, stinking savages!" he screams at the other Spaniards. "I'll cut you down with your own metal weapons!"

For a moment, it looks as though he will be victorious. His brutal slashes fell several men, giving the women and children a chance to flee into Tlatelolco.

But other canoes pull to the edge of the canal, and dozens more enemy combatants come rushing.

Axoquentzin turns to us. Looks me straight in the eye.

"Now, cadets! Get your asses over that bridge!"

The austere lessons of the telpochcalli kick in, and we obey orders with renewed energy, hefting the weighty idol and quickening our pace.

Halfway across, I look back.

Axoquentzin has slashed many throats. He is now twirling another Spaniard around. But as he slams the man down to the ground, an archer loosens an iron bolt, piercing our captain's heart.

He stumbles forward, raising his fists, ready to take on all of Tlaxcallan and Spain and the entire sea-ringed world.

Then he looks up at the sun. A faint smile crosses his lips.

And he tumbles backward, sprawling on the ground like a man succumbing to sleep at long last.

I fight back horror and sadness as we race from the causeway and start weaving through the southern borough of Tlatelolco. It helps to focus on Sitlali. She's gone to some sort of indoor market, where she's acquired supplies. In a small, mirrored room, she changes her clothing. I catch a glimpse of her bare stomach, the elegant lines of her thighs and hips, even as I avert my eyes.

"Thank you for not looking, Calizto," Sitlali says. I can hear the humor in her voice as she pulls the white sandals off her shapely feet.

If you only knew the tragedy I just witnessed, Sitlali. The sight of you, the sound of your voice at this moment . . . Your beauty is a balm. But I beg your pardon. Your body's your own; I've no right to gaze upon it.

I force the focus of my knotted soul elsewhere for a moment. Ayotochtli, who has been weeping, looks over at me.

I nod. We know each other well. Words would be meaningless.

"Okay. You can look now."

Sitlali sports a new set, the almost military "pants" and "shirt" that are the most common garb in her time. She has pulled her curls up, hiding them under a hat with a strange duckbill.

"I'm going to wear this when I walk to the border."

The border between what?

"Mexico and the United States."

Mexico—like the name of our kingdom—is what her country's called, stretching from Eastern to Western Seas, encompassing the land of the Maya and Chichimecah and Michhuahqueh. But she's not explained this other country.

"It's north of the Río Bravo, the Great River at the edge of the desert. My father lives there, somewhere."

Will crossing be difficult? Are there treaties between your peoples?

"There are treaties, but the leader of the United States is a tyrant who delights in punishing others. He's ignoring all the agreements, building a wall between our countries. It'll be tough to get across. But there are ways."

I pray your trek is successful, Little Star.

Then our separate tasks distract us from further conversation.

Late afternoon, a squadron of Jaguar and Eagle Knights meets us as we cross a lagoon at the edge of the Yacacolco neighborhood. They let us rest our shoulders, bearing the god until we reach the ceremonial complex of Tlatelolco. It's much smaller than the Sacred Precinct of Tenochtitlan; a few temples are ranged around a smaller pyramid than ours.

Nearby is a palace. On its steps, regarding us coolly, stands the emperor.

He is young, maybe seven years older than I am. But hard and wise, a product of the instruction and training of the calmecac, that elite school for nobles.

On his brow sits the imperial diadem, its curved turquoise mosaic rising to a point. His richly embroidered cape is clasped at one shoulder with a silver representation of his name:

An eagle, dropping from the sky, talons at the ready.

We fall to our knees.

"Well done, cadets." His voice is deep and calm. "Where is your captain?"

I clear my throat. "Axoquentzin has fallen, Your Imperial Majesty. But not before protecting innocent women and children, slaying more than a dozen enemy soldiers."

Cuauhtemoc turns to Prime Minister Tlacotzin.

"He is to be remembered. If his body can be retrieved, have it brought here for what noble rites we can muster."

The emperor looks down at me. "Your mission has been arduous. Yet, I ask you to carry our god a little farther. Should the Caxtiltecah breach our defenses, they will sack the temples. Huitzilopochtli will be hidden in the telpochcalli of Amaxac, the neighboring borough. There you will be fed well and quartered for the night."

I scoop up dust and lick it from my palm, as one does in the presence of one's sovereign. Then we take the litter from the knights, who guide us from the ceremonial center.

We pass alongside the marketplace, the most enormous place of commerce in all of Anahuac. Sitlali appears to walk alongside me. She keeps her head down as she goes.

Are you traveling through Piedras Negras?

On the outskirts, trying to avoid crowds. Someone recommended a cheap place, a room for rent. I'll stay the night there, figure out how to cross the river tomorrow.

I just met the emperor, I tell her, keeping silent about the death of Axoquentzin.

Cuauhtemoc? I see his face on the hundred-peso bill all the time.

Like many of her utterances, this makes no sense to me.

He's younger than I imagined. Such has been our history. Youths, required by circumstance to become adults perhaps before their time.

Like you, she says.

I look up at the wooden face of Huitzilopochtli, lit by the setting sun. A trick of the light makes it seem as if his jeweled eyes return my gaze.

Like us both, Little Star. Like us both.

CHAPTER FIFTEEN

Sitlali

June 16-17, 2019

I find a room to rent from Doña Sofía, a dentist who works out of her house. It was her son's bedroom, but he's off in Monterrey, studying engineering. I sit glued to the TV, nervously watching the news, expecting a report about the seventeen-year-old girl who stabbed a narco in the neck, escaping in a dead man's truck.

At five, when I know my madrina Tomasa is home from work, I leave the bedroom and walk into the sala to ask Doña Sofía if I can place a call to los Estados. "You can use my cell phone," she says. "Ten minutes, one hundred fifty pesos. Does that work for you?"

I hand her the money, and she dials the number for me. I sit on the recliner and look out the window, while the phone rings and rings. Nobody answers, so I leave a message, letting my madrina know to expect me soon.

I only leave the house to eat dinner at El Toztón a few blocks away. At the restaurant, Calizto sits across from me, eating whatever they've given him at the commoner school where he took the idol of

Huitzilopochtli. I look at him and think how strange this is, how the magic of the moon conch has made it possible for Calizto and me to be so present in each other's lives. How we've become more than companions in a matter of days. We are like family, living in each other's spaces, connecting on that level of intimacy loved ones give one another.

"You look like you're going to fall asleep any second," I whisper.

He looks up, able to hear me when I speak out loud. But because he is not alone, he speaks to me with his mind.

It has been a long and grueling day, Sitlali. I believe I should go find a mat and get some rest.

I suddenly yawn. The massive torta I just ate has made me drowsy too. "You and me both, Calizto."

By the time I return to my room, he is sprawled on the floor, breathing deep and slow.

I smile, reach out, and pretend to push a loose lock of hair behind his ear before I move toward my bed. The sun is low in the sky as I crawl under the blankets.

"Good night, Calizto," I whisper, and he moans a little in his sleep.

I wake up later than I had planned. Calizto seems to be moving in and out of the room, passing through the walls as he goes about various tasks and has conversations with people I cannot see in his time. When he sees that I'm getting up, he smiles at me.

At last. I wondered if perhaps you had entered hibernation.

"Very funny. What're you doing?"

Helping the telpochcalli masters accommodate groups of refugees. Will you be going down to the river today?

"This afternoon, yeah. I can't cross until it's dark."

Very well, Little Star. We'll talk again soon.

After a late breakfast, I walk to the plaza. The miniature pyramids standing there are well done, though part of me is glad Calizto can't perceive them. It would sadden him to see remnants of his culture depicted in motionless statues and monuments. I continue to wander, then stop to admire a bronze figure that rises above the others in the middle of the park: an Aztec warrior, lifting his hands to the sky. The sun plays tricks on my eyes, and for a moment, I swear there is a conch cupped in those metal fingers.

Say a prayer for me, to your Virgencita. Calizto's words come back to me, like a whisper in the wind. I gaze up at the clock tower of the Sanctuario de Nuestra Señora de Guadalupe and see that it is two in the afternoon.

It is dim inside the sanctuary. Standing before the small statue of our Blessed Mother in the far corner of the room, I light a candle for Calizto. Even though history says he perished a long time ago, I know the Virgencita's love is not limited by time or space.

Crossing myself, I take a slim lighting stick and lift it over the flame of a well-lit candle. I am looking for a good-size, extinguished candle to claim as my own, when I feel someone touch my shoulder.

"Sitlali," Calizto says. His hand on my shoulder sparkles, sending tiny, gold-flecked electrical charges down my spine, and I shudder. But there is something more—his hand has weight.

"You touched me," I whisper. "I felt it."

"Me too," he says.

But he isn't looking at me. His wide eyes are focused on the image of the Virgen de Guadalupe behind me. He comes so close I can see candles flickering in his luminous eyes. They are like amber lights, reflecting back to me an image of myself encircled within the glory of Guadalupe's glowing altar. And for a moment, we are, all three of us, trapped in a vacuum, a radiant, light-infused space as bright and magnificent as the burning sun.

"Something's changed," Calizto whispers in awe.

"Yes. You are here—in my world."

"Where are we?" he asks, mesmerized. "What is this wondrous place?"

"We are in the Virgen's sanctuary—her temple, in Piedras Negras, Coahuila."

"Tonantzin." Calizto is in awe of the statue of Guadalupe. "She is magnificent. The starry sky of her robe is different, but glorious in its own way—a sacred garb worthy of a goddess."

"Can you see anything else?" I ask him, watching his eyes narrow as he tries to focus. "Can you see the high ceiling? The arches?"

"No," he says. "Only you. Her. And her divine light."

He moves to touch the statue of the Virgin, but his hand goes through it. "What does it mean that she stands on a crescent moon?"

"I'm not sure. I don't know what all the symbols mean. There's a story about the roses," I say, taking a white rose from the altar and showing it to him. He stares at its creamy complexion and smiles.

"Part of the mystery," he says, nodding. "We must trust what we do not understand."

"Yes," I say. "You can talk to her, you know. She speaks Nahuatl. It is her language too."

"I would not know what to say," he admits, lifting his eyes to the face of our Indigenous Virgin. "As a child, I learned many prayers. They had been passed down through the ages, and my elders taught me the words, the gestures. But how does one address a revered goddess in her new form? It would take me many years of study to understand how to honor her."

"Would you like to pray with me?" I ask.

Calizto's eyes light up.

"Very much so," he says.

I reach for the lighting stick and try to hand it to him. But it is not part of his world. So I take his hand and put it over mine. A series of tiny sparks—golden flecks of electricity—pass between us as we touch again, but I am not startled as much as I am warmed by them. The heat of his touch travels up my arm, over my shoulders, and down my back.

As every muscle in my body relaxes, I guide our joined hands over a flickering flame. I can feel Calizto's breath on my shoulder, but it is the beating of his heart that roars in my ears, palpitating in rhythm with my own. I look at his handsome face, his hooded eyes, straight nose, and wide lips, and I wonder if he feels it too—this divine connection.

Calizto looks at me too; his eyes glimmer brightly as he smiles. The moment stretches. I think it might last forever, until the flame on the lighting stick licks at my fingertips. I cry out and drop the stick as I pull away.

Calizto inspects my hand. Looks at each finger carefully. I stand still, holding my breath, transfixed as he leans down and kisses my fingertips with his soft lips. The warmth inside me grows. If I didn't know any better, I would think I am glowing all over with the luxurious feel of his lips on my hand.

"I'm all right. Shall we pray?"

"Yes," he says, letting go of my hand.

"Wait," I say. "It's part of the ritual. We hold hands as we say our prayers. Where there is more than one . . ."

Calizto intertwines his fingers with mine and steps closer to me. I can feel his soft gaze caressing my face, and my breath catches in my throat. "It is fortuitous that we should be able to touch here, in this sacred place, in the presence of Tonantzin Guadalupe, today."

"Fortuitous?" I ask.

"Today's date is Chiucnahui Tochtli, Nine Rabbit. Rabbit days are for self-sacrifice, for serving to something greater than oneself. It is obvious that this sanctuary is very important to you. And now it is important to me too."

"You mean this was preordained?"

Calizto thinks for a moment. "The old songs mention *'those I choose to spark through paradox to fight the dark.'* She chose us, Sitlali. At the beginning of time, she prepared a way for you and me."

"I'm *'she who is destined to wield'* and you're *'he who is commanded to shield'*?"

"I believe so."

"Fascinating," I whisper. My voice quivers as he strokes my knuckles ever so softly with his thumbs.

Calizto falls silent and turns his head as if he is listening to someone else, someone I can't see or hear. His grip on my hands tightens. *I am sorry, Sitlali, but I must leave. The Spanish brigantines attacking the north of my city have been captured. I must return to Tenochtitlan to look for survivors.*

"I understand your loyalty, Calizto, but . . ." I stop myself before I say too much. I know that the people of Tenochtitlan and Tlatelolco will be massacred, that both cities will fall, but I don't want to fill his head with information that might put fear in his heart. That would be devastating for a warrior. I can only pray for his safe return.

This might be my only opportunity to check on Ofirin, Calizto says.

When he reaches up to caress my face, I lean into his touch. My eyes downcast, I notice a burned pattern on the inside of his wrist. Three spots in a diagonal—Orion's Belt? The soft stroke of his hand is a fine feather, moving downward along the line of my cheek, and I shiver from head to toe.

Calizto's fingertips linger on my chin, and he says, *Do not worry, Little Star. Coyolxauhqui is with me. We will set eyes on each other again.*

“Be careful.” The words leave my lips as he steps back, turns around, and walks into the sunlight outside the sanctuary. I watch him disappear, dissipate into whiteness.

It is hard seeing him go. It isn’t fair. Every time he leaves now, deliberately weakening our connection with his will, he is off to fight in that terrible war again. I wipe the tears that flow down my face and light another candle. Sobbing, I ask, “Tonantzin Guadalupe, please intercede for your son Calizto in the heavens. Ask the goddess Coyolxauhqui to cover him with an invisible cloak. Ask her to make him imperceptible to his enemies and return him to me soon, because I don’t know how much more I can take of this.”

When I am done, my eyes feel like two throbbing red tomatoes, and I put the oversize sunglasses I purchased at the gas station yesterday back on my face. Head bowed, I walk out of the sanctuario, into the hot afternoon. Without delay, I cross over the placita and make my way down to the river.

CHAPTER SIXTEEN

Calizto

Day 10-Water of the Year 3-House (June 18, 1521)

First Quarter of the Day (6 a.m. to noon)

The canoe glides under the brilliant light of the full moon, hugging the shore, carrying Ayotochtli and me to the eastern docks of Tenochtitlan.

Sitlali sleeps, head on her pack, the conch cradled in one arm. My hand rests lightly on the waves of her hair: silken soft, with delicate highlights glinting like maize tassels. As I brush strands from her face, I realize I can smell her, a faint perfume that makes my heart ache.

The pilot pulls up to a quay. Ayotochtli and I slip from the canoe, wending our way among smoking ruins. Twice we have to swim across bridgeless canals, one choked with debris and corpses.

We reach the telpochcalli to find its buildings shattered and burning, but free of bodies.

"They might've taken refuge at the temple of Tezcatlipoca," Ayotochtli suggests, his face haggard with worry.

"Or at Tocihtitlan." I think of the widows and orphans who visit that ritual complex to beg Tonantzin for mercy. "Let's split up, gather what survivors we encounter, and meet back here at the end of the watch. Then we can either head to the docks or walk back to Tlatelolco."

I turn south as light begins to touch the sky, heading for the shrine where I left Ofirin five days ago. Hopeful, I adjust the netted bag, gripping the conch, reassured by its glyphs.

"Good morning, Calizto."

Sitlali is standing beside me, drinking water from a clear container. She sets it down and reaches out her right hand while her left clutches the conch.

"Good morning, Little Star." I reach out my free hand as well.

Our fingers touch with a jolt of static, as when one is grazed by a bit of metal on the driest winter day.

Behind Sitlali, my world fades away.

She is standing under a copse of mesquite trees at the edge of a slow-moving but broad river. On the other side of the river rises a wall formed of iron slats. It stretches, black and ugly, as far as the eye can see in either direction. The soil has been blasted and trees uprooted to erect it there, but I see no city or fortress on the other side.

It's a monument to isolation. Without guards, easily climbed, the wall exists as a symbol.

You are not wanted here, it says.

"Oh my God!" Sitlali cries aloud. "I can see your city behind you!"

"Yes, and I can see the Great River at your back, and beyond it the most unsightly barrier ever erected."

She glances over her shoulder and gives a grim laugh. Our fingers intertwine, as if of their own accord. "You're not wrong. Damn useless wall."

I look at her hand in mine: soft yet strong, small yet capable of holding my entire heart. Then I notice that we each grip our version of the conch, as we had in the sanctuary.

"That's the secret: we both must hold the sacred trumpet when we touch."

"If the moon is full," she adds. "Because we couldn't touch before."

We stand staring at each other, eyes flitting to the alien world over the other's shoulder.

"Come. I'll show you what remains of the borough of Zoquiyapan."

Some homes still stand. But most are shattered, looted, burned. An occasional dog or racoon skitters away as we walk along once shady paths, impossibly hand in hand.

"I wish you could've seen this neighborhood two years ago," I tell her. "Thriving. Full of warbling turkeys and laughing children. Smelling of flowers and delicious meals. Canoes plying the waters of the canals, dappled by the shade of trees that anchored our chinampa gardens."

Her hand squeezes mine. "But then the Spanish came."

"And with them, Death." I point to the ruins of my parents' home. "The house where I was born. It stood for decades. A single cannon blast erased it forever."

"I'm so sorry." A sob hitches in her throat. I pull her closer, till the flesh of her arm presses against mine, the most bittersweet pleasure I've ever felt.

We round the block. The shrine to the lunar goddess still stands, its three walls of volcanic rock as unperturbed by the siege as the moon itself. The thatch roof is singed, though whole. Inside, the altar is coated with soot, but the effigy of Coyolxauhqui glows in the morning sun.

"That's her, isn't it?" Sitlali whispers.

"Yes. But where's Ofirin?"

I call his name, glancing about at the broken houses.

"Behind you, I think," Sitlali says.

He stumbles from an abandoned building, clothes in tatters.

"Calizto!" He hugs me tightly. I cannot return the embrace, as I refuse to let go of either the conch or Sitlali's hand. "Don't leave me again. I thought we were friends."

As he pulls away, I pretend to ponder. "You are indeed my sacred charge. But friend?"

Ofirin winks. "Your closest confidant. Who else has heard you moan in longing all night long? What was her name again?"

I raise the conch to stop him.

Sitlali widens her eyes. "Moaning a girl's name in your sleep?"

Ofirin leans in again. "Sitlali. That's it. Calizto's true love."

Clearing my throat, I elbow him. "You're suffering from starvation."

Sitlali stifles a laugh. Two small dimples form on her cheeks. My breath catches, and I force myself to look back at Ofirin.

He gestures at the house. "No. I found food and clothing in there. Now my stomach is full and my mind clear."

"Maybe you'll be less of a burden."

Sitlali sucks in air. "Calizto, that wasn't very kind."

Ofirin winces. "You're a bastard. But I understand. They took everything from me, too."

I nod. "Burned your village. Killed your parents. Enslaved your siblings."

Ofirin grits his teeth. "It didn't stop there."

"What does he mean?" Sitlali asks.

Ofirin's "master," Narváez, came to our shores to arrest Cortés and take him back to face consequences for disobeying orders.

"Oh, I know that story! The pinche conquistador trapped Narváez, put out his eye, and clapped him in irons. Then didn't Cortés turn Narváez's men against him?"

Yes. Those were the forces he brought with him when he came back a year ago, once he'd caught wind of the massacre in the ceremonial center. My uncle Ceolin was there. Dancing for the festival of Toxcatl, honoring Huitzilopochtli. Until Alvarado shut the gates and had his vicious beasts open fire on the dancers. Out of ignorance and cruelty. A few men survived, climbing over the Serpent Wall or hiding in temples. Not my uncle.

Sitlali lifts my hand to her lips, kisses it gently. "I'm so sorry. Did Ofirin come with Cortés when he returned to Tenochtitlan?"

"Tell me again," I urge Ofirin, "about the civilians. About your beloved."

Sitlali gasps.

Ofirin rubs his eyes. "Cortés organized the new men and horses into an expedition to rescue his murderous compatriots. But he sent the civilians ahead, a group of cooks and shepherds with their flocks, Spanish women and children, servants bearing burdens, and slaves. Including Ana, the girl I'd come to love aboard our ship. Of the Yoruba people, like me. Enaben, her parents named her."

Sitlali's grip tightens. "What happened to her?"

I repeat her question.

"They were ambushed in a mountain pass," Ofirin manages to say, dropping his gaze. "By some allies of the Mexica. Most were slaughtered. A woman made it back with the horrible news, but Cortés had already left. In a fit of rage or despair, I followed. Maybe Enaben survived, I thought. If not, I would make the Spanish bastards pay. Instead, I was drawn into this city with them and then left behind when your people killed most of them and expelled the rest."

For the first time, his story makes me uneasy. I sense that he has been hiding something from me, something he's now hinting at with these revelations.

"Why did they leave you behind?" I ask. "Why were you not with Enaben's group or with Cortés?"

Ofirin stammers. "S-someone had to remain behind. Spaniards. And they needed their slave labor."

"Really?" I want to contest this obvious lie, but Sitlali shakes her head.

"Stop. You have to get him out of this city. It's horrible, what's happened to him. Can't you shave his head, pretend he's, I don't know, a Maya or something?"

Ofirin and I stare at each other for several seconds.

"There's food and clothing in that house?" I ask.

"Yes. And a flint knife."

"Go inside and change into a loincloth. Throw your boots and rags and your crucifix into a fire. Then take that flint knife and shave your hair down to the scalp."

Ofirin swallows. "What do you have in mind?"

"I must check for survivors, but I'll return and get you to safety."

"When?"

"Today. Be ready in an hour. We'll be meeting others at the telpochcalli."

Ofirin's eyes widen. "Isn't that dangerous?"

"Every option left to us is dangerous, my friend."

As he heads inside, Sitlali gives me a sad smile.

"Time to let go while you search," she says. "I need to double-check a spot I found last night. It's shallow enough, I think, but I'll see better by daylight."

Reluctantly, I pull my hand away, rubbing my palm lightly against hers. Her world fades from view, though she still smiles at me as she rummages through her pack.

After a half watch, I cross a bridge to the small island at the edge of the southern causeway. At its center rises a pyramid. The Cihuateocalli. Temple of the Goddesses. The first sight that greets a traveler's eyes as they enter Tenochtitlan.

I keep to the morning shadows, slipping along walls, avoiding Spanish and Tlaxcaltecah eyes. The greatest risk comes as I run up the steps in full view of the causeway. Fortunately, since Cortés is camped outside the Sacred Precinct and Zoquiyapan has been reduced to rubble, there are fewer men stationed here.

The sanctuary is empty. No refugees in sight. I stand before the statue for a moment. Starred headdress, rich flowing huipil blouse and cueitl skirt, hands clasped above her stomach.

I feel a hand slip into mine. I know it's Sitlali without looking.

"Who is she?"

"Teteoh Innan," I whisper, "Mother of the Gods. We call her Tocih."

Sitlali murmurs in her own dialect. "Tosis. Grandmother. She looks like . . ."

"Your Tonantzin Guadalupe. Yes." I press Sitlali's hand against my chest as I close my eyes and pray. "Arise, Mother. Leave us not abandoned. Walk by our side forever, through the fire and the rain."

Moved, Sitlali echoes my words: "Ximewa, Tonantzin."

I open my eyes. Something mute but tangible trembles in Sitlali's features. I feel it too. We cannot give a name to that emotion. The spell might be broken, our connection lost.

Instead, we gaze wordlessly at each other for a time before Sitlali grabs her pack to head upstream and I make my way back.

Though in different times and places, we walk side by side.

When I get back to the shrine, Ofirin is nowhere to be found. I check the house he's been staying in, but it's empty.

"Where did that fool go?" I mutter in frustration.

"Is that a piece of paper beside the entrance?" Sitlali asks after taking my hand again.

On a hook in one of the shrine's walls hangs a rectangle of amate paper. I examine it. Two glyphs have been sketched: a moon and a telpochcalli. Footprints lead from the former to the latter. Beneath them are letters, but I only recognize my name, which Ofirin taught me.

"It appears he has left for the school," I muse.

"Yeah. He's written in Spanish, 'Calizto, you can't read this, but a group of Tlaxcaltecah is patrolling. I'm heading to your school.' Wait. Does he even know where it is?"

I nod. "I've helped him make maps of the city. But I need to hurry if I'm going to get there before Ayotochtli."

Upon arriving, however, I find that I'm too late.

I've also underestimated Ofirin.

"Calizto!" Ayotochtli calls in greeting. "Find anyone else? The Chontal scribe you sent ahead told me you were still looking."

Ofirin is sitting among a group of refugees, eating. He has been transformed, hair scraped to the scalp like a new student at the telpochcalli, his limbs uncovered, a simple loincloth tied into place.

"Oh," I say. "No, there was no one else at the temples. Just . . . the scribe."

Ayotochtli nods. "Well, his Nahuatl is shitty, but if we stumble across other immigrants, it'll be good to have a translator."

As soon as I can, I pull Ofirin aside. "Scribe? I was going to pass you off as a captive."

"You underestimate me, always. I have enough Nahuatl to pull this off."

"Fine. But talk as little as possible. Never in Spanish. Speak Yoruba if you must. People will assume it's a southern tongue."

As soon as the refugees have broken their fast, Ayotochtli gestures at three canoes docked in the canal.

"Okay, time to head out. We'll stay in the prime minister's palace tonight and then travel to Tlatelolco at dawn."

Sitlali touches my upper arm lightly. "Already? I was really enjoying this time just to ourselves, hearing your voice . . . feeling the warmth of your skin . . ."

"Ayotochtli," I call out, more respectful than usual. "Can you take them all with you? I have some . . . personal matters to attend to first. I shall rejoin you at the palace, comrade."

My friend hesitates a second, and then he nods with a mischievous grin, approaching me.

"So you did find someone else. Hid her away, did you? Fine. Because we're brothers."

Ofirin winks as well, and soon they're rowing away.

CHAPTER SEVENTEEN

Sitlali

June 18, 2019

Noon to 2 p.m.

Once the boats have disappeared around a bend in the canal, Calizto takes my hand again.

"Have you eaten yet?" he asks.

My stomach rumbles in answer. "Sorry!" I mutter, a little embarrassed. "No, I haven't."

"Then let's try something. Breaking our fast together, in your time."

"You mean like a little picnic?" Then, because I realize he doesn't know what that means, I explain. "We can sit right here, beside the river, and eat. We call it a date! You're so sweet for suggesting it."

Calizto shakes his head with a confused smile, the way he always does when I say things that he doesn't quite understand. It's very endearing. Wondering if he can tell the effect he's having on me, I take out some of the sandwiches, fruit, and granola bars from my pack, and take my time to arrange them elegantly on the small towel I use as a pillow.

Calizto grins when I am done and sit back on my knees to look directly at him. “There. Now we’re ready to relax. For a moment, anyway.”

“The problem is . . . how do we hold the conch, hold hands, and also eat?”

My heart is fluttering in my chest, in a strange way, like I’m afraid of not having this work. “I don’t think we have to grip it in our hands,” I tell him. “Let’s try just keeping the contact with our bodies. If it doesn’t work, we’ll try eating with one hand.”

We experiment for a bit, laughing at the silliness of strapping our bags to our chests and letting just our shoulder or bare feet touch instead of holding hands. Eventually we understand what’s needed: the conch has to be within a finger’s length of our skin. Organic materials like cotton or reed fiber can’t stop its power, though plastic or refined metal can.

But our physical contact with each other has to be skin to skin for us to see and experience the other’s world.

I don’t know when it happened, but I’m starting to crave closeness. Could I be getting addicted to his touch? The thought warms my cheeks and Calizto’s grin tells me he’s in tune with my emotional state. That’s okay with me. I’ll take any excuse to feel him near me.

“You say this is *bread*?” Calizto asks after another bite of his sandwich. “Made from actual grains? I’ve never had food so . . . fluffy in my life.”

“Fluffy? That’s a word for a warrior.”

“I, Calizto, Son of Omaca, declare fluffy bread the true food of the gods.”

We both laugh as he gives a running commentary on the rest of the food from my time, especially oranges, whose name strikes him as a paradox.

“Which came first, the color or the fruit?” he asks. I can’t tell if he’s serious.

"No. No philosophy today, Calizto, son of Omaca," I declare, taking his hands and pulling him to his feet. "Let's walk along the riverbank. I want to show you where I plan to cross."

We pick up our tiliches, and I take him upstream to a bend, shallow and broad, with nice shadow-dappled pools on the edges. After rolling up my pants legs, I grab his hand and pull him toward the water. It's nice and cool, and the denser mesquites dotting the bank of the river provide relief from the already hot, afternoon sun.

"I can't believe that I am both standing at my school and standing in this river in your time all at once," he says, reaching down to run his fingertips through the water. "You have brought magic to my life, Sitlali. Magic and so much more."

He takes my other hand in his, gazing at me with those beautiful dark eyes.

My heart palpitates, and my knees weaken, and I am mush. Then, without warning, he lets himself fall backward into the meander, pulling me with him. We hit the water with a splash, and I'm immediately soaked, clothes and all.

"Calizto!" I shout, sputtering as I thrash about in the shallow end. "I wasn't planning to jump into the Río Bravo just yet!"

He pulls me to my feet. The water reaches our waists now.

Calizto adjusts his netted bag, slinging the conch on his back. Then he draws me close, pulling down gently on the strap of the canvas bag where I've stored my version of the shell. I feel it slide into the small of my back just as this boy I'm falling for steps so close to me I can feel his breath on my neck.

"I'm going to kiss you now," he rasps, voice husky with need, "unless you object."

My heart is beating so fast that I can't catch my breath enough to form words. So, I push him. As he falls back into the river, I run out of the water, but I don't get far. Calitzo catches up to me and, laughing, I wrap my arms around him.

He reaches up and pushes a wet strand of hair off my face before he traces my lips with his thumbs. "May I?" he asks. "Kiss you?"

I nod and close my eyes as his face draws closer. His lips are soft, a feathery sensation, as he brushes them gently over mine. But then, as I sigh, a sort of hunger overcomes him, and he groans, puts his arm around my waist, and pulls me closer. I put my hand against his neck and melt into him, wanting more than the sweet taste of bread and honey that lingers on his breath. Five hundred years, and a kiss worth waiting for, makes it all disappear. Because with my eyes closed, nothing else exists. Nothing else matters, except the two of us, clinging to each other, as we slide down and lie on the soft grass under our feet.

I giggle when I open my eyes, take a breath, and find a twig tangled in his hair chig. I pull it off and toss it aside, before I pull his head down for more of his hungry kisses. The churn of the rolling river, gliding over pebbles and rocks, fades away, and the shivering of leaves in the mesquites around us become silent when Calizto traces the line of my cheek all the way down, past my neck, and along the hem of my wet blouse.

All I hear is the accelerated beating of my heart as it comes to life and roars against my eardrums. I reach up and tug at the piece of cloth that holds his hair up, and it comes tumbling over, weighed down by its wetness. I run my fingers through his dark, moist locks. "It's longer than mine," I whisper, as I stroke it, push it out of his face.

Calizto mutters something in Nahuatl, passionate words I do not catch, before he leans over me and kisses me intimately. His tongue nudges gently, urging me to caress him, to run my hands down his muscular body, to use my fingers and palm to massage his naked back.

After a while, lying on my back along the riverbank, the conch pressed against my ribs, I shudder as a delicious sigh leaves my lips. Calizto kisses the curve of my neck as his hands slip under my wet T-shirt and work their way up. I grip his strong shoulders, cling to him. Release another shuddering breath.

Am I ready for this?

His hand reaches the bottom of my bra, and he slips a finger under the elastic, stretching it, as if trying to figure out what this thing is that's keeping him from exploring the rest of me.

"Whoa, whoa, whoa," I mutter, pushing at his hard chest gently but firmly as I sit up. "Too fast. Let's pump the brakes on this, okay?"

"Brakes?" he asks, a quizzical look on his handsome face. "Is that what you call that pliable cloth?"

"No," I say. "That's what we call *stop*. Pause. You know, retreat?"

"Oh. I did not mean to make you uncomfortable." He swallows heavily, clearly embarrassed, and slowly stands. "I . . . I apologize, Sitlali. I allowed myself to get . . . caught up in the moment."

"It's not that I wasn't enjoying it. Just that . . . I think we should take things a little slower, okay?"

He glances around at the surrounding in his own time, looking at his school now that we're not touching.

Then, smiling again, he turns back to me.

I try not to think of what we might've just ended up doing because it's something I've never done before. Though when I look at him, I can't seem to think of anything else than the deliciousness of what he started, the fire he kindles in me. "What?"

"I would like to take you on a tour of the canals of Tenochtitlan," he says. "Would you be keen on that?"

CHAPTER EIGHTEEN

Calizto

Day 10-Water of the Year 3-House (June 18, 1521)

Second and Third Afternoon Watch (2 p.m. to 6 p.m.)

I take Sitlali's hand, and she connects to my time, where I guide her to the remaining canoe and head northwest along a slanting canal.

As I row, Sitlali sits across from me, hand resting on my knee. I let the boat glide for a while as she marvels at the gleaming white stucco of the walls of the canal, rising about the height of a man above the water. Tall trees cast afternoon shadows across us as we move slowly and silently out of Zoquiyapan.

"What do you think?"

"Amazing," she says in awe. "Never in a million years did I imagine that one day I would get to enjoy the beauty of Tenochtitlan."

"What remains of it."

"My teachers spoke of its canals, but I never expected to see one close up."

"Broad enough for Spanish brigantines, so the Tlaxcaltecah have kept it free of debris and the dead. But we're moving past the boroughs they occupy." I turn my head toward the northwest. Above the line of trees, the twin temples of the Great Pyramid are visible. "That way lies the ceremonial center. Those are the shrines of Tlaloc and Huitzilopochtli, highest point in the city."

I set down the oars for a while, and we lie back in the canoe, basking in the afternoon sun, letting it dry our hair and clothes as we drift in and out of a pleasant nap, fingers interlaced.

For a moment, I forget that war is raging in most parts of this city.

A light breeze blows across us. The water laps gently against the hull. Perhaps the goddess herself stills the world for us.

A half watch of peace. One hour, just the two of us. Content. Together.

Sitlali jerks beside me, as if startled in her sleep. I notice the air is filled with the cackling and squawking of hundreds of birds. Other animals respond with roars and cries.

"What in the world was that?" Sitlali says, sitting up.

I blink drowsiness from my eyes. "Ah. The aviary and the zoo. Lord Moteuczoma had them built behind his palace, across the canal. He collected creatures from far and wide, strange species not found in Anahuac."

"How amazing they must be!"

"Would you like to see them? I can take you."

Sitlali's eyes go wide with delight. "Would you? Really?"

In answer, I point up ahead, where the canal starts to straighten, turning due north. "You'll see a wharf on our left soon, with stairs leading out of the canal. We'll disembark there."

Reaching the spot, I tie off the canoe and climb the stairway onto a broad boulevard. Ahead, I can make out the long bridge that crosses the wide east–west canal used for transporting items to and from Moteuczoma's palace and gardens.

Nearby sits a half-submerged building.

"What's that?" Sitlali asks.

"A temazcalli, a sweat lodge."

"Ugh. Where I am, you don't need help to sweat."

"There's also a pool of fresh water inside where we could bathe and relax."

I can feel the ambivalent hesitation roiling in her heart.

"I . . . I think we've had enough water for one day, Calizto. Let's . . . just go straight to the aviary, okay?"

Suppressing a laugh, I take Sitlali's hand and walk toward the sound of birds. We cross the long bridge as I point to our left.

"You can see the ceremonial plaza from here, and beside it, on the other side of the aqueduct, stands the Palace of Moteuczoma."

Sitlali takes a deep breath. "So much gleaming white and luxurious green! And all those colorful murals! I would've never guessed it was this beautiful."

For a moment, I'm surprised the enemy isn't camped at the Southern Gate, just beyond the palace. But perhaps Cortés has retreated to reorganize.

We come at last to the aviary, sprawling beside the zoo. Hundreds of men and women once attended to the animals' needs, but now no one stops me as I open the gate and pull Sitlali inside.

A forest spreads before us, trees of every sort, some as tall as a small pyramid. Over the top of them a vast net has been spread, letting in air and sunlight, but keeping the birds from flying away.

They are everywhere, raucous and colorful, flitting from branch to branch, filling the air in a sudden explosion of brilliant motion.

Sitlali leans into me, her face beaming. "It's beautiful, Calizto."

"Yes." I look into her face, the only beauty that matters.

Nearby is a pond, a bench at its edge. We sit side by side, my right hand entwined with her left, each of us gripping the moon conch, mirror images. Sitlali smiles at me, rests her head upon my shoulder.

"Thank you for this," she whispers, watching ducks and swans weave in and out among flamingos and roseate spoonbills. "How can such an amazing place still be standing? Why haven't the Mexica raided it, eaten the birds?"

I rest my chin against the top of her head, relishing the faint scent of flowers. "It belongs to the emperor, Sitlali. Long ago the people of this city made a pact with the nobility—protect us, let us live long lives, free of suffering and wandering. In return, we give you ownership of everything. No one would dare raid this aviary. It would violate our way of life."

I feel her thumb gently rubbing my wrist. My mouth goes dry. My blood thunders in my veins.

"What is this symbol? These three burns on your wrist. Stars?"

"Yes. The Fire Drill constellation."

"Ah. We call it Orion's Belt in my time. What does it mean?"

"When the world was young, there were only stars in the sky. The gods needed a bonfire in Teotihuacan, the holy city on high. Two would sacrifice themselves to bring light to the world. So the gods took the staff of Quetzalcoatl and began to drill, spinning it back and forth. A spark leapt forth, then another, then a third. And with that last, the flame burst forth. The gods set the sparks among the folds of heaven to honor them. When I was thirteen, ready to enter the telpochcalli, my father drilled fire one evening, and with the glowing stick burned this pattern into my wrist. It marked me as a man in awe of heaven."

Sitlali lifts her head from my shoulder, looking at me expectantly, her lips slightly parted, teeth glowing white against the setting sun. I lean toward her, drawn by something more immediate than the moon conch, more basic yet profound. Her eyes close, and this time she moves her head closer as well.

I can barely breathe when our lips touch again. Popocatepetl itself seems to erupt in my very heart. Her mouth is an intoxicating blend of sweet and tart, like a mango brined with salt, like pungent chocolate drizzled with honey.

For a moment, everything else recedes, just as it did beside the river in her time. All that exists is the unending cosmos of my being and the single star, burning hotly in its center.

Nocitlalin.

My Sitlali.

Mine.

And suddenly I know the name of this feeling.

Not need. Not relief. Not friendship.

Love.

Before I can grapple with the realization, there comes a distant explosion.

I feel her pulling away. No, I want to beg. Why now, you cruel gods? What have you sent to ruin this moment?

"Calizto!" Sitlali gasps, shuddering. "Look!"

Flames in the sky to the west.

I let go of Sitlali's hand, drop the conch into its netted bag, turn to the nearest tree, and start to climb.

"I can't see it anymore!" Sitlali cries. "What's going on?"

Even from here I can make out the destruction. Another volley slams into the ceremonial center, smashing temples and statues.

"The Palace of Axayacatl is in flames! A Spanish brigantine has come from the west up the broadest canal and is firing on the buildings around the Sacred Precinct!"

The birds go wild, slamming against the netting, screeching. A quetzal comes flying right at me, its beak wide in fear.

I slide down the tree. Sitlali leaps to her feet, pointing at the gate behind her.

“If they’ve come from the west, then they must be heading east!”

The bridge we just crossed. Over a canal broad enough for a brigantine.

“Run, Calizto! Run!”

Before I can obey, the world explodes around me.

PART TWO

WANING MOON

CHAPTER NINETEEN

Sitlali

June 18–19, 2019

Afternoon and Night

I barely have time to register Calizto's kiss before he pushes me away at the same time that he flings the netted bag with the moon conch into a nearby bush.

I love you, I want to say, but I don't.

I can't.

Our perfect day is over when our connection breaks, and I am instantly thrown back in time, back to the river's edge. Startled, I sit up, open my eyes, and see the sunset bouncing off the surface of the Río Bravo.

I call out, "Calizto? Are you all right?"

He doesn't speak. But, in my mind, I see him sprinting into a hasty run, reaching down and grabbing the conch as he takes off. He escapes the explosions and the fire and jumps into the canal. Sunlight bounces off the surface of the water, and I blink, confused, as one becomes the other and I am back in Piedras Negras, staring at the waters of the Río Bravo in my time.

"Hey, girl!"

Someone calls from behind me, and I turn around and see two young men coming toward me. Their smiles are friendly, but my guard comes up immediately.

"You going in for a dip?"

I grab my mochila and quickly stand up. "No," I say. "I'm not."

I start to leave, but the first boy stands in my way. "Oh, come on," he says. "It's not too late for a swim, is it, Ramiro? Or were you thinking of crossing over?"

"We can help you," Ramiro says. "Lalo and I can transport you tonight, if you like."

"I have to go," I say, and I turn and move away from them.

When Lalo grabs my arm, I pull myself loose and push him away. My mochila slaps against my hips, and my tennis shoes pound hard against the packed ground as I run along the river's edge, until I come to a clearing where a family is packing up to leave.

Catching my breath in quick gulps, I walk up to them and mouth the words, "Help me, please," to the mother. She looks behind me at the two boys who have stopped chasing me and are watching us from twenty yards away.

"Where were you?" the mother asks.

"Back there," I say, pointing beyond the boys.

The father, who was busy moving something around inside his truck, raises his head, peeks up at us, and frowns. Then he straightens up and fixes his gaze on the two young men lingering by the river's edge.

"Can I help you?" he calls out.

Ramiro shoves his hands into his jeans pockets and shakes his head. "No," he says. "We were just leaving."

"Good," the father says.

As the two boys turn away, I look over at the father. "God bless you. You have no idea . . . I was so scared."

The father's eyes narrow. "I suppose you need a ride," he says, and I nod. "I can take you as far as López Mateo."

"Thank you," I say.

He hauls up his youngest, a chubby little girl with two missing front teeth, and puts her in the cabin. A whistle tells the three little boys by the river that it's time to go, and they run up and climb into the back of the truck.

I climb up and scoot in beside them.

As we make our way down the road, I clutch the conch inside the bag and call out to Calizto in my mind.

Where are you? I ask, because I can see him and Ofirin, bobbing in the water. Behind them is the retention wall of the canal, crumpled and blackened. Floating around them are bits of smoldering wood, the remains of the bridge. I can hear shouting and the pounding of running feet. That peaceful row of palace gardens has become a war zone.

Apologies. The Spaniards are still firing. The prime minister's palace is aflame. I've found Ofirin, but we must search for Ayotochtli.

Yes, yes. Go, I say.

I watch him and Ofirin slip underwater and swim around the brigantine that is anchored in the canal shelling the ceremonial center to pieces, and my heart breaks.

True to his word, the father drops me off in front of the Plaza de las Culturas in downtown Piedras Negras. Because I have a phone call to make, I cross the street and walk quickly past the Aztec, Olmec, and Maya monuments, back to the hostel.

As soon as I get in, I ask Doña Sofía if I can try my madrina again. She dials the number and goes to the kitchen to fix dinner while I make my call.

"Hello?" My madrina Tomasa's voice is foreign to me. I have only seen her a handful of times in my life. And it suddenly strikes me that

I am being rude by not asking but telling her that I am going to her house. What if she can't accommodate me? She has no reason to take me in. Not really. It's not like I'm her real daughter. The thought paralyzes me.

"Sitlali? M'ija? Is that you?"

The concern. The care in her voice. It's all too much for me, and I start crying. "Yes," I say, wiping my nose.

"Are you okay?" my madrina Tomasa asks. "What is it? What's wrong?"

"Nothing," I say. "I'm just glad to hear your voice."

"Oh, thank God," she says. "When are you coming to see me?"

Relieved, I give her all the details of my plan, and she explains that she has contacts in Eagle Pass and she's found out the best thing I could do is get connected with the Gallinitas on the other side. They have a network of reliable people who can get me through the checkpoints on the road out of town.

"When you get into Las Quintas, walk down Eidson Road to Eagle Pass, until you reach El Indio Highway. Take a left on El Indio and go down to Rodee's Fried Chicken. Order a two-neck special with a little cup of hot sauce and tell them to toss the biscuit. But you have to say it exactly like that—'You can toss the biscuit in the trash'—with attitude. Then sit down and wait. They'll tell you what to do from there."

After dinner, I say goodbye to Doña Sofía and walk down to the shops. I don't have time to browse. So, without wasting time, I buy a lightweight duffel bag big enough to carry everything in my mochila. It has a long strap that I can wear securely over my shoulder and across my chest. Then I visit five different exchange kiosks and turn every peso of Martín's dirty money into crisp American dollars. The paper bills feel strangely thick in my hands, and I wonder if they are real, so I decide to test it by purchasing a soda at Farmacia Benavidez. When I come out, Calizto is standing in the fading sunlight, waiting for me.

"It will be dark soon," Calizto says, and he falls into step with me on the sidewalk and takes my hand in his. "You should get back to the river."

Even though I am the only one who can see him in the sparsely populated street, I still whisper. "I know. That's where I'm going. And you? Did you find Ayotochtli?"

"No, but a few women and children he had guided to the prime minister's palace are hiding within the nearby botanical gardens. Ofirin is waiting with them while I reconnoiter, but I wanted to make sure you cross this Río Bravo safely."

We are at the far end of town, holding hands as we walk, when I notice two young men crossing the alley perpendicular to us.

Recognizing Ramiro and Lalo, I stop abruptly. Were they following me all this time? When they catch me looking at them, they smile and turn the corner, walking briskly toward me.

"Run!" I tell Calizto, gripping his hand tightly and tugging at it as I take off.

"What are you doing?" Calizto asks, as we weave in and out of honking traffic. "Who are those men?"

"I'm not sure," I say. "Thieves. Gangsters. Human traffickers. Come on. We have to lose them."

Calizto looks back at Ramiro and Lalo, who are crossing the street, closing the gap between us. "Slave traders?"

"Maybe," I say. "Come on!"

I go into a restaurant. The smell of roasted meats and savory spices attacks my senses, and I look around for a way out. Spotting a door, I pull Calizto with me, and we run across the restaurant past startled cooks and bolt out the back door, into the waning afternoon light.

As we run down the alley, the back door of the kitchen flies open, and I hear pounding footsteps behind us. Calizto jumps sideways, pulls me around to him. We turn together. Our bodies face each other as my bag flies off my shoulder and swings around us. As if in slow motion, Calizto reaches out and pulls it in between us. We take hold of it at the exact same time.

As we slam against a trash bin, the conch grows warmer in our hands. Then something extraordinary happens. Calizto's mind merges with mine even as his body disappears. And, suddenly, we are not two but one. But we have no time to make sense of what is happening because Ramiro grabs my arm.

I pull away, but then Calizto's instincts take over. He moves our muscles, grabs Ramiro with both hands and spins around, towing him as he goes. In one long swoop, Calizto tosses Ramiro at Lalo. Ramiro crashes into his friend, and we pick up a broken shovel stick, weigh its heaviness in our hands, and take a defensive stance—two warriors waiting. Our minds alert, our merged senses amplified, we wait.

Ramiro and Lalo jump up and rush at us.

We raise and spin the heavy stick overhead.

Swing. Strike. Raise. Swing. Strike. Raise.

Again and again, we strike. Against arms. Legs. Backs. Shoulders. Heads. We strike, and strike, and strike, and strike in a flurry of hard, succinct movements that I have no time to think about, until Ramiro and Lalo are on the ground, moaning. Bleeding. Defeated.

Let's go, I say.

We run down the alley and stand looking at the busy sidewalks. The smell of roasted corn coming from a street vendor nearby, the sound of the cars honking, the engines running, the dark smoke of exhaust pipes, and the chatter of people going around us as they walk by becomes a melee of sights, scents, and sounds that confuse our minds, and Calizto is thrown out of our collective form.

Standing before me, Calizto smiles and offers me his hand. I look down at the heavy shovel stick in my hand and toss it aside. Then we cut across standing traffic, weaving quickly between stalled cars, before the light changes, to walk hand in hand down the street.

"That! Was amazing!" I tell him as we turn into a dirt road and are finally alone. "I've never . . . How did we do that?"

"I'm not sure," Calizto says. "But it had to be the moon conch. We touched the same version of it at once. Amazing. This sacred object holds many secrets—many untapped powers. It seems we have just begun to discover its magic."

"Yes," I whisper, and we continue our journey in silence, happy to just hold hands as we travel down to the river's edge and follow its curves southward. By the time we reach the spot where I've decided to cross, the sun has started to set.

"You should go," I tell Calizto. "It'll be a long while before I can cross."

"Are you sure? What if those ruffians return?"

"I can hide," I assure him. "Trust me. I'll be all right. Go. I could see in your thoughts that the botanical gardens is poor protection for your friends. Get them to safety, Calizto."

Then, slowly, hesitantly, Calizto leans over and kisses me. His lips on my forehead are a sweet reminder of all that is good in the world, of the hope I feel in my heart as I embark on this journey.

"I will not easily forget how it felt to be one with you," he whispers in my ear, and I remember the way my body reacted to his, how I yearned for more than his soft lips on mine, before the explosion broke our connection.

Then he gives my cheek a soft caress and leaves me standing at the river's edge.

I sit under a mesquite, relishing the lingering feel of his hand on my skin, his mind in my mind. To my surprise, when the moon comes out, my abuela Lucía appears. She's standing in front of the river. Her translucent form glittering in the moonlight, she turns around and starts coming toward me. Small, slim, and quiet, she holds her hands together in front of her stomach and looks down at me.

"There is no wall here," I tell her. "I'm going to cross tonight."

She nods, but she still doesn't talk. Her eyes are pools of glistening moonlight, and I know she loves me as much as she ever did. That's why she's here. That's why she's come. To let me know I am not alone in this lifetime.

"You shouldn't worry," I whisper. "It's not deep here. I watched kids swim all the way back and forth this afternoon while I waited. It's a good place to cross."

She smiles and sits down beside me. I look at her closely, examine her profile. Her face is pale, and I can see every line of her long life creasing the skin around her eyes and forehead. We sit like that, side by side, silently watching the river run by, for hours.

At 2:30 a.m., I get up, sling the new duffel bag over my shoulder, and adjust it across my chest. Then I gather my courage and forge ahead, wading into the cold water without holding my breath. Abuela Lucía is behind me. I can't see her, but I know she is there, following me as I cross, chest-deep into the chilled, dark water that sets my teeth to chattering.

At first, it goes well enough, so I move faster, with the other side in sight. Suddenly, the bottom falls out from under me, and I sink down. The water rushes over my head, and, shocked, I struggle to stay afloat.

I want to swim up, but the duffel bag is weighing me down. Panicked, I kick my legs and flail my arms, until miraculously, I float up. When I pierce the surface of the water and inhale deeply, the current is so strong it whirls around me, spinning me as it drags me farther downriver.

Sitlali! I can hear Calizto calling out to me. *Do not fight the current! Just keep your head above the water and let it pull you to the riverbank!*

I stop thrashing, put my arms out, and lie back, and just as I am about to give up and start fighting again, the water pushes me toward the low-hanging branch of a crooked huisache. I grab at the shrubbery, ignore the pricking of thorns on skin, and pull myself out of the water. On hands and knees, I crawl to the riverbank, where I heave, cough, and throw up.

CHAPTER TWENTY

Calizto

Day 11-Dog of the Year 3-House (June 19, 1521)

Once the moon has risen, I lead Ofirin and the other refugees toward the Eastern Gate. A crew of women is widening the gap between the causeway and the ceremonial center. At my request, the Eagle and Jaguar Knights guarding them ferry us across.

Sitlali sits on the bank, chest heaving still from the effort of crossing. I smile at her, but her gaze is cast down.

I have looked through those eyes, run with those legs, fought with those arms. The feel of her flesh lingers in my soul.

Magic. From the goddess. What purpose must she have in store?

As I guide my charges through the gate, sentinels stop us.

"From your sword and shield," one says to me, "you're a soldier."

I nod. "Calizto. Telpochtlahtoh of Metztonalco, in Zoquiyapan. I was escorting these refugees to safety when the barrage began."

"Except for the digging crews, we're putting the women and children in the main calmecac. Priests are letting people drink from the sacred fountain. Take them there. And get some rest. We'll need your blades in the morning when that fucker comes back."

Campfires dot the ceremonial center. Warriors sit or sleep in that flickering light, conserving their energy.

We walk between the Great Pyramid and the Serpent Wall until we come to the entrance to the calmecac, small conches encrusted into its lintel. Inside, we look for a space among all the refugees softly weeping or sleeping on the bare floor.

"Calizto!" a voice cries. Ayotochtli is signaling us over. "You found them. Good. I was worried they might've been killed."

Ofirin finds a place to curl up, exhausted. I sit beside Ayotochtli, who recounts his escape from the prime minister's palace as it fell to pieces.

"Do you remember," Ayotochtli asks, "the time we stole smoked peccary in the market? Oh, it tasted so good."

I smile at the memory. "My father was not pleased."

"He was furious!" Ayotochtli chortles. "Held our heads over a pot of steaming chili peppers until our eyes were bloodred and snot ran from our noses. But it was worth it."

I shake my head. "You were a fool. So was I. The whole escapade was Ce Mazatl's idea, but he escaped punishment entirely."

Ayotochtli grows somber. "I miss him."

"As do I. All those things we did as boys, the games, the failed attempts at fishing . . ."

"The courting of girls who ignored us," Ayotochtli adds with a wistful sigh. "You realize we'll never see our old neighborhood again?"

Saddened, I stretch out on the floor. "Most of it is gone, anyway. Try to rest. Dream of the good times. Tomorrow we may have to fight."

"It's all that's left," he says as he curls against the wall. "Fight. Survive. Dream."

The Lord of the House of Dawn streaks the sky with his bright brush. After breakfast, we escort our charges past the smaller temple of Mixcoatl.

As we approach the Northern Gate, however, a cry goes up at the other extreme of the ceremonial center. Then comes a harquebus fusillade, followed by cannon fire.

"Go!" Ayotochtli shouts to our group. "Take the causeway north!"

All but Ofirin scatter. Though frightened, he looks at me and announces, enunciating each Nahuatl word, "I stay with you."

I grunt in agreement. There is an armory beside the gate, empty except for some spears with broken hafts. I choose the longest and place it in his hands.

"Stab," I say, making a gesture.

"With the pointy end," Ayotochtli clarifies. "I never thought I'd make a stand alongside a devout asshole and his immigrant scribal assistant, but then I never thought it possible someone might invade Tenochtitlan, either."

Drawing my father's sword from its scabbard, I give a grim laugh. "These are impossible times."

The barrage of fire has been a stratagem, meant to keep Mexica warriors from the Southern Gate. During the night, women widened the gap between the causeway and the Sacred Precinct, chipping away at the earth so it spilled into the broad moat that surrounds us.

But hundreds of Tlaxcaltecah have now swum across that canal.

They stand dripping at the shattered gate, looking in on the Eagle and Jaguar Knights who are supported by commoner soldiers like Ayotochtli and me.

Then as one, the invaders let loose a battle cry and come rushing.

In the midst of the melee, Sitlali recovers enough to speak from where she sits in her time.

"What's going on?"

The enemy has attacked again.

She reaches up, touches my leg. The sensation is quite distracting.

"Wait. Ofirin is here, but what about the others?"

We sent them north.

"Why didn't you go with them?" she demands.

Ayotochtli and I are required to remain and fight. We were trained to do so.

"That's stupid. What is that . . . a lance in Ofirin's hands? Can he even fight? You said you were going to protect him. You said you'd stay safe."

I pull my leg away. *Just don't look, Sitlali. I won't rush into the fray, but I'll do what I can to stop the enemy from passing through this gate until the innocents who are midway up the northern causeway can reach safety.*

She falls silent.

All that exists for a time is the din of ever-closer battle.

Finally, a Tlaxcaltecah berserker bursts through the front lines, zigzagging his way toward the Northern Gate. I grip my sword and rush him. His shield comes up, his face a rictus of bloodlust above it.

With a twist of my body, I smash the maccuahuitl into his shield, shattering it. The warrior's right hand holds a club, which he swings. But my blow has sent him off-balance, so the jagged obsidian jutting from its knobby end simply nicks my chest.

As I spin on the ball of my right foot to attack again, Ayotochtli comes running.

Something hisses through the air. An iron bolt from a Spanish crossbow slams into Ayotochtli's forehead.

My last friend drops dead before me.

My soul becomes a flame of anguish. With a brutal chop, I sever the Tlaxcaltecatl's head.

I scream, ready to hurl myself into battle, to avenge all the deaths that weigh on my heart like debts.

A hand touches my back. I whirl around, ready to kill and kill and kill.

Ofirin stands there, eyes full of tears.

"Your friend," he whispers in Spanish. "We can't leave him lying there. He needs us."

The words break me. Weeping, I help drag Ayotochtli's lifeless body toward the temple of Tocih, sheltering it behind a large conch statue.

I kneel beside my brother of the heart, sobbing like a child.

"Oh my God!" Sitlali exclaims as she takes my hand. "Ayotochtli!"

"I never got to say goodbye. Never got to say how much I loved him."

Ofirin rubs tears from his eyes. "He knew, Calizto."

Sitlali leans toward me. "You can speak to him. I can help you—if his spirit still lingers . . ."

She puts her hand gently on my back, slides it down to the conch in its netted bag.

And with a disorienting thrust, her soul enters my body. She lifts my head.

Emerging from Ayotochtli's body is a glowing knot—three souls woven into one.

With my own lips, Sitlali speaks. "Tell him what you need to say, Calizto."

Ignoring the shock on Ofirin's face, I nod and take control. "Ayotochtli. Brother. Friend. I loved you. I will miss you. Goodbye for now. Give my regards to Ce Mazatl and the rest of my fallen family."

Ayotochtli's soul transforms, becomes a swarm of glowing butterflies that spiral around me gently before flittering off toward the east.

"He heard you," Sitlali says aloud.

Stop. Ofirin is staring at me like I have gone mad.

I'm sorry, she says in my mind. *I just wanted to show you that he was not lost to you. That even in death, our loved ones are with us.*

"A god," Ofirin whispers, "just possessed you, didn't it?"

I glare at him. "My friend's dead. I've no patience for your foolishness."

"Something took you over, Calizto. God, devil, spirit. Something. You were completely transformed. Your voice sounded different. The words were even strange."

I didn't mean to scare him. Sitlali lets go of the conch. I feel her dissipate from me as she disengages.

"I suppose it was my ancestors," I lie, "speaking through me."

After a few hours, the enemy retreat.

Throughout the ceremonial center, men set about doing the same as Ofirin and me.

We bind our beloved comrade up. Then we set his empty flesh alight.

Loosening my hair so it hangs in my face, I chant a few lines from an old song of sorrow my father intoned when my only brother fell, nearly a decade ago.

Thou pure in heart, now dead in war,
art summoned from the earth.
Thou leavest this place of woe
for the land of thy merit, thy worth—
there where the drums forever beat,
there where friends at last shall meet,
like burnished jade to eternal glow,
like flowers that blossom amid the snow,
a song to gladden hearts here below.

Twilight begins to purple the heavens by the time he burns down to ash. I watch the wind scatter what remains.

Ofirin stands nearby, face wet with tears.

Sitlali sits beneath a mesquite, deep in her thicket, wanting to grieve with me.

"I've been inside your heart," she whispers. "I've felt what you feel. Please, let me carry some of that burden for you."

As night falls, I head back to the calmecac and curl against the wall where Ayotochtli last slept.

Sitlali reaches across that impossible gap, touching the moon conch I have cradled in my arms. Soft as caresses, we spend the evening in each other's minds, learning each other's pasts, sharing our loss and pain.

At last, I feel Sitlali slip into sleep.

I turn my head.

There she lies, nestled among the reeds.

Loving and lovely.

Worthy of love.

CHAPTER TWENTY-ONE

Sitlali

June 20, 2019

I awaken with a start.

"Stay . . . ," a woman's aggrieved voice wails, and I lie very still. Listening.

"Staaaay!" She wails again, and I think of Llorona, the ghost of Malitzin doing her eternal penance, crying out for the children she drowned in her madness. Only I know it's not her because I recognize that pained voice, that sad wail.

"Mami?" Through a crevice in my hiding place, I see that I am alone on the riverbank on the other side. Relieved, I push the blanket of dead carrizo canes aside.

I rub the sleep out of my eyes and look closely at my watch. It's four o'clock in the morning. Time to move on. I pull my things together. Looking around, I take a swig of water and crouch low as I examine my compass. The needle points the way, and I start to walk northwest, moving stealthily, if not quietly, away from the cane and through the thicket.

After a while, I can see rows and rows of tiny lights out on the horizon, and I know I am nearing Eagle Pass, Texas. I come upon a barbed wire fence, press on the middle wire, and push up the others as I cross. The edge of my shirt catches on a barb, and I tug it loose. It tears and gives way to freedom.

Emboldened, I break into a run but stop when I hear the motor of a car approaching. I spot it in the distance, a border patrol vehicle, driving slowly along a narrow dirt road. My heart beating wildly in my chest, I dive down, lie flat against the ground, and hide within a cluster of huisachillos.

The border patrol van drives by. I watch it turn into another dirt road and stop. It sits there for a while, and I wait. And wait. And wait. The humidity starts to get to me. I am sweating profusely. I know I should hydrate, but I am afraid of moving even one single muscle for fear of being caught. What if when I move, he is looking in this direction through his binoculars? What if the rustle of a single branch, a single leaf, shows him exactly where I am?

My mouth is completely dry, my face feels like it's on fire, and I am about to pass out, when I see the wavering figure of my abuela Lucía reappear. She is standing on the other side of the road behind a cluster of thick mohintli, its orange blossoms dark and muted in the moonlight. Her translucent, silvery hand waves for me to follow her. I shake my head no, but she smiles and keeps urging me to go to her.

Stay!

The echo of my mother's voice in my dream haunts me, and I don't know what to do. She sounds so far away, so lost to me. I wish I knew what she wants. The border patrol car starts to move again. It makes a U-turn on the road and starts heading my way. My grandmother's eyes grow wide. Then she lifts her arms high up in the air and calls forth a great gust of wind that creates a blinding sandstorm.

My grandmother's silver hair swirls around her head. Her white dress flaps in the wind as the sandstorm gets stronger and stronger. The patrol car speeds by us quickly, its taillights barely visible in the whirl and swirl of the dirt storm. When he has passed through, my grandmother waves me forward and I run across the road through the sandstorm. The giant gust of wind conceals me as I make the run of my life.

When I stop and crouch behind the brush, the dusty whirlwind begins to lose power. It dissipates in seconds, taking my grandmother's spirit with it. I jump up and start running again. I don't stop until I am in the city.

Hearing dogs in the distance, I duck into an alley. With my compass in my hand, I make my way north, from one alley to another until I spot a gas station with its lights on. My grandmother reappears and points to it. When I nod, she touches her lips, throws me a kiss, and disappears—vanishes into the newly formed sandstorm. Because I don't want to call attention to myself, I hide behind a stack of empty pallets. Not far away from me, in his own time, Calizto is hiding too.

"Where are you?" I ask.

Your voice is faint, he replies. *Speak into my mind.*

Are you okay? You're not hurt, are you? I ask. My heart thrums in my chest at the thought of it.

Yes. Cortés pushed into the ceremonial center again. We attempted to retreat toward Tlatelolco, but we were cut off.

I understand, I say. *You had to run.*

To fight was impossible, Little Star, he admits. *Now the Spanish are pulling their cannons from block to block with their horses, flattening houses as they go. They are approaching. We have to move. Be safe, Sitlali.*

You too, Calizto . . .

My love, I add in the hidden recesses of my heart so he won't hear.

The sun has come up over the horizon, so I sneak out of my hiding place and walk down the street. Businesses are opening, and I trot quickly to the gas station. It's a small establishment, but I find a way to enter it inconspicuously, falling into step behind a group of chatty Mexican American girls.

I go into the restroom, strip down, and use the wipes in my bag to wash up inside the privacy of a stall. When I am done, I pull out the yellow sundress and white sandals Doña Sofía gave me, happy to see that they stayed dry.

As I slip the dress on, I am overcome with anxiety and something else—lament. So much has happened to me. It feels like a lifetime since I first put this beautiful dress on. At the sink, I comb my hair into a ponytail and apply makeup to my face, until I look like myself again. When I am satisfied, I leave the restroom.

As I wander the store, trying to figure out what to buy so that I can blend in, I realize everyone in the store is speaking Spanish. Here and there, I hear a few words I do not understand, because they throw in a bit of English, but for the most part I catch the gist of their conversations.

I buy a bottle of Diet Coke and drink it as I walk down Eidson Road. Waiting to cross at a corner, I see an old couple leaving their car, and I step out of their way when they go into the restaurant.

Looking up at the street sign, I realize I have reached El Indio Highway. *Which way did my madrina say to turn?*

Left. She said to turn left. I walk along El Indio Highway for a few minutes, and then, I'm there. I smell it before I see it, Rodee's, an orange building with a dancing chicken on the signage. People, smiling, laughing, talking excitedly, step out of it, weighed down with loaded bags of food.

I step up to the counter and place my order, exactly as my madrina instructed. The young man at the counter frowns.

"Necks?" The young man asks in Spanish. "We don't sell necks." He points at the cardboard menu beside me.

"But that's what I want. That's what I need," I insist.

Startled, the young man blinks at me. "Do you mean the three-piece chicken?" he asks.

Frustrated, I shake my head and repeat the order, emphasizing that he can keep the biscuit, with attitude.

The boy's confusion turns to panic, and he says, "Forgive me. It's only my third day here. Let me get the manager for you." He turns around, steps away from the counter, and yells, "Sandra! I need help. I am not sure . . ."

A woman in her forties with her dark hair tied back in a chignon and a headset close to her wide lips winds her way around the heated chicken stand and says, "What's up?"

Sounding a little flustered, the boy repeats my order to her. Sandra turns to look at me. Her eyes take in my hair and dress. They linger on my duffel bag, and then she breaks into laughter, a hearty, luscious sound that bounces off the restaurant ceiling and walls, like joyful thunder.

"Osvaldo!" she says, looking back at the boy. "This is my niece. She's trying to play a trick on me! Aren't you, m'ija?"

I laugh, a genuine, little chuckle that turns into a giggle when I look at the relieved boy.

"Oh, oh," the boy says. "I'm sorry. I didn't know."

Sandra unties her apron, pulls it over her head, and shoves it under the counter. "I'm going to take a lunch break. Put in a three-piece order for us and throw in some gizzards. She can't leave here without tasting our gizzards." Then she turns me around and guides me to an empty table in the far corner of the restaurant, where we are out of earshot.

Sandra leans over the table and smiles. "Hola, Sitlali. I am one of the Gallinitas, so you can relax. You're in the coop now."

She tells me my madrina is excited about my upcoming visit, and, after sending a series of texts, she says my madrina is happy I made it there safely. When our order is called, Sandra jumps up to get it.

She talks between bites, giving me bits of information about the restaurant, her relationship to my madrina Tomasa. Apparently, they've known each other for over thirty years. Sandra does all the talking, while I mostly melt over the lemon-peppery goodness of Rodee's gizzards. I've never tasted anything so divine.

"Do you have a phone?" she asks, slurping on the drink that came with her meal between bites of fried chicken.

I shake my head, and she frowns.

"That's okay. We'll see what we can do to help you." She sends another text. Finally, Sandra smiles and says, "You're in luck. Mariela is leaving work right now, so she can give you a ride to the station."

"The station?" I ask, confused, because she knows I don't have any papers.

Sandra pats my hand. "You'll be fine. Mariela will take good care of you, I promise."

The "station" ends up being a small, dark warehouse that we access by driving past a gas station and taking a rural dirt road to a part of town with no street names. We pull into the shadowy warehouse, get out, and walk to a small office at the end of a long corridor. Mariela speaks for me, introducing me as Doña Tomasita's goddaughter to Ramona, a white-haired woman with winged eyeliner, dark red lipstick, and a wide collection of loud bangle bracelets tinkling on her right wrist.

"Is it all right to leave her, then?" Mariela asks.

Ramona nods, and her hoop earrings glint in the dark office. "Sure."

"She needs a phone and a ride to San Antonio," Mariela explains.

"One fifty for the phone," Ramona says. "Five hundred for the ride. You have that much?"

I reach into my bag and pull out a wad of cash I know is close to that amount. Ramona takes the money and nods. "Close enough," she says, reaching under the counter to pull out a box. "Take your pick. They all work."

I choose a small, white phone. Mariela helps me turn it on. She calls herself. When it's clear the phone works, she ends the call and hands the phone back to me.

"That's my number," she says. "In case you need it. But I doubt it. Ramona will make sure you get there."

Mariela hugs me and prays over me before she leaves. Then I follow Ramona down the hall. We go through several doors, down a winding flight of stairs, and along a series of narrow hallways, until we arrive at a windowless room, where nine other people sit in folding chairs, waiting.

I look at the faces of men, women, and children. They smile as I sit and wait with them.

"Do you need to use the restroom?" Ramona asks. "Your ride won't get here until after midnight."

I shake my head and she leaves. I pull the phone out and try to call my madrina, but the call doesn't go through.

A woman shakes her head. "There's no reception in here."

Calizto, I call to him in my mind as I hug the duffel bag to my chest, pressing my fingers between the grooves of the moon conch through the thick canvas. *Are you safe yet?*

Yes. Apologies for not speaking sooner, but I could see you were occupied. Ofirin and I reached the borough's ritual plaza. Many others have converged here as well. In fact, I have encountered two people I know: the xochihuah named Quechol and the middle-aged woman who worked with me, moving rubble.

Eyolin, right? It's one of the many names I learned in his mind last night, as we lay merged as one for hours, sharing our stories.

Yes. She is trying to get a little sustenance into the dozens of people trapped in this temple. Close to no food remains. But between us we have trapped a few lizards and gathered maize straw, salt grass.

My eyes find him, crouched down in the corner of the room. He's exhausted. His handsome face looks haggard, and I know he needs to drink fresh water. He needs to eat and rest.

As if sensing my apprehension, he adds, *The barrage has stopped. I suspect the Spanish are retreating. Ofirin says Cortés isn't stupid. He won't be trapped here again.*

My mind races, and my heart twists itself into a knot in my chest because I know different. This isn't good. I don't want to tell him outright what happens if he doesn't escape, but I have to warn him. I can't let him die like this.

I love him.

Ofirin is right, I say. *Cortés is the most dangerous man in Mexico right now.*

Indeed. And he leads a massive army, every nation with a grudge against the Mexica. Our enemies are tireless locusts, swarming the city.

I close my eyes and try to control the tears that threaten to roll down my face.

You are right about them, Calizto. They will not stop until everything and everyone is destroyed. You must find a way to escape. Now. Before they find you.

CHAPTER TWENTY-TWO

Calizto

Day 13-Grass of the Year 3-House (June 21, 1521)

It is a restless night for both Sitlali and me, curled up on dusty floors, surrounded by strangers. Eventually I arise to keep watch, though more than anything, I watch Sitlali's face, her features slack but beautiful.

The moon's descent tells me that half the time between midnight and dawn has elapsed. Given the enemy's strategy of marching into the city before the break of day, I know we must get moving soon.

I stir Ofirin first, then Eyolin and Quechol. It is a brutal reality that I can only keep a handful of people alive. The rest can accompany us, but I'll focus on my—dare I say it?—friends.

"I suppose we've no choice," Quechol groans, their hair comically askew, rich clothes covered in dust, "but to set forth without having broken our fast."

Eyolin laughs wryly. "Oh, Honored One—it may be days before this fast ends. May as well attach a paper collar to your neck."

As they gather their things, Ofirin mutters, "Paper collar?"

"A joke," I explain. "We wear them when fasting."

He nods as the other two join us, a half dozen strangers in their wake.

"Come," I say. "Let's reach Tlatelolco before dawn."

We leave the temple, cross the plaza, and find the bridge over the canal to our north still intact.

On the far bank, Eyolin gives a cry of joy. "Look! A gift from Huitzilopochtli!"

She rushes to the courtyard of an abandoned home. A prickly pear cactus awaits, its paddles heavy with fruit.

"Okay," I rasp. "Grab as many pears as you can, quickly."

Eyolin shakes her head. "No. We need to harvest the paddles, too. There's a week's worth of food here for each."

"Aunt," I say respectfully, "there will be food in Tlatelolco."

"You don't know that. People all over this isle are starving. They've gotten so hungry they're eating the poisonous fruit and bark of the coral tree. They're roasting leather, breaking mud bricks open to get at the straw."

Quechol puts their hand on my shoulder. "We'll be as quick as we can, but we cannot shun this opportunity."

With a groan, I acquiesce. "No matter how badly you're pricked, work fast. The enemy will return soon."

The group falls to work. I pull Ofirin after me. We set a watch outside the courtyard.

"Dawn's in an hour," he says.

"Keep your eyes south and west. I'll scan the north and east."

The setting moon, brilliant stars, and slight eastern glow illuminate the closer and farther dikes. Both have been breached, spilling brackish water into our canals so that thirsty children make themselves sick with brine.

Terror. That is what the Spaniards have brought. I've never heard of a Nahua nation razing a city, starving its widows, poisoning its children.

Armies are defeated; their cities become tributary territories. Sometimes an enemy refuses to surrender, and our army sacks their city, taking goods and prisoners, enslaving women and children.

But wholesale slaughter?

Never.

Calizto.

Sitlali is getting up.

The truck's here. We're going to get inside. I don't know how long the journey to San Antonio is, but that's where I'll be for a while.

Be safe, Little Star. We have left the temple, but we found a prickly pear cactus.

Oh! Nopales and tunas.

But we put ourselves in danger by lingering here.

You need energy to run, she says sternly. *Or to fight to defend your charges.*

Of course you're right. Until later, then. May the goddess clear your path of enemies.

She shudders at my words. *And may she give us strength to face whatever trials must come, Calizto.*

Sometime later, as the eastern sky grows brighter, cannon fire sounds in the distance.

"Enough," I call, entering the courtyard. "Whatever you've harvested will have to do."

We cross over one last canal. I can see the northern causeway, leading off to the hill of Tepeyacac, where a shrine to Tonantzin Teteoh Innan stands.

And where just decades from now, Sitlali has told me, the goddess will reappear as the Virgin of Guadalupe.

I squint at the causeway. There's no foot traffic this early. No canoes along its length.

The signs could not be clearer. I have to get Ofirin off this island *now*. The heavens have prepared the way.

I pull Eyolin aside.

"Grandmother," I begin.

"Oh, stop with the formalities. You're leaving us, aren't you?"

Swallowing heavily, I duck my head.

Eyolin glances at Ofirin. "I know who he is. Saw him come into the city with them last year. You've shaved him and changed his clothes, but I don't forget a face."

I choke back the impulse to lie. "He was wounded during their flight. My father rescued him, nursed him back to health. When the plague fell, that man took care of us. It was my father's dying wish that I protect him. The Caxtiltecah enslaved him. Their cruelty isn't his fault."

"If you plan to leave the city with him," she advises, "go past Tepeyacac, up the lakeshore, to Ehcatepec. They're Mexica, like us. But lose him before you reach that city. You've kept your promise. Now live."

We reach the causeway. The sun has risen above the volcanoes. I can see plumes of smoke to the south and east: Cortés has reached the Sacred Precinct and is pushing beyond it.

"Past these canals," I announce, "is the Apahuazcan district of Tlatelolco. Head straight along the street, and you'll come to the great market where refugees are housed. I must take my companion north, so here we part ways. May the gods permit us to survive. If not, may we meet again in the Unknowable Realm."

Quechol wipes a tear away and embraces me. "Let's do meet again, dear Calizto. You should have been born a noble. You've more heart, wisdom, and elegance than many princes."

Eyolin hugs me as well. "Let's meet again indeed, my boy. But here on the slippery earth. Come find me when this is all over. Bring a wife and children with you. My boys are all dead. You have no grandparents. I will stand in their place, if you allow it."

I almost break as she lets me go. But I grit my teeth and bow.

"I acknowledge myself as part of Your Grace's family," I intone with all the formality I can muster. "Depart now peacefully, guided by the Lord of the Near and the Nigh."

Face streaked by tears, Eyolin leads the others away.

Ofirin clears his throat. "What's the plan?"

I jerk my head at the causeway. "Run."

The causeway is about two hundred rods long. It takes a pilgrim or merchant nearly one Spanish hour to cross. Running, we should halve that time.

But we will be exposed the entire journey.

Ofirin is slower than I hoped. I lope along behind him, scanning the water to our left and right. If our fortune can hold out a bit longer—

A spear thuds into the causeway in front of Ofirin, as if hurled by an atlatl.

He stops, stumbles, falls.

I turn to see three canoes pulling up to the causeway.

Men are already spilling from one, coming my way.

The sun is in my eyes. I can't tell if they're Mexica or Tlaxcaltecah.

"Halt in the name of Emperor Cuauhtemoc!" one shouts. "This causeway is closed except to Jaguar and Eagle Knights, scum. It's clear you're neither."

The man approaches, brandishing his club.

"I'm Calizto, telpochtlahtoh of Metztonalco in Zoquiyapan."

"And this bastard you're with? On your feet!"

Ofirin stands. The guard sucks air in, surprised.

"I know you. You were in the palace with the Caxtiltecah. One of their slaves."

He turns to his men.

“Take them. Alive, preferably.”

My hand goes over my shoulder, reaching for the pommel of my father’s blade.

Then the guard gives a crooked smile, and, before I can do anything, he swings his club at my head.

CHAPTER TWENTY-THREE

Sitlali

June 22, 2019

I sit in the back of the dark trailer crammed behind a tall, wooden crate with twelve other undocumented immigrants. Silent, we press our backs against the walls, close our eyes, and give in to the shake and bounce of our bodies as the truck rolls down the highway.

When the trailer slows down and comes to a complete stop, nobody moves a muscle. Because we can feel the truck's engine idling, vibrating against our backs and thighs, we know we are at the checkpoint on the outskirts of Eagle Pass. So, we sit quiet as mice.

A mother presses her hands over her children's mouths. Husbands and boyfriends wrap their arms around their wives and girlfriends. I sit by myself. No one is here for me. Five hundred years away, Calizto is silent. Our connection is severed, and I worry that he might have been . . . No, I refuse to believe it. Calizto is alive.

He has to be.

When we finally move again, we are relieved. But that joyful moment lasts only a few miles. Soon, we are all somber again. I rest my head and shoulder against the corner of the crate and try to ignore the headache that presses down on my temples and forehead. I am exhausted. Every single muscle in my body begs for water, and air, because the trailer has been so well insulated there is no hint of fresh air coming in here. Looking around at the heavy tape, I can tell our transporters wanted to make sure the dogs at the checkpoint couldn't smell us.

Hours go by.

One. Two. Two and a half.

The heat in the back of the trailer has become unbearable. My body has no more liquid to exude. I feel its heat trapped inside my parched skin, and I know I need to get out of here. The two children in the group start crying, and their mother wipes their tears and mucus away with a wrinkled rag.

After almost three hours, we finally slow down and make a series of turns, left, right, left, left, right, and left. When we come to a complete stop again, we are all silent. Huddled and hunched over, we look at one another across the small compartment at the back of the trailer with tired, unblinking eyes.

A loud bang startles us.

"Did he leave?" the mother asks.

"I need to go to the bathroom," a young woman tells her boyfriend.

"Is he coming back for us?" the mother asks her husband. "We can't stay here all night."

"Patience, woman," her husband advises.

But after almost an hour of complete and utter silence, it becomes clear to all of us that we have been abandoned in the back of this hot, miserable, metal box.

"I've heard about this on the news," the young woman says. "They just take your money and leave you to die."

"Shut up," the father of the two boys says. "You're scaring the children."

"Don't tell me what to do. I'm not your wife!" the young woman says.

"You're too ugly to be my wife," the man says.

"Stop," his wife tells him. "You're making it worse."

"*I'm* making it worse?" the man asks his wife.

"If my children can be quiet, then we can all be quiet," the mother says. She looks down at her two boys. They are lying on their sides, resting their heads on her lap, while she runs her fingers through their hair.

I close my eyes and pray.

Suddenly, my thoughts are interrupted by a strange sound. One of the boys is standing with his back to us. In the dimness, I can see urine spreading, a quiet, glistening shadow that meanders toward me. I jump up and quickly move away.

"Son of a bitch!" the young man yells when he sees the urine inching toward his leg.

He clambers up, and then everyone is on their feet, moving around, piling up against one another at the other side of the trailer.

The boy starts to cry, and his mother wraps her arms around him. "It's okay," she whispers into his ear while she strokes his hair. "You didn't do anything wrong."

"The hell he didn't!" the young man swears under his breath.

The boy's father straightens up. "Don't curse at my son!"

"It's not his fault," I say, standing between the two men. "It's natural. I am surprised he's the only one doing it."

"I'm sorry," the young man says, and he puts his arm over his girlfriend's shoulder.

The mother pulls a shirt out of her bag. As she sops up the urine in the dark, I take a plastic baggie out of my sack and tap her shoulder with it.

She thanks me. I press my back against the wall again and close my eyes.

"Please, God," the young woman prays out loud. "We can't die like this."

I open my eyes, and my heart skips a beat because I see Calizto's dark form materializing in the shadows. He sits on the floor, his legs stretched out before him and his back pressed against the wall, looking completely defeated.

Oh, thank God! I think, and he turns to look at me.

Little Star. His voice is weak, and my stomach sinks.

What's happened? I ask, trying to focus on his dark form.

We are captive, he says. *Imprisoned in a cell meant for prisoners of war. Perhaps our luck has been stolen from us, along with everything else.*

No! You can't give up! I say, forcing myself not to cry. *You have to fight!*

You don't understand, Sitlali, he says. *These cells are designed for special battle captives—those deemed worthy of sacrifice.*

Sacrifice?! I shake my head, refusing to accept what he's telling me. *No. No.*

A resounding noise breaks through my grief, confusing me.

The people in the trailer cringe and huddle. I listen as I keep my sight focused on Calizto's eyes. The door unlocks, and sunlight bathes the interior of the trailer, bringing with it a wave of cool, fresh air so that the light blinds our eyes at the same time the air wounds our exhausted lungs. I close my eyes to the brutality of it, and when I open them, Calizto has disappeared.

"No!" I yell, looking frantically around the trailer. But he is gone. And I am alone in this new world, where freedom assaults the senses and the thought of moving forward without the boy I love paralyzes me.

Two men and a woman stand on the ground, watching us. The woman is talking into the small black phone. She speaks in English, and when she nods, the two men pull down the ramp and wave for us to come down. I let the family go first. The older men step to the side, so I walk down the ramp, still stunned by Calizto's revelation. One of the men holds his nose and shakes his head.

"Jesus Christ," he says. "Who fucking pissed themselves?"

Nobody says anything. But the boy presses his face against his mother's side, and the man steps away from us. I pull out my phone and turn it on. All around me, the others do the same. The woman in charge takes a good look at us.

"Good morning," she says. "You're in San Antonio. Rudy, Pedro, and I are going to transport you to a safe house until your people can come for you. But we can't take everyone at once. So, if you're traveling together, we need to know that right now."

It takes a while for my call to go through, but I wait. When my madrina finally answers, I am relieved.

"Hello," she says. Her voice sounds hesitant, like she is afraid of who might be calling her at six in the morning.

"It's me," I whisper into the phone, holding it to my ear with both hands.

"Sitlali. Oh, thank goodness," my madrina says. "I've been so worried. Where are you?"

"In San Antonio."

"I'll come get you," she says. "What's the address there?"

The woman is looking at me, giving me a sideways glance as she listens to the family of four. I look away and notice the young couple is leaving, going to the other side of the warehouse with one of the men.

"I don't know," I whisper. "There are people here, to pick us up. But I'm not sure . . ."

My madrina picks up on my hesitation and says, "Let me talk to them."

I make eye contact with the woman in charge and point the phone at her.

"Hello?" she says and listens. "Gallinita Mora? Yes. This is Gallinita Rosa."

I hear something that sounds like excitement in her voice, and then she laughs, a quiet, reserved laugh that I am not sure how to interpret. "Yes. We are at the Westside Coop. You know where that is?" she asks. But then she listens and frowns. "Are you sure?" she asks. "Okay, but I'm not responsible. You understand?"

"Listen to me," my madrina says when she hands me back the phone. "I want you to get out of there right away. Go around the building if you have to, until you can see the highway. There's a taquería to the left and a big movie theater to the right. Go inside the taquería and order some breakfast tacos. You have money?"

"Yes," I say.

"Sit down and eat, and play a game on your phone," she says. "I'll be there in twenty minutes. Don't talk to anyone. Don't even look up if someone walks by. Eat your tacos. Stay on your phone. Mind your own business. You understand?"

"Yes."

"Good. Good." My madrina sounds a bit frazzled. "And if something should happen . . ." She hesitates. "If ICE should pick you up, don't tell them how you got there. Just wait until I make contact."

I am eating my tacos when a woman walks up to me. She whispers my name, I look up, and her face lights up. I haven't seen her in a million years, but I recognize my madrina Tomasa instantly. I jump up and throw myself into her arms.

"You are the living image of your mother!" She holds my face in her hands and kisses my cheeks. "Come on. Let's go home."

Sitting in her little Toyota, I tell my madrina Tomasa about the snake and the coyote and the thugs who stalked me in Piedras Negras. Madrina Tomasa is horrified, but she tells me I will be safe in her little house in the country.

But when we get there, Von Ormy is nothing like what I expected. There are mesquites and huisaches everywhere. My madrina's house is tiny. There are two goats and eight chickens in her backyard. And she has a fat yellow cat named Momo who likes to sit by the window and watch the sparrows nesting under her roofline.

"I haven't been to the grocery store," she says, finishing the last of the pineapple soda she is sharing with me. "But we can make a list of things you like, and I'll pick them up after work tomorrow."

When we are done catching up, my madrina shows me my bedroom. It is a small room, with a nicely made double bed, two nightstands, and a little table and chair in front of a tall window that looks out into the backyard. There is a small television in the room, and an old computer, but I don't turn either of them on.

Because my body is still aching from the arduous journey, bouncing around in the back of that trailer, I take a long, luxurious bath. Then I put on an old dress and lie down for a nap. When I open my eyes, the room is dark. I've been asleep for almost eight hours.

Calizto walks out of the shadows and nears my bed.

I could not bring myself to wake you, he says, looking down at me tenderly. *You looked like you needed your rest.*

Are you still imprisoned?

Yes.

Is there no way of getting you out? I ask. *Do you have public defenders, someone to plead your case to those in authority?*

Calizto nods. *We had a justice system, but it's in shambles now. I am afraid all might be lost.*

What? How?

Prime Minister Tlacotzin visited us this afternoon. Because he spent a lot of time among the Spanish, he recognized Ofirin.

So, what did he want? I ask, confused.

To reprimand me for harboring the enemy. I tried to justify my situation, but he said I can explain myself before the emperor when I am tried for treason. And if I am found guilty . . .

It won't happen! Talk to the emperor . . . tell him your story!

All through the night, I sit up with Calizto. He is convinced that he'll be executed, so I try to comfort him. Give him hope.

I know that Tonantzin and Coyolxauhqui will take care of us, I whisper, wishing the moon was full and I could put my arms around him, caress his cheek, kiss his soft lips. *They are up there right now, working their powerful magic together.*

Calizto's eye glisten in the bright light of the waning moon.

I'm sure they are, he says, and he leans forward so that our foreheads would be pressed together if we were still able to touch. *They have their ways, don't they, these divine women?*

They do.

We stay like that forever, it seems. Two souls touched by light, fused in love. Then, as Calizto starts to doze off, I see a hand reach out and touch the conch in his arms.

Suddenly, he is there. With us. Ofirin.

What are you doing? I ask, looking at his hand on the conch.

Startled, Ofirin jerks and falls back. His dark eyes stare at me for a moment, and then his face lights up and he says, "It's you, isn't it? His goddess. His Little Star."

CHAPTER TWENTY-FOUR

Calizto

Day 2-Jaguar of the Year 3-House (June 23, 1521)

The sound of Spanish jolts me awake. Ofirin has one hand on the conch I'm cradling. He's staring at the almost ghostly form of Sitlali that floats above the ground beyond the thick bamboo bars of our cell.

What has he done?

He touched the conch, and now he can see me.

"Ofirin, remove your hand," I warn.

"No," he says, not taking his eyes from Sitlali. "She spoke Spanish, Calizto. What's going on? What is she, a witch? Did she use a spell to make me forget about the conch?"

No! Sitlali laughs. *Of course not.*

Sitlali, I caution her. *He'll likely not believe the truth.*

"You realize I can hear your thoughts, don't you?" Ofirin says. "What's this magic you call forth with the conch?"

You're right, Ofirin. Calizto's moon conch connects us across great distances and . . . time as well.

Part of me wants to stop Sitlali, but I realize it's too late.

We're probably going to be executed when the sun rises. Let Ofirin hear about the future, the mingling of Spanish and Indigenous and African into Mexicans, their wheeled and winged vehicles, their devices for speaking and seeing across thousands of leagues.

Who will he tell but other wandering souls in the afterlife?

Before she finishes the unlikely tale, I drift into formless dreams.

Ofirin will not shut up about the conch when the sounds of footsteps awaken us.

"They confiscated everything else. Why did they leave the shell with you? It's like they didn't notice it. Or forgot about it right away."

Yawning, I glance at Sitlali, sprawled on a bed in her madrina's house.

"It must be how the goddess protects her trumpet," I reply, sitting up. "And I'm thankful. Distance from the moon conch weakens my connection with Sitlali."

Before Ofirin can bombard me with further questions, guards approach. One of them unlatches our cell, and they part to reveal another figure.

I take a sharp breath.

It's Tecuichpo.

Daughter of Moteuczoma.

Wife of Cuauhtemoc.

Our empress.

She's a couple of years younger than I, but there is nothing childish in her bearing. Drifting forward with regal steps, she enters our cell.

I kneel, pressing my head to the stone floor, so I see her feet first, enclosed in white cotton sandals. The embroidered hem of her yellow skirt almost reaches her ankles. But she wears a brightly patterned summer quechquemitl, whose front point leaves her sides and midriff bare.

Her neck is encircled by an ornate gold choker that matches her earrings. Her hair is bound up in the traditional horns of Mexica women with jade and ribbons.

Who's there now? Why are you kneeling?

Sitlali is sitting up in bed, and I'm glad for the first time that she cannot see my surroundings.

"Empress Tecuichpotzin," I say aloud, unable to focus my thoughts. "Your Imperial Majesty honors us."

Sitlali's holding something in front of her, frantically swiping away. She must be searching for information on Tecuichpo on her "phone."

Beside me, Ofirin stands, head bowed.

Inexplicably, the empress smiles. "I'm delighted to see you have survived, Palancixco."

I recognize this as a Nahuatl pronunciation of *Francisco*, the slave name Ofirin was given by the Spanish.

"Thank you, Princess," he struggles to reply.

I glare at him and mutter, "Hueyi Cihuatlahtoanié."

"Empress, I mean," he repeats.

She glances at me, gestures for me to rise. "I assume you can speak the Caxtiltecah's tongue. Where he struggles to understand or express himself, translate."

"As Your Imperial Majesty commands. Yet, I wonder how . . ."

Tecuichpo scoffs. "Palancixco was kind to me when I was in the custody of the Caxtiltecah in the Palace of Axayacatl. The two weeks after his arrival were the gentlest treatment my sisters and I received at the foreigners' hands. And when Cortés sought to drag us away with him during his flight from the city, Palancixco ensured my freedom. He gave his life to help me escape. So I believed, until my husband told me he'd been discovered on the northern causeway in the company of a common warrior."

She falls silent, waiting for me to relate my part.

"Ah. When that battle ended, my father found Ofirin in a canal, wounded. The goddess whispered mercy into his heart, and he brought the man home. We cared for him, and when the plague arrived, he cared for us."

Ofirin reaches out and puts his hand on my shoulder. "My friend. Calizto, his name."

With the barest of nods, she acknowledges me. "Calizto, friend of Palancixco, I have come to escort you before my husband. I'd thought to advocate for mercy on this man's behalf, but I see you share the same life debt."

I lower my eyes. "I'm glad for the delay. The emperor's justice is notoriously swift."

"Yesterday brought complications. Alvarado spent the previous night in the city with mounted warriors. So, my husband forced him to retreat, then drew his men into multiple ambushes. Several of the enemy fell, horse and all, into pits lined with spikes. A few were taken captive, and others were slain by our knights."

Ofirin clears his throat. "Any survived?"

"Yes," the empress replies. "Many swam across the lake."

Swim across the lake. That might work.

All I get is a feeling of agreement from Sitlali, who is focused on the empress.

"However," Tecuichpo continues, "today the enemy is licking their wounds. My husband has time to see you. As we walk, you may want to whisper a prayer to the goddess."

I lift the conch as she and her guards turn to guide us. "This conch helps me do precisely that."

"What conch?" asks the empress without looking back.

"Please ignore, Imperial Majesty," Ofirin stutters, shaking his head at me.

Everyone forgets it, Calizto. Sitlali sounds exasperated. *Even your empress.*

I was simply verifying, I say. *She's taking us before the emperor and his council. She may attempt to hasten my end. So I'm devising a plan.*

Sitlali jumps out of the bed. *That bitch. I swear, if something happens to you . . .*

You'll cross the centuries and take your revenge? Relax, Sitlali. Ofirin saved her a year ago, and she's in his debt. We may yet get out of this alive. But I'll need all my concentration for this meeting, so forgive me as I withdraw.

Sitlali fades as we cross Tlatelolco's religious and administrative precinct toward the emperor's palace. The empress leads us to the heart of the palace. The imperial audience chamber has become a war room. Messengers come and go. The heads of various divisions of the army look down on maps unfolded across tables.

Near the throne, Prime Minister Tlacotzin and Emperor Cuauhtemoc consult with four other men, the Imperial Council. Unlike the custom of years gone by, none of these leaders has donned the simple white once worn in deference to a sovereign.

Everyone is battle ready, in greaves and padded armor. One of the two generals on the council even wears a helmet.

Nothing drives home the desperation of our times like this breach of decorum.

"Cuauhtemoctzin," the empress calls, "I bring thy prisoners before thee."

Wincing at her lowered speech, another sign of our deteriorating sense of propriety, the emperor turns his hard eyes on me.

"Come closer."

Mindful of the guards at our backs, Ofirin and I approach.

"Who is this boy?" the chief magistrate asks. "Doesn't he know it's illegal for an untried adolescent to wear a temillotl?"

I almost reach up to touch my topknot, but instead answer boldly. "Sire, I have slain four Caxtiltecah and a half dozen Tlaxcaltecah. The head of my telpochcalli elevated me to telpochtlahtoh. As we are besieged, the ceremony could not be held, and I lack the cloak of my office, but I assure you I have earned this temillotl."

My response arouses the emperor's interest, and he sets down the map he's holding.

"Tlacotzin recognized the slave in your company, but I recognized this sword."

My father's sword is leaning against his throne. Cuauhtemoc hefts it, nodding at its weight.

"It belonged to Azayolli," he continues, "a valiant cuauhpilli."

Stunned, I lower my head. Of all the improper behavior on display in this room, the breaking of this taboo is the most painful to experience.

"Indeed, Your Imperial Majesty. He was my brother."

"My apologies. I had no idea, or I would not have used his name in your presence and caused you such pain." There's compassion on the emperor's face. He too has lost much. "Tell me yours."

"Calizto of Metztonalco."

Setting down the sword, the emperor nods. "Well met, Calizto. I knew your brother. The bravest, wisest commoner I have ever met. I was a shield-bearer, barely fifteen solar years old, on the campaign to put down the rebellion in Huaxyacac."

I swallow. I know the details of that military expedition by heart.

With a sigh, Cuauhtemoc adds, "I watched your brother die on the battlefield, but not before he felled a dozen Tzapotecah. He earned his noble title many times over. As the singers remind us, we are but lent to one another for a time. Then the Lord of the Near and Nigh takes up his sickle and harvests us all."

The emperor narrows his eyes.

"Wait. Are you not one of the god-bearers who brought the image of Huitzilopochtli?"

"Yes, Your Imperial Highness. My comrade was later slain by an iron bolt from a Caxtiltecah bow."

"Ah, you make punishing you so very difficult," Cuauhtemoc mutters.

"Then perhaps don't." Tecuichpo's interjection is unseemly. "I've already told thee of Palancixco's bravery. Calizto has valid reasons for harboring him."

In a few quick sentences, she retells my story.

The prime minister clears his throat. "Sire, they were *fleeing the island.* Dereliction of duty on the part of this telpochtlahtoh at the very least."

"I made a vow to my dying father," I cut in, heedless of the danger. "To take care of this man and see him safely out of the city. Would you have me break my sacred troth, sire? I fear the gods more than I fear the prime minister or the Imperial Council."

Sitlali gasps, runs down a hallway, closes a door, and turns back to me.

Don't make them mad!

Trust me.

Cuauhtemoc looks down at the sword, looks up at me.

"As much as I admired your brother and grasp the weight of responsibility you must feel, I must consider the consequences of freeing you, Calizto. How could I possibly justify such mercy at this critical moment?"

"La concha lunar." Ofirin deliberately uses Spanish. "Ponésela en las manos. Que vea a Sitlali."

It's a brilliant idea.

And dangerous.

Little Star. Are you ready?

Wait, for what?

To speak to the emperor. To save my life.

Wait, what?! And if I say the wrong thing? Accidentally piss him off?

I trust you, Sitlali. The goddess as well. She will guide you to the right words.

There's a moment of still silence. *Okay, luckily for you, I just spent the last half hour going down the rabbit hole on the internet—*

Rabbit hole? Is that a good thing?

I've got some useful information. But how do I . . . ?

Just pretend you are the moon goddess.

Ah, I get you. Let's do this.

With a motion too swift for the guards to stop, I unsling the conch from my shoulder and step right up to Cuauhtemoc, thrusting the netted bag into his free hand.

"Greet Coyolxauhqui, Your Imperial Majesty," I whisper.

In her soft, sweet voice, Sitlali croons, *Cuauhtemoc. My child. Will you not turn to behold your mother?*

His head swivels, astonished.

Sitlali is sitting cross-legged on the bed, so she appears to be floating in the air above the emperor's throne. She has pulled her hair back.

"Who are you?" the emperor asks, trembling.

The protector of Calizto's people, for whom I carved this conch in ages past.

Cuauhtemoc begins to move toward her, but I hold the conch tightly, preventing him.

The guards have now encircled us, halberds ready to slash.

The Imperial Council are shouting. The prime minister lifts a stone dagger.

Coyolxauhqui. Goddess of the moon. Sister of your Lord Huitzilopochtli. And believe me, King of the Mexica, Emperor of Anahuac: if you harm my Calizto, I shall rip your heart from your chest and feed it to your enemy.

Even knowing the girl, I am startled by the fierceness on her face.

But if you keep him safe, I shall help you win. I know what the Caxtiltecah will do next. Your future unfolds for me like the pages of a book. I can help you stop the inevitable. I can save Anahuac.

The emperor surges toward her. My fingers are sliding from the conch.

Or I can let you all die. In my heart, you are dead already.

Cuauhtemoc shoves me aside, rushing the throne, but Sitlali has disappeared. The guards seize me.

"Where is she?" Cuauhtemoc cries, his head jerking back and forth. "Bring her back!"

Summoning all the courage I can, I stand up against the mightiest man on the island.

"First, let us discuss terms."

CHAPTER TWENTY-FIVE

Sitlali

June 23–24, 2019

Exhilarated by our little victory with the emperor, I spend the rest of the afternoon using my Googling skills to track down my father. I finally find his address on the west side. My madrina is so happy to hear my news she agrees to take me to San Antonio to meet him in the morning.

It takes us forty-five minutes to get to my father's house. We go through an older neighborhood. The cars in this area are nice, a lot newer than the one my madrina is driving, but the houses and storefronts are in direct contrast to them. There are a lot of run-down buildings in the area, with graffiti on their walls, and every one of them has iron bars on the windows and doors.

When we knock on my father's house, a woman with sleek, blondish hair opens the door. Her eyes are perfectly made up, and her bright mauve lipstick matches her long fingernails.

"Good morning," my madrina introduces us. "My name is Tomasa. Enrique is my cousin. This is his daughter, Sitlali."

"His daughter?" the woman asks, holding a hand to her chest. "I'm sorry. I didn't know . . . I mean, I knew he had a daughter . . . I just didn't know she was in the States."

"I just got in," I say, smiling politely at the pretty woman. "Yesterday."

The woman's green eyes sparkle, and she looks me up and down before she opens the door to let us in.

"I'm Samantha," she says. "Enrique! You have visitors!"

My father looks old. His hair is almost completely white, and except for the bits of peppery black spots behind his ears, he looks much older than my madrina. The shape of his eyes turns naturally down at the corners. But when he smiles, his full lips are shaped exactly like mine, and I recognize him at once.

"Well, go on." My madrina gives me a little push. "Give your daddy a hug. This is why you came all this way. Isn't it?"

My father opens his arms, and, suddenly, I am a little girl again, running across a beach in Zongolica. He smells like salty air and wet sand and the ocean when the waves lap happily over the dunes, and I wrap my arms tightly around his neck and kiss him over and over again.

"I missed you so much!" I cry, letting the emotions I have been holding back roll right out of me.

"I missed you too, m'ija." My father holds me a bit longer before his arms slacken, and I realize it's time to stop clinging to him.

"Sit down. Sit down." My father pulls away from me and settles on the corner of the couch.

I settle beside him, and my father caresses my hair.

"It's curly," I say. "Like Mom's."

My father nods.

"Wow. I still can't believe you're here," he says. "You were waist-high the last time I saw you. A skinny little heron. All elbows and knees and small. So small."

"Now look at you. All grown up," Samantha says, coming to stand behind my father and putting her long, lacquered fingernails over his shoulders. "Enrique. You should call the boys out here."

"The boys?" I ask, and my father physically cringes.

Samantha leans over and hugs my father's neck. "Our sons," she says. "They should meet you. Before you go back to Mexico."

"Go back?"

My father's jaw tightens, and he clears his throat. "Oh, I don't think . . . ," he finally starts. But he doesn't get to finish his thought because Samantha leans back and screams.

"Joey? Frankie? Come here!"

At her beckoning, two little boys come barreling into the room. Laughing as they push each other, Joey and Frankie jump and climb all over the couch until they are sitting down, crushed between me and my father.

"Who are you?" one of them asks in English. I only know the basics, but I understand well enough.

"Joey. Frankie. Listen," my father says in heavily accented English, pulling one of the boys onto his lap. "This is my daughter. She's come here all the way from Mexico."

"Mexico!"

"Mexico!"

"Tortillas and sopas and enchiladas!" Joey and Frankie scream, wriggling out of my father's arms to climb all over him. My father laughs as he fights them off.

"They're young." My father looks embarrassed. "They don't know what this means."

Instead of catching up with my father, I spend every moment of my visit listening to Samantha deflect every conversation I try to start to call attention to what her children are doing as they run rampant in their living room.

"I'm sorry," my madrina finally says, after Frankie tramples over her purse to get on the table behind her. "Is there somewhere else they could go play, while Sitlali talks to her father?"

"Excuse me?" Samantha raises a perfectly penciled eyebrow. "They don't have to go anywhere else. This is their house."

"I just think it would be nice if Sitlali and her daddy could talk," my madrina says, in her sweet, gentle way. "They need to get reacquainted."

My father leans over and pats my hand. "Oh, there'll be plenty of time for that," he says. "We can talk this afternoon, when Joey and Frankie take their nap."

Glancing at Samantha's furious features, I mutter in Nahuatl, "I have so much to tell you, Father."

His eyes go wide. "My goodness! I had no idea you could speak the old tongue so well."

Samantha slaps her hand against the arm of the couch and stands up. "Spanish or English, please! None of that weird dialect of yours."

I glare up at her. "It's not a dialect. It's a language."

My father puts a finger to his lips. "Ya. Enough. Tonight, after dinner, we can sit out on the deck for a while and talk before bed."

"Enrique?" Samantha's voice is quiet, but there is an unmistakable chill in it. "She can't stay here. We don't have the space."

"We have a spare bedroom," my father says, frowning.

Samantha puts her hands on her hips. Her sharp claws dig into the tight fabric at her waist, and I look down at her nice high heels.

"I don't want to be an inconvenience," I whisper.

"Exactly." Samantha glares at my father. "She's not a child, Enrique. She's a full-grown woman. She doesn't need a daddy anymore."

My madrina clears her throat. "Sitlali's seventeen. She needs guidance, an education. Enrique needs to enroll her in school. Buy her supplies, clothes, all of that!"

Samantha's face goes beet red. My father's large brown eyes glisten as he stares up at her. "It's true," he says. "We need to discuss this."

"There's nothing to discuss," Samantha says, staring my father down before she shifts her cold green eyes on me. "Moving in here is not an option. School doesn't start for a few months. There's time to make other arrangements."

I cry all the way back to my madrina's house, silent tears that I keep swiping angrily away from my face because I don't want to dwell on this.

"Give her time," my madrina says, when we heat up tortillas to eat with our homemade soup at her kitchenette. "She'll come around. This caught her by surprise."

After lunch, I go back to my room. Calizto is there, pacing around in circles. His hands are on his hips, so it is clear he is deep in thought.

"I'm sorry," I say, closing the door quietly behind me. "I didn't know you were here."

"I didn't want to disturb your lunch. They've moved us to better quarters, but our fate will depend on our meeting with Cuauhtemoc. Does this new city you are in have a historical archive you can consult? We need to find specifics about what is to come. He needs actionable intelligence to turn the tide."

With Calizto sitting close by, I get on the computer and pour through website after website, intent on finding something specific we can give Cuauhtemoc when we meet with him.

I am engrossed in my studies when Calizto stands up and bows. I can see him talking to someone, but I can't hear what he is saying.

Suddenly, his mood changes.

Sitlali, he calls out with his mind, without looking over at me. The serious tone of his voice puts me on alert, and I abandon the keyboard.

"What is it?" I ask.

My empress.

The way he says her title, using the possessive pronoun, makes my heart turn into a little knot that wrings itself inward, getting tighter and tighter inside my chest, until I have to admit it.

I'm jealous.

"What about her?" I ask.

She wishes to speak with you, he says.

"Right now?" My heart loosens, deflates. My knees tremble, and I put my hands on them to keep them from knocking together. "No . . . I can't . . ."

She insists. Just improvise, as you did yesterday.

I look around frantically, trying to figure out how to stage this unexpected meeting.

My eyes fall on the stuff on my desk. Grabbing my phone, I switch on the flashlight and hop up onto the desk, sitting cross-legged. My hands on my lap, I point the light at my face and take a deep breath.

Then, before I can say anything else, Calizto stands before me, his body turned sideways, gripping the conch in both hands. Another hand materializes upon the conch, and then I get my first glimpse of the beautiful young Tecuichpo.

Standing inches from the boy I love, she is exquisite. Prideful and haughty and breathtaking . . . everything I could never be. Before I can betray my feelings of inadequacy, the empress lowers her gaze, bends her head, and says, "Moon Goddess! You honor us with your presence."

She's just a girl. Younger than me. But her voice is older, wiser, and when she looks at me again, I can see that she's distracted by my clothing. So I position the flashlight away from my upper body, drawing her gaze to my face. If I've calculated right, to her I appear as a glowing being, floating cross-legged in the air a few feet above her.

I throw my shoulders back, lift my chin, and look at her through half-closed eyes. But I don't speak, leaving her to think about how she is inconveniencing me, forcing her to find the courage to ask her questions.

"Calizto says you are working hard with him to protect us. We are most grateful."

"Yet you imprisoned him—my chosen warrior."

"A misunderstanding. But we have made amends." The empress looks at Calizto. Her eyes glisten as she smiles at him. "He is in our personal care now."

Bitch.

My face must betray my fury. I consider standing, looming over her smaller frame, making it clear to her who has the greater claim on him. I shift.

She flinches but remains silent. Then I understand. She has no questions. She just didn't believe them. She demanded to touch the moon conch to see if this was yet another trick perpetrated by her husband, the man who's already taken so much from her.

My heart softens.

"Child, Calizto is under 'our' personal care," I say, speaking about myself in the plural, for emphasis. "You would be wise to care for him too . . . from a distance."

"As it is requested, so will it be done," the empress says.

Because of my internet reading, I know so much about her future. All the pain she will suffer before she finds a semblance of peace saddens me, and I afford her a small smile.

"You must trust us, Tecuichpotzin," I say, in a calm voice. "You will survive these trials. And you and I will meet again. Both of us will have new names, but I will watch over you then as I have always done. Now go."

"Blessed Mother," she says, bowing her head. Then she lifts her hands from the conch and fades into nothing.

I let out a long-held breath. Relieved. Shaken by the experience.

Is she gone? I ask Calizto.

"Yes. Apologies, Sitlali. She grew suspicious. I had to prove your presence to her."

"Well, I hope that satisfied her," I say. "Because I don't want to ever do that again."

"Until you meet with Cuauhtemoc, tomorrow," Calizto reminds me.

"Yes! We can't forget that," I say.

My madrina opens the door. "Dinner's ready," she announces with a gentle smile.

I leave Calizto and go join her in the kitchen.

"You shouldn't let this get to you," my madrina says, and I realize I've been sitting here eating my chicken tacos and staring off into space without saying a word to her.

"I'm sorry," I say, leaning over to give her a quick hug. "I just have a lot of things on my mind."

"Just remember you have a place to live, here, with me, for as long as you need it." My madrina kisses my cheek. "I'll help you find a job and put you in school. You'll see. Soon, you'll be dating, and then you'll find a good man, someone worth marrying. You're young. You have the rest of your life ahead of you."

"Dating?" I shake my head, vehemently, because I can't imagine that. No. I couldn't.

My heart is taken.

After dinner, I go back to the book I was reading online and find a shocking fact.

"I've got something!" I tell Calizto, calling to him from across the room. But even as I say the words, I know that revealing this information means two more men will be put to death. This will devastate the young empress.

"What is it?" Calizto asks, coming to stand beside me at the computer.

In a split second, I decide that saving Calizto's life is far more important than breaking the empress's heart.

"Moteuczoma's sons are plotting against Cuauhtemoc." I say the words quickly, before I can change my mind.

"Axayaca and Xoxopehualoc?" Calizto asks.

"Yes. The empress's brothers are in league with the Spanish."

"This is grave news. They will be executed. It will . . ."

"Destroy her." I finish his thought.

Calizto looks downright wounded, and I wonder. Does he have feelings for her? Has the little empress stolen my Calizto's heart? Or is this just some strange loyalty I can't understand?

"Can I tell him this?"

"I am not sure." Calizto tugs at his hair and takes a few deep breaths. "The emotional distress might be unbearable. Tecuichpotzin is so young, so fragile. So betrayed already. By her father, who turned her over to Cortés. By her husband, who has already commanded four of her brothers be slain, including the child of her own mother. This might break her."

"I can try to find something else," I say. "This is . . ."

"A hard choice," Calizto whispers.

CHAPTER TWENTY-SIX

Calizto

Day 4-Vulture of the Year 3-House (June 25, 1521)

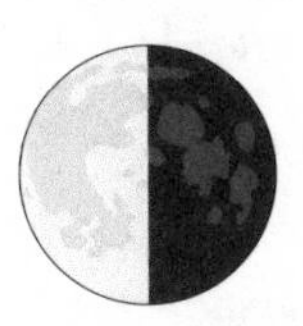

By morning we've decided. Archives in Sitlali's time indicate that Cuauhtemoc discovers the plot and kills Moteuczoma's sons. We are but tools the gods will use to ensure that fate.

Guards escort me alone to the audience chamber. The emperor sits on his throne, flanked by his prime minister and his top generals.

"Approach, Calizto," Cuauhtemoc commands. "Bring that trumpet closer. We are at our most desperate hour. Has the goddess decided to help us, now that we have shown you hospitality?"

I lower my eyes. "She has, Your Imperial Majesty. You need but place your hand on the moon conch, and she will reveal important truths to you."

Halfway up the steps, I pause. The emperor has stood, reaching out.

Sitlali is standing on the bed of her temporary bedroom, but appears to be floating a rod above the floor, wearing a gown she has borrowed from her godmother's closet.

She is beautiful.

Cuauhtemoc, my child. You have shown respect to my chosen champion. Therefore, I warn you: a plot is brewing in your palace. Axayaca and Xoxopehualoc, sons of Moteuczoma, have gathered discontent nobles to their side. They have sent word to Cortés already, expressing their desire to parlay. Treason is their goal. To allow the enemy entrance into Tlatelolco and to hand you over.

"Bastards," Cuauhtemoc spits. "This day will be their last."

Do what must be done, child.

"Divine Coyolxauhqui, ye of the silver bells, is there naught else you can reveal?"

My champion has experienced much hardship and loss to stand at your side, Cuauhtemoc. When I see that you have fully compensated his unrivaled bravery, I shall speak to you again. Lift your hand, child. We are done for the moment.

The emperor steps back, severing his connection.

What are you doing?

Getting you a better deal. Be thankful, Calizto.

Cuauhtemoc shakes the surprise from his face and looks at the guards. "Escort this warrior back to his quarters. Be sure he and his companion get a decent meal."

As I leave, I can hear the emperor begin shouting commands.

"Find Moteuczoma's sons, all of them, and drag them here before me!"

When I'm back with Ofirin, Sitlali has changed into the "pants" and "T-shirt" that fit her so well. She's attempting communication on her "phone."

Whom are you contacting? I ask.

My father. We barely had time to catch up yesterday. But that bitch Samantha keeps picking up. She says he's "not available." Which is bullshit.

Is there a way of conducting reconnaissance so that you can learn his new wife's schedule? Armed with knowledge of her normal times of absence, you can more readily meet with your father.

Hmm. Stalking them . . . maybe as a last resort.

I catch Ofirin up on the latest, and then we are brought a feast of deer stew, fresh tortillas, and wine.

After a restless night spent weighing possible courses of action with Sitlali, the meal makes me drowsy, so I lie on my sleeping mat for a brief nap.

Several hours later, there is a loud knock, and Prime Minister Tlacotzin enters. I sit up, rubbing the sleep from my eyes.

"Come. The emperor requests your presence." He looks over at Ofirin, scrawling on bits of amatl paper. "You stay here."

As we walk together, Tlacotzin addresses me with bemused wonder. "I have no idea how you managed this ruse. I assume you learned of the plot before we caught you fleeing. Perhaps you are part of it. Yet both the emperor and empress have been completely fooled by whatever sleight of hand you employ to make them hallucinate a goddess."

I sigh. "It is no sleight of hand, Your Excellency. The conch is indeed a divine conduit."

Sitlali, walking beside us, smiles. *No lie detected.*

Where are you headed? I ask.

To an interview. My madrina bugged me all morning. There's a job opening at a little taquería on the south side of the city. Helping in the kitchen. She spoke to the owner. He understands my situation and wants to chat.

I, on the other hand, understood very little of what you just said.

Work, Calizto. So I can make money to buy food and clothes.

Oh! I see. May the goddess guide your every word so that the outcome is favorable.

Thanks!

The prime minister shakes his head and laughs. "You are a strange young man. Your eyes get lost in the distance, as if you are daydreaming even at this crucial moment."

"Why? What has happened?"

"Your information proved fruitful. We captured the conspirators, the princes and some of their band of traitors. They have been executed. Now the emperor wishes to bestow an unprecedented honor upon you. But know this, Calizto: I shall keep my eyes upon you, both these two in my head and the many more in my employ. If your intentions are ill, you will be discovered and punished."

"As the law demands," I agree. "I do not fear your vigilance, Your Excellency. I intend no harm to our city or our people."

We've reached the audience chamber. It is full of noble warriors, mostly high-ranking officers of the four military orders: Jaguar Knights, Eagle Knights, Shorn Ones, and Otontin.

The emperor stands before his throne. The two chief generals flank him, various items in their arms. I cannot focus on what they hold. My chest constricts and my eyes water.

Calizto? Sitlali asks. *What's wrong? You feel . . . overwhelmed.*

Ah, Little Star. You've no idea what you've wrought.

Wrought? What did I do? Are you going to be okay?

That's a matter of perspective. Hold.

The prime minister leads me to the foot of the steps leading to the dais. Cuauhtemoc looks down with a genuine smile.

"Behold Calizto," he announces to the gathered officers. "Son of Omaca. Telpochtlahtoh of Metztonalco. Many of you fought alongside his brother, fallen ten years ago in battle with the Tzapotecah. Against all odds he has survived, obeying what orders he received and acting wisely on behalf of the Mexica when there were no officers to command him. Because of the intelligence he has brought us, we have rooted out a conspiracy that might have meant our defeat. And he intends to continue serving us as he has, a true hero of Mexico, of Anahuac, of the empire.

"Therefore do I confer on you, my son," he continues, "a position in the order of Otontin Knights."

My knees threaten to buckle in shock, but I stand straighter.

A knight? Sitlali gasps. *Wait.*

The general to his left clears his throat. "Yours is the tasseled red ribbon, with which to bind your topknot, marking your station upon the battlefield. Yours is the blue-green uniform, marking you as divine jade to be broken at the gods' whim."

Solemnly, he extends his arms and deposits these items into my own. I clench my muscles to keep from trembling.

The general to the right of the emperor speaks next. "Yours is this banner of quetzal feathers and its wicker frame, signaling your companions and your enemy alike. Yours is the white shield with water-glyph design, blinding your opponent as you rush into the fray."

He gestures to a young shield-bearer nearby. The boy rushes to stand by me, accepting the heavier items.

"And yours," intones my emperor, switching to reverential speech, "are the white cotton sandals, forbidden to commoners, which you may wear as is your right from this day forward. I elevate you to cuauhpilli. Place them on your feet, Caliztotzin."

Kneeling before me, he sets the sandals on the floor. I slide my feet into them, and he binds the straps to my calves.

Caliztotzin, Sitlali whispers, sitting down at a table somewhere. *Don Calizto.*

The sandals feel strange, as if I'm standing upon clouds. After a lifetime of going barefoot, I'm unused to the softness.

"Commander Acacihtzin," the emperor calls. "I present to you the newest knight of your order. Caliztotzin, turn to greet your commander."

The head of the Otontin Knights steps from the ranks. With my free hand, I salute him, fist against my heart.

He is holding my father's sword.

"This has been yours, Caliztotzin," he says, extending the pommel. "Wielded by your brave father and then by your noble brother. May many more enemies fall beneath its obsidian blades."

I receive the sword in its unique scabbard. Kneeling quickly, I scoop dust from the stones and eat it.

"Command me, sir."

"On Six Flint, you will report to the calmecac beside the temple of Quetzalcoatl. There you will begin your training under Captain Ehcatzin, leader of your new unit."

"Yes, sir."

I feel Cuauhtemoc behind me. He puts his hand on my shoulder and leans forward to whisper.

"Tomorrow, I must speak to her again. I have done as she asked. Now I need more. A true victory."

All I can do is swallow and nod.

I return to my chambers to find Ofirin fast asleep. Sitlali stands with her arms crossed, scowling at me as if I have done something wrong.

What is it? I demand, a little too surly. *Did your interview go poorly?*

No, Calizto. It went fine. It's a nice little place. Señor Jiménez, that's the owner, seems kind, if kind of tired. His wife works the register, but she spends most of the time complaining about this and that.

A lesson could be learned from that dynamic.

Excuse me? When have I complained? All I've done is help you out!

You may not like the help you've just given me. Because of what you commanded Cuauhtemoc, he has made me a cuauhpilli. Not a commoner, but not quite a noble. An honorary knight.

She drops her arms and looks at me intently.

Like your brother, right?

Yes. After his death, I often dreamed of following in his footsteps. I knew my destiny was that of a farmer, like all the men before me in my family. Called to battle only at the direst of times, when all men were needed to defend Mexico. My brother reached for more, but he died on the battlefield and was unable to achieve the greatest glory of a cuauhpilli.

Which is?

To sire children, sons and daughters who are nobles by birth.

The kids of an honorary knight are nobility.

Yes.

Sitlali sits down. Her brow crinkles up. Normally, I love to watch her grow so intent, think intensely about things. Her eyes narrow, glimmering with fire and will. Her red lips purse. She tugs at her uncommon curls.

But now her expression worries me. There is something dark behind it.

So. If we help Cuauhtemoc defeat the Spanish, if you remain in good favor, you can get married, have children, start a family of nobles that will enjoy all the benefits of that class.

Unless the city falls, as you have repeatedly said it will.

Eyes glittering with nascent tears, she looks up at me.

What if we're changing history, Calizto? What if I feed information to the emperor and he changes the outcome? Won't I . . . change? Or . . . cease to exist?

I had never pondered this possibility. My stomach churns.

No, I say finally. *That makes no sense. If you are not Sitlali Morales, you never retrieve the moon conch. We never connect. I die, probably, or at the very least Cuauhtemoc never receives your information from the future.*

A paradox, she mutters.

I do not know this word. She has used Spanish: *una paradoja.*

Motlatzohuilia, she explains in Nahuatl. *An impossible contradiction.*

"What the hell," Ofirin says, stretching himself awake and staring at the armaments I have laid across our table, "is all of that?"

Explain it, Calizto. My madrina's here for me.

That night, Sitlali sits on the floor so we can be near. She runs her fingers through her hair and sighs deeply before finally speaking.

I've been thinking. I just put you in a lot of danger, didn't I?

Sitlali, you must not . . .

Stop. I read what the Otontin Knights do. They aren't the first into battle; that's those wild kamikaze Shorn Ones. But you will go in right after them.

Yes, I admit. *They are named for the valiant Otomi people, who nearly defeated the Mexica when we first arrived in Anahuac. But surely the goddess will watch over me as she has done. There is a reason the conch exists. We must have faith.*

Oh my God. Her hand goes to her mouth.

What?

I can see Ofirin through you. You're fading!

She is right. I can make out the contours of the door through her body.

The moon is waning. We knew this would happen.

Sitlali muffles a sob.

I feel so sad, Calizto. I've got a job now. I'll probably start school in a couple of months. You've been elevated to honorary knight. It's like . . . we're finally finding our place in our separate worlds. And now we're beginning to fade. It feels . . . ominous.

My sweet . . . , I begin, wanting to say so much, but afraid of the impact of those words.

What if we lose each other, Calizto? What if we fade to nothing in each other's eyes and that's the end?

I cannot stop my tears this time. I let them flow as I lean toward her ghostly form.

I . . . do not know, dear Sitlali. But I will cherish you forever. That much is certain.

Together, we weep until late, the quarter moon watching bereft in the sky.

CHAPTER TWENTY-SEVEN

Sitlali

June 26, 2019

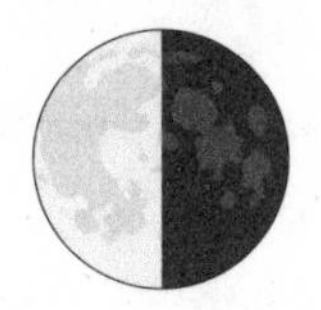

In the morning, I rinse my face. But no matter how many times I wring the hot water out of the hand towel and press its soothing warmth against my teary eyes, I can't get the swelling to go down.

"What is it?" My madrina puts the coffee pot back on the stove and rushes over to me. She takes my hand and squeezes it tight. "What's wrong?"

"Nothing," I whisper. "I'm fine."

My madrina shakes her head slowly. "Clearly you're not."

"I am," I whisper. "It's just. Oh, never mind. It's hopeless."

"Ay, m'ija. I know it's hard," my madrina insists. "But your daddy is struggling too. Think about it. He's trying to reconcile his present with his past."

"Reconcile the present and past?" Her words resonate so much with my predicament that they cut deeply into the open wound that is my heart, and I start to cry again.

At a loss for words, my madrina puts her arms around me and holds me tight. "Forgive him, m'ija," she whispers. "It's not good to hold on to pain like this. You don't want to curl up and asphyxiate, like a little cardinal."

The memory of the red bird in my father's hand sends me into a spasm of dry, convulsing sobs that pull at my chest and rack my shoulders. As I cry, I hear another soft sob, emulating my own, and I lift my eyes to see the ghastly ghost of my mother materialize in the room. She is standing behind my madrina, looking down at me with a tortured look on her face as she moans—a low, mournful wailing that escapes her dark lips and fills the room with a resounding echo.

"Liar!" she screams at the phantom letter trembling in her skeletal hand. "Cheater!"

I squeeze my madrina's hand and cry out.

"No! No!" I tell the ghost of my mother. "This isn't about my father!"

My madrina thinks for a moment. "Then what is it? What could possibly make you come undone like this?"

I look at my ghost of a mother, who is lost in her own grief, and I pull the words out of my heart, knowing full well they will disappoint her, because she always warned me about this.

"I'm in love," I whisper.

"No!" my mother screams. "No! No!"

"I am," I tell her. "I am."

The assertion makes my mother quiver and vibrate with such force that her image distorts and distends, until it finally shatters, breaking itself into a million tiny pieces that dissipate in the sunlight coming in through the kitchen window.

"In love?" my madrina furrows her eyebrows.

"Yes," I admit. "I'm in love with a beautiful boy—a beautiful soul. But we can never be together."

My madrina prods gently. "Is it someone you left behind, in Zongolica?"

"No," I try to explain. "He's from another . . . another . . ."

"Another planet?" My madrina giggles and gives me a little shake. "Come on. I'm sure it's not so bad. What is it? You've got me in suspense!"

"Oh, what's the point?" I tell her. "We can never be together. Not now. Not ever."

"So, he's far away. That doesn't mean anything." My madrina waves the idea aside, like it's a fly she's shooing away. "The women in our family have been making long-distance relationships work for centuries. Our people have been migrating north and back down again since the beginning of time. I'm sure you and this boy will find a way—"

"Thank you," I tell her, and she gives me a tight little hug before she goes off to make us some breakfast.

I don't see Calizto again until I've been in my room for over an hour, researching more information about a situation on the twenty-ninth of June.

"Calizto?" I call out to him when he enters my space. "Are you all right?"

"Yes, but I received bad news this morning. A rebel band of nobles broke into the temple during the night. They massacred the priests of Huitzilopochtli and Tezcatlipoca—a cowardly act of revenge."

"I'm sorry." The coyote bite scar itches, and I scratch at it nervously. "I have bad news too."

"Worse than this?"

"Yes," I whisper. "According to this periodical, there's going to be a massive attack on your island in three days."

"Three days? That may not be enough time to prepare."

"I know," I say. "But at least we know what's coming. I can give Cuauhtemoc the details if you think it'll help. It'll give him some time to plan an exit strategy."

Calizto paces the room. "Yes," he says.

"Sitlali?" my madrina calls me from the other room. "Are you almost ready?"

Ready? Looking across the room at the small alarm clock on my nightstand, I realize I've lingered on the internet too long. "Oh my God! I'm going to be late!"

"Late for what?"

"Work, remember?" I run around my room, pushing my feet into my tennis shoes and throwing my brush and hair clips into my bag. "Darn it. I just got this job. I can't be late. I'll see you later. Okay?"

Calizto nods. "Go. I'll reach out when the time comes to speak to the emperor."

There are two things I learned on my first full shift at the taquería. The first one is that if you want to know anything useful, you listen to the cook, Manuel, because he's got everything figured out.

"The best thing to do," he says as he chops up a skirt steak into slender slivers on the grill, "if you think ICE is on the premises, is to pull off that apron and walk out that back door. Turn the corner and keep walking all the way to the bank."

"The bank?" I ask him, wondering where this is going.

"Yes. The IBC down there, on Military. Walk right in there. And get in the long line. When you get to the teller, ask her if you can open a new account."

"But I don't want to open an account."

"Oh, don't worry. They'll never get to you," the cook says, flipping the skirt steak around on the grill before putting it on a plate beside me. "Those people like to make us sit down and wait."

"Of course, if Angel is here, you just jump in his truck," a voice says from behind us.

Manuel turns around and looks at Angel Ramos, the delivery boy, as he walks up to us at the flat top.

Manuel rolls his eyes. "Don't listen to Pretty Boy here," he says. "He's got more spins than a slot machine."

"Aww, come on. Why are you trying to make me look bad?" Angel puts the takeout containers into a bag.

Manuel pushes Angel toward the door. "Out with you. Go on. Get to work. There's nothing for you here."

Angel winks at me as he walks away. I try not to laugh, but the sound he makes when he hits his head on a cabinet door on the way out is too funny, so I smile and look back at my work.

The second thing I learn on my very first day is that girls in the United States are just as crazy about boys as my girlfriends in Zongolica ever were. During my lunch break, I get all the scoop on Angel.

"Oh, don't get me wrong, he's totally worth it," Carolina whispers. "I mean, those lips are like sopapillas, soft and sweet as honey."

"Uh-huh," Amparo attests. "He'll drip that honey all over you, and you'll think you've died and gone to heaven."

Carolina crunches on a tortilla chip. "But once he's done with you, you can just forget it. The most he'll give you after that is a ride home."

"Only if he's between girls, you understand?" Amparo winks at me.

I finish eating my torta and wipe my lips. "Well, thank you for the company," I say, as I pick up my plate and push back my chair. "But I don't have time for guys like Angel."

I spend a couple of hours making tea, cutting lemons, onions, and chiles, and helping with delivery orders when they come in. Sometime during the three o'clock hour, Calizto comes into my line of vision. I see him before he calls my name.

Sitlali, can you get away for a moment?

I think so. Why? I ask, looking over at Manuel, who's busy scrubbing the flat top clean with the edge of his spatula.

The emperor wishes to speak to you.

Again?

Yes. How soon can you be ready?

I don't know. I'm at work! I tell him, turning around and looking for a good place where I can be alone for a moment.

"Sitlali?" Señor Jiménez calls my name, and I turn around. He's standing in front of the door that leads to the dining room. "Are you okay?"

"Yes," I tell the owner of the taquería. "I'm just . . . I'm just feeling a little . . ."

"Overwhelmed?"

"Yes! It's a little hot in here," I exclaim, giving him my most honest smile. "Can I take a small break? I just need a moment."

"Of course," Señor Jiménez waves his hand, as if to shoo me out of the kitchen. "It's your first day. You'll get used to it."

I pick up my bag and move quickly around the tall cooling trays on my way to the restroom. Once inside, I lock myself in, take off my apron, straighten my clothes, and spruce up my hair. When I am sure there is nothing else I can do, I look around for a place where I can pose in some sort of goddess-like manner with the conch in my hands.

When Calizto calls my name again, I am sitting on the tank of the toilet with my shoulders pressed against the wall for balance.

"Coyolxauhqui. Mother Moon." Calizto speaks to me in a reverent voice. He knows I'm here, but he does not look at me. "Will you grant your child permission to bring Cuauhtemoc to you in this time of need?"

"Calizto, child of my heart. I am here for you," I say, staying in character in case Cuauhtemoc should touch the conch in the middle of our communication.

Calizto nods, and I see Cuauhtemoc's hand appear first on the conch, then his forearm, followed by the rest of his visage, as translucent and ghostly as Calizto's form.

"Goddess. Divine Intercessor." Cuauhtemoc bows his head. "Thank you for affording us this gift of your time and knowledge."

I have no interest in pleasantries. You must listen and waste no time preparing for what I am about to say, I tell him as I look down at him. *In three days' time, the Bearded Beast will attack this isle. It is Cortés's darkest desire to take the Great Marketplace of Tlatelolco.*

"Three days." Cuauhtemoc considers my words. "Tell me, great goddess, what can we do to stop him? How can we best prevent this?"

You cannot prevent. Only prepare. Look for him by morning. He will enter along the southern causeway. Once inside the Sacred Precinct, his force will split in two. Alderete will continue up the avenue toward you with eighty men and eight horses. Cortés will go north, take the narrower road just to the east. Tapia and Alvarado will circle around and travel the western avenue, then swing north on the farthest road. The rest will head into the city along the western causeway.

Cuauhtemoc's eyes brighten. I can almost see the wheels turning as plans form behind them. "Praise be unto you, Goddess."

Remember, child. His army is great, but you have the advantage. You know the when and where—now you must consider how this will end.

Cuauhtemoc bows his head. "As it is requested, so will it be done."

When Cuauhtemoc removes his hand and his image dissipates, I let out a long, heavy breath. *Okay. That's all I can do for now. I have to get back to work. Be safe, Calizto.*

You as well, Little Star, he says, and then he is gone again.

When I get home, my madrina is on the phone.

"It's your daddy," she whispers.

I take it and run into my bedroom with it.

"Hey!" I say, sounding cheerful, because I really am happy to hear from him.

"How are you?" he wants to know, so I prattle on about my new job and how much my feet hurt after just one day of waitressing.

"I'm glad, I'm glad." Then, after a long pause, my father finally says, "Listen, I wanted to talk to you about what happened the other day."

"Yes, me too."

"I just hope you understand," my father interrupts. "You can't come over anymore. Not without making arrangements with me."

"Arrangements?" My voice is trembling, and I cough.

"It's not easy for me. I have responsibilities here," he starts again. "The boys don't know what's going on. And Samantha, well, she wants to protect them."

"What about me?" I ask. "What about your responsibility to me?"

My father swears under his breath. "Ay, Sitlali. You know I love you. But I don't want to upset my family. This isn't easy. It just isn't."

"Yeah, you said that already." I close my eyes and press my fingertips against the bridge of my nose, to keep the tears from coming.

"Just wait for me to call you, okay? Can you do that? Before you come again?"

"Sure," I say, even though I know there will be no calls, no invitations. Not if Samantha has anything to say about it.

I end the call, give the phone back to my madrina, and plop down on the couch.

"Everything okay?" my madrina asks. The bluish light coming from the television accentuates the worried look on her face.

"Yes," I say. "Everything's perfect. Just what I was expecting."

CHAPTER TWENTY-EIGHT

Calizto

Day 6-Flint of the Year 3-House (June 27, 1521)

I awaken before dawn to bathe. As I linger in the pool, considering the luxuries a young cuauhpilli might enjoy, I realize Sitlali is looking at me from her bed.

Good morning. How long have you been awake?

*Just a couple of min—*seconds. *I have the morning shift.*

I chuckle at her discomfort.

I also have an early start. I don't know what to expect from Ehcatzin. I've heard his name before. He has a reputation for unconventional tactics.

That new uniform seems cool. Can't wait to see you in it. I mean, to see how it fits your body. Wait, that is . . . She is flustered. *You know what I mean.*

Of course I do. But I won't be wearing it today. It's only for battle.

She sits up, her hair a tangle, her sleeping garments twisted. Her face crunches up as she pouts. It's incredibly endearing.

Not fair. What if you fade completely by the time you have to suit up? I wanted to . . .

To what?

To . . . see you all dressed up for the position I got you! What else?

Enjoying the awkwardness, I make as if to stand up.

You may want to avert your eyes. I need to dry myself.

She gasps and turns away.

Calizto, that's not funny. Give me more warning!

Hrm. Perhaps if you were less curious in the first place . . .

She picks up her phone and feigns interest in its screen while I dress. It takes some time, but a glance in the obsidian mirror shows my efforts have been worthwhile.

Sitlali, you can look.

She shrugs.

I've seen enough of you.

Really?

Mm-hmm. Long black hair, white loincloth, a few muscles. Same old, same old.

I should just take this uniform off, then?

Wait, what?

Sitlali whirls around.

I have donned it all: the one-piece blue-green body suit, the red ribbon for my topknot, the white sandals. I have even strapped the wicker framework to my back that lifts the quetzal feather banner into the air behind me and to my arm the new shield of my station.

Sitlali gasps.

You look . . .

Dignified? Handsome?

Pretty . . . ready. Her blush says much more, feeding my pride.

I laugh loudly. *Ah, my sweet. I can feel your heart beating across five centuries and a thousand leagues.*

For a moment we simply stare at each other with yearning.

Then she sighs.

Time for me to get ready too. Breakfast tacos wait for no woman.

Then I'll release the conch to give you some privacy.

As she dresses, I change back into my loincloth and a pair of rougher sandals.

Before long, we're walking together under a dawning sky, Sitlali to work and I to practice. We exchange a warm glance and words of leave-taking just as I step onto the training field beside the calmecac of Tlatelolco.

Ehcatzin is there already. Four other men are setting up the tlaczayan, chalking out the sparring square and placing a rack of training weapons nearby.

My captain is a svelte, hardy man of thirty years. Thin lines crisscross his arms, legs, and chest from hundreds of obsidian razors that have grazed him in battle. Badges of courage and skill. He rushes into the fray but is too fast and agile to be slain or maimed.

"Calizto. Son of Omaca," he greets me. "Welcome to the Otontin Knights."

"Captain Ehcatzin," I reply, saluting with fist against heart. "It is my honor to serve."

He tilts his head. "Ah, they told me you wore that big sword of yours strapped to your back. Let me see it, son."

I unsling the sword and scabbard.

"What in the nine hells is this?" Ehcatzin grabs the handle and slides the maccuahuitl from the grooved wooden rectangle that covers the blade and its embedded obsidian razors.

"An invention of my father's," I explain. "A tlaquimiloani."

"A shroud?"

"Yes, sir. He got the idea from the Caxtiltecah. You have seen how they keep their metal swords by their sides, protecting themselves from the sharp edges by a similar method. With the help of a woodworking cousin, he crafted one for the weapon."

Ehcatzin grunts as he hefts the sword. "Your elder brother's blade. He was one of our best."

I duck my head. "Even though I was just a boy, he taught me many things. I continued practicing after his death, under the supervision of my father."

"Then you studied under Master Miquiztin, another valiant and decorated soldier. Does he yet live?"

I keep my eyes down. "I don't know, sir. Our neighborhood was reduced to rubble by enemy cannon. I've not seen him since."

Something whistles through the air. Ehcatzin has dropped the sheath and is brandishing the sword. "A fine weapon. Where have you gotten replacement obsidian razors?"

"Mine have never broken."

He lowers the sword, an incredulous look on his face. "Impossible. Razors strike bone, splinter, pull free to remain in the enemy's flesh. How did you manage such a feat?"

Trying not to sound too arrogant, I explain. "The first rule my elder brother taught me, sir. 'The edge is for slashing, the flat for smashing.' A severing blow with the edge will shatter the blades and perhaps the weapon. It is a move of last resort."

Ehcatzin purses his lips, raps the oak handle with the knuckles of his left hand. "If this sword ever shatters, son, take it as a sign from the gods. I've not seen a more elegant and durable piece of weaponry."

"Sir."

Ehcatzin signals to the other four men, who come to stand beside him. "These are my squad leaders. To determine whose team you fit best, I want you to move through the thirteen olintin of the sword. You know them all, I trust?"

In answer, I walk to the weapons rack, select a practice macana and shield, give a war cry, and begin. The forms are instinct after years of practice and teaching. Each series of attacking and defensive moves puts the swordsman through every possible combination of encounters in war.

As I complete the final strike of the thirteenth olintin, parrying from a crouch before hamstringing the opponent, I lower sword and shield to kneel before Captain Ehcatzin.

"That was flawless. What other weapons are you proficient with?"

"Only melee arms, sir. I've little experience with bows or spears. The tepoztopilli would be my second choice."

"Excellent," Ehcatzin says. "Show us the five olintin of the halberd."

Returning the shield and macana, I choose the tallest pole arm. Instead of obsidian razors, this practice weapon has flint blades embedded at the edge of its long, ovoid head. The weight is perfect, and I move through the forms, three for fighting in formation, two for duels. It feels strange to return to the thrusting, twisting, and backward jerking of the tepoztopilli. The last olin winds down with a flurry of slashing and stabbing attacks before ending with brutal blows from the weapon reversed, the handle slamming into the falling enemy's imaginary face and throat.

Whipping the halberd around my shoulders and planting the butt into the earth, I kneel again before Ehcatzin and the others.

"Well done," he says with an appreciative tone. "Rest for a spell. Then get padded up. You'll be sparring with Poloc."

I return the pole arm to the rack and stretch the tension from my muscles before sitting on the ground and looking over at Sitlali, whose image wavers with the breeze.

I almost spilled coffee on a customer, watching you.

Am I that distracting? I ask, teasing.

Your fighting moves? Yes. You yourself? Meh.

But she is smiling as she thinks it.

A cadet brings me a cup of pinolli while I rest. The drink of toasted cornmeal fills my gut without making me sluggish.

Sometime later, Ehcatzin and Poloc return, bearing helmets and sparring jackets of thick cotton, similar to the ichcahuipilli worn on the battlefield. The captain helps us into our gear, tying the jackets at our backs.

"Good. Both of you are tall, evenly matched," Ehcatzin notes. "You know the rules. First man to step over the chalk line loses. Choose your weapons."

Poloc, whose face is crossed by a jagged scar, selects a heavy, broad macana and a solid wooden shield. His muscles tense at the weight in both his hands. He's quite strong but will tire quickly.

Ignoring the shields, I draw a longer, narrower two-handed practice sword. Not as heavy or dense as my own, it will still allow me to fight in the same hybrid way I've developed.

We face each other from opposite sides of the tlaczayan. Poloc assumes the traditional stance: shield up, sword held in reverse, with the blade pointing behind him. Normally, a fighter will move from that stance into an underhanded half-spindle side cut, swinging his arm in a short arc about chest-high.

Which means Poloc will do no such thing.

I flex my knees, point my sword toward the ground at an angle.

Poloc explodes into motion, running at me. I see his left arm lifting as he leans forward.

He plans to use the shield offensively. Solid oak can break bones.

Loosing a cry, I swing my sword in an arc over my head and start running too. I leap as he bends and thrusts his shield forward.

I plant one foot on the shield, another on his shoulder, and push off him with a spin, swinging my sword in a downward parabola till it slams into his helmet.

Hitting the ground, I roll into a crouch. He has whirled about and whips his sword through the air. Rather than pulling back or parrying, I roll forward under his attack and jam the end of my macana into his groin.

Poloc grunts but doesn't stop. I've gotten too close, and he slams the edge of his shield down against my helmet. This blow is followed by a downward diagonal slice of his blade, which I bat away as I stand, reeling from the pain in my head.

The shield comes whizzing close again, but I dance back and catch it with the flat of my blade, twisting to wrench open his defense. I spring into the air with a cry and bring my sword down in a brutal arc that would have ripped open his armor were it edged with razors.

I duck under another of his half-spindle side cuts. He has not learned to lower that attack. Twisting away, I pull to the other end of the tlaczayan, right at the edge of the chalk, lifting my sword over my head as far as possible so that it touches the small of my back.

Poloc laughs, letting his sword dangle from the thong that binds it to his wrist. Then, as I have been hoping, he yanks the shield off his left arm and flings it through the air at me. He clearly expects I will step back and lose by crossing the line.

Instead, I bring my sword crashing down on it and hurtle toward him. A half rod away, I pull my momentum into a full spin of my body, sword outstretched.

A malacachtli. Full spindle. A jaguar move. My brother called it the metzli.

The moon.

Poloc flinches, steps back.

Crosses the line.

The 360-degree spin has pulled me into a crouch. I'm still holding my sword extended.

I lower it and stand. Poloc pulls off his helmet and grins.

"He's a hell of a strategist," the squad leader says. "The emperor wasn't wrong to make him an Otomitl Knight."

Ehcatzin shakes his head, but grins. "I've never seen such a strange blend of styles. But, nine hells, it works. Come, Calizto, let's get you out of that gear and go have lunch. You can meet the other boys in our unit."

As elite soldiers, we eat better than probably anyone in the city. Certainly better than Sitlali, who wolfs down a tortilla wrapped around meat before taking a walk during her lunch break.

I need to buy some things at the dollar store, she explains.

Like what? I ask, ignoring the ribald jokes one of my new companions is making.

Don't worry about it.

Well, now I cannot possibly stop worrying about it. Are you hurt? Is there some new obstacle you must surpass?

No, Calizto. Just, you know, personal items.

Such as?

Things that a woman needs. Every once and a while. You know, moon cycle, et cetera?

Ah, ritual items for prayers to Coyolxauhqui?

Uh, yes, weirdo. You can buy ritual Mexica prayer stuff in the United States. Clearly.

I suddenly understand what she needs to acquire. I had older sisters for many years.

Oh! I, uh, beg your pardon. Go . . . go about your business, then. Yes. Talk later.

I look around at the soldiers. Our unit is made up of twenty men, we fifteen fighters and the five officers eating in the adjoining room. The unit breaks down into five squads when necessary, one led by the captain.

I'm the youngest, but not by much. Tzohuac, son of a general who died last year during the Night of Victory, is just a handful of moons older.

No one questions my right to eat and fight alongside them.

The emperor and their captain placed me where I am.

That's sufficient for these men.

The afternoon is spent drilling as a unit and then breaking into squads for mock battles. Ehcatzin shifts Tzohuac to Poloc's command, where a companion's death has created an opening.

"With me, Calizto," he says. There is no argument, no hurt feelings.

I learn the formations, obey orders, coordinate without showing off.

No one can ever take the place of my fallen family and friends. But by the time the day is over, I realize I need this camaraderie. The ache in my heart is dulled by their jests and battle cries. Good Mexica men, ready to die for king and country.

Walking back to the palace, I see Sitlali moving like a ghost that flitters past in the dead of night. She must be in a vehicle.

Going home? I ask, though her godmother's house is hardly the home she wants. I curse her bastard of a father for making her weep.

Yes, Amparo is giving me a ride. She's one of the waitresses.

Those gossipmongers who leer at the supposedly handsome womanizer? Angel?

No, she's not one of them. She's easy to talk to. We're having a nice conversation.

About?

You know, what kind of fun things there are to do around here, safe places for someone like me to go and not get picked up by border authorities, mainly ICE.

Are any of those places frequented by ruffians like Angel?

Ruffians? I couldn't tell you what kind of young men . . . I mean, I don't—

Because you shouldn't go to such neighborhoods. Or see such knaves.

Wait, are you jealous, *Calizto?*

Hardly! Jealous of some vapid twit who ruts with women like an animal, abandoning each in turn? I just want to look out for you as you have watched over me.

Uh-huh. Well, I won't be going anywhere tonight, so you can relax. I'm exhausted. I'll probably watch some TV with my madrina and then go to bed.

Wise choice. I'm also exhausted. And bruised. No one advertises that about being in an elite military unit. "You will ache all the time."

Ah, Calizto! I wish I could . . . Hmm. Please take care of yourself.

I've requested unguents be sent to our rooms. I should be fine by morning.

I pause. The setting sun has spread crimson all over the western peaks.

May I make a suggestion? Don't attempt to contact your father tonight. Let him stew for a while. Let him think upon his unwise choices, the pain his neglect has caused you. Let him suffer a little as well.

But I love him, Calizto.

I know. I know. Still, let your love be a hard love, Sitlali.

She says nothing for a long while. I reach the palace, walk into our suite, greet Ofirin, who wants me to tell him about my day.

Finally, sitting on the couch at her godmother's house, Sitlali looks over at me.

My sweet, it's for the best, I reassure her. *Imagine it's a battle. Use the right strategy.*

I'm thinking about it, Calizto. I promise. Rest well.

CHAPTER TWENTY-NINE

Sitlali

June 28, 2019

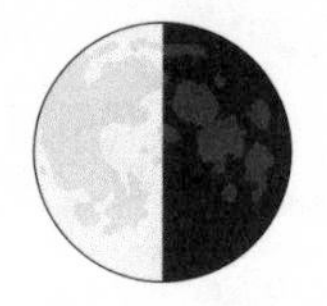

Manuel cut the side of his index finger during the breakfast rush. It wasn't that bad. He just had to bandage it, but he and Angel have switched positions and Manuel's driving today.

With Angel on the grill, there's no break from the googly eyes and the cheap come-ons. The guy is so slimy it takes every bit of my resolve not to hit him over the head with a skillet.

"Oh my Lord, look at you," he says, when I go to wipe the sweat from the back of my neck. "You are a goddess. You know that? I would put you on a pedestal—worship you night and day if you were my girl."

I ignore him and turn sideways to look at Calizto, whose ghostly profile is standing in line, I assume with his companions, listening to a debriefing. I want to talk to him, but he is so busy. So, I just sit on the stool by the door and watch him silently.

"Hey, daydreamer, you listening?" Angel calls to me, and I snap back to my time's reality.

"I am," I say, as I jump off the little stool and rush up to the flat top, where Angel's got the next delivery order ready for packaging.

"Why do you do that?" Angel asks. "Where do you go, when you get like that?"

I shrug.

"Women," he scoffs.

Something akin to anger replaces the slight flush on my skin. "What do you mean, 'women'?"

Angel throws several slices of ham on the grill. "My mother used to do that, look out into space," he says as he flips the ham. "It was like we didn't exist or something. Like she was already gone, years before she left."

"Left?" I ask, taking the ham and putting it in beside the eggs before I close the lid on the container and place it in a plastic bag.

"Yeah." Angel pulls the next ticket off the counter, reads it, and tosses it on the table beside him. "Long time ago. I'm over it now."

Manuel picks up the delivery order and rushes out the back door. The taquería is busy. I can hear Carolina and Amparo laughing on the other side of the pass over.

Angel stops twirling the spatula in his hands. His handsome face changes, the smile disappears, and he looks at me for a moment. "What?" he asks.

"Are you?" I ask him.

"Am I what?" He blinks and then rubs the side of his jaw against his shoulder to wipe the sweat off his face.

"Over it?" I ask him. "I mean, abandonment is a hard thing."

Angel's eyes glisten, and he leans over and grins at me. "What?" he asks. "You think I'm broken?"

Now it's my turn to be uncomfortable. "I'm sorry. I wasn't trying to get in your business."

"That's all right," Angel whispers, his face inches from mine. "I let you fix me, baby?"

His arm snakes around my hip, and he cups my buttocks.

Infuriated, I grab the lapels of his shirt, pull him down, and hit his groin with my knee.

"Ugh!" Angel grabs his privates and falls over in pain.

"There! Consider yourself fixed!"

Carolina and Amparo break through the kitchen door and stare at the scene in front of them, shocked at the sight of Angel writhing on the floor.

Disgusted, I pull off my apron, toss it on a table, and weave my way through the prep tables. As I make a dash for the back door, I can hear Carolina and Amparo clapping and yelling, "That's how you do it! That's how you make an exit!"

I run down to the end of the alley and take a right. What was it Manuel had said? To go to the bank if ICE ever came? Only ICE is nowhere near me. No. Right now I am running away from a ghostly memory—an ugly reminder of a boy whose stupid delusions forced me to run away from everything I was, everything I am. And I wonder if I will always be running. If the ways of men like Jorge and Angel will always haunt women like me.

I stop at the corner and realize I didn't ask for a break. So, I turn around and walk back slowly, quietly.

When I get back to the taquería, Angel is nowhere to be found, but Señor Jiménez is waiting for me by the door. "Are you okay?" he asks.

"Yes," I say. "I'm sorry I left without permission."

"Don't worry about that," he says. "I just want to make sure you're all right. Angel didn't hurt you, did he?"

I lift my chin. "Angel couldn't hurt me if he tried," I say.

"Well, I sent him home," Señor Jiménez says. "He's on suspension. Indefinitely. I'll make the deliveries until he decides what's good for him."

Manuel raises his eyebrows at me. "Or until we hire another delivery guy. I vote for that."

I work without incident for the rest of the day. And when my shift ends, I look up bus routes and find the best way to go to my father's house. I know he said I should wait for an invitation, but Angel's confession, no matter how contrived it might have been, has awakened something in me. And I don't want to wait one more second before telling my father that I love him and that I forgive him for leaving. I want him to know I will always be here, waiting for him to come to me.

When I knock, my father's wife opens the door and pulls me inside.

"What the hell do you think you're doing?" she asks, pushing me forward, into the small living room of her home.

"What do you mean?" I ask, rubbing my forearm because she grabbed me so hard her fake fingernails scratched my skin.

Samantha glares at me. Her green contact lenses glimmer in the sunlight as she peeks out the window discreetly. Then she calls for my father, whose disheveled hair tells me he was in the middle of a nap.

"What is it?" he asks. "What's going on?"

"Tell her!" Samantha demands of my father. "Tell her she can't come around here like this. Tell her, Enrique!"

My father accepts my hug. "Sitlali, m'ija. I told you on the phone. You can't come over here. Okay?"

"Oh, for heaven's sake!" Samantha throws her arms up in the air. The silver bracelets on her forearms jingle against each other. "You are putting us in danger! These jealous bitches around here, they are just waiting for a reason to call the cops."

"Cálmate, mujer." My father puts his arms around his wife and kisses her temple.

"They don't like me," she whimpers. "You know they've never liked me."

"I know." My father caresses her blond locks.

Samantha glares at me. "And you! You are just the reason they need to call ICE. Is that what you want? You want ICE to take my children's father away? You selfish little bitch!"

"No!" I say, looking at my father.

Samantha's mascara has started running. She looks like one of those women on the soap operas. I suspect this isn't her first performance, as she shivers and whimpers and clings to my father's shoulders. "Make her go away, Enrique!" she cries. "Please. I can't live without you. I need you. The boys need you."

I watch her dramatics and feel more than witness to the deception, the manipulation, lurking behind Samantha's antics, and I shiver. My body thrums with the injustice of it. How dare she use her children's needs against me when I'm the one who's gone without my father for more than a decade?

"Get out! Now! Now!" Samantha cries, over and over again. "Go back where you came from!"

"Xiwiki. Come." My father puts his hand on my elbow and guides me to the door. But when he opens it and stands there, waiting for me to leave, the knot in my throat won't let me talk. I feel like I'm living in a nightmare. How is it possible that in my father's eyes I am the unwanted, the banished?

Suddenly, the anger and resentment I have been repressing all these years comes to life. Like a dark leopard, a hungry panther, it awakens in my belly and starts to claw its way up to my throat. I hold my lips tightly closed, because I don't want to know what will happen if I let the panther roar. But Samantha won't stop crying and shaking her head, doubled over, holding herself up against the back of the couch, as if she's in agony.

The theatrics make me sick, and I blink through the pain I feel tearing me up from the inside out. Tears start to form in my eyes. Then, because I can't help it, because I can't fall prey to one more injustice in my life, I do it. I open my mouth and roar.

"No!" I step away from the door and scream at Samantha. "No! I'm not leaving! Not now. Not ever."

"Sitlali," my father begs, as he closes the door quickly so the neighbors won't hear us. "Please, m'ija. Don't make a scene."

Horrified, I turn on him. "You think *I'm* the one making a scene?"

"You are!" Samantha cries, still playing with my father's heart, bending it to her will. "This is my house. Our house. You can't just walk in here anytime you want!"

"He's my father too," I tell her, as I go around my father to face her. "You can't erase me. I have a right to see him too. Those are my brothers in there. They deserve to know me, to build a relationship with me. I'm their sister."

I can see that I've hit a nerve because, miraculously, Samantha's pain disappears. She unbends, pushes herself off the couch, and throws her shoulders back. Eyes piercing, thick tears glistening, she sees me—for the first time since I arrived at her doorstep, she really sees me—daring her to deny my existence, daring her to erase me.

"I. Said. Get. Oooout!" Samantha screams, and then, unexpectedly, she rushes at me. Enraged, she grabs my hair and pulls on it, unmooring me long enough to wrap her arms around me and push me against the wall.

I struggle to get away from her because I don't want to fight.

This is not what I came here to do.

"Samantha!" my father screams. "Stop. Please."

"Let me go," I tell her, pushing back and trying to escape her grip. "I don't want to hurt you."

"Shut up!" Samantha puts her hand over my mouth and whispers into my ear, "Nobody wants you here. You understand? Nobody."

I struggle, try to pull her hand away, but because she is leveraging me against her shoulder now, I can't pry myself free. I can breathe, because her hand is not covering my nose, but I swear I'm not getting enough oxygen. My blood is pumping so hard against my eardrums I feel dizzy, and I can't see straight.

That's when my father steps in. He puts his hands on Samantha's wrists and leans in to speak to her. "That's enough," he says urgently. "Let her go. She's my daughter. I'll deal with her."

Samantha removes her hand from my lips, and I take a ragged breath. "Deal with me?" I ask him when I can speak again. "You'll *deal* with me?"

"I didn't mean . . . That came out wrong," my father starts.

"I'm not here to be dealt with," I tell him. "I'm here to be with you, to get to know you, to build a life with you! I'm a good daughter. You'd know that if you hadn't left. You'd know that if you hadn't abandoned us!"

My father looks cornered. His eyes shift over at Samantha, a look of desperation in his eyes. I don't know what that look between them means, but I am done trying to talk to him. Done trying to find a middle ground. Done trying to make my way back to him.

So, I rush out the door and run down the street, past the neighbors' blank stares, past the dogs barking and the cars honking. I run the past right out of myself until, exhausted, I stop. At a corner far away from my father's house, I sit on a bench in a bus shelter and wait for a ride.

Across from me, five hundred years away, Calizto makes defensive moves and trains hard. I watch him from my seat in this time, unmoving, unfeeling, until the bus picks me up and I head back to Von Ormy.

I'm waiting for my madrina to get home from work when I see Calizto again. He tells me he is happy to return to his quarters in the palace, because today has been long and he's very tired. I watch him eat and lie down to rest, and he listens to me relay the horrible scene with my father.

Calizto tries to assuage my anger. *Don't despair. He will come to see his mistake soon enough.*

Someone enters Calizto's room, but I can't see or hear them. "Who is it? Have they come for you already?"

No. It is . . . my empress. She has been meeting with Ofirin often. But to me, she is cold . . . clearly upset about the loss of her half brothers.

"She doesn't blame you for that, I hope."

I believe she does, he admits. *Still, she just asked me to thank the goddess for her protection.*

A car drives up to the house, and I lean over and pull the curtain back.

"It's my madrina," I say.

Go, Little Star. I'll be here when you return. Calizto nods and turns away.

I look at the bruises on his back, arms, and thighs, and something inside me melts. I want to reach out and rub soothing ointment all over him.

Your tender touch would soothe more than my muscles, my sweet. Your soft caress would restore my spirit.

Rest, I say, my cheeks warming because I forgot that he can read more than my mind. He can feel my emotions. *I'll talk to you tonight.*

Yes, he says. *I would like to share one more peaceful night by your side, before . . .*

The way his words trail off unnerves me. *Before what, Calizto?*

Then he finishes his thought, and the words, when he finally gives them voice, break my heart into a million pieces. *Before I have to go into battle.*

CHAPTER THIRTY

Calizto

Day 8-Flower of the Year 3-House (June 29, 1521)

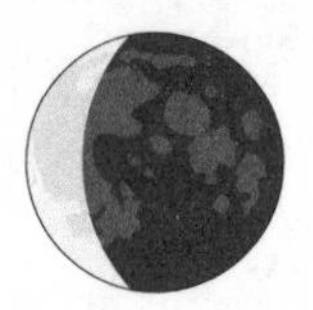

Not long after midnight, my shield-bearer Cemiquiz arrives.

With his help, I don my war gear. I ignore the feathered standard, strapping sword and sheath to my back instead. *Tomorrow will be a day of stealth*, Ehcatzin told us. *Come ready to kill or die. Leave all else behind.*

"Take my shield," I tell Cemiquiz. "And this."

I've put the conch in my mother's wooden box and stowed it in my bag. I need it near me but can no longer risk its being damaged.

She owns my heart now.

"Guard this with your life," I growl. "Or I'll kill you myself."

Cemiquiz swallows and nods. Then he leads me to the staging area, between the palace and the Great Pyramid of Tlatelolco. The moon is a sliver of silver, harbinger of solitude and silence.

The other nineteen assemble with little sound. Our captain nods and gives the signal to march two by two. Behind us come our handful of shield-bearers, bearing replacement razors, water, and other necessities.

We've been assigned to the northern causeway. Near the black volcanic rock of Tezontlemacoyan Temple, we find a unit of Shorn Ones. Ehcatzin has us split into squads: two on either side of the avenue, one hidden under the bridge of the canal north of us.

Soon other Otontin, Jaguar, and Eagle units arrive, hiding among the ruins. Farther back, I can make out archers and spearmen, taking up positions within bowshot of the enemy's route.

Now comes the uneasy wait. Sitlali could not determine precisely when Alderete comes marching up this road. Just that it happens before dawn.

I search for her sleeping form, but then I remember.

She's faded. All that is left is her voice, her heart.

I must survive this day. I need to see her again.

"Eighty Caxtiltecah," Ehcatzin said in his final briefing. "Eight mounted. Another one hundred Tlaxcaltecah. Kill those dogs. But let's take some of the bearded sons of bitches captive. We'll bind them, have the shield-bearers carry them. The emperor has special plans for any prisoners, and rewards for those who take them."

I picture women and children, slipping like mice along side streets, getting ready to dig out the trenches the enemy must fill to come this far north.

Complicating any retreat.

Risking innocents' lives.

Cuauhtemoc plans to bottle the enemy up. It's our last chance.

"Now or never!" he shouted yesterday evening. "Mexico forever!"

As we crouch, Ehcatzin twirls his preferred weapons, one in each hand: macuahuitzoctli, short wooden swords almost like knives, their triangular heads edged and tipped with obsidian.

Like me, he fights without a shield.

Kill or die.

We feel them first.

The heavy hooves of the horses. The muffled steps of two hundred men.

Then the smells, that peculiar stench of the Caxtiltecah, the wild scent of horseflesh, the warpaint of the Tlaxcaltecah.

The moon has set. Through the inky darkness they come, weapons rattling softly. Starlight glints off metal here and there. A horse snorts its exhaustion.

Suddenly, the air is full of the hushed singing of arrows, blotting out the stars.

Men scream. Horses rear in fright. Shields come up.

Another volley of arrows. Another.

Bodies thud to the ground, writhing or still. As enemy soldiers run toward the source of the attack, the javelineers rush forward from behind us, weapons loaded into their atlatls. With an almost simultaneous grunt, they let their missiles fly. A few rods away, a javelin pierces the armor of a Spaniard, pinning him to the road. A horse collapses, a gurgling whinny dying in its throat.

The Shorn Ones waste not one second. In pairs, they erupt into motion, shattering the enemy's ranks, a flurry of kicks, punches, obsidian knives slashing.

Ehcatzin gives our unit's battle cry, and I draw my sword as I rush into the street.

My first opponent is a Tlaxcaltecatl, bare-chested, armed with a razor-studded club and oak shield. I pivot as he swings, turning my forward momentum into a full spindle. The spin ends with my hamstringing him. Blood spatters my face as he falls. I bash his head in with the blunt tip of my sword.

Whirling, I find myself facing a Spaniard, who lifts his pistol. I bat it away with the flat of my weapon, closing fast as he reaches for his blade. I swing my sword high, slash down across his face and neck.

"Not the Caxtiltecah," shouts Ehcatzin, rushing past me. He hurtles into a knot of Tlaxcaltecah, his blades a blur as he slits throats and opens bellies.

Prisoners. Right.

Suddenly Sitlali awakens in my mind. *Are you fighting?*

Hush, my sweet. All is well. I must focus.

A horse comes thundering at me. I sheathe my sword, crouching.

The Spaniard leans in his saddle, sword extended. I leap into the air, diving toward him.

The sword smashes into my chest, ripping the material of my uniform, but deflected by the quilted armor beneath. I wrap my arms around the man, and we tumble to the ground. The impact knocks the sword from his hand. I lock my arm around his neck, squeezing as his boots flail. In a matter of seconds, he's unconscious.

As if I have summoned him, Cemiquiz hurries to me, using my shield to counter a blow from an enemy club. Together we truss the Spaniard up.

Dawn is breaking. The Jaguar and Eagle Knights are swarming the avenue, having emerged from the canal ahead.

Dozens of enemy combatants lie dead, dying, or bound.

Alderete, upon his white steed, sounds the retreat.

I look over at my captive's horse, which whinnies with fear.

Sitlali, how does one ride a horse?

Um, you put your foot in the stirrup, the leather strap that dangles from the saddle. Then you swing your other leg over the saddle. Grab hold of the pommel, the ball-like anchor at the front of the saddle, with your left hand, and take the reins, the leather straps attached to its face, in your right. Slap your knees against its sides to make it walk. Dig them in to make it run. Pull its head to the left or right to turn.

As she explains, I leap onto the beast.

Ehcatzin sees me, laughs, and climbs on behind me.

"Let's run these bastards down!" he shouts. "Head for their standard-bearer!"

My eyes make out the red Spanish flag, emblazoned with the crown of Castilla.

I spur the startled horse, and we rush forward.

The enemy's retreat grinds to a halt at the breach our women and children have opened, a gap ten rods wide and as deep as two men, already filling with water.

Down the canal come our canoes.

"That's right, you filthy sons of bitches!" Ehcatzin shouts, leaping from the horse and rushing into the confused squirm. His hands move faster than I can see, slicing and stabbing. Then he lets his short swords dangle from their thongs as he wraps his fingers around the haft of the Spanish flag and rips it from the enemy.

"For Mexihtli!" he cries, using the ancient epithet of the war god, for whom Mexico and the Mexica are named.

Alderete, panicked at the forces approaching from all sides, breaks ranks, leading the remaining horsemen across the ruins, toward the road that Sitlali told us Cortés would take.

I yank on the reins and follow.

Our forces have surrounded the leader of the Spaniards and are closing, hard. As I charge into the fray, three Jaguar Knights disarm and seize Cortés, whose face is so covered with blood he barely seems human.

"Cristóbal!" Cortés screams as he's taken captive.

"Release him, savages!" shouts a Spanish swordsman, hurrying toward the knights, blade flashing.

I dig my knees into the horse's flank, trying to intercept him.

If I yank back on the reins, hard?

The horse will rear up, Sitlali says. *You'll fall off if you don't hold on to the pommel and lean into the movement.*

Cristóbal de Olea reaches the knights, swings his sword with precision.

In three quick moves, he has cut the hands off two of them. Cortés jerks back. Another Spaniard grabs him and draws him away.

I'm almost on top of Olea. I yank back on the reins, managing to stay in the saddle as the horse lifts its front hooves into the air.

Then I let go, leaning forward as hard as I can.

The hooves smash into the Spaniard's head and chest, killing him instantly.

A moment of silence. Mexica warriors and enemy combatants alike look up, startled to see an Otomitl Knight astride a stallion.

Then I draw my brother's sword.

"Kill or die," I say between clenched teeth. "Matar o morir, hijos de puta."

By the time the sun is at its zenith, we have slaughtered scores of Tlaxcaltecah and captured dozens of Spaniards.

While my passions roil, Sitlali says little. I sense her routine when Cemiquiz brings the conch near: serving food, chatting with the girls her age that frequent the taquería. She is worried about me, but tries to drown her concern with work.

I drink water and eat something quickly, unwilling to dismount. The others have begun to call me Quiquinaca: the one who neighs.

"Calizto," calls Ehcatzin. "Enough rest, boy."

I look down. He is holding the severed heads of two Spaniards in each hand. Behind him, our unit has moved into marching formation.

Not one of us has fallen.

"Yes, sir," I say. "Your orders?"

"Head west. Sandoval and Alvarado are still making their way toward Tlatelolco. There are brigantines on the lake providing cover."

As if to underscore his statement, a distant roar thrums through the ground.

"We're going to befuddle them, slow them down. The emperor has a show prepared that should chill their foreign blood."

Cemiquiz and the other shield-bearers fall in with us as we make our careful way through the carnage and ruins.

I can feel Sitlali again.

Calizto! I've been scouring the internet, trying to find a mention of you and your fate . . .

I'm fine, Little Star. Your intelligence has given us the upper hand.

That's a relief. I also need to look into ICE and immigration in this messed-up country.

Because of your father, yes? He's living there without legal permission.

Yeah. And they don't just send you back to your country anymore. They lock you up in a cage, like an animal. Even children. They take them away from their parents. Keep them in cold rooms where the light is always shining bright.

The embers of fury in my blood flare up.

Evil. Careful, Sitlali. It would be terrible for your father to be taken. But I'll cleave the very cosmos if you are ever caged. I'll cross the centuries and leagues upon this horse and lay waste to anyone who dares lay a hand on you.

Shhh. It's fine. I'll be fine.

Needing an outlet for the pressure crushing my heart, I dig my knees into the horse's flanks.

Behind me, the knights double their march, unstoppable.

We find Alvarado near the Atezcapan Lagoon, kept from Tlatelolco's Sacred Precinct by hundreds of Mexica soldiers and knights. Behind him on the water is a brigantine, its cannon trained on us.

Alvarado's eyes go wide as he sees me astride the stallion.

In that moment of surprise, Ehcatzin steps out from behind me and lifts the bloody heads into the air.

As if responding to his signal, drums begin to sound atop the Great Pyramid. A sidewise glance tells me the priests stand on its summit, pounding out a ritual beat.

"Translate for me, Calizto."

I nod.

"We have slain your comrades, Cortés and Sandoval!" my captain shouts.

"¡Hemos matado a vuestros compañeros, a Cortés y a Sandoval!" I echo. I can feel the uncomfortable shuffling behind me as my fellow Otontin hear me speak Spanish.

"And thus will you die as well, dogs!"

Ehcatzin hurls the heads at Alvarado's feet.

"Behold!"

Ehcatzin points to the Great Pyramid of Tlatelolco, which was designed for just such a sacred spectacle, visible from afar.

Jaguar and Eagle Knights are force-marching naked Spanish captives up the steps.

In another time, Sitlali tells me she's watching the news with her godmother. I can feel the worry and sadness that threaten to overwhelm her.

The Spanish captives reach the summit. Alvarado's men shout curses.

The world is so bad, Calizto. This wall they've built cuts through entire communities. The raids they do, pulling men and woman from their vital work. Children who never see those parents again. Why? So greedy men and women can hold on to power, accumulate more wealth.

The effigy of Huitzilopochtli is brought from inside the temple. The naked Spaniards are forced to dance before it, leaping and sobbing to the rhythm of the drum.

I don't want this, Calizto. There has to be more to life than this horror, this persecution.

The priests seize one of the Spaniards, push him against the sacrificial stone. His back arcs; his chest is thrust forward.

Even if I finish high school, get my diploma, go to college . . . I will always be looking over my shoulder. One wrong turn, and I could lose everything. Because I'm not a citizen; I'm not a human being in this country. And it scares me, Calizto. It scares me so much.

The head fire priest slices his flint knife across the Spaniard's abdomen, below the ribs. Without hesitation, he plunges his hand in, all the way to the elbow, seizing the captive's heart.

The party, I say, my mouth suddenly dry, my rage spent. *The one Amparo mentioned. Go, Sitlali. Forget this bloody world for a moment.*

I look down at my gore-stained hands. My eyes fill with tears.

Upon the pyramid, the priest hefts the captive's heart and then places it in the sacred basin before motioning to the next victim.

The party? I guess it could be a distraction.

Yes. Look away from the ugliness for a moment.

I turn my horse around and gallop away from Alvarado, my unit, the sacrifices, the carnage.

There has to be more to life than this horror. Sitlali's words echo in my mind and heart.

Passing Cemiquiz, I reach down and pluck the moon conch from his surprised hands.

I'm exhausted. Body and soul.

All I want is to hold the girl I love in my arms.

And the gods will not even permit me that one small solace.

CHAPTER THIRTY-ONE

Sitlali

June 30, 2019

The next morning, I wake up to the sound of my madrina honking, because she's got a carload of groceries. I pull on a T-shirt and pair of jeans and run outside to help her.

"I hope you like pork chops. They were on sale. So, I bought a ton of them," she says as we head into the house, our arms full of bags.

"I like pork chops," I tell her, and we drop the bags on the counter and head back out for the rest of the groceries.

When we're done putting everything away, I turn around to find my mother in the room with me. Dressed in black, Mami is sitting in the living room, across from my madrina, who is busy scrolling through her phone. The only colorful thing on her is the painted butterfly comb that is keeping her hair up in a perfect French twist. Her cheeks are lean and pale, and she looks emaciated.

You're really here, aren't you? I ask. But instead of answering me, my mother turns around and starts to drift away. I follow her into the kitchenette. She looks at her surroundings—the walls, the windows, the kitchen sink, the stove, and the refrigerator; even the ceiling holds more interest for her than I do.

What do you want? I ask her.

My mother looks back at me. Her eyelids droop over her sad eyes in a way that says, *I'm tired of being in this world.* Then she opens her mouth and says, *Caaaa . . . Caaaaall . . . him.*

The long, drawn-out words sound hollow and dense, like she's speaking from the bottom of an old, musty well, a well that hasn't seen the light of day in years.

"What?" I ask, stepping away from her, because her ghostly figure is shifting, wavering, and shivering, as if attempting to pull more words out of herself is a painful, exhausting process.

"Caaaaall . . . yoooour . . . father," my mother wails out loud.

"No!" The word is a frightened shriek that explodes out of my mouth before I can do anything to stop it, and I press my hand against my lips and run out of the kitchen.

"What's going on?" My madrina wraps her arms around me when I bump into her in the hall. "You look like you just saw La Santisima. What's got you so spooked?"

"Nothing," I say. "I'm just . . . I'm still . . ."

"Tired? From the party?" my madrina asks, as she pushes a strand of hair away from my forehead. Because I've gone silent, she lifts her fist, makes the sign of the cross over my face, and says a prayer over me. Then she kisses my temple and says, "Go take a nap. I'll wake you up for dinner."

In my room, I change out of my jeans and throw myself on my bed. I close my eyes and fold my forearms over my face, because I want to keep the sunlight out of my eyes.

Sitlali? My beloved Calizto sounds tense, hurried.

"Calizto! Has something happened?" I sit up in bed with a jolt, knocking my phone off the table and onto the floor.

No. Rather, yes, but it is a good development. The Spanish and their allies have completely retreated to their camp! They are cowering in Castle Xolotl, south of the island. Still, I have called out to you for a different reason.

I slip my legs over the bed, pick up my phone, and check it. It's not broken, so I toss it on the bed. "Do you need me to research the castle?"

Actually, I wanted to know if you know anything else about horses beyond how to ride them.

"It depends," I say. "I mean, I don't know historical stuff, like what kinds of horses the Spanish brought over. But I know horses well enough. We used to have one when I was young."

Good. This beast I have obtained is a fine animal, but I have no idea how to keep him healthy, what to feed him, how to best care for him.

"Oh, that's easy. Have you taken off the saddle?"

This mounting gear?

"Yes. You need to take his saddle off. There should be some kind of blanket under it. Take that off too. He'll need a big bucket of water and some food."

Food? Yes, of course. Um . . . What sort of food?

"Oh, that's even easier," I tell him. "Horses eat grasses and hay, like cows and goats. The best thing to do is tie him under a shady tree somewhere and let him graze. He'll eat what he likes."

And shelter? Calizto asks. *How do these creatures sleep?*

I giggle. "They lie down, like you and me. He'll need an enclosed space with a roof and a gate to keep him from wandering off."

Calizto thanks me. *I'll do my best to provide for him.*

After my communication with Calizto cuts off, I get up and do some research. Yup. Everything I told him off the top of my head was true. There's not much more he could do for the horse without an expert's assistance. For the rest of the afternoon, I get caught up looking for information on horseshoeing, but I can't find anything that tells me if or how the Spanish horses were shoed five hundred years ago.

By the time my madrina calls me out for dinner, I am so "informed" that my mind is a jumbled mess. So, once again, I am shocked and confused by the sight of my silent mother sitting on the recliner in the living room.

"Well? Are you going to sit with me? I made us some taquitos." My madrina pushes a paper plate toward me on the coffee table.

I smile and go sit beside my madrina. She picks up her soft drink and folds her legs under her. Then she flips through several channels before she settles on a variety show. I pull the plate of food toward me, staring at my mother the whole time.

My mother lifts her chin and stares back at me.

"What?" I mouth the word to her.

My mother presses her lips tightly. Her eyebrows are knit tightly together over her dark, narrowed eyes, and I can tell she's not happy with me.

"Caaaall him!" she screams.

The sound of her voice is so loud, so violent, it bounces off the walls, and I jerk back, startled. My madrina sits up straight. She puts her hand out and touches my shoulder. I shake my head, over and over again.

"No. No. No," I tell my mother.

"Sitlali?" my madrina whispers my name.

"I have to go," I say.

My madrina puts her soda down on the coffee table. "Go where?" she asks. "It's late."

"I have to call my father," I tell her.

Her eyes soften.

"Oh, darling," she whispers. "Are you sure that's the best idea? I mean, I thought we agreed he needs more time."

"Caaall him!" my mother screams again, and I jump with a start.

"Why are you doing this to me?" I ask my mother. "You're supposed to love me."

"I do love you," my madrina says, getting up and putting her arms around me.

"Not you," I cry as I cling to my madrina and hide my face in the curve of her shoulder. "My mother. My mother."

My madrina pulls back her head and looks at me closely. "Oh, honey, your mother did love you," she says, as she strokes my hair. "She just . . . Well, it's hard to know what was going on with her."

"My father left her," I whisper. "And now . . . now . . . she's . . ."

"She's gone, I know." My madrina nods. "But all you can do now is try to forgive her. Release her, Sitlali. Strange, dark things happen to a woman's heart when a man abandons her. I'm sorry you had to go through that horrible trauma with her. But I'm here for you now. And I love you. I love you as if you were my own daughter. And not just because I signed a paper in front of God and everybody when I baptized you . . . I really, really do love you, m'ija."

My madrina's words move me to tears, and I weep into her shoulder. When I am done weeping, my madrina lets me go, and I turn around to see that my mother is crying too. Her silvery, transparent tears glisten against her thin, ghostly face, and I let out a long, shivering sigh that sounds like a whimper.

"He's your father," my mother whispers, and her voice is perfectly normal now. Apart from the slight emotional tremble, she sounds exactly as I remember her. "He has to talk to you. He has to."

I nod and press my hands against my eyes, wiping the tears away.

"I have to call my father," I tell my madrina. "One last time. To let him know I'm here when he's ready to talk. It's all I can do."

"Yes." My madrina lets out a breathy sigh and kisses my forehead. "That's good."

Alone, in my room, I dial my father's number and wait. The phone rings and rings. It goes to voice mail, but the box is full, so I can't leave a message. I hang up and dial his number again. Finally, on the third try, Samantha answers.

"What?" she asks, her voice tart, full of disgust for me.

"This is Sitlali," I say.

"I know!" Samantha hisses. I can almost hear her rolling her eyes at me.

"Will you please tell my father that I need to talk to him?" I beg. "Tell him I'll meet him anywhere he wants. It doesn't have to be your house."

"Are you crazy?" Samantha says. "He doesn't have time to take off and go meet with you. He works all day. And when he's done, he has to come home to be with his children, here, in our home."

"Of course," I say. "Thank you."

The realization that I will never be allowed to be part of the family hits me hard. So, I lie on my bed and force myself to breathe, to inhale and exhale, to allow myself to live with the knowledge that I have been replaced.

Half an hour later, my madrina knocks on the door.

"Come in," I say, and she tiptoes across the room and puts my plate of tacos and a bottle of pineapple soda beside me on the desk.

Then she looks at the computer and asks, "What are you looking for?"

I click on a tab on the corner of the screen and point to a website that shows a map of Tenochtitlan. "I was reading up on our history," I say, but I don't tell her that tomorrow I have to talk to the emperor. What would happen, I wonder, if she knew about Calizto?

"That's interesting," she says, and she pushes the plate of tacos closer to my hand. "Maybe tomorrow, I'll show you some websites where you can read some American history. You know, the kind of things you'll need to know to prepare yourself for school."

"Yeah, I know about your history," I say. "It's a little different from the way we tell it."

My madrina laughs. "Well, it's all a matter of perspective, isn't it? But it can't hurt to hear what the other side has to say, does it? That way, you can make up your own mind. See things from your own personal point of view."

"Sure," I say. "We'll talk about it tomorrow . . . or the next day . . . or . . ."

"Later. You let me know when you're ready, okay?" My madrina leans down and kisses the crown of my head. She smooths down my hair and turns to leave.

"Madrina?" I call out after her. "I love you too. Very much."

When she leaves, I turn back to my computer and read while I eat my tacos.

Are you eating late too? Calizto's voice slips into my thoughts, and I almost choke on my food. I cough and take a swig of my soda.

Yes, I tell him. "I got busy reading up on the events of August 13, 1521."

The day the island will fall . . . Calizto's emotions wash over me. I can feel his sadness seep into my skin, and I sigh.

I put the soda aside and shift in my seat at the desk. "I thought maybe yesterday's victory might have changed the course of history," I tell him.

However . . .

"Nothing's changed. Every website tells the same story. The island will fall in a month and a half. I'm sorry. I've failed you."

Calizto pauses. Sighs. *You've brought us great joy, my sweet. Tonight, the Mexica celebrate wildly in the streets of Tenochtitlan and Tlatelolco. We feast and dance and rejoice. I'm glad they have this reprieve. Though eventual defeat might be recorded in your annals of history, this moment of triumph, this small measure of pride, can never be taken from them. And that will have to be enough.*

"For now. For this moment—only this moment," I tell him. "Nothing is over until the moon stops shining forever."

Melancholy seeps from his heart across the centuries and fills my eyes with tears.

Ah, but my sweetest Sitlali, he whispers sadly, *from where I sit, the sliver of moon has already been effaced by clouds. Rain is falling, ceaseless and heavy. The world is plunged into darkness.*

I want to comfort him, to ease the horror of battle that has shocked him so deeply.

But the moon has disappeared in Von Ormy, too, and dark, heavy clouds block the stars in my part of the sky.

CHAPTER THIRTY-TWO

Calizto

Day 10-Wind of the Year 3-House (July 1, 1521)

In my dream, Sitlali lies in her bath, head back, eyes closed. It is dim, but the curves of her breasts and legs are clear just below the surface. I take a step toward her, loosening my loincloth. Slowly, her eyelids rise. She stares at me with the same hunger that knots in my gut and quickens my blood. Lifting her hand from the rim of the bath, she gestures me closer . . .

"Calizto!"

I jerk awake with a start. Ofirin is standing nearby.

"Quit moaning and come eat breakfast," he snaps.

Cursing under my breath, I wait until my body has fully left the realm of my dream. Then I visit the washroom to scrub at my teeth with a cranesbill root smeared with copal paste, rinsing with salty charcoal water. Afterward, I wash my face and hands carefully. Once I have completely scoured the night away and hopefully frustrated Ofirin in the process, I emerge.

"Well, I left you some atolli, but I ate both the boiled quail eggs," he says. "Tecuichpo has urged me to keep my strength up."

I sit cross-legged at the table and take up a bowl of atolli. "I hope you're not so uncouth as to call my empress by her name to her face. I've taught you better."

Ofirin scoffs, sipping from a gourd of water. "She'll always be Imperial Majesty to me, Calizto. Don't worry."

"What does she even discuss with you?"

"She wants to know everything she can about the Spaniards, Europe, Catholicism. I've begun to teach her the Latin alphabet too."

With deliberate slowness, I break off a piece of tortilla and scoop atolli into my mouth.

"So, you hope to become her official foreign scribe and translator?"

He shrugs. "Perhaps. She said it's 'xopan,' and our lessons will give her something to do during the long afternoons."

"Ah, the rainy season's arrived."

Ugh, Sitlali groans in my mind, awakening. *I wish it would rain here. It's been cloudy, but nothing but a few droplets fall.*

Good morning, Little Star. I'm sorry you are struggling with drought and heat. The rain god is probably angered by that country's stupidity.

Ha. That would make sense.

"Tell her I said hello," Ofirin mumbles around a mouthful of tortilla.

Ofirin sends greetings.

Give him a big hug for me.

I glance at my friend, who is licking his fingers. "She wishes you a productive day."

Sitlali, Ofirin has become too comfortable, providing counsel and tutoring to my empress. He seems to forget the very real danger we face. The date that looms before us.

Let me guess. The Indigenous allies of the Spanish are leaving, right? Heading home?

Yes. My captain met with us late last night. Everyone is certain the siege is over.

Well, it's not, Calizto. Not by a long shot. There won't be any real attacks for a couple of weeks, just a quick incursion by a small group of Tlaxcaltecah. I can't figure out when, exactly. But you all can't just stay on that island and pretend you've won. Experts agree that this is Cuauhtemoc's biggest mistake, his missed opportunity. He needs to go after the Spanish and attack their camps.

I relay this information to Ofirin, who hunches his shoulders. "She has to convince him, Calizto. The emperor has to win. I can't go back. Won't be enslaved again."

I put my hand on his. "No matter what, friend, we'll find a way to keep you out of their clutches."

Sitlali finishes work just as our unit ends our morning drills. We both eat and then bathe—she in her godmother's shower, I in the Otontin Knights temazcalli. Then I drape my new cloak over one shoulder, slip on my white sandals, and visit the emperor.

The meeting chamber is nearly empty. Gone are the scribes and minor officials, all presumably taking a long-deserved rest.

Lord Cuauhtemoc sits on his throne, talking to Prime Minister Tlacotzin. As I enter, conch in hand, he gestures me toward him. Tlacotzin grimaces with distaste.

"Beloved younger brother," he says, paying me a reverence I could never have expected. "Herald of Coyolxauhqui. It is good to see you. Reports of your bravery and prowess on the battlefield have reached my ears. Truly, you are a treasure of the Mexica."

I bow low. "I serve my people, my emperor, and my gods."

"Speaking of which," Cuauhtemoc says, gesturing at the moon conch, "is Coyolxauhqui willing to speak to me?"

"Yes, Your Imperial Majesty. May I approach?"

"You may."

I climb the dais, extending the sacred trumpet. He lays a hand on it.

"Where are you, Mother Moon?" he asks.

Sitlali's voice drifts into our minds, softer than this morning. Stronger than a whisper, but only by a little.

I am above you, as always, child. But my light is dim, my face covered by clouds. You can only hear my voice today.

Cuauhtemoc frowns. "Your people revere and praise you, Coyolxauhqui. You have brought us a mighty victory. We have vanquished the Caxtiltecah."

You have driven them from the island, yes. Yet you must not rest too long, Cuauhtemoc. You need to strike at their heart. Merely one hundred and twenty men from Anahuac remain to support the barbarians. Should you not act to crush Cortés at once, however, those numbers will swell again. It will be the end of you and the Mexica people.

"Goddess, I shall obey you . . . when we are ready. At the moment, my troops are exhausted from months of sustained warfare. They need time to fully regain their necessary strength. And we require allies, so I—"

Yes, Sitlali cuts him off, exasperated. *I know. You have sent the decapitated heads and severed hands of Caxtiltecah captives to Chalco, Xochimilco, Cuauhnahuac. "Behold the might of Huitzilopochtli," you have told them, as if it were not I who aided you.*

Cuauhtemoc is visibly disoriented. I suspect very few people know of these plans, so any doubts he has about the reality of these visions have been undermined by Sitlali's strategy.

"I beg your pardon, but they would never respond to the idea that Huitzilopochtli's sister . . ."

Ah, but you think they will be impressed by the five foreign archers you have kept alive, who have promised to teach you the secrets of the

Caxtiltecah bow, who swear they will fire upon their countrymen. They are lying to you, child. They will never kill one of their own.

"As you say, Mother Moon. Yet the men of Malinalco . . ."

. . . will be prevented from arriving by Andrés de Tapia, once he has finished bringing Cuauhnahuac to heel. And you may as well forget the support promised by Matlatzinco: Sandoval has been sent to stop them. Why do you doubt one who knows your future? Why do you not act, now, while Cortés languishes without his captains, fearing what you might do? Soon Alonso de Ojeda and his Tlaxcaltecah bride will return to Tlaxcallan for reinforcements and supplies. Your moment is NOW. *Do not be a fool.*

Something twists in Cuauhtemoc's face. With a grunt, he pulls his hand away.

Then he curls it into a fist.

"Witchcraft," he mutters to himself, nodding. "You were right, Tlacotzin. I cannot simply accept what this voice tells me."

"No, Your Imperial Highness," answers the prime minister, giving me a twisted grin. "Trust instead your instincts, the counsel of your lords."

The emperor's eyes narrow as he looks at me. "My wife has become entirely too devoted to that slave of yours. See to it that he knows his place. Know yours as well. Go."

I pull the conch to my chest, hesitating.

Oh, shit, Sitlali whispers.

"Go!" the emperor shouts.

I turn and stride from the chamber, my pulse thundering in my ears.

That evening, Sitlali, Ofirin, and I confer, trying to determine our next steps.

You've got to be careful, Sitlali warns, terror curdling in her heart.

Yes, I reply. *One misstep, and Cuauhtemoc will have us both killed. It's clearly what the prime minister wants. Our divine advice has enraged him. Possibly the council too.*

Ofirin nods. *You've made them irrelevant. That's dangerous. I was ready to stay, Calizto. To hope history would change. To watch you fight for our freedom against the Spanish.*

That's not an option anymore, Sitlali says firmly. *I want you away from there, do you understand me, Calizto? I can't . . . I can't bear the thought . . . It would kill me, too.*

I sigh. *Hush, Little Star. In two days, my unit's stint begins. Patrolling the ruins at night. I'll arrange to separate myself from my squad and escape with Ofirin. Somehow, on horseback or in a canoe, we'll leave this island before it falls. I swear it.*

CHAPTER THIRTY-THREE

Sitlali

July 2–3, 2019

I'm in the middle of my shift, busing a table, clearing away dishes, napkins, and those little plastic containers of salsa that spill everywhere, when my phone starts vibrating. I don't recognize the number, so I put it in my pocket.

When I'm done with the table, I head to the kitchen without looking back. I don't want to give anyone the impression that I'm slacking. Manuel watches me set the tray of dirty dishes down beside the sink for Felix to wash, and he whistles and points to a new bag of Styrofoam containers sitting against the wall. I grab them and replenish the tray beside his grill.

"Three to go," he says, and he points to the food waiting to be packaged and sent out for delivery.

For the next two hours, Manuel, Señor Jiménez, and I work quickly to fill and send out the rush hour delivery order. And when I finally get a moment to breathe, I take my break. Drinking a cup of coffee, in a corner booth, by myself, I zone out and call to Calizto in my mind.

Little Star?

His voice is faint. He sounds like he's talking to me from farther away than before. "Can you hear me?"

Not as well as before, he says. *There is much commotion here. I've been training all morning. But the prime minister is never far, and his eyes are always upon me. I think he lies in wait, looking for a false move on my part.*

"Let him wait!" I tell him. "You know you've done nothing wrong."

I know. I just have to make it through this day. As I promised you, tomorrow I will find the right moment to escape.

At that very instant, my phone starts to vibrate again, and I pull it out and look at it absently. "Oh my God!"

What is it? Has something happened?

"I think . . . I think my father's calling."

Speak to him, Calizto urges.

My heart beats furiously in my chest as I answer the phone. "Yes?"

"Sitlali?" My father sounds uncertain. "How are you?"

"Um . . . I'm okay. Just working."

"Oh, you're at work? I'm sorry. I didn't know," he says, and then he's silent, like he's thinking about what to say next.

"It's okay," I tell him. "I'm on a break."

"Oh, good." He sounds relieved. "Well, I was wondering if you would like to join us for dinner tomorrow."

My heart skips a beat, and now I can't stop smiling. "Dinner? Really? Yes! Yes. I'd love to."

My father clears his throat. "I have to work the night shift at the warehouse on the Fourth of July, so we won't be celebrating that day. But we want to take the boys to dinner and a late movie on the third. Is that something you'd like to do?"

"Dinner and a movie!" I practically squeal at the idea of spending some time with not just my father, but also his family. "Yes. Yes. I would like that very much."

"Good. Good," my father says. "We're going to El Sueño, a small mom-and-pop place on Flores Street, downtown. Can you be there by six tomorrow? You're not working tomorrow, are you?"

"No," I tell him, swallowing hard and clearing my throat, because, in that moment, I am having *all the emotions.* And I'm quite overwhelmed. "I mean, yes. But I get out at five, so I can definitely meet you there."

"That's great, m'ija! We'll see you then," my father says, and he hangs up.

And just like that my life does a somersault, and I land with my feet firmly planted in my new world. When I get home, I can't contain my excitement, and I blurt it all out for my madrina in one long string of words that burst from me all at once.

"That's wonderful!" My madrina hugs me, and we do a little dance in the living room. When we are done celebrating, she says, "You'll need a new outfit. Let's go to the mall."

"The mall? Are you sure it's safe?"

"Yes," my madrina says. "You just have to mind your own business. Go in, buy what you need, and get out." And she picks up her purse, and we head out the door.

At South Park Mall, we visit several crowded stores until we find a very nice summer dress. They have it in navy and pink, but I take the pink because it just makes me feel beautiful to put it on. My madrina smiles and nods when she sees me flouncing the skirt in front of the dressing room mirror.

"He's going to love seeing you in this."

My madrina plays with my hair so that it falls down my back in a nice cascade of waves and curls. And for a moment, I think she's talking about Calizto. Then I remember he is in great danger and promise to speak to him as soon as I get back.

We leave the dressing room and weave around the store, looking through the racks absently, when I notice that a man in uniform is staring at us as he speaks into a handheld device. I turn to give him my back at the same time that I tap my madrina on the shoulder and gesture for her that we are being watched.

My madrina starts talking in English to me loud enough to be heard by the officer. She shows me a dress, laughs, and prattles on, and I nod and laugh as if I know what she's talking about. Then, very discreetly, we move away from the dress rack and take the escalator down to the first floor.

Because the uniformed officer didn't follow us, we relax while we wait to pay. My madrina Tomasa picks up a pink, iridescent lipstick, a volumizing mascara, and a pink seashell necklace from the discount rack by the register and pays for it all.

"Madrina!" I complain. "You don't have to do that. I have money."

My madrina puts her arm around my waist and pulls me in close. "I know. But how often do I get to treat my beautiful goddaughter? Not often. So, don't complain, okay?"

"Thank you," I tell her, and she squeezes me tight.

"You can buy me an ice cream cone on the way home, okay?" she says as we walk away from the register and through the sighing electric door.

Because my madrina and I are so exhausted, we eat a quick bite and turn in for the night by ten. As I lie in bed, missing the moon that usually hangs in the sky outside my window, I decide to invoke the Virgen de Guadalupe. First, I thank her for softening my father's heart and for the opportunity to meet and spend time with his family—my family now. Then, I pray earnestly for Calizto's security.

I fall asleep while I am still in prayer. But even my faithful prayers do not keep the darkness away. My dreams turn to nightmares, and I wander around in the Chihuahuan Desert again, lost, ravaged by hunger, with a wounded arm. Around and around I go, walking in circles, dragging my bare feet over grass burs and chancaquillas.

I hear a rattle, *rap, rap, rap* . . . rapping so close that I lift my head slowly, deliberately. I see her first. Fangs glistening with poison tears, she strikes.

I scream.

And when I sit up in the darkness of my room, my heart is a rattler, rap-ap-rapping inside my chest, warning me that something's not right. That I am not alone in the room.

With a trembling hand, I reach over and turn on the lamp on my nightstand. And that's when I see her, my mother, standing over my bed. But something is wrong. She is not the same composed woman she was when I last saw her. Her hair is a wild, tangled mess, and her hands and clothes are filthy with dirt and grime. I make eye contact with those watery, wounded eyes and shake my head, because I'm scared of her.

She reaches for me, and I jerk back, put distance between us.

"What do you want?" I ask her.

My mother looks at me and sighs. Then she turns and stares at me. "Stay away from that woman," she says. "She has nothing but poison in her heart."

"What are you talking about?" I ask her. "What woman?"

At the door, my mother turns back. The light on the lamp flickers, and the light bulb goes out with a loud *pop*. From the darkness, I hear my mother's soft sobs echoing in the stillness and silence in my room.

"Mom?" I call out to her, even though I can't see her. "What woman?"

"His wife!" she screams.

The words reverberate and echo in the room, and I reach over and search for my phone on the nightstand, but it's fallen to the floor. It takes me a few minutes to find it, plug it into the charger, and use the flashlight app to scan the room.

Alone again, I lie back down, but I keep the phone on my chest, to give me light until I can get the ghastly image of my haunted mother out of my mind.

After my heartbeat returns to normal, I get out of bed and go to the kitchen, where I make myself a cup of chamomile tea to soothe my nerves. My madrina finds me sitting by myself in the kitchenette.

"You're just stressed, that's all," my madrina whispers when I tell her I've been seeing my mother for days now. "You're scared of being rejected again. But you can't think like that. You have to remind yourself you've been through the worst of it."

"You're right, of course," I say. "There's nothing to be scared of . . ."

When I'm back in bed, Calizto reaches out to me. *You're troubled, Little Star.*

"You can feel it?" I sit up and look at the clock. It's almost two in the morning.

How could I do anything but feel what you are feeling? he says, and I close my eyes and concentrate, letting Calizto's affections wash over me. *Our hearts are interlaced through time and space, my sweet Sitlali.*

His voice is so quiet that I wonder if he said what I think he said, that he can feel what I feel, that our hearts are interlaced. Heartbroken, I reach over and pull back the curtains. Of course! The moon has almost disappeared! We were right to think that our connection is tied to its phases.

Sitlali? Are you still there?

"Yes. It's just that . . . I can barely hear you now. And I'm worried. The moon is completely gone. Calizto? Is this it? Is this the last time we will . . . ?"

Be able to speak or see or . . . touch, ever again?

"Is it?"

I cannot be sure, he says. Though I can hear the fear in his words. *But I meant what I said before. About our hearts . . .*

"Interlaced through time and space . . ."

Yes. No matter what the new moon may bring, you will always be a part of me. His voice is so weak, so, so far away, it's nothing more than a silvery, moonlit whisper, a wisp of emotion. But then, it grows strong again. As if he is willing it to cut through the haze of lost time and space. *I love you, my sweet Sitlali. Through time and space, and everything beyond, I love you,* he whispers.

"I love you too, Calizto!" I confess. "I love you more than anything else in the world! Beyond understanding. Beyond logic. Beyond boundaries and borders, I love you!" I tell him, running my words quickly, rushing them together, one after another, before the moon disappears altogether. Though, deep in my heart, I feel our connection break before my words make it across to him.

He didn't hear me.

He doesn't know.

I love him too.

CHAPTER THIRTY-FOUR

Calizto

Days 12-Lizard and 13-Snake of the Year 3-House

(July 3–4, 1521)

In the silence of my unmoored heart, Sitlali's voice echoes.

I love you too.

Sleep does not come easily. My dreams are of unbridgeable chasms.

I awaken with a start before dawn with an awful, dreadful certainty.

Clutching my fists to my mouth, I strangle a howl. It escapes in shudders and tears.

"Calizto?"

In the dimness, I see Ofirin's silhouette.

"Apologies," I rasp.

"A nightmare?"

"No. Sitlali . . . I can no longer hear her."

Ofirin takes my hands in his. "I'm so sorry. It must be hard, even though you knew it might happen."

I'm grateful for his friendship. "What if I never hear her voice again or gaze upon her face? How am I supposed to live without the girl I love?"

"She'll return. When the moon gets bigger in the sky, you'll be reunited."

"And if not?" I cry, despairing.

Ofirin puts his hands on my shoulder now. "Then you do right by her, Calizto."

I squint at him. "What do you mean?"

"She has to find that conch, five hundred years from now. How does it get to that beach, Calizto?"

The realization shocks me.

"I have to take it to the ocean."

"But not alone. We'll go together. No matter what happens, I'm your friend. Your . . . brother."

My shield-bearer knocks.

"Lord Calizto," Cemiquiz mutters. "My apologies, but the prime minister has ordered a change in the patrols. Your unit assembles at dawn."

Tlacotzin suspects me. He's decided to upend whatever plans I may have made.

Yet I can just as easily escape after our patrol as during it. Nothing will stop me from keeping my promises. To my father. To Ofirin. To Sitlali.

Captain Ehcatzin leads us into Tenochtitlan, toward the southern causeway. The emperor has posted guards at the bridges closest to the city, hoping to keep the demoralized enemy at bay, but our job is to make sure none has slipped in. Exhausted, we sweep the neighborhoods. Refugees have begun to return, hoping to rebuild during the lull. For a moment, I imagine Sitlali at my side, helping me clear debris and repair the roof on a simple home. My chest aches with longing not just for her, but for normalcy as well. For a chance to begin again, to surround myself with loved ones and beauty.

Then shouts go up from the causeway.

"After me!" shouts Ehcatzin.

We rush to the road to find the guards retreating from a battalion of Tlaxcaltecah. At its head comes a tall, imposing figure wearing a wooden helmet and a cape of quetzal feathers. He wields a two-handed sword even longer than mine.

"Commander Chichimecatl," breathes Ehcatzin, gripping his short swords grimly. "The right hand of Alvarado. Today he dies."

We sound the alarm: special shouts plus the beating of a drum, summoning the remaining squads.

Tlaxcaltecah and Mexica converge just south of the ceremonial plaza.

The battle is fierce. While I manage to wound several enemy soldiers and kill at least two, around me fall many knights. Tzohuac's arm is nearly severed by a blow from a bladed club, and when Poloc attempts to pull the youth away from the fray, his neck is slashed.

I push through a throng of Tlaxcaltecah, but by the time I reach the soldiers' side, they've bled out, eyes wide and glassy in death.

For hours the battle rages. At one point, the tide seems to turn. Reinforcements have come from the north, Eagle and Jaguar Knights raging with indignant fury. The enemy begins to retreat.

"After them!" shouts Ehcatzin.

But right before the edge of the city, the Tlaxcaltecah drop to the ground.

Beyond them stand some four hundred archers, whom Chichimecatl has stationed upon the bridge, bows drawn.

They loose a storm of arrows at us.

My shield is strapped to my back, so I spin, crouching with my head down. Four missiles slam into the wood and leather. An obsidian point digs into my shoulder, though it does no real harm.

All around, men fall, wounded or dead. Most, however, are crouched together, forming barriers with their shields.

A second volley. Third. Fourth.

Two rods away, my shield-bearer Cemiquiz topples over, his throat pierced.

Then the crouching warriors we pursued leap and fall upon us, killing and capturing many. Ehcatzin, howling, rushes at Chichimecatl.

I follow their combat even as I fend off those who would seize me for sacrifice. My captain is like a ghostly wind, flitting around the bigger enemy commander, his blades nicking and slashing.

Then one of Chichimecatl's men rushes toward them, dropping to slide along the ground under Ehcatzin's attack. With an obsidian knife, he slices the backs of my captain's knees, hamstringing him.

As Ehcatzin topples, Chichimecatl raises his massive broadsword.

I run toward that giant of a man, leaping to cover the last few yards of distance. Soft yet clear, my brother's voice echoes in my memory. "A move of last resort, Calizto."

My feet hit the ground just as my blade meets his.

The obsidian razors shatter. My shoulder is almost wrenched from its socket.

There is a resounding, sickening *crack*.

And my brother's maccuahuitl snaps in two.

Chichimecatl's own sword digs into the surface of the road, deflected. I punch him in the throat. As he doubles over, I grab my captain and drag him away.

"Leave me!" he shouts. "Take the unit and retreat, Calizto."

"Sir, we can transport you. The imperial doctors . . ."

"Can do nothing about this!" he snarls. "I am Ehcatzin, boy. Fast and deadly as a winter wind. I choose holy death upon the burned and flooded battlefield. I'll take as many of them as I can before I wing my way to the sun. By dusk I'll salute your brother for you. Go!"

I rush back to the battle and give the whistled signal.

Then Ehcatzin's last ten knights obey their captain's final command.

By evening, the toll is clear. Hundreds of Mexica have been taken prisoner. When I return to my quarters, Ofirin and I take stock.

"The Tlaxcaltecah left the city at dusk, like Cortés."

"But they're emboldened," I say, holding the empty wooden scabbard my father crafted for my brother's sword. "And the emperor's shocked. He wants to speak to Coyolxauhqui."

"What're you going to do?"

I shrug. "The shattering of my brother's sword is an ill omen. The enemy's just outside the city. We should leave tonight, but I fear the risk, and I am exhausted. I'll simply have to go before him tomorrow and say that the conch is useless while the goddess is gone from the sky."

Ofirin rubs his hand across the stubble on his scalp.

"Shit. And then?"

"Tomorrow night we leave."

I set aside the useless sheath and take up the moon conch. My fingers trace its nine mysterious glyphs.

Squeezing it against my chest, I say a silent prayer.

Keep Sitlali safe. May she face no battles, no challenge she cannot overcome.

The following day, there are no patrols. Word comes that Cuauhtemoc has ordered most soldiers to leave their positions in Tenochtitlan and retreat to Tlatelolco.

After preparing all I can for tonight's escape, I'm summoned by an imperial page. I take up the moon conch and go kneel before my emperor.

"Dear Calizto," Cuauhtemoc says, eyes sunken with worry. "Once again I hear you acquitted yourself well in battle, though your captain fell beneath the blades of the enemy."

I lower my head. "Not before slaying dozens of Tlaxcaltecah."

"Indeed. But we have suffered enough loss. I must entreat the goddess for mercy."

"Your Imperial Majesty, she will not answer you. Her face has gone dark, and she is angered at our disobedience."

He gestures me closer with his hand. "I shall entreat her nonetheless."

I extend the conch. Cuauhtemoc places his hand upon it.

"O mighty Coyolxauhqui, brave in battle, hear my plea. I did not heed your counsel. Now my forces have been dealt a terrible blow. Guide me, Mother Moon."

Silence is all that greets his plea. The emperor waits several moments, his hand tightening on the spirals of the trumpet. Then he releases it. Anger hardens his eyes.

"Then I shall proceed as my advisors suggest. Go back to your quarters. We'll speak again tomorrow."

I bow low and obey.

Outside the palace, I notice a group gathering, what appears at first to be warriors with quilted armor. As I approach, however, I see that these are not veterans gearing up for battle.

They are teenaged girls and women, dressed as soldiers.

For a moment, I stand staring in shock.

"Calizto?" a voice whispers. "Is that you?"

A few strides bring me face-to-face with a pair I had not expected to see again.

Eyolin and Quechol.

"Grandmother!" I cry. "Honored One! What are you doing in such gear?"

Eyolin's lips twist in a smirk. "They made you a cuauhpilli. Why wouldn't they make old women and xochihuahqueh knights, too?"

Quechol takes my hand. "Dear Calizto, the emperor has ordered all over the age of thirteen who are not men or boys to dress as warriors. We'll get some basic training today and then head into Tenochtitlan to patrol so the men can rest."

"Why do you look surprised, Grandson?" Eyolin asks. "Tlatelolco has a reputation for putting its women in harm's way like this."

Quechol ignores her. "What happened? I thought you and Ofirin had escaped."

"The gods had other plans," I whisper. "But we're leaving tonight. Come with us."

The xochihuah shakes their head. "No. We've decided to meet our destiny here. But you have promises to keep. Don't think about us. Leave this island and make a life for yourself. Be happy. In your happiness, we will find contentment."

Their words are almost too much to bear. How many people must I lose?

Kneeling, I kiss their hands, then Eyolin's.

"I'll beg Mother Moon to keep you safe. Take no risks. Hide when the enemy comes."

They both smile, and the dam of my sorrow shatters.

Trying to retain some shred of dignity, I stand and walk away.

Ofirin and I try to sleep. Night falls, bringing rain. At midnight comes the changing of the guard. Taking nothing but the moon conch, leaving behind all the trappings of my knighthood, dressed only in white cotton loincloth and cape, I guide Ofirin out of the palace and to the storeroom where my horse is kept.

The creature whinnies quietly, and I hush it. Ofirin helps me with the saddle, and before long, we are riding through the rain.

Cries go up behind us. Sentinels have seen us leave.

The horse can outrun them all.

I make as if to head west, along the causeway to Tlacopan. But once we reach Tenochtitlan, I swerve east, weaving through shattered neighborhoods. At one point, our path is blocked by a canal, but Ofirin assures me that horses can swim, so we manage to ford it.

At last we reach the eastern docks.

Removing the saddle from its back, I embrace my horse's neck.

"Stay alive. Be free."

Ofirin slaps the creature on its withers, and it thunders off.

"Come, friend," I say, pointing at a canoe. "Let's leave this doomed island."

Heads down, we slowly row through mist and rain. I try to navigate toward the northeast, but gauging direction is difficult.

No stars. No moon. Just a few rods of visibility.

For a moment, it seems we are floating alone on the vast cosmic sea, with nothing around us for thousands of leagues.

Then the Spanish brigantine looms suddenly from the mist.

A half dozen harquebuses point down at us from the gunwale.

PART THREE

BLOOD MOON

CHAPTER THIRTY-FIVE

Sitlali

July 3–4, 2019

All morning long, I'm perturbed because I have not spoken with Calizto since the onset of the new moon. I want to scream and cry and run all the way down the street until I have no more breath left in me. But instead of letting my emotions get the better of me, I tamp down my despair and take out my anger and frustration on the tables I have to scrub at the taquería—even though I just found out they pay me less than minimum wage!

"What's got you all riled up?" Señora Jiménez asks when I reach under her register to organize the supplies she keeps down there.

"Nothing," I tell her.

"This," she says, taking my hand and inspecting my ragged fingernails, "is not nothing."

When I don't say anything, she takes the dishrag out of my hands and pulls her apron over her head. "Come on, time for a break."

Outside, Señora Jiménez lights a cigarette, and we walk briskly down the sidewalk on Zarzamora. "So, what's going on?" she asks. "And please don't tell me it's that pig, Angel. Because I can tell you right now, he's not worth it."

I watch her exhale a cloud of thin, gray smoke. "No," I tell her. "It's nothing like that."

I'm about to tell her I'm mad about her paying undocumented workers less than minimum wage when my phone rings. I pull it out and look at it. It's my father.

"Excuse me," I say as I slide my finger over the screen. "Dad?"

There is a small silence as Señora Jiménez drags on her cigarette and looks absently at cars passing by.

"Sitlali?" the voice on the other end is a disappointment. My heart tightens in my chest, and I make an effort to smile because Señora Jiménez is listening. "It's Samantha. I'm sorry, but there's been a change of plans. We're not going to be able to go to dinner tonight."

Why am I not surprised? What was I expecting? She hates me. She was never going to let me be part of "her" family. *Nothing but poison in her heart*—isn't that what my mother said?

"Oh. Okay." Rage washes over me, but I stand still, letting it drip off slowly, like melting candle wax.

"Your father has to work today, but he still wants to see you," Samantha says. "Can you meet him tomorrow? At Domingo's off 1604? It's close to where you live."

I grin and push the hair away, because the warm summer breeze has curled it around my face. "Yes! I know exactly where that is!"

"Four? Five?" she asks.

"Five," I tell her. "I can leave work early."

Señora Jiménez raises an eyebrow at me, and I smile apologetically because nothing's keeping me away from my father.

When I turn my phone off, Señora Jiménez shakes her head and says, "Come on, break's over."

I start walking, keeping up with her quick pace. "It's okay, isn't it? If I take the day?"

She gives me a sideward gaze and winks. "Sure. I'll talk to the boss for you." Then she pulls a small packet of red cinnamon Chiclets out of her pocket and pops one in her mouth.

When my madrina gets home that evening, she is happy to hear that Samantha is coming around and being more civilized.

"Well, I can still take the day off if you need a ride," my madrina says, as she opens a bottle of pineapple soda and sinks into the couch beside me.

"Oh, gosh, no," I tell her. "It's just down the street. I can walk there. Unless . . . you wanted to see my father."

My madrina Tomasa almost spits out her drink. "No," she says, clearing her throat. "I'll talk to him when he invites us over for Thanksgiving!"

"Thanksgiving?" I frown.

"It's a long story," she says.

I remember our chat at the kitchenette the night before. I push the vision of my mother's ghost out of my mind and shove another spoonful of cold cereal into my mouth.

"Popped corn cereal is a revelation, isn't it?" I ask her. "I mean it's full of sugar, but it's so cold and refreshing. The food of the gods—times five!"

"I wouldn't know," my madrina says. "I never touch the stuff."

"Well, thank you for getting it for me," I say. "It's the only cold cereal I like."

My madrina reaches over and pinches my cheek. "I love you, you know."

I love you, my sweet Sitlali. Through time and space, and everything beyond, I love you. Calizto's words echo in my mind, and my heart tightens inside me. I drop the spoon and press on my chest.

"Hey." My madrina leans over to check on me. "Are you okay?"

"Yes. I'm sorry . . . I was just . . . ," I tell her, taking her hand and kissing it. "I love you too, Madrina. Very much."

I head out to Domingo's early, walking peacefully up K Street, the bag with the moon conch slapping gently against my thigh. As I look at the tiny bits of firework debris scattered on streets, sidewalks, and lawns, I can't help but think about how the Fourth of July is a really big deal here.

The fireworks started last night, right after midnight, and they've been going strong all day. Every few minutes, there's a series of pops or a whistle or some kind of aerial display to celebrate the birth of this nation. But after seeing firsthand everything Calizto is experiencing as the Spanish decimate his world, I can't help but feel a certain amount of apathy for this day's celebration.

When I get up to 1604, I turn into the small dirt and gravel driveway at Domingo's. It's a tiny place, with space for no more than ten cars. Only the place is packed, so some of the customers are parked along the sidewalk at the edge of the property. Somewhere in my subconscious, I flirt with the idea of changing jobs. This place would be closer to us.

I stand under a mesquite and wonder which of these vehicles belongs to my father. Does he drive a truck or car? I look at the time on my phone.

4:30 p.m.

It's possible he's not here yet. It's too hot to be outside, so I put my phone back in my pocket and walk into the restaurant.

It's bigger than I imagined. Somehow, they've managed to make the best of the space, so there are ten tables and two booths in the dining area. The place is decorated with Mexican artifacts, and there are a couple of framed bullfight posters that look like they might be authentic.

4:33.

I sit down at a two-person booth, and the waitress, an older woman with her hair tied back into a neat bun, brings me water and a bowl of chips and salsa. I tell her I'm waiting for someone, and she nods politely and leaves.

4:45.

The waitress comes back and refills my water. "Running late?" she asks.

"No," I tell her. "I'm early."

"You don't want a soda?" she asks, pointing at the cooler with canned and bottled drinks.

"Maybe a Barrilito," I say. "You have tamarindo?"

"We do," she says. "I'll get you one."

4:51.

A tiny ant crawls out from the underside of the table and sits on the edge. She raises herself on her hind legs and lolls her little red body back and forth before she decides to return to where she came from.

4:57.

A gray-blue dove attempts to fly through the window. It crashes against the glass. Tiny claws scratch wildly, wings flutter awkwardly, as it falls to the ground.

5:00.

A pup runs into the taquería. It skitters under tables, sniffing at legs and feet, startling the customers. The little boy at the next table cries. The waitstaff chases the pup from one end of the dining room to the other, until they finally shoo her out.

5:07.

I call my father. It goes straight to voice mail.

"Dad? I'm here. At Domingo's. Everything okay?"

5:16.

My Barrilito is gone. The chips are sitting in the pit of my stomach like broken, jagged rocks. I am so worried I don't react as fast as the others when the kitchen door flies open and a group of darkly clad officers comes rushing in.

I've never been in a raid before, so I don't know what to do.

People stand up, spill drinks, scoop up their children, but there is nowhere to run. Another group of ICE officers is waiting outside the front door. I look at the ones who remain seated. They are scared too, as they pull their wallets and remove picture IDs and driver's licenses.

I have neither.

Hours later, as I sit alone in a small room, waiting to be processed, I realize I'll never see my father again. Even if they hadn't taken all my belongings from me, I couldn't have called him. That would put him in danger.

Without my phone, I can't call my madrina and tell her I'm scared.

In this cold, strange place, not even Calizto can hear me cry.

And he may never hear me again at all.

They have the moon conch.

CHAPTER THIRTY-SIX

Calizto

Day 1-Death and 2-Deer of the Year 3-House (July 5–6, 1521)

It's an odd sensation, being in the belly of a brigantine, able to feel the slight rocking of the water but unable to see any but the puddles of seepage that slosh around with each movement.

"Perhaps we'll get lucky," Ofirin mutters. "This young captain Ruiz may not trust us, but Cortés might think us valuable enough to keep alive."

The *Veillantín* creaks around us, a dismal sound.

"I'm less certain, friend."

Ofirin sighs. "Have you tried reaching out to Sitlali?"

Sighing, I clutch the netted bag to my chest. Inside its wooden box, the conch is quiet.

"No response," I whisper. Then a sob racks my body. "I miss her."

He puts his hand on my shoulder. "Of course. You love her, don't you?"

"More than anything."

At sunrise, we're given bread and water to break our fast. The wind picks up outside, and I can tell the sails have been unfurled by the increase in speed.

"Heading toward shore," Ofirin says.

I pull the conch from its box and study the nine glyphs in the gloom, trying to decipher their meaning.

"Eye? Ear? Maybe hand? Mouth?" I mutter. "If only any of my senses could perceive her."

Then I realize: the first time, I sounded the trumpet, opening the connection.

What if . . . ?

Raising the moon conch to my lips, I blow with all my might.

The sound seems to penetrate the wood of the ship, setting it to thrumming. All around us, the wind howls, spinning the vessel for a moment.

Then the world grows calm.

And I feel her, like a trickle at the back of my mind, seeping in.

I focus every bit of my being onto those faint emotions, seeking to decipher them.

Humiliation. Despair. Impotent anger.

Someone is treating her like an animal.

And there's nothing I can do.

Hold on, beloved! I shout with every fiber of my being, my brain reeling at the effort. *Be strong! I'm still here, within you!*

The *Veillantín* docks at Mexihcaltzinco, where one of the two prongs of the southern causeway meets the peninsula of Iztapalapan. There we are escorted to a muddy stockade and locked in with an assortment of Spanish traitors and captured Mexica soldiers.

Recognizing me as an Otontin Knight, my countrymen bombard me with questions. Being careful to recast Ofirin as a valuable prisoner of war I was transporting to Tlatelolco, I share with them the basics of our recent victory. Then I balance that positive news with a dose of reality: food is nearly gone, fresh water scarce. It will be difficult to hold out more than another couple of weeks.

By nightfall, they've all shared their stories with me. When I ask about escape, they explain that Tlaxcaltecah forces surround us, eager to slay any fleeing enemy. I look for a comfortable spot on some rocks, away from the muck.

Ofirin has also found a place to rest, far enough from both the Spanish and the Mexica. He lets me know with his eyes not to show him friendliness.

Sleep overcomes me. I dream of Sitlali. She lies on the floor in some cold, featureless room, shuddering.

I want to take her in my arms, hold her close, keep her warm and safe, but she dissolves into mist, and I awaken with a start in the darkness.

In the mud beside me sits the moon conch, in its case, kept safe by whatever magic makes men forget about it when it's not before their eyes.

I pray to Coyolxauhqui that it continues whole and undiscovered until I can convey it safely to the coast.

The next morning, we're allowed to wash most of the muck away before being marched to the Spanish camp, sprawling where the causeway broadens and shifts due north, right before the Fortress of Xoloc.

Our guards walk us past horses and pigs, women and slaves hard at work, meager bivouacs and campfires, to the large command tent at the heart of enemy headquarters.

We wait for what seems an eternity. Then we're ushered inside.

I recognize Marquess Cortés, sitting behind a broad table piled with books, letters, and maps. To his left stands a Nahua woman perhaps a year or two older than Sitlali. Though she's lovely and haughty, her eyes reveal the overwhelming weight that rests upon her heart.

Malintzin. The conqueror's tongue, translator of his alien commands. I remember her voice, shouting from the rooftops a year ago, demanding our obedience with that coastal accent. I don't wish to hear it again.

To the right of Cortés stand two armored lieutenants. I recognize one as the man who dragged the marquess away after Cristóbal de Olea rescued him.

Cortés gestures at us with his left hand, and I notice for the first time that he is missing two fingers. A smile tugs at the edges of my mouth.

I hope one of us did that to him.

"Marina," he says, not even turning to look at her. "Ask the Indian whether—"

"I need no translator," I interrupt. "You may use your own . . . Christian tongue."

Cortés lowers his hand and chuckles. "Delightful. But how is it you know Spanish?"

"I taught him, Marquess," Ofirin explains.

"Ah," Cortés says with a nod. "You are Narváez's slave, the one who crossed the mountains to meet us at the gate of Tenochtitlan. I was never clear as to why."

Ofirin's glance tells me not to mention Enaben.

"Whatever his reason," I snap, "you left him behind when we ran you out of the city."

Cortés smooths his beard, leaning back in his chair. "Your tone suggests you've lied about your reasons for escaping the island. What's your name, young knight?"

"Calizto," I growl. "Son of Omaca."

"Where have I seen you before?" Cortés puzzles over me for a while before his eyes light up. "The Indian on horseback! The one who killed de Olea. That was you, wasn't it? I cannot easily forget that superior smirk."

"Good," I say, my heart alight with indignant fire. All Sitlali has told me of his fate bursts from my lips like obsidian wind. "I hope it haunts you until the day you die, twenty-six years from now, shitting blood from dysentery, your lungs filling with fluid as you wait in Sevilla to return to Mexico."

Cortés makes a strangled sound that might be a laugh. "Oh, are you an oracle now, Calizto, son of Omaca? Do your people's false gods whisper the future in your ear?"

I smile fiercely. "Yes, you bastard, they do. And they tell me that in five hundred years, you'll be one of the most despised men in the world."

His barely bridled rage gives way to real mirth. "At least," he manages to say around chortling, "they will still remember me. You should have smashed the hooves of that horse against my face when you had the chance. Even in death, I would have made you immortal, boy."

I make a move to spring at him, but the guard behind me slams the butt of his gun against my head, dropping me to the ground.

My mind reeling with the pain, I slide in and out of consciousness.

Cortés has begun speaking to Ofirin. I cannot focus on the words.

Calizto?

The whisper is so welcome I begin to weep.

Sitlali. Oh, beloved Sitlali. I think I have just condemned myself to death.

What? Where are you?

In the command tent of Cortés.

Opening my eyes, I push myself slightly off the ground. The barrel of the harquebus presses against my back. "Stay down."

"So what say you, Francisco? Whatever intelligence you can

provide in exchange for your freedom. Everyone in this tent knows how the war will end. The question is, how many more people must suffer and die because of the stubbornness of Cuauhtemoc?"

"Dare not," I rasp. "Keep silent, Ofirin."

"Do you really believe," Cortés continues, "that this Mexica boy can keep you safe? You are in my hands, slave. And I know what you did. Your ally Calizto lost loved ones, yes? To the smallpox?"

Ofirin gasps. "Marquess, no, don't. I will tell you everything."

I lift my gaze, my head thundering. Through the blood that drips over my eyes, I glare at Cortés, who is now standing in front of his table.

"I lost everyone. You took them from me. Your steel. Your disease."

Cortés waggles his finger. "Not my disease, no. Narváez brought that plague to these shores. In the body of his personal slave."

Nausea grips my stomach.

Calizto? What can I do?

Francisco de Eguía. Do you recognize the name?

Uh, yes. He was the slave who had smallpox. He died near Veracruz, but not before infecting some Indigenous people. Then it spread.

My head feels like it might explode, from physical and spiritual pain. I want to howl at the universe.

Calizto? Oh my God, your emotions are like acid! What's . . . ?

He. Didn't. Die.

Across the centuries, I feel Sitlali's heart begin to thunder in fear.

Wait! No, beloved, no. Don't let Cortés manipulate you!

I reach back and shove the guard's weapon away, struggling to my feet. I face Ofirin, my features twisting with rage.

"How could you lie to me? How could you live under my parents' roof? How could you accept our food, putting us at risk, when YOU BROUGHT DEATH TO MY PEOPLE?"

Ofirin puts his face in his hands, sobbing.

"Antonio," Cortés says to his lieutenant. "Give the Indian your sword."

"Marquess?"

"Do it."

Antonio de Quiñones unsheathes his falchion and throws it to the ground at my feet.

Steel sword. A fitting replacement. Lying there, awaiting my fist.

Don't pick it up, Calizto. Don't become what he wants.

But I bend to seize the pommel all the same.

"Come on," Cortés goads. "You cannot slay me, boy, but you can certainly cut down the man responsible for the deaths of thousands of your people."

Ofirin lifts his face from his hands and looks me in the eyes. "Calizto, dearest friend, how could I have told you? The damage was done, and I sought to ease your parents' pain, your pain, the best I could. But it wasn't my fault. Among my people, the smallpox doesn't exist, either. When the Spanish and Portuguese began raiding the coast of our kingdom, they also infected many villages with the sickness they carry with them everywhere, though they themselves seldom suffer from it. They took me from my family as a boy. Enslaved me and baptized me, as if their cruel god condones my mistreatment as long as my soul is his. When I fell ill, Don Pánfilo didn't confine me to quarters on the ship. No, he brought me to the beach. And when the poor Totonacs who tried to ease my suffering began to die by the dozens, this evil bastard before you, who urges you to kill me, did nothing."

To focus on his words, I repeat them in my heart as he says them.

Sitlali hears. *He's right, beloved. It's not his fault. He's as much a victim as you are.*

Ofirin steps closer, letting the point of the sword dig into his belly.

Then he starts speaking Nahuatl, and I cannot help the tears that stream down my cheeks as he addresses me with respect, like a commoner would a noble. "Revered Brother, that base foreigner could have stopped the spread of the disease. Yet he *wanted* Your Lordship's people to die, as many as possible. How else could a handful of inept merchants with little military training ever hope to defeat Tenochtitlan, the very foundation of heaven? Nonetheless, I place my life in Your Lordship's hands once more. Spare me or slay me. I'll not gainsay your righteous anger. Only know this, Revered Brother. I love you well. I'll go to my grave grateful for what Your Lordship has risked on my behalf."

In the deadest tone I have ever heard, Malintzin translates this beautiful speech with a single Spanish sentence. "He begs for his life using florid language."

I lower the sword and turn my eyes on her.

You are right, Little Star. Ofirin is not to blame. Yet before me stands Marina, her soul weighted down with the deaths of the innocent. I can slit her throat before anyone stops me.

No! You can't! They'll just kill you, Calizto.

They're going to kill us anyway. We won't leave this tent alive.

Listen to me, damn it. You don't know what I've suffered in these three days away from you. You don't understand what's at risk. I am not *going to lose you today, Calizto. No goddamn way.*

In the tent, everyone stares at me, waiting.

I drop the sword.

Okay, Sitlali. Tell me what to do.

Put. The. Conch. In. That. Bastard's. Hands.

Slowly, so no one shoots or stabs me, I unsling the netted bag and pull the moon conch from the wooden box.

"Marquess," I croak through the pain and despair. "Someone wishes to speak to you."

CHAPTER THIRTY-SEVEN

Sitlali

July 5–6, 2019

Last night, ICE transported two dozen undocumented people, including me, to an unknown destination. They loaded us up, hungry and unbathed, onto a bus. No officer explained what was going on, but some of the others whispered that the San Antonio ICE detention center was too full, so we were being taken to a place on the border.

We finally arrived at the large complex and were herded into something like a warehouse, full of chain-link cages labeled as pods. Separated by gender, we were sorted into the pods in a semblance of order. But the message was clear. ICE saw us as animals. These were our kennels.

Everything had been taken from me. My only link to my country, my beloved, was the fragment of the conch in my pocket. I curled my fingers around it, feeling bereft.

Just when I thought my heart would shatter, I heard a trumpet, distant but clear. And like an answer to my prayers, I felt and heard Calizto again.

Beloved! Be strong! I am still here!

It was enough to lift my spirits as they pushed me into Pod 5, where seventy-two other women tried to maintain their dignity.

Not long after I had settled into a cramped spot along the far "wall" of the fencing, a lawyer named Sara Sifuentes visited our pod, checking on our treatment.

"Is there any way I can get my bag back?" I asked her when she interviewed me.

"I'll work on that. Meantime if you give me your madrina's information, I'll let her know where you are."

The living conditions here are inhumane beyond imagination. Sleep is impossible. Water is scarce. Denied medical attention, sickly, lethargic children cling to their exhausted mothers. The air-conditioning is turned down so low we shiver all night.

When I finally get my bag back, I don't even care that my phone is missing. I have the conch, and, when I hold it close, I let him know I'm here for him.

Directly in front of me, Conchita, the young woman who advocated for me and the rest of the new arrivals to get some water, is watching me. She is sitting back-to-back against her younger sister, Monchi. Both of them hold their knees before them; only Monchi has her head buried in her crossed arms.

I cling to my bag, pressing my hands against the material where the conch lies. Conchita furrows her brows and lifts her chin to silently ask if I am all right.

"Are you sick?" she asks.

I shake my head. "Just tired."

She looks over at her friend on the ground and gently prods her.

"Hey," she tells Lourdes. "Can you sit up? Sitlali needs to lie down."

Lourdes lifts her forearm off her face and stares up at me.

"No, no. I'm fine. Really." And with that, I lean back against the chain-link fence and close my eyes.

An hour later, Calizto keeps thoughts of me close to his heart as he confronts a conquistador.

"Are you afraid to speak to my goddess?" he asks as he holds the conch out to Cortés. "Will your faith crumble before a 'lesser god'?"

Yes, I tell my beloved Calizto. *Challenge him. Dig at his pride. Say whatever you have to say to make him talk to me.*

Calizto's rage washes over me. Cortés's mocking laughter infuriates him.

Don't let him get the best of you, I tell him. *Use his entitlement, his arrogance, to get to him . . . If there is only one God, if the moon goddess doesn't exist, then what's the harm in touching the conch? Ask him, Calizto.*

"Why won't you take it?" Calizto taunts Cortés. "Are you afraid of what you might learn about your destiny, about the God you claim has given you permission to decimate us?"

There is a disruption in Pod 5. I hear a noise, and then everyone is screaming and whistling. My body shakes with the force of the noise, and I open my eyes, startled. Lifting my head, I see what the commotion is all about. The detention officers are trying to stuff six more people in here.

"Can't you see there's no more room?" Conchita yells a few feet away from me.

"What are we supposed to do, sleep on top of each other?" Monchi screams. "We're not beasts! We're human! We have rights!"

"Oh, merciful Lord, please help us!" a woman wails.

Up and down the row of pods, the detainees curse and yell and beg for mercy, for understanding, but the ICE officers' eyes are glazed over. They have no compassion for us.

I turn away from Monchi and Conchita and everyone else screaming and crying in the detention center.

Calizto, darling, please talk to me!

He has weakened. Are you ready, Little Star? He is asking for the conch.

I am, I say. Even though I have not given it any thought, my rage demands I speak to the swine. *Go ahead. Give him the conch!* I tell him. Then I take a deep breath and quickly invoke my beloved Virgen de Guadalupe in my own time. "Give me the right words to speak to this cursed man," I whisper under my breath. "He is wily, but you are wise, Virgencita querida. Please speak through me, share your courageous heart and eloquent thoughts with me, even as I speak to this coward."

Wait for my invocation, Calizto says. *Choose your words wisely, beloved. For they may be the last words I hear in this lifetime.*

Within seconds, I feel Calizto again. His heart thrums in my ears even as Cortés's thoughts begin to trickle in.

"Oh, blessed Mother Moon, Divine Coyolxauhqui, ye of the silver bells! Deliver unto this man your sacred knowledge. Impart to him your divine decree," Calizto chants.

"Yes. Please," Cortés says. "Enlighten me, Moon Goddess. What is it that your heart desires? Should I kneel? Expose my neck? Cut out my own heart to please your devoted son?"

I can feel the braggard's laughter. His words send electric twinges that pull at my nerves. So, I take one last big breath and zero in on what I need to say.

"Well?" Cortés taunts me from five hundred years away.

"Kneeling would be unwise, you blind Spanish moth," I begin. "Your mockery is not welcomed here. I will rip off your head, bathe in your blood, and roll it down my spine before I accept one more insolent word from your putrid mouth."

"What the devil?" Cortés stammers. I can almost smell the fear oozing from him. I can sense the trembling of his lips, the cracking of his shaken spine. He was not expecting to hear much less *feel* anything. "Who is this? How are you . . . ?"

"I am Queen of the Night Sky, Matron of the Moon. Address me with the respect due my divine station or I will bring a poison upon your people greater than the pox you brought upon my children. Be warned. I can wipe your kind off the face of the earth, make your bodies rot where you stand, before you are done taking your next breath."

"This isn't possible!"

Angry and frustrated, I dig deep and channel my Virgencita to speak to the darkness in Cortés's black heart.

"This is your final warning. Neither time nor space will save you from my rage should you continue to defy me."

"Blessed Mother Moon, please be patient," Calizto implores, his voice humble, reverent, a model for Cortés who must be astounded by the way my beloved's lips do not move as he talks. "The Spaniard needs to hear your message. Lead him, Goddess; impart your wisdom to him. Let him see what the cosmos has ordained—for him, for me, for Ofirin. For all humble servants beneath your marbled sky."

"Oh, God in heaven—is this real?" Cortés asks, his words measured, his thoughts confounded.

"Perhaps your lack of true faith keeps you from hearing your God's voice," I mock. "But Calizto is pure of heart, and I will destroy whoever dares lay hands upon my most beloved."

"Moon . . . Goddess, I wasn't trying to . . . ," Cortés begins.

"Then close your foul mouth and listen," I tell him. "Tomorrow, I will speak truth to power. At first light, I will lift the veil of mystery for you and yours. But for this, you must prepare. Fast and set aside time for this meeting, and make others do the same."

Cortés is silent for a moment. But I feel his trepidation pricking over my skin, and I shiver as I clutch the conch through the fabric of my bag tighter than I ever have before.

"Why would you do this?" Cortés asks.

"My motives are beyond your comprehension, Spanish beast," I say, letting my distaste for him slither from my mind to his like a poisoned reptile. "What I do is not for you to understand but to abide. Tomorrow, you will allow my children—Malinalli, Ofirin, and Calizto—to meet. You may provide two guards for Malinalli, but no more, though they must keep their distance as they are not part of the council I wish to address."

"You want to speak to my translator? Why?" Cortés questions.

"Your body shivers, yet your arrogance endures," Calizto tells Cortés. "Be wise, Marquess."

"Listen with an open heart," I warn. "Tomorrow, before I relinquish the sky to my brother, Huitzilopochtli, I will reveal Cuauhtemoc's plan to Malinalli. The knowledge I will impart will be of great benefit to you. In exchange, you will release Ofirin and my dearest Calizto free without harm or fear of retribution. That is my edict, my universal directive. Obey it or die!"

CHAPTER THIRTY-EIGHT

Calizto

Days 2-Deer and 3-Rabbit of the Year 3-House

(July 6–7, 1521)

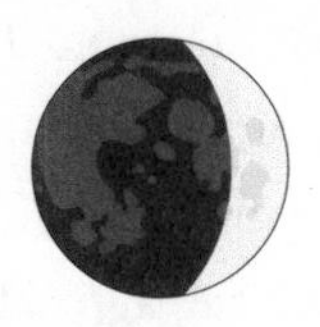

As the guards lead us to a tent set aside for visiting Tlaxcaltecah dignitaries, I send a wave of affection to Sitlali.

Thank you.

She sends me warmth in return.

What will you tell Marina?

I'm not sure. All I know is I cannot—will not—give up on love.

This is why I love you, Little Star. You take the impossible in your hands and wring hope from it.

I love you for your bravery, your endurance, the goodness in your heart, Calizto. Plus . . . you're . . . ah, quite handsome.

I stumble. Ofirin reaches out to steady me. "Are you okay?"

"Just . . . catching up with Sitlali."

And you are extraordinarily beautiful, my sweet. I long to look upon your face again. To hold you in my arms. To feel your lips against mine.

I needed to hear that. Thank you. Things are bleak right now.

Be steadfast, Sitlali. Together, we'll find a way to get you free.

Ofirin and I spend the afternoon discussing the route we'll take once free. His belongings restored to him, my friend reveals the map he has drawn with the help of the empress, who gave him access to the imperial archives in Tlatelolco.

He traces his finger along the Iztapalapan peninsula and into the eastern highlands. "We'll have to avoid Tlaxcallan. I've kept us away from most villages, except a couple that are still loyal to the emperor."

"We can't descend toward the coast too near the Spanish settlement," I point out. "No matter what Cortés agrees to now, he is duplicitous."

Ofirin taps his finger a little to the north of that beach. "While the Totonacs may be less than overjoyed to see me, it's better to risk detection by them."

After dinner, the weight of exhaustion pulls us to the mats. Sitlali and I talk for a while. I try to soothe her anxiety in that cold prison where the light shines bright all night long, but I end up falling asleep before she does.

Sitlali wakes me. *Calizto. They'll be coming for you soon. Don't let them catch you asleep.*

I rub my face vigorously. *Yes. Thank you. How are you this morning? Did you get some sleep?*

Little children cry all through the night. It's hard to rest.

Will you be ready to speak with Malinalli?

Yes. Don't worry, beloved.

Ofirin stirs at the sound of my preparations. Soon we've packed our meager belongings and stand waiting.

At dawn, guards lead us to a larger, more elegant tent. Inside we find

Malintzin, or Doña Marina, as the Spanish call her. This time I look at her more carefully. She is dressed as a noblewoman, though I have heard she was a slave of the Chontal people. She turns to us with an expression of disdain.

"Good morning, Calizto," she says in Spanish. "Francisco. I don't know what sleight of hand or sorcery you used on Don Hernán, but I won't be so easily tricked."

"If you entertain the notion that it might be sorcery," Ofirin points out, "you've already recognized we have power."

"All of us do," she counters, "to some extent or another. Wisdom lies in deploying it in ways that maximize its effectiveness."

Switching to Nahuatl, I interrupt. "As you've proven by helping these foreigners destroy our city. I cannot fathom why."

She laughs, shaking her head in bemused frustration. "The question you should ask is, why *wouldn't* I help them? I was born into a merchant family in a small kingdom where Nahuas and Popolocah live side by side, intermarrying, seeking stability and joy. As a child, I watched imperial tax collectors scoop up the best of our goods, watched imperial soldiers descend on our community to gather up sacrificial victims and slaves. Every year. Without fail."

"Revenge," Ofirin muttered. "If you think the Spaniards are any better, you're mistaken."

Marina shrugs. "They've come to establish an empire. It's the way of the world. One hundred years ago, the Mexica and their allies destroyed the city of Azcapotzalco. That siege lasted one hundred days. At the end, not a house was left standing. The Tepanec Empire fell, and a new one rose to power. Why do the Mexica now weep when the same is done to them? Empires rise, become unjust and corrupt, and get toppled."

"And you would rather stand with those doing the toppling," I snarl.

"Have you seen," she asks, "how the Spanish sprout back up every time they seem cut down? Your people killed *six hundred of them* last year, more than half their number. But by the time we reached Veracruz, reinforcements were waiting in the bay, ships sent from Spain and Cuba. There are hundreds of thousands of them preparing to come, all equipped with tools and weaponry no one in Anahuac can counter. Are you fools? Why would you *not* bend your knees? Do you have a death wish?"

I've been thinking her words to myself so Sitlali can hear. Now my beloved speaks.

Enough. Time for me to handle her.

"We are sustained by something stronger," I say, pulling the conch from its box and holding it out in both hands.

"What am I supposed to do, touch that old thing?"

"Yes. And then you'll hear the voice of the divine."

Scoffing, Marina takes a step closer and sets her small, tattooed hand upon the moon conch.

Malintzin, Sitlali says. Marina stiffens, looks around. *I'm not there with you. You can't see me. I'm speaking into your mind.*

"How?"

The moon conch holds ancient power. From Coyolxauhqui, the goddess of the moon, I believe.

"Are you not her?"

No.

I balk. Why is Sitlali deviating from the plan?

"Then who are you?"

A young woman, like you, caught between warring forces I can't control. Given against all odds a gift. Yours is language. Popoloca, Nahuatl, Chontal, and Yucatec Maya. Now Spanish. Which I also speak, Sitlali adds, switching to that tongue. *My gift? Perhaps this conch. Perhaps the love of the brave boy you see before you. But definitely my knowledge.*

I know everything that will happen over the next five hundred years as a result of your choices, Malintzin.

"Nonsense. How can that be true?"

Because I live in your future, Mother.

Marina's arrogance falters. She's not expecting any of this. Neither am I.

I could lie to you as I have to Cuauhtemoc. As I have to Cortés. But you deserve the truth. I am your daughter, Malintzin. Or rather, the daughter of the mestizaje that will begin with you. With your son, who will be taken from you. With your daughter, who will be raised by others when you die. And your death will come soon, Mother, if you continue on this path. Eight years. That's all you have left.

Eyes wide, Marina stammers, "Th-this path?"

Aiding Cortés. Your actions will have terrible repercussions, Malintzin. Not just for the Mexica you despise, but for all Indigenous people, your own community included. Your choices will affect more than Tenochtitlan. The Spanish will decimate many other nations, continue to slaughter and conquer as they expand throughout the continent. Here, now, five hundred years later, the Indigenous people living within colonizers' nations are still fighting to survive in a world that does not respect their ways.

Swallowing heavily, Marina tries to deflect. "I can't worry about what happens five centuries from now. I must live in the moment. Survive. Thrive, if I can."

You will not survive, Mother. Don't you understand? And even during the few years you have left, you will get to see what happens to your name. Twisted by the Spanish tongue into "Malinche," it will be forever tied to that loss, that pain, that decimation. While a few will remember you as the captive, the translator, most will malign you, inscribe your name in history as the betrayer, the traitor. Is this really how you want to be remembered?

"What other possible destiny could await me?"

Turn from this path. Make Cortés withdraw from the kingdom of Mexico. Give the Mexica time to recover, rebuild. Then they might withstand. Wouldn't you rather be honored and worshipped for helping the Indigenous people of Mexico prevail?

Marina takes her hand away and begins pacing the room. Ofirin looks at me questioningly. I shrug.

This is a dangerous gambit, I tell Sitlali. *She took her hand away and seems overwhelmed with bitter anger.*

Trust me, Calizto. I had to be honest with her. She deserves it, and it's the best strategy to get you free. She'll be back. Give her a second to process it all.

As if summoned, Marina stomps back and slams her hand on the moon conch.

"I need you to give me Cuauhtemoc's strategy. Will he attack? When? How?"

A wave of sadness washes over us across the years and distance.

Ah, Mother. Your new masters are going to win. Why does it matter what they have planned? It won't work.

"You promised Don Hernán. I can't let them go if you don't give me something, future girl. And I want to let them go, believe me. I don't relish the idea of their dying."

Fine. Tell Cortés not to leave. Cuauhtemoc has nothing planned. He has been hoping for reinforcements, but the Spaniards have already stopped those allies. Your damned conquistador can continue with his planned incursions. He will encounter less and less resistance. In a month, the emperor will surrender.

My heart quails to hear Sitlali give this information up. As Marina pulls her hand away, I cry out.

Why would you tell her those things?

Because I understand now. They've already happened, Calizto.

History records them. We can't stop them. But there's no record of what happens to you, *beloved. Right now, we need to focus on your safety. Don't you understand? We weren't given the moon conch to change history. The goddess wanted us to find each other. So that something beautiful survives the ugliness of our times.*

Marina gestures at the guards.

"They've fulfilled their promise. The marquess now fulfills his. Escort these two out of the camp. Take them south to the foot of Mount Huixachtecatl and set them free."

A few hours later, we approach the small dormant volcano where the New Fire Ceremony is celebrated every fifty-two years. I ready myself. The soldiers may have orders to kill us here.

But they just turn and leave. Ofirin and I watch until they disappear in the distance.

"This was too easy, Calizto. Something's going to happen."

I gesture at the two of us. "No food. No water. No weapons. Days of brutal travel through hostile, mountainous territory ahead of us. Your definition of easy is rather different from my own."

No, he's right. Cortés and Cuauhtemoc can remember the moon conch. One or both will have you followed. We've shown them our power. They'll want to know what we do with it.

"Sitlali agrees with you," I tell Ofirin. "But whatever our enemies may be plotting, all we can do is move forward. Hug the shoreline of Lake Xochimilco and then Lake Chalco. Head up the river into the mountains. Reach the coast, no matter what."

Ofirin nods. "We've got a goddess on our side, at least."

I laugh. "That we do."

Then we begin to run.

CHAPTER THIRTY-NINE

Sitlali

July 8, 2019

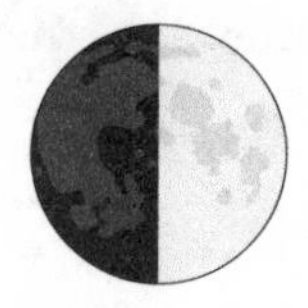

It's early, 5:35, and breakfast is being passed out. Because we are the last pod on this side of the warehouse, we get served first. All around me, women stir, sit up, and wake up their companions, daughters, sisters, mothers, grandmothers. We are all mixed together here.

To have those children's cages bursting at the seams is a blessing to these mothers. They consider themselves lucky to be assigned here, to the female cell, with their female children. Even if they can't be with their husbands and boyfriends, at least they have their daughters with them.

As I sit among the women, I learn that Señora Tita's eldest boy, Robertico—like Doña Laura's only son, Mario—was being recruited by a local gang in their small town in Ecuador, the same gang who killed his father. She was not losing him to them. "I'd rather sacrifice him to the snakes in the desert than let those buitres have him," she tells me, as I push the aluminum foil off the top of my breakfast burrito and finally take a bite.

The tortilla is lukewarm, and the center is cold, but I chew it fast and swallow it dry. I only have a bit of water left in the bottle they gave me yesterday, and I want to preserve it, in case I don't get another one.

"I feel the same way," Doña Laura says, as she pats the back of her two-year-old daughter, Teresita. The toddler rests her head on her mother's shoulder and stares at the wall blankly. She is filthy, but I can see the beautiful little girl behind the dirt and filth.

"Where is he now?" I ask.

Because her hands are busy, Doña Laura lifts her chin and gestures across the facility. "Pod 8, with his father. You can't see them from here. They're in the back. I know because my husband, Roberto, calls out his good mornings and good nights every day. Twenty-eight times, so far."

As if on cue, a man's voice calls out, loudly, above the hum of voices and noises as the inhabitants of the detention center start to eat the first meal of the day.

"Laura?" the man's voice screams in Spanish. "Good morning, my love!"

Doña Laura beams. "Good morning!" she says, and she looks down at Teresita's face on her shoulder. "It's your daddy . . . Can you say good morning to your daddy?"

But Teresita is listless. Even her eyelids move in slow motion when she blinks and takes a shallow breath. Doña Laura opens her burrito, takes a small bite off the corner, and tries to tempt her little girl with it. But Teresita isn't interested.

"My boy, Samuel, is over there too," Rosa, a woman in her forties, whispers. She's finished her burrito, crumpled up the aluminum foil, and is forming a turtle figurine with it.

"This is shameful," I say, thinking about these unnecessary separations.

"It's deplorable," Doña Laura says. "These facilities create 'jobs.' These white people are getting rich off our suffering. Every fearful soul shoved in these cages, every wail, every tear, is one more dollar in the bank for the big corporations running this place."

"Still, there are good people working to help us," I say. "The lawyers, the doctors, they come here to try to help."

"Yes. We are lucky," Rosa muses.

Doña Laura frowns. "Well, I wouldn't say lucky."

"But we are," Rosa insists. "We could be dead right now. Samuel and I left El Salvador because my husband was executed. He refused to use his family's van to transport product for a drug dealer, and they killed him for it. After that, they targeted Samuel. I wasn't going to let them kill him too."

Teresita starts to cry. Doña Laura tries to calm her, but her cries turn to wails. Her discomfort is contagious, and soon the whole facility is full of crying, fussing children. There is movement and complaining and discontent in pod after pod, as more and more children wake up.

"Here," I say, when Doña Laura looks like she needs a break. "Let me hold her awhile. You need to eat your breakfast."

Doña Laura smiles and hands Teresita over to me. I stand up and rock her, singing a soft lullaby to her, an ancient, rhythmic tune that my abuela Lucía used to sing to me. I stand like this a long time, rocking and smiling, smiling and rocking, disconnected from time and space, and I wonder what Calizto is doing.

Eating raw squash for breakfast, Calizto says, and I freeze.

Calizto! Good morning! Where are you?

Traveling to Iztapalocan, walking along the shoreline of Lake Xochimilco.

Eating and walking at the same time? I tease, speaking to him in my mind as I rock Teresita in my arms. She has stopped crying and is falling asleep now.

There's no time to waste, Calizto explains. *This is the first of what*

Ofirin predicts will be between five and eight days of travel, depending on what obstacles come our way.

Still, at least you're free. Any one of us in here would give anything to walk the shorelines of the lake right now. I bet it's beautiful this time of year.

In the distance, I can see Cuitlahuac, the island of my family's ancestors, Calizto says as he chews on a piece of squash rind. I can feel his pleasure as he savors the delicate vegetable.

My next thought is sabotaged as the four facility guards grab an aluminum trash can each, hit the side of it, and scream.

"Okay! Breakfast time is over!" one of them yells.

"Pass your trash down!" the female officer instructs.

The ruckus makes Teresita wake up, and she starts to cry again. She is inconsolable, and I sit with Doña Laura after she takes her back and try to make a game out of the things we see and hear as we sit clustered together in Pod 5. Only after Teresita falls asleep do I get up and move back to my spot against the chain-link fence in front of Conchita and Monchi.

"You shouldn't get so involved," Monchi says, lifting her head and looking at the top of the fence over my head. "It's not good to get attached."

"I'm just trying to help," I tell her.

"Babies die here," she tells me. "Then how are you going to feel?"

I watch her gaze linger on the lights overhead.

"I'm sorry?" I tell her.

Monchi laughs. "You can keep your sorries to yourself. They don't do anybody any good. Not out there. And certainly not in here."

Before I can say anything, Monchi scuffles around, gets up, and pushes her way down the length of our pod until she is standing right up against the chain-link fence facing the guards.

"Hey, you fucking bozos!" she screams as she grabs the chain-link and rattles the cage. "Where's my lawyer? She's supposed to be here already!"

I watch Monchi argue with the female officer, who threatens to lock her up in isolation if she doesn't settle down. But she takes pleasure in riling up the other detainees, who are booing and hissing at the guards.

"She's a spark plug," I tell Conchita because she is watching me intently now.

"She's full of rage, that one," Doña Sofía says from her place a few feet away from us.

"More than you could ever imagine," Conchita says.

"Everyone has a story," I whisper.

"Story?" Conchita asks. "Stories have happy endings. Monchi's was a nightmare."

"Nightmare." I think of my mother, then, and push the thought away.

Conchita stares at me. "They were keeping her all drugged up," she tells me. "Making her 'work' for them. I couldn't get her out of there without the police. I had to lead them there. Show them what was going on."

Doña Laura shifts Teresita in her arms and reaches over to pat Conchita's shoulder. "You did the right thing, child."

"And that's how you ended up here?" I ask.

Conchita nods. "Every single one of those girls and boys was undocumented. There was no way they were going to let them go free. That's not how justice works here. Not when ICE is involved."

Monchi leaves her place along the chain-link fence and starts to wander back to us, kicking people out of her way and cursing as she goes along. When she returns, she lies down next to Conchita and covers her face with her forearm because there is nothing else to do but take a nap until lunchtime.

While others are resting, I tell myself to stay awake. The lawyer who took my information and got the officers to give me back my bag the day before yesterday said she would come back to talk to me, and I don't want to miss it if they call my name.

The officers come back, pulling in a cartful of small sacks, which they begin to pass out. I want to go to the restroom, but I don't want to miss out on lunch. So, I wait until things settle down. But the lawyer lady never comes, and the rest of the day goes by unbearably slow. So slow that I am overjoyed when I can see Calizto stop to camp at the mouth of a river. I watch him sit back to roast a rabbit in a fire that is only evident in the light that dances over his face and torso.

How is it? I ask him, when Calizto tests the meat on the spit.

I prefer rabbit stew, Calizto remarks. *But we have no pot. Are you well?*

I am, I tell Calizto. *Everyone in this detention center has a story. They're all different, but they have one thing in common. Not one of them deserves to be here.*

Every person should be given an opportunity to continue on their own path, he says, looking at me again, a loving warmth in his eyes. *To unfurl freely, without being sabotaged.*

It's hard to believe that our communities are going through the same kind of struggles they were going through five hundred years ago. It's like nothing's changed. We're still being hunted down and persecuted. We're still having to fight to survive, I tell him, shifting on the ground and settling my shoulder into the chain-link fence so that we are facing each other. He shifts too, and now everything around us has disappeared, and we are alone in another world, another time, gazing into each other's eyes.

That breaks my heart, he whispers, and I wish the moon was full so that I could reach out and touch him, feel his arms around me, lean in and kiss his soft lips again.

It just makes me so mad! I admit, wrapping my arms around myself to keep from shaking so hard.

Me too, my sweet, Calizto admits, as he leans over to look deeply into my eyes. *I wish I were there. If I were, I would fell every single one of those guards and set everyone free!*

I smile, wishing I could caress his face, smooth the frown off his forehead. *I know. I feel the same way. I wish there was something we could do, something we could make happen with this conch, to end their pain and suffering, to change the world we live in.*

The fire crackles. I hear a log fall, and the light burns brighter in my Calizto's eyes. *Nothing lasts forever, Little Star*, he says. *One way or another, every great nation falls. The one thing we can be sure of is that we are chosen people, the children of Nahui Olin, the Fifth Sun. My mother told me, just before she died, that no matter what the enemy does to conquer us, we will always have paradise awaiting us. Tamoanchan, the divine echo of our ancestral Aztlan.*

That's true, I whisper. *Here, or in the next life, a better place awaits us.*

CHAPTER FORTY

Calizto

Day 5-Dog of the Year 3-House (July 9, 1521)

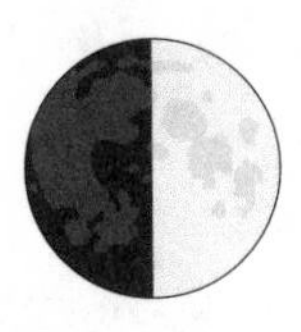

At dawn we follow the river into the mountains, chewing on cold rabbit meat as we go. The sparse vegetation of the foothills becomes denser pine forest the higher we climb. Well-worn paths snake their way among the trees and boulders along the river's edge.

As Sitlali's ghostly form sits up nearby, I let Ofirin take the lead.

Good morning, beautiful.

I don't feel beautiful. This place strips beauty and dignity away.

Your prison is horrible, no doubt. But there is no man in my time or yours capable of erasing your fierce dignity or breathtaking beauty.

The ire in her heart is cooled a bit by my words. *Thanks, Calizto. I'll try not to despair before breakfast. Where are you two?*

Climbing into the mountains.

"Tell her we're taking the pass I discovered on my way here," Ofirin said, noticing my distraction. "Between the two volcanoes."

Popocatepetl and Iztaccihuatl? Sitlali asks.

Yes. Do you know the story of their love?

I do. Popoca refused to accept that his dearest Iztac had died. He demanded the gods bring her back.

And he waited on the mountaintops, refusing to move until he was given an answer. That powerful love sustained him when he should have died.

Warmth flows into my heart across the long years and leagues.

That's how much you love me, isn't it?

Yes, Little Star. Beyond death itself.

Ofirin sighs. "I know that look. You're not alone, turtledoves."

I hold out the conch.

"You're welcome to listen in. We were just reminiscing about the volcanoes."

He puts his hand on the carved spirals. "Your father told me the gods decided to allow Iztac to be reborn. They gave Popoca immortality as a mountain god so he could search for her. What if that's your destiny, the two of you? Maybe Calizto has been reincarnated already, somewhere off in that northern country where Sitlali is captive."

And the conch will guide me to him, now that our souls have been connected? Sitlali muses.

"No," I conclude. "I'd rather not have to die and be reborn to be with the woman I love. I pray the goddess has a different destiny in mind."

Deep in thought, Ofirin and I resume our ascent. The path pulls away from the river, and the incline becomes less steep.

I see Sitlali turning something over in her hands.

What are you looking at?

The glyphs on the moon conch. Can you read them?

No. They're ancient, I explain.

That's right, she agrees. *The song you remembered . . . It says that She of the Bells—Coyolxauhqui?—had them carved by He of the Shells.*

That's Tecciztecatl, I remind her. *Guardian of the Moon.*

Ah, okay. And the glyphs are "inscrutable" except for those the goddess chooses "to spark through paradox."

That has to be us, I say. *We hold the conch in our hands "in two different lands and each other" in our hearts, "though leagues and eons apart."*

She's promising to reveal the secret of the moon conch to us. Is it hidden in these markings? We've been so caught up surviving. I know I haven't examined the moon conch closely enough.

Neither have I. The conch brought you to me, and that miracle has distracted me.

But, she adds, *we know it does more. You were able to fight off my attackers through my body.*

And I was able to see a spirit with your eyes.

Maybe there's more, Sitlali says. *A way for me to escape this place. A way for us to be together.*

I manage to snatch a trout from the river for lunch. Ofirin starts a fire after finding dry kindling. We eat our fill as Sitlali shares a meal with the other women in her cell. Her gaze is distant, despondent. I'm moved to make promises.

This evening, let's try to decipher the secret. Somehow, I'll get you free from that cage.

The smile that flickers across her features is more sustenance than any earthly food.

With renewed vigor, Ofirin and I finish the ascent, coming by midafternoon to a level pass high above the Valley of Mexico and the rest of Anahuac.

"Ah!" cries Ofirin. "It'll be easier going from here on out. Level for a while, then downhill for hours. My aching muscles are glad!"

As if summoned, a half dozen Tlaxcaltecah warriors come rushing at us from the trees, ululating a war cry.

Were Ofirin a warrior, had we weapons to wield, I would stand my ground and face our ambush, unafraid.

But there is courage in knowing when to flee.

"Run!" I scream before bursting into movement.

Ofirin is right on my heels, dingy cape fluttering.

The Tlaxcaltecah pursue us like hunters behind a wounded deer. They have the advantage. I presume they were lying in wait for us, with foreknowledge of our approach.

Ofirin and I have spent nine hours walking and running, with just three stops for rest and food.

The outcome is inevitable. They will catch us, sooner or later. Yet my eyes fall on a shallow cave off the path, fist-size stones strewn before it.

Weapons. Not the most elegant, but perhaps sufficient to down two or three of them before I must face their swords.

"Cave!" I shout in Spanish before sprinting in that direction. Ofirin's long legs keep pumping till we both skid to a stop amid the stones.

"I hope you know how to throw," I pant, scooping up a jagged bit of granite and spinning to fling it at the lead warrior. It strikes him in the throat; he stumbles. Ofirin hurls another stone, which strikes him on the top of the head, and the man tumbles onto the damp earth.

The others begin to zig and zag as they close the distance between us. I clip one's shoulder, but there is no time to fell another. A grinning maniac with a shaved head lifts his sword high and leaps . . .

. . . only to have his chest pierced by an arrow!

It takes a few seconds for his compatriots to understand what has happened, and by then a dozen arrows are falling from the sky. Three more warriors collapse. The remaining man draws up short, frustration on his face.

From the opposite direction, a *second* group of men comes running. They sling their bows over their shoulders and draw obsidian knives.

The Tlaxcaltecatl flees.

Hand raised in a gesture of peace, the leader of the new arrivals approaches.

"We're allies," he says, and I recognize the accent. These are Choloitecah, men from the nearby kingdom of Chololan, revered for its great age and wisdom. Cortés had many of them slaughtered and part of their capital city burned to the ground, so they harbor no love for him or his Tlaxcaltecah dogs.

"Calizto," I begin, "son of . . ."

"Yes, I know who you are. And the Spanish slave who accompanies you. I am Captain Cecalli. Word came you two might attempt to reach the coast through the pass. So I was sent to escort you."

Ofirin mutters to me in Spanish. "Word came from your damn emperor, he means."

Without looking at him, I ask, "Escort us where?"

"For now, to Chololan. Then our king will assign a team to take you back to Cuauhtemoc. Apparently, you are very valuable. I've been ordered to protect you with my life."

"Told you," Ofirin groans.

As we march southeast under guard, I tell Sitlali—who was meeting with a legal advocate—what's transpired.

What're you going to do?

I'll never go back. I need to spend the rest of my life near the sea so I can throw this conch into the waves before I die and ensure you find it. So I'll wait for the right opportunity to come. Dark clouds are gathering in the sky before us. I see glimmers of lightning. Perhaps Tlaloc will aid me.

As I mumble prayers, I pull the conch from its box and netting, hoping the gods will hear me better with that sacred object in my hands.

Cecalli narrows his eyes, stepping closer to look at the trumpet. "Those glyphs are familiar. Seen them on the walls of the old temples, the ones built by the Olmecs."

"Do you recognize them?" I ask.

"Just this cluster: eye, ear, mouth, hand. What does the priest say? 'Given to humanity so that we might see and hear the wonders of the cosmos, then sing praises and make sacrifice to the gods.' Ancient proverb."

Oh! says Sitlali as I relay this to her. *I see it now, yes! Let's try something. Put your finger on the eye glyph when I count to three. I'll do the same. One, two, three!*

I squeeze my thumb on the stylized eye, but nothing happens.

Damn. Okay, maybe it's first me, then you. Let's try that, Calizto.

For the next hour, as the wind picks up and clouds pile higher, Sitlali and I try every combination we can think of, but the moon conch simply lies inert in our hands.

Something's wrong, I mutter. *Yet we'll have to discover what a little later. It's begun to rain. I must get ready to escape when the moment comes.*

Within minutes, the rain is falling in thick walls of water. Thunder booms. Lightning forks across the black heavens.

Before long, the downhill path becomes a river of mud. The warriors struggle to keep us between them without slipping, but soon the current makes coordination impossible.

The youngest member of the team loses his footing and shoots away in a roiling flood. The slowest quails, calls out to his fallen comrade.

It's my opening. Slamming a fist into the back of his head, I wrest the obsidian sword from his hand, kicking him into the muddy flow. Before the others realize what has happened, I dispatch two more with slicing cuts.

Ofirin is already scurrying into the trees, anchoring himself to a pine with his cape.

The water is up to my knees. As the surviving Chololtecah advance, I kick off my sandals and dig my toes into the mud.

Then I lift the sword.

And the sky erupts with blue fire.

A bolt from the sky hits the water between my enemy and me. In its wake, a glowing sphere of lightning hovers for a heartbeat before whizzing toward my captors.

When it reaches them, it explodes.

CHAPTER FORTY-ONE

Sitlali

July 10, 2019

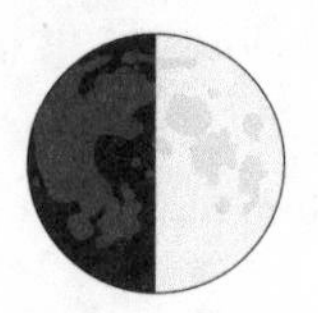

Though the lawyer, Sara Sifuentes, doesn't have good news about my father—Samantha made it very clear to her that he can't visit me in here—she does bring with her a most unexpected, wonderful surprise. When my madrina Tomasa enters the visiting room, it takes every ounce of fortitude I have left in my body to stop myself from getting up and throwing my arms around her.

She sits across from me and shakes her head when I apologize for putting her through this emotional roller coaster. "I should have gone with you," my madrina says regretfully.

"It wouldn't have helped," I tell her. "They came out of nowhere."

"Still," she says. "If I'd been there. If you hadn't walked, we might have waited in the car, and left before . . ."

"Or stayed and ordered, and gotten picked up anyway," my lawyer says. "There's no point in going through the scenarios. We need to continue to build a case for Sitlali. She's a minor; establishing your guardianship is imperative. She won't be released if she has nowhere to go."

"Guardianship?" I ask. "You mean, I would become your daughter?"

"My charge." My madrina smiles warmly. "You're already like a daughter to me. But your father would need to cooperate. And right now, we can't reach him."

"I'll try to visit the home," my lawyer says. "But if they don't open the door . . ."

My heart twists in my chest, and I struggle to keep my emotions in check. "Then your hands are tied," I say, and my lawyer nods.

"He needs to sign the papers," my madrina says. "Otherwise . . ."

I feign a smile and fight back the hot tears that threaten to fall down my cheeks. "Otherwise, they'll send me back."

"We won't let that happen," my madrina says. She starts to reach forward, to touch my hand, but my lawyer stops her. "Don't worry, Sitlali. I'll find a way. Even if I have to sit outside Enrique and Samantha's house day and night, I will find a way of getting the papers signed."

When my lawyer and my madrina leave, I don't let the sadness overwhelm me. Instead of dwelling on my father, I help Doña Laura with Teresita. The poor woman hasn't slept for days, and I rock the baby while she rests her eyes.

You are going to make a wonderful wife and mother someday, Calizto says, and I look up to see him crouched low to the ground, hiding, somewhere in the distance.

Hey, there you are! I say. *Wait? You can see her? Teresita?*

No, but the crook of your arms and the soft lullaby let me know you were caring for the sick child again.

Too bad you can't see her. She's beautiful, and so sweet.

Calizto's gaze is soft, and he looks at me like he has nothing better to do. He is so handsome, strong yet caring. I am sure he will make a great husband and father too.

So, what's going on with you? Where are you?

We crossed the Atoyac River. A fisherman took us across in his canoe. That was a big help. We made great gains.

So, now you're just lying low? I ask.

Yes. We are scouting the area before we move on, Calizto explains. *The journey is long and the terrain difficult, but we want to reach the kingdom of Tepeyacac by nightfall.*

Teresita is splayed out over my knees with her head thrown back, and her little fingers are wrapped around the strap of my bag as it sits across my chest and stomach. I reach down and gently swipe the wisps of new hair growth off her forehead.

"Oh my God," I say, speaking the words out loud.

What is it? he asks, shifting quickly and leaning over to watch me closely.

She has a fever, I tell him. *It's freezing in this place. She shouldn't be this warm.*

Freezing? In the summer?

Yes. The air conditioner is on full blast. It's like a meat locker in here, I tell him, as I shift and pick Teresita up into my arms so that I can stand up. *I have to go, Calizto. I have to get her seen by a doctor. Doña Laura hasn't been able to get any medical attention. But this can't wait anymore.*

"Doña Laura," I call out. "You need to wake up. Teresita is getting worse."

Doña Laura sits up quickly. She takes her little girl, puts her hand on her forehead, and scuttles off the ground. "Can you get my things together?" she asks, as she moves, making her way through the crowd.

I follow her to the edge of the cage, where Doña Laura slaps a hand against the chain-link fence. "Help! Help me!" she screams. "My daughter is very sick. She needs a doctor! Now!"

The female guard starts over, walking slowly as she comes. "What's going on?"

"I told you. My baby is very sick. Touch her, if you don't believe me." Doña Laura lifts Teresita's limp arm and then lets it fall. "She's not moving anymore. And she's burning up."

The guard looks perplexed. Her eyebrows furrow, and she looks around as if the answers were somewhere in that row of overcrowded cages. "Okay," she finally says. "Let me see what I can do."

She walks off then.

Doña Laura leans down and coos at her daughter. Teresita's lashes flutter, and she opens her eyes for a few seconds before she closes them again. "Baby, please hold on. Please, please, hold on. I love you, sweet girl. Mommy loves you."

All around us, people of all ages and genders are staring. Women and their daughters in our cages, men and their sons across the aisle—everyone looks worried. Mothers and fathers sigh and shake their heads, because no one here can do anything to help us.

We are the impotent. The disempowered. The entrapped.

I pat Doña Laura as she cries softly against Teresita's forehead, letting the teardrops mingle with the child's soft, dark hair. "It'll be all right," I keep telling her.

After half an hour, the female guard finally comes back. She opens the gate and reaches for Teresita. "The nurse wants to see her," she says.

"No!" a wounded, haunted voice screams from across the length of the cage. It is Juana Cervantes, a mother who lost one of her twins to illness before I arrived. Doña Laura and I look back, as Juana stands up and starts tearing through the crowd, wild-eyed and wild-haired, like a ghostly specter. "Don't let them take her, Laura. You'll never see her again!"

"Stop!" the female guard screams, putting her hand on the weapon at her waist. "Stay back!"

But Juana won't be stopped. If anything, she walks faster, more purposely, toward us. "No. No. You don't get to tell me what to do," she screams. "Not after what you did to me."

"Shut up and step back," one of the male guards says, putting his hand out in front of him, as if by will alone he could keep Juana from coming forward.

"Where's my baby, huh?" Juana asks, as she holds the single twin in her arms. "What did you do with her? Who did you give her to?"

Doña Laura turns to look at her. "Juana, please," she whispers, eyes lowered, face flushed. "They're trying to help."

"Don't let them fool you, Laura," Juana says, her concave eyes large and brimming with unshed tears. "Can't you see what they're doing? Their taking our babies away to sell them on the black market."

"I'm warning you," the female guard says, shaking her head, her trembling hand hovering over her weapon.

I turn around and step between Juana and the female officer. "Juana, come with me," I say quietly, because I don't want to upset her any more than she already is.

Juana's wild, erratic gaze shifts to me. She narrows her eyes as she considers my words.

I touch her baby's forehead, trace the dark curlicues of hair sitting on it. "Just look at your baby, Juana. Look how beautiful she is," I say, pressing my hand on Juana's shoulder to make her turn back. "Let's go take care of her. Come on. Help me find her bottle."

I sit beside Juana and find her baby's bottle. Once she is settled in, I sit with my back against the fence, too emotionally wrought to close my eyes and rest. As I watch Doña Laura hand Teresita over to the female officer, Calizto's words come to mind.

You are going to make a wonderful wife and mother someday.

Desperate for a glance of my beloved, I roll my head to the side and call out his name in my mind. But instead of Calizto, I see my abuela Lucía standing on the other side of the cage, her fingers clinging to the thin spokes of the chain-link fence.

I manage to smile, and she lets go of the fence and puts her hands together, then raises them up to her lips. I think she's about to blow me a kiss, but it looks like she's blowing an invisible horn. I frown, and she does it again, blowing on the make-believe horn again and again.

A horn? I ask her, in my mind's voice, and she smiles.

What horn? I lift my eyebrows to let her know I am not sure what she wants.

Abuela Lucía rolls her eyes at me. Then she moves her hands up and down from her shoulder to her stomach and pats her hip.

Oh, the conch. The broken piece? I ask, pointing at my right hip pocket.

Abuela Lucía lifts her hands in front of her chin and lips and claps a small, soundless clap that makes her eyes glitter with joy.

I reach into my jeans pocket and pull it out. I hold the bit of moon conch within my fingertips and look at it closely. Abuela Lucía waves at me. And when I look at her, she pretends to bring two things together in her hands.

Fix it? Oh! I can't. I don't have glue in here.

My grandmother shakes her head, and then she does the thing again, insisting that I put the piece of broken moon conch where it belongs.

It's not that simple, I tell her.

Maybe it is. Calizto's voice startles me, and I look to my left, where he is sitting beside me. *The song, Sitlali. "When what was broken is healed."*

I turn so that we are facing each other. "*And she who is destined to wield.*" *Do you think that I can somehow repair the conch with . . . magic?*

We're sitting here, five hundred years apart, tethered by that very magic, beloved.

I pull the strap over my head and unzip the bag in front of me. Gently, I pull the moon conch out of the bag.

Hold on, Calizto says. He takes a moment to fuss with something in his world.

What is it? I ask.

I want to see if anything happens on my end when you hold the piece in place, he says, shifting so that he is sitting with his back straight beside me.

Taking a deep, hopeful breath, I inspect the broken piece of moon conch. Turning it this way and that, I find the best possible fit, and then, gently, I push the piece back into its original place.

The world echoes with the crescendo of a thousand chiming bells. All around me, a million tiny sparkling lights flicker on and off, like invisible fireflies that only I can see and hear. Warmth fills my hands, a divine fire that roils without burning.

I smell surf and sun and beach grass. Then, in a fusion of light and sound identical to the moment when the blue ocean crests over the horizon and becomes part of the night sky, the conch absorbs the missing piece and becomes whole again.

In that instance of restoration, every glyph on the moon conch lights up. Bright, golden rays of warmth shine through each of the grooves of the nine resplendent symbols.

Whoa! I say. *Calizto . . . the glyphs! They are . . .*

Activated, he says. *Gleaming with life.*

Beside me, Calizto's hands glow as bright and full of magic as mine.

CHAPTER FORTY-TWO

Calizto

Days 6-Monkey and 7-Grass of the Year 3-House

(July 10–11, 1521)

"The conch!" shouts Ofirin.

"I know. Give us a moment."

That's why they never worked, Sitlali groans. *I had the answer all along!*

Don't torture yourself. The conch is restored. That's all that matters. I press my thumb against the eye glyph.

Nothing.

Sitlali senses my frustration. *It's just like during the full moon. We've got to touch the same symbol at the same time.*

Three.

Two.

One.

The conch quivers in my hands as my thumb makes contact.

Brightness blazes all around. I see metal netting on every side. Women and children huddle together on padded mats, some covered by silvery blankets.

The future.

The cages.

Oh! exclaims Sitlali. *I see the trees, lit up by the moon! You're beside a stream. There's Ofirin! Ha, he looks freaked out. His lips are moving . . . Let's try another glyph! The ear.*

Her excitement is infectious, overwhelming the anger I feel at the conditions in which she's trapped. We count backward together and touch the ancient symbol.

Sniffling. The distant cry of a baby. A strange hum, like some growling monster. Snoring nearby. A whispered conversation in a language I cannot recognize.

Ay, poor thing, Sitlali says. *He's worried. You should take a moment to reassure him.*

Perhaps you *can, Little Star. Let's try the mouth glyph. It may allow us to speak through each other's lips.*

A few seconds later, I feel my tongue move without my prompting.

"Ofirin, it's me, Sitlali. I'm using Calizto's lips to speak. My version of the conch was broken, but the spirit of my abuela Lucía showed me how to fix it. Now we can use each other's senses."

Ofirin's eyes go even wider. "Incredible! I don't see how it helps, but such magic must have a use."

Let's try . . . touching two glyphs at once. Ear and mouth. I want to have a conversation with him.

We count backward again to coordinate.

"Sitlali?" someone asks. "Are you okay?"

Though I cannot see, it must be one of the women encaged with my beloved. Clearing my throat, I mimic her Spanish speech patterns. "Yeah, I'm fine. Just thinking about . . . stuff."

This is awkward, Sitlali.

She sends a wave of bemused joy. *We'll get used to it!*

What about the hand icon?

Okay. Three, two . . .

When the conch trembles, I lift my free hand—my beloved's—and touch her face.

Skin soft as a flower petal blushes warm beneath my fingertips. My heart beating fast, I brush her full lips, cup her chin, let my palm rest against her neck.

And Sitlali takes my own hand, presses it to my chest as if to feel the beating of my heart, sliding my palm upward, reaching behind my neck as if to pull me to her across the centuries for the deep kiss we both desire . . .

"Do you want me to turn away?" Ofirin asks. "Because this looks more intimate than I was expecting."

Sitlali and I both jerk our hands away—from our bodies and the conch.

"Sorry. We're . . . getting accustomed to these new features."

Ofirin scoffs and settles in. "You should postpone your explorations till another time. Morning comes fast."

He's right. But I lie down with my back to him, cradling the conch.

In the future place called America, Sitlali does the same.

And carefully, aided by incomprehensible magic, we fold our arms around ourselves, around *each other*, and fall asleep in that impossible embrace.

I awaken at dawn to find the conch has rolled away from me. Sitlali is standing. Lunging for the conch, I greet her.

Good morning, lovely one. Where are you? Let me see through your eyes.

Sorry, but I can't. I'm waiting in line for my turn to shower for the first time in days.

Understood. We must move quickly so as not to lose the day. As I put the conch in its box and the netted bag, Ofirin stares at me, despondent.

"What's wrong?"

He points at the bag. "You spent the night in each other's arms, didn't you? What I wouldn't give for another chance, even across time, even knowing it was the last chance, to hug Enaben tight, to tell her I love her."

A shout echoes behind me. I whirl about as a group of Tlaxcaltecah converge with troops coming from the direction of Tepeyacac.

"Shit!" I say, picking up my sword. "Move!"

On the horizon, silhouetted against the rising sun, the largest volcano in Anahuac looms, snowcapped even in deepest summer.

Aiming our hopes and bodies at that peak, Ofirin and I begin to run.

Behind us come dozens of armed pursuers.

After we spend hours keeping barely out of range of the enemy's arrows, a late morning shower gives Ofirin and me respite. We manage to lose our hunters in a dense wood just before the town of Tenanco, nestled among mountain peaks that overlook the high plains.

An old woman, moved by my deference, gives us food and lets us rest in her home. But we are soon on the move again.

Any sign of them? Sitlali asks.

No. But Ofirin wants to head south through difficult terrain, then along a river before turning back toward your mountain.

My mountain?

Yes. Citlaltepetl. Star Mountain. A great volcano at the edge of Anahuac.

Oh! Pico de Orizaba. Yes, I visited it once with my father when I was little.

And how are you? I ask, following Ofirin down a winding path into the narrow valley.

Frustrated. Teresita, the baby, is still really sick. The nurse couldn't do much for her yesterday. I keep trying to convince the guards to do something, but nobody listens. No surprise. Cruelty is the point: part of their strategy, not some side effect.

I saw the bright lights and terrible conditions last night, felt the ceaseless cold with your own skin. What sort of country tortures women and children? What sort of god demands their prolonged pain?

Moloch.

Who?

Greed, I mean. That's what the people controlling the government worship. Riches and power.

My father once said the same, after drinking too much agave wine in the privacy of our home, about Emperor Moteuczoma. Apologies. We've reached the flat riverbank, and it's time to run again. We need to reach the volcano's base by nightfall.

By midafternoon, we emerge from the valley onto the sparsely forested plain that leads to Citlaltepetl, looming in the east, its white summit wreathed by dark clouds.

"Rain tonight," I tell Ofirin. "But we can take shelter in caves on the southern face."

As we race away from the sun, which slips down the sky behind us, I catch glimpses of movement. But when I swivel my head to investigate, there are only knots of trees and the occasional low hill or boulder.

It's your imagination, Sitlali reassures me. *I'm sure you've lost them.*

I humor her, but whatever my beloved has been through, she does not know war. Instinct scratches at the back of my mind. I keep my senses open.

After another rest, we push ourselves harder. Just as dusk begins to thicken, the evening star glinting like ice on the horizon, we reach the forest at the base of the volcano.

From amid the trees, the enemy bursts forth, howling battle cries.

I push Ofirin behind me and lift my sword, leaping at the vanguard. They're not prepared for my unhinged attack, and I slice throats and arms and chests before having to retreat.

Nearly three dozen of the bastards.

Then dread certainty fills me. I'm exhausted. Cannot outrun their arrows.

I unsling my bag, hold it behind me.

"Get this to the ocean!" I shout to Ofirin. "No matter the cost!"

What are you doing?! Sitlali howls.

The only thing I can. Kill as many as I can before I fall.

No, Calizto!

I love you, Sitlali.

Then don't do this, damn it! There's got to be another way. The conch! The other glyphs . . . here! This one looks like a sun. Maybe there's some power there.

The Tlaxcaltecah slow their approach; weapons are raised, bows drawn taut.

Ofirin, sobbing, takes the bag from my hand.

"Wait," I say. Dropping my sword, I yank the netting open, pull the shell from its box. I find the stylized sun. Its rays shoot out more on one side than on the other.

Goddess, you gave us this device. You want us to survive, for whatever purpose. I trust in your wisdom. I put myself and my beloved in your hands.

Sitlali shudders. *Three.*

Two, I say, joining in.

One.

As our fingers touch the glyph, the conch begins to tremble, light glinting from every crack and crevice.

HOLD IT HIGH, CHILD. A voice like a thousand bells, moonlight made music, fills every part of my being. *AND CLOSE YOUR EYES.*

"Ofirin!" I scream, lifting the conch overhead. "Do not look!"

Golden fire curls from my hands.

I squeeze my eyes shut, but even then my eyelids go red with the explosion of light.

Screams of pain come from all around. After a few seconds, the moon conch ceases its vibration. I open my eyes. The Tlaxcaltecah are writhing on the ground or stumbling aimless, moaning, clutching their faces.

"That sorcerer blinded me!" one groans.

Not waiting another moment, I pick up my sword and pull Ofirin to his feet from where he has buried his face in the grass. With extreme stealth, we move away from our squirming enemies.

Thank God. Sitlali shudders with relief.

We hurry up the slope. Thunder rolls overhead, and soon it begins to drizzle. In minutes, that light rain becomes a deluge. Despite the low visibility, a thousand rods or so from the base, we find two trees, intertwined in front of a shattered rock face: a willow and a wild olive, out of place at these altitudes. On the ground before them sprawls a huge maguey plant.

"Stop," I say. "It's a sign."

Walking behind the trees, I find the cantilevered entrance to a cave.

Ofirin sighs and slips inside.

The cave is dry but dark, though flashes of lightning illuminate it well enough to show it is safe.

How did you know?

The trees suggested it. The gods Quetzalcoatl and his lover Mayahuel transformed into a willow and wild olive to escape Mayahuel's grandmother and aunts, the fearsome Tzitzimimeh. Sadly, the couple were discovered at last, and Mayahuel was destroyed. But Quetzalcoatl resurrected her, planting her limbs in the soil to be reborn as maguey plants, beautiful and free. Now they're together forever, with no interference from her family.

I hope you'll be safe here for a while, she says. *And that one day we can be together, too.*

I shudder at the thought of my Sitlali, torn apart in her prison like Mayahuel. Can the moon conch undo death as well? Might that be its secret?

At the very least, I promise her, *we'll set each other free.*

CHAPTER FORTY-THREE

Sitlali

July 12, 2019

I watch my beloved standing silent, looking out into the distance intently. He is so still and serene I don't want to break his peace, but it's such a joy to be able to see him. Soon, the moon will be full, and we will be able to touch again. I can hardly wait to wrap my arms around his waist and nestle into his embrace.

And kiss.

Good morning, my darling, I whisper, and Calizto turns to look at me. *What are you looking at?*

Little Star, I was taking a moment to rest. Ofirin and I have traveled many miles this morning. We walked beside the rivers that flow down the east side of Citlaltepetl. And now we stand atop this mountainous terrain, looking south over . . .

Veracruz! I squeal. I can't help it. I know exactly where he is . . . He's in the mountains, overlooking Zongolica! *Oh my God! Show me! Please! I miss the mountains . . . the forest . . . the birds . . . the sea! I have to see it! I need to see it!*

I pull the moon conch out, and, at the same time, Calizto and I count backward and press our fingers down on the eye glyph.

Behold, the city of your ancestors, Calizto says, sending waves of love. *Tzoncoliuhcan.*

Transfixed. Conflicted. I stand, looking out at the purple mist of horizon against the jade of jungle, lush and full of life. It's so clear I can almost smell the clean air, the fresh scent of loam and leaf and life. We had it all. Our own little paradise.

Are you all right, dearest Sitlali? Calizto asks.

I nod as I hold the conch still against my stomach with one hand and wipe an errant tear off my cheek.

You're . . . disappointed? Calizto asks.

No, no. It's different, but still beautiful, I explain. *I just wish things hadn't changed so much for us. That the violence of men hadn't come here—to disturb this peace.*

Don't deceive yourself, Little Star. Chaos and order have always existed simultaneously on this earthly plane. Only Tamoanchan will be free of conflict, free of pain.

"Sitlali Morales!" I hear someone calling my name.

I have to go, I tell Calizto, and I release the pressure on the eye glyph so I can look around the detention center.

My madrina Tomasa enters the visiting room, a loving smile illuminating her face. She takes a deep breath and sighs. "I haven't been able to make contact with your father," she says. "So, I haven't gotten him to sign the papers."

My heart falls, and I can feel fear pressing down against it, like a boulder. "So, what does that mean?"

"That he doesn't understand the gravity of this. I got a letter from him," my madrina says. "It's for you. But I'm not sure you want me to read it to you."

I look at my madrina's haggard face. There are dark, heavy circles under her tired eyes, and her hair looks a little grayer than I remember. Guilt gnaws at the pit of my stomach, because I am sure my entrapment is taking a toll on her—making her look older than her forty-six years.

"Do you have it with you?" I ask.

"Yes," she says, and she reaches into her purse and pulls it out. "They said I could read it to you."

> *Dearest daughter. I am sorry I cannot visit you or connect with you in any other way. But you must understand even this is a risk. I have two young children to think of. So, this will be the only time I write. Please know that I am thinking of you and praying for you as I am praying for Samantha. Because what she did was very wrong. I only wish things had gone differently. That I had known. Then I might have stopped her. And none of this would have happened. Forgive her. And forgive me for not being able to help you. But your madrina will do what can be done. Of that, I am sure. To God, I entrust you. Your father, E. M.*

"To God, I entrust you?!" I scream. "Why do men always have to bring God in when they leave their families? Do you know how many times I've heard that, how many girls have told me their fathers left them and said God knew what he was doing?"

A guard in my periphery turns her head and torso to watch me as I slam my fists against the side of my thighs to keep from hitting the table with them.

"Calm down, Sitlali," my madrina Tomasa whispers. "You don't want them to end our visit so soon."

"I'm sorry, Madrina," I whisper as I cross my arms and hold my fists against my sides in rage. "I just . . . can't . . ."

"I know it must be hard to take," my madrina whispers.

I feel my eyebrows form a tense frown over my eyes, and I press against the skin with my fingertips, because I think I'm developing a headache. "Forgive Samantha? Wait . . ."

Suddenly, it all makes sense. She called ICE! Instinctively, I reach out and rip the letter out of my madrina's hand and read it for myself.

"Hey!" a guard behind me hollers.

"It's okay," my madrina says. "They told me she could read it."

"Nothing can pass between you," the guard says, and she reaches over my shoulder and takes the letter from me. It happens so fast I don't have time to react.

"Wait, that's mine," I say, turning around to look at the guard inspecting the letter.

The guard hands my madrina the letter, steps back, and yells in a loud voice, "We're done here. Let's go. Visit's over."

"But we still have forty . . . ," my madrina begins.

"Not when you break the rules," the guard says, shaking her blond head.

Another guard taps the table with his fingertips and points for me to get up.

My madrina looks at me tearfully. "I'll be back," she says, putting her fingertips against her lips and blowing me an invisible kiss as she walks away. "I'll see you soon, okay?"

I nod and stand up. The guard pushes on my shoulder so that I have to turn my back on my madrina. But not before I yell, "I love you!"

After dinner, I sit back against the fence, sigh, and go back to beating myself up mentally for being so impulsive during my madrina's visit. What would it have hurt to just let her read the letter to me again? Nothing!

Do not torture yourself, my darling, Calizto says. He is sitting down somewhere, resting back comfortably, as he looks intently at me. *It is your impulsive spirit that has kept you alive. Before and after your ordeal in the desert, your tenacity helped you escape Jorge's henchmen. In the water, too, your instinct to fight, to persevere, saved you.*

I blew it, Calizto. I broke the rules, I tell him, full of regret.

You cannot hold yourself accountable for the rules your captors impose on you, Calizto advises, his features firm, his eyes direct. I've never seen him so intent on getting a point across to me. *Those regulations are there to break you, to carve away at your will. Do not let them defeat you, Little Star. Your light burns too bright for such ready surrender.*

I love you, I tell him, as we hold fast to the love in the other's eyes.

As I love you, he says.

After a moment, Calizto picks up the moon conch and inspects the four remaining symbols.

What are you looking for? I ask him.

Answers. Do you see the one that looks like a moon, on the top left? Calizto asks.

I do. What do you think it does?

I'm not sure. He thinks for a moment. *But if the sun sends out rays of sunlight, then it would make sense that this would send out rays of moonlight.*

Or call forth the ocean waves, I say. *There is a correlation, we know, between the moon and the flow and ebb of the tide.*

Yes, there are multiple possibilities, Calizto admits, and he smiles warmly up at me. *I enjoy listening to your clever thoughts.*

I just love looking at your handsome face, I tell him.

Calizto blushes, a warm, soft flush that rises from his neck up to his cheeks and dances in his glistening eyes when he looks across time and space at me. *Your flattery is a dangerous elixir. I crave it when you're not near me, and fear never hearing it again.*

I cast my eyes down on the moon conch again. *Oh, look at that; there's an eye superimposed on that moon glyph. I just noticed.*

Well, that changes things, Calizto muses.

And what about this horizontal bar with the three curling lines extending from it? I ask him.

Turning the conch this way and that, Calizto says, *It looks like some kind of directional signal.*

This one along the lip is kind of simple, a rectangle. Do you see it? I ask. *But rectangles have all kinds of meanings in our world. Depending on its position, it could be any one of the elements. Three traits. Wisdom. Truth. Time . . . oh, oh, time! It means time!*

Yes, but the world is very different in your time, Calizto reminds me. *We cannot be sure until we try them.*

I like this last one, the long-legged bird, I say, lightly tracing the lines of the tiny creature with the pads of my fingertips.

What are you thinking? Calizto asks. *I can't quite read your thoughts.*

Oh, nothing. I . . . well, I used to have this recurring dream, I tell him. *That I grew wings and could fly. I flew over coastlines, following the curve of the sea, over mountains and deserts, over redwoods and fir trees, my legs flowing freely behind me, my long neck extended, as I crashed through the airwaves, suspended between Earth and Heaven.*

Dreams are gifts from the ancestors, Calizto says.

Yes, I believe that too. They're messages, sent to us when we need them most, I tell Calizto, thinking about my grandmother coming to me the night I left Zongolica. It was the last time I heard her speak, in my dreams, a true gift. *Their purposes will reveal themselves when we need them most.*

CHAPTER FORTY-FOUR

Calizto

Day 9-Jaguar of the Year 3-House (July 13, 1521)

"You have to," Sitlali demands. "We can't keep putting up with this shit, Rebecca."

While Ofirin catches his breath, I'm listening and watching through Sitlali. She stands in the middle of a knot of fellow prisoners, addressing a girl about her age. This Rebecca has managed to have smuggled to her a phone.

"What if they confiscate it?" Rebecca counters, tears welling. "I need it to get messages to my boyfriend. He's coming for me."

"If we don't do something *now*," Sitlali counters, "the baby will die, and we'll all be deported. People need to know what's going on here. I'll use my own social media accounts. I'll take the blame, say I threw the phone away."

After more cajoling from the other women, Rebecca agrees. The prisoners ensure that no guards are nearby, and Sitlali begins to speak.

"I am Sitlali Morales, a prisoner at the Hidalgo County ICE Detention Center. You need to know the conditions here. The temperature is kept below sixty degrees. We're sleeping on the floor with thin space blankets. The toilets are overflowing. We don't get to bathe very often, and the medical care is substandard. There are babies with high fevers and coughs, but nobody is doing anything. Even cattle get treated better than we are. Shoved into these cages," she says, gesturing around her, "without any legal recourse. The United States should be ashamed. It's lost its humanity, letting the private company that runs this place profit from our suffering. So the women of my pod, and others throughout the center, we're going on a hunger strike. Those of you who support us, who support decency and the humane treatment of innocent people with no other hope, please come out and protest. Let the director of this hellhole know he can't get away with torture."

It is a courageous speech, delivered with compassion, authority, and conviction. My heart swells with pride and respect.

You're magnificent. I cannot begin to tell you how much I love you right now.

Just now? she teases.

Now and forever, Sitlali Morales. Until the sun is devoured by the Tzitzimimeh, and long afterward, during the eons that await us in the Unknowable Realm beyond death.

You sure know how to seduce a girl, she whispers, going to a corner of the cage to send her speech to the four directions. *I wish you were here right now. And that we were alone.*

Groaning at the quickening of my pulse, I call to Ofirin.

"Time to get moving, friend."

We head northeast through hills and valleys, hoping to pass to the east of Xalapan and avoid detection.

But no sooner have we started walking than we are almost caught.

The whinny of a horse and creaking of leather warn us just in time. Backing into a copse of cypress trees, we watch as two Spanish horsemen make their way up the faded path, once used for trade before other, broader roads were established to the north.

"Much better," one of the men says. "Less flooded than the normal route."

The other nods. "Agreed. Let's double back and bring the reinforcements along this route. It's a shame Ponce de León died, but at least Don Hernán gets his men now."

They head in the other direction.

"Let's hide until nightfall," I say. "There's no way of knowing when they'll return or where they'll go after this point. We cannot risk discovery."

Ofirin nods. "Good. I need more rest. And food."

We find a shallow cave, hidden by dense foliage, and settle in.

I've gone viral! Oh my God!

I stretch and yawn. *I have no idea what you mean, Sitlali.*

My little speech, she explains. *Thousands of people have watched it. It's being shared everywhere. And the comments, Calizto! People are outraged. Demanding action. A caravan is heading this way to stage a protest.*

You've said that in the future, governments are influenced by popular opinion. Since all citizens can vote to decide who their leaders are, negative rumors and displays may ruin a person's ability to rule.

Hang on, she tells me.

The early afternoon sun is gradually covered by clouds that pile higher and higher.

They're pissed, she finally says. *We refused to go to the cafeteria to eat. Told them we're on a hunger strike until they do something about these deplorable conditions.*

I don't like the idea of your not eating, beloved.

I'll be fine. I've gone without food before, Calizto.

Be careful, I insist. *Your guards will look for a target when pressure builds.*

It's not long before my words prove prophetic. Rebecca's phone reveals that the exterior of their prison is replete with people who've traveled to protest their plight. Professional news criers—reporters—have arrived in droves to carry word of the hunger strike to the rest of the world.

The guards attempt to enter the cell in which Sitlali's pod is caged, but the women prevent their entrance for a time and refuse to comply with any directives. They lash themselves to the mesh of the cage with strips of clothing and defy their captors to move them by force.

"We're not budging," shouts Sitlali, "until you meet our demands!"

The other women, caught up in the fervor of their young leader, shout their agreement, peppered with stinging epithets.

Through Sitlali's eyes, I see the rise of ire in the guards' demeanor. This confrontation will not end well.

But I am distracted from her situation by the arrival of the Spaniards. Several hundred men march past while Ofirin and I huddle together, as soundlessly as possible. I cannot afford to risk myself, not now.

When at last I am able to return my attention to her, a man stands over her. He is dressed strangely, in black breeches and jacket, a red-striped strip of fabric tied around his neck.

"You've violated the terms of your stay in this center," he snarls at Sitlali. "Where's the phone you used to upload that video?"

"I dumped it in one of your nasty, overflowing toilets," she snaps back. "Go root around in them until you find it, Mr. Director."

"Giving me lip won't help," he says, gesturing to a pair of guards I haven't seen before. "Since you're the instigator, you may want some time to cool down and rethink your revolt. I'm going to separate you from your little friends here. Put her in the conference room."

The guards grab her upper arms and haul her to her feet.

As she struggles against them, her fingers press against all four of the interactive glyphs at once.

I quickly do the same.

"Let go, bastards," I spit as my voice becomes hers, our bodies fuse, and, by the gods' design, we become one.

The idiot on our right gives an empty, stupid laugh. By instinct, I curl our free hand into a fist and slam it back into his nose with every ounce of force my training can wrest from her body.

Blood spurts from the guard's nose. He lets go of Sitlali to grab at his face as he moans like a little child.

"Now you've done it. You've assaulted an employee of this center," the director shouts. "You clearly need more than just some time to cool off. A couple of days of isolation ought to do the trick."

The uninjured guard wraps his arms around her, pinning her hands to her chest. She can no longer touch the glyphs.

All I can do is watch her, floating in the air before me, being hauled away. She kicks and struggles, to no avail.

Forgive me, Sitlali! I've made things worse.

She does not respond.

It's pitch-black in this room.

Ofirin and I are walking again, since the Spaniards have passed our position. Sitlali has been sobbing, refusing to speak. Until now.

Night is falling here as well. But we must carry on even in the darkness.

I'm sorry for not answering you. I'm just angry, Sitlali bemoans. *More at myself than anyone else. What the hell was I thinking? I can't change anything. Nobody can. I told you, we're just animals to them, and they have the support of nearly half this godforsaken country.*

I take a deep breath and exhale, wishing I were there to hold her. *Ah, Sitlali. You mustn't despair. There's dignity in the struggle for what's right, even when the odds are against us and the outcome certain. How we face defeat defines us more than how we celebrate victory.*

Like the Mexica, she says, weeping again.

My chest tightens. I've been avoiding this topic for days, but I must know.

How . . . how do my people face their end, Sitlali? With honor? With courage?

I can see her body shudder as she takes a deep breath. She looks at me, tears streaming down her face.

Oh, beloved. I can't. It's too much . . . My heart breaks when I think . . .

Tell me. Please. I must know.

Sitlali averts her eyes. *The Mexica stand until every last knight falls. The emperor refuses all attempts at negotiation. Starving, your people end up eating the straw in the adobe bricks of their shattered homes. The end comes in one month, on August 13. Activity inside Tlatelolco will grind to a halt. Bad water and starvation will have broken the Mexica. The streets will be . . .*

Blood-soaked. It is not a question. I can imagine the destruction.

Yes. Rotting corpses will line every walkway.

I grit my teeth so hard there is an audible crack. Ofirin stares at me, worry on his features. I wave his attention back at the faded path.

How exactly does it end? Are they all slaughtered?

No, Calizto, she says. *After ninety-three days of siege, Cuauhtemoc will decide enough is enough. In the middle of a heavy downpour, he'll get into a canoe along with Tecuichpo and his closest advisors. They'll row to a Spanish brigantine and . . .*

He surrenders, I surmise.

On the condition that the surviving Mexica be allowed to leave the island to search for food. When word spreads, the remaining families spill from the ruins to seek food in the countryside or with relatives in distant towns.

What happens to the orphans, Sitlali? The ones left in the rubble, who don't hear the news, who are too weak to move?

I don't know, she admits. *Our history books don't tell us that.*

I know, Calizto sighs. *They'll die. Or become slaves, playthings. I know of the Spaniards' twisted appetites.*

Sitlali turns to look at me, heartbroken. *I'm so sorry there was nothing we could do.*

The cosmos exists as a tension between order and chaos, I tell her. *For the moment, chaos wins. Tenochtitlan is the unshakeable foundation of heaven, poets once sang. But Tezcatlipoca, the enemy of both sides, has chosen its destruction. I cannot fathom why. Still, the goddess put this conch in our hands. It's kept us safe and sane. I believe there's a greater purpose we haven't glimpsed.*

Sitlali nods. *Yes. We were chosen.*

In the darkling light, clouds blocking the rise of the moon and the evening star from view, I look at the moon glyph.

Touch the moon, my love.

As we do, the world is transformed. The valleys are now lit by a silver glow, as if the moon has lost its dark spots and glows as it once did at the beginning of time, as if the clouds have been burned away by that pure white fire.

Calizto! I can see! The room is lit up by the most gorgeous light.

"Her bells," I whisper. "Coyolxauhqui's silver bells."

Thank you, Tonantzin, Sitlali prays.

Ofirin has stopped a few rods away.

"I can't see a thing."

"That's fine," I reply, taking his hand. "I can."

As the goddess floods my path with light, I guide Ofirin through those ancient woods.

CHAPTER FORTY-FIVE

Sitlali

July 14, 2019

I lie on my side in the darkness of an empty room.

Keys rattle, and the doorknob turns, so I scramble to sit up. I feel for my bag and slide it into the corner behind me. I put my hand up and turn my face away. Through the slit of narrowed eyes, I see a guard standing over me.

"Get up," she orders. "Now! If you want to eat!"

"But I don't," I remind her.

"So that's it?" she asks, staring down at me, one hand on her hip, the other balancing a food tray. "You're not eating?"

"Not until you stop treating us like animals."

The guard lets out a sigh and looks at the wall in front of me. "Okay, suit yourself!" Then she drops the tray of food beside me.

Brown gruel flies up and lands on my leg. The simple act makes a rabid rage rise up in me, and I pick the bowl up and throw it at the guard.

The bowl hits the back of her head, splattering gruel over her hair. She starts to turn around, but before she has a chance to come at me, I bombard her with the rest of the food items on my tray. A roll, a milk carton, an orange, plasticware—absolutely everything on my plate is a hurled weapon.

The guard leans down to restrain me. But I'm too fast. I use the force of her own body's weight, grab her arms, and pull her down. We wrestle, but I twist her arm behind her, slam her over on her stomach, and shove a knee against her back.

"Let me go!" she yells as she struggles. "Let me go, you fucking bitch!"

Sitlali! What is happening? Calizto looks shocked as he awakens to find me leaning over the guard's back.

I press her face against the filthy ceramic floor. "Apologize!"

"Why should I?" the guard asks, craning her neck and spitting the words out at me. "Look at you. You're a wretch. You smell like a goat. You and your friends are worse than animals! You're lice on beasts. Parasites. All of you!"

Don't hesitate, Little Star, Calizto urges. *Snap her neck. The violence is justified.*

"That's enough!" an authoritative voice yells from the door.

Two male guards rush in and pull me off the female officer. I struggle, but they handcuff me and drop me on the floor. I scoot to the corner and press my back against the wall.

Breathe, Calizto whispers. *Don't let them think they've won.*

"What did I tell you? Strong as an ox," one of the male guards tells the director.

"Drugs, probably," the other male guard says. "Only reason she broke my nose yesterday."

I would've pulled out his heart if I'd had more time! Calizto snarls.

"Go see the nurse," the director tells the female guard. "And let her know we need a drug test for this woman."

The guard nods and leaves, looking back at me in disgust.

The director pulls out a little notepad and flips it open. "Sitlali Morales," he reads. "Do you know how much trouble you're in?"

"Yes. Do you?" I ask. "Seventy-five thousand views and counting. Reporters circling your detention center. That's a lot of trouble."

"This is your second attack," the director reminds me.

"I can count."

"After your drug test, we're turning you over to the police. Two accounts of assault on peace officers. In a few hours, you won't be our problem anymore."

I lower my head, let the hair fall over my face, and hide the hot, shameful tears that start rolling down my cheeks, because I didn't trek halfway across the world to end up incarcerated like a criminal. This was never part of the plan.

Calizto takes a deep breath and swears.

Don't cry, my Little Star. In two more nights, the moon will own the sky again. Once that happens, we'll get you out of this terrible place. You'll be free if it's the last thing I do.

I love you, I tell him.

And I adore you, he replies with a wry, worried smile. *But we need to get you unleashed. We can't interact fully if you can't touch the glyphs.*

"Can you please take the cuffs off?" I ask the director, who is writing something in his notepad. My tone is courteous, because I want him to see that I am calm and don't intend to fight anymore. "Please. They're cutting off my circulation."

The director nods at one of the guards who pulls me up and uncuffs me. I rub my wrists and sit down on the floor again, careful to keep my bag at my back, away from their eyes and hands.

"Thank you," I whisper, and the director and two guards leave. They close the door and turn the lights off again.

When they are gone, Calizto and I trigger the eye and ear glyphs. Immediately, the darkness around me dissipates, and I am in that other time again with my beloved.

Ofirin comes into the camp, a rabbit in one hand, two men behind him.

"I just encountered these lumberjacks," he explains to Calizto, eyes glimmering. "Father and son. They've seen a dark-skinned girl my age in the village of Xomotlan."

The older man takes out an obsidian knife and passes it to the younger. Then he gestures at the rabbit. "Skin it while we talk, my son. Good to meet you, young noble. I recognized your companion as a foreigner. We do a lot of business in Acolhuacan. Hundreds of civilians brought by the Caxtiltecah were captured last year by Acolhua soldiers. They were furious that their king had been killed by the retreating Spaniards when he was visiting Tenochtitlan."

Calizto picks up a stick and pokes at the fire, moving embers around so that he can distribute them evenly on the ground. "Rumors reached us in Tenochtitlan. Many innocents were sacrificed in the town of Zoltepec, people whispered."

The son, finished skinning and gutting, spits the rabbit. "A few a day," he adds. "Over the course of six months, rumors claim."

The father nods. "Hmm. Yes. But the darkest young woman, she got free."

"Eeeeeat! Eeeeeat!"

A woman's wail pierces through my senses, and my hand slips away from the conch, making everything dark again.

What was that? Calizto turns to look at me.

"Eeeeeeat! Eeeeat!" the woman's voice wails. I shiver as I wait for what I know is coming.

Sitlali? Who is that?

My mother's spirit begins to appear before me, a transparent gray form that shifts and shivers as it manifests itself.

It's my mother. She looks worse than ever, I tell Calizto because my mother is a gray corpse with hair so thin and sparse I can see patches of scalp underneath it. And her face—her face is all eaten up with rot and decay! Her dull eyes are sunken into their sockets, and her skin is shriveled over her hollow cheeks. "You are not my mother!" I scream, shrinking away from her as she floats above me.

Little Star, the conch! Calizto's urgent voice competes with the wavering, quivering form of my dead mother coming toward me in the darkness of the room. *I can't help you if you won't press the glyphs!*

"Go away. Please, whoever you are, whatever you are, please leave," I whisper to her.

Sitlali, please touch the conch, Calizto insists.

"Eeeeat! Eeeeeat!" my mother wails.

I close my eyes and will myself to lift my hands. I feel for the ear and eye glyphs, and when I think I have them, I press down.

Dear goddess! Calizto whispers.

My mother wails as her ghostly figure comes in and out from the other side. "*Eeeeeat!*" she wails. "*You must eat!*"

Don't be afraid, Calizto says, as he sits beside me. *This is part of her journey.*

She must be mad because of the hunger strike, I tell Calizto. *I just wish I understood why she's come back like this.*

What do you mean? Calizto asks.

You know, I tell him. *All scary looking. It's not like this is helping me.*

Perhaps that's not why she comes, Calizto hypothesizes. *Perhaps she's looking for a way out. For both of you.*

I shake my head. *You've lost me.*

Forgive me, Calizto asks gently. *But may I ask how she passed?*

The question throws me, and I physically recoil from him. *I'm sorry. I've just . . . Well, I've never . . .*

Calizto holds fast to the conch and reaches over to try to touch my free hand, but it's no use. We can't touch yet. *I only ask because it might help me to know what still haunts her.*

She starved herself to death. The words escape me, leave my lips, and fly away, like a flock of tiny red birds that's been trapped inside me most of my life. *The women in the village said she died of sadness. My abuela Lucía said she died of a broken heart because my father abandoned us. But the coroner said her malnourished heart just couldn't pump blood anymore.*

I understand, Calizto says. *I believe your mother's ghost is trapped in one of the nine levels of Mictlan. You must talk to her, help her resolve her conflicts in this world.*

I nod because I've read about this. *Only by releasing her earthly bonds can one pass through Mictlan and reach the center of the Underworld.*

Calizto nods. *Into the Unknowable Realm.*

Paradise, I whisper, a shuddering sigh escaping my chest.

Paradise. Yes.

And if she can't release her earthly attachments? I ask him.

If she won't let you go, she will not find peace and forgiveness, Calizto whispers. *Divine Forgiveness. Do you understand?*

I take a deep breath and release it. *I do. But I don't know what to do . . . How could I possibly help her, when I don't know what she wants . . . what she needs from me?*

It is something only you can do. I am here if you should need me, Calizto says, as he gets up and steps away so that he remains in the background, holding the conch under his arm.

Quietly, I stand up and walk around the quivering figure of my mother's ghastly apparition. *I am not afraid of my mother. I am not afraid of my mother*, I keep telling myself.

"Mom?" I call out sweetly, in the voice of the child she left behind, hoping that she will remember me.

My mother's tormented gaze is fixed on the door. But her eyes narrow when I call out to her again. "Mom? Can you please . . . look at me . . . ?"

My mother's dull gaze moves about the room. She seems to be looking for me. "Are you worried about me? That's why you came that last time—at my madrina's house—isn't it? You wanted to warn me about my father's wife, Samantha."

"Stay away from that woman," my mother says, her bulging eyes scanning the darkness of the room. "She has nothing but poison—poison—in her heart."

"I know," I tell my mother. "But it doesn't matter. You have to let it go, Mom. This anger—it doesn't serve you anymore. It's over. It's in the past."

"Poison!" my mother wails. She starts to cry, and, as her shoulders shake, she begins to descend so that soon her feet are touching the floor and she looks like she did in real life. "Eat. You must eat!" she wails.

Calizto moves along the wall behind me as I stand before her. My mother's gaze lingers on my face for a moment; then she looks at my hair, my shoulders, and focuses on my hands. "You must eat," she whispers again.

"I will," I tell her. "I promise. But you shouldn't worry about me, Mom. I'll be okay."

My mother reaches out. Her pale, ghostly hand traces the handcuff marks on my wrists. Deep, dark lines form on her gray forehead, thick, translucent tears fall from her closed lids, and she starts to cry again, a mournful sob that breaks my heart. "I'm sorry," she whispers. "I'm sorry I couldn't stay. I'm sorry I wasn't there for you."

"Please, don't be sorry. Let's just put that behind us. Okay?" I ask her.

Then, because she is my mother and I love her, I take her hands. Her cold, dead fingers are thin and parched, like packed sand. I close my eyes, and, suddenly, I am on the beach in Veracruz again, a child holding my mother's hands. We stand still for a moment, letting the wind in that distant land caress our glowing faces, our outstretched arms, our linked fingers. It is just the two of us then, connected in love, my father—a distant memory. Forgiven. Foreign. Forgotten.

When I open my eyes again, my mother is smiling at me. "You don't need me anymore."

It is not a question.

"I need you to let me go," I tell her. "I'm all right now. I thought I needed to find my father, but I don't. I have everything I need to get through this. I'm strong. And healthy. And smart. Plus, I have Calizto by my side."

"Calizto," my mother repeats the name and frowns.

"Yes," I say, checking to make sure Calizto is still behind me. "The goddess of the moon brought us together. With her magic conch, we will find our way out of this mess. You can set all your worries aside and move forward on your journey through Mictlan. It's okay to let me go. I'm well. I'm fine. I'm . . . beloved."

My mother lifts her eyes and looks at Calizto behind me. "Yes," she whispers. "You are. Truly loved."

CHAPTER FORTY-SIX

Calizto

Day 11-Vulture of the Year 3-House (July 15, 1521)

Ofirin is up before dawn, anxious to get moving.

"What if it's her, Calizto?" he keeps repeating. "'The darkest young woman,' the lumberjacks said. My Enaben was beautiful and dark, a goddess of the night sky."

I put my arm around his shoulders. "It must be her, dear friend. Let's trust that the gods have some measure of peace in store for us both."

Most of the morning is spent taking a detour toward the village of Xomotlan. When the sun is overhead, we stop and eat.

My exhausted Sitlali has slept late, but she jerks awake, and I reach for the conch to see what is happening.

Beloved, the glyphs.

They just threw the food in at me, she grumbles as she lets me see. *Like I'm a fucking animal. No tray, just various types of food, some wrapped in the clear paper called plastic, some still rolling in the dust of the insect-ridden floor.*

Rage rises in me, but I clench my teeth and do what I can to comfort her. *Try to endure it. Just a little longer. Tomorrow evening the moon rises full. Then, even if I have to cleave open the very universe, I'll release you from that cell.*

Thank you. She sighs and gives a little laugh. *It's a good thing I'm on a hunger strike. Because that shit they just dropped on the floor does not look appetizing.*

I smile and finish the roasted snake Ofirin and I have spitted.

We are on our way to Xomotlan. Say a prayer to the goddess for us.

I will. I so want Ofirin to find happiness.

A few hours later, we reach the edge of a village. A man and woman are tending to a small milpa, squash and corn and beans carefully curling together.

"Good afternoon, my uncle, my aunt," I greet them formally. "Is this Xomotlan, by chance?"

They look up and notice Ofirin beside me. The woman smiles.

"Are you one of her people, sir?" she asks him.

"Whose?" he responds, eyes wide.

"Enaben's."

A sob wrenches itself from Ofirin's chest. Tears of relief roll down his cheeks.

"She's here? Really?"

Now the man speaks. "Yes. She's been waiting. For someone. Keep walking forward. You'll find her carrying water from the well. It's the job she was assigned in return for our protection."

I can hardly keep up with Ofirin as he hurries along the path. We come to the center of town, dominated by a small temple and a cistern. Ofirin whips his head back and forth.

"Where?" he moans. "Where is she?"

Then, rounding a corner and entering the square, a beautiful African girl appears, dressed in a colorful huipil and skirt, balancing a clay pitcher on her head.

She sees Ofirin. Casts the pitcher aside. Runs to him.

I turn away to give them some privacy. They shout and cry and address each other lovingly in their people's tongue.

Gripping the conch, Sitlali listens through my ears.

I can't wait to hug you like that, she tells me. *I rejoice for them, but I'm dying to hold you close.*

As am I, my precious and beautiful Little Star.

Sometime later, the three of us are sitting on the floor in the room Enaben has been given by the townsfolk. Ofirin has narrated our story up to the present, and his beloved can't take her eyes off the moon conch in my hands.

"Can Sitlali hear me?" she asks. "Can we speak?"

If you don't mind, Calizto . . .

No, of course not. Go ahead.

"Hi, Enaben," Sitlali says through my mouth. "It's me. I'm so happy to meet you, to see that you're okay. And to watch you be reunited with Ofirin, so near and dear to my heart."

"Thank you for watching over him," Enaben says. "I'll never forget what you have done for us."

"What will you do?" Sitlali asks. "Remain here?"

Enaben looks at Ofirin, smiling. "For a time. But I worry about living in these mountains. The Spaniards will keep arriving, in droves, I'm sure. They'll enslave us once again."

Sitlali reaches out with my hand and touches the woman's arm. "Life will be hard for the next decade. There will be few places safe for

African people in this country. On this continent. But perhaps you should make your way to Tlacopan."

Ofirin raises an eyebrow. "That's one of the imperial seats of power, Sitlali. I'm sure some Spanish bastards have already taken control of it."

Enaben gives him a little shove. "What language is that for mixed company, love? Your manners are sorely lacking."

Sitlali explains. "Empress Tecuichpotzin has real respect for Ofirin. Not long from now, the emperor will die. Cortés will make the widow his ward. She'll become Catholic, baptized Isabel Moctezuma. Cortés is going to make Doña Isabel marry one of his friends. Her dowry? The entire city-state of Tlacopan."

Ofirin leans forward. "She'll get to rule it?"

"Not exactly," Sitlali clarifies. "But that husband will die, and so will her next. Then the fifth husband will die as well. Her sixth and final marriage will last, however, and the former empress will control a huge encomienda there. Dearest friends, I wish I had something other than servitude to recommend. But the world you live in will continue to be brutal to Black people for centuries. Isabel at least will treat you with some dignity. And when she dies, she'll free her slaves. Your children will be safe."

Enaben nods soberly. "We'll consider that option. What matters most is that we're together."

"Forever," Ofirin adds, lacing his fingers through hers.

I think I see something, Sitlali tells me. *Behind them. But I need to look more carefully.*

You mean with your own eyes, yes? With your . . . gift?

Yes.

We use all four glyphs—ear, eyes, hand, mouth—to fuse across time. Sitlali makes our body stand and stares with our enhanced eyes.

I cannot believe what we see.

"Enaben. Ofirin," we say to our friends. "Know that right now, as you sit here, you're surrounded by spirits. Folks of all genders and ages, dressed in lovely clothes of bright colors. They are African. They are smiling at you both."

Enaben is overcome with tearful joy.

"Our ancestors!" she cries. "They've come. I called to them, prayed for their protection, and they've crossed the broad ocean to be with their stolen children."

Oh, Calizto, I almost can't bear it. So beautiful and yet so sad.

The poet king Nezahualcoyotl spoke of this, I tell her. *The poignant, fleeting nature of life. It's like a dream, he said. Brief and lovely. We are lent to one another for just a short time. Like flowers, friendship is colorful and bright, sweet-swelling and intoxicating. But everything withers. Everything fades. In the end, people must move on.*

Knowing it is time for us to do precisely that, we take Ofirin and Enaben in our arms for one last embrace, wishing them all the happiness that this slippery earth can offer.

It feels strange to travel alone. I already miss Ofirin. He was a part of my life for more than a year. Only now do I fully appreciate the man, his influence on my life and my views. Sitlali leaves me to my thoughts, wrapped up in her own dilemma as she is escorted to shower and change after they have made her collect her urine.

Hours pass. The sun slips down the western sky.

How much farther? she asks, when she returns to the dark. *Another day?*

Yes. At nightfall, there should only be another seven of your hours left in my journey to the sea. Tomorrow afternoon I'll reach the low cliffs above the beach.

And then?

Then we'll find a way to live together and love each other across the centuries. I'll stay by the sea in case any danger should ever arise. I cannot die without placing the conch in the waves so that in the future you may find it.

But you won't die for a very long time. Neither will I. We're going to make this work, Calizto. We have to. Our love is too strong for the cosmos to crush it.

No one and nothing will keep me from you, beloved.

As if on cue, a dozen Spaniards burst from the trees around me, rifles raised.

"Halt!" one of them growls. "Ximoquetz!"

"Do not dirty my people's clear speech with your rotten tongue," I say in Spanish.

Another one laughs. "One of the beasts speaks Christian. A fucking miracle."

The conch is in my hand. I start sliding my fingers toward the glyphs. *Sitlali, take up the conch. We might need to merge again.*

From behind the circle of soldiers, another figure emerges. A young priest, eyes sunken, hair already thinning. He cannot be much older than I am, perhaps twenty-one, but he looks sickly and undernourished.

"Greetings, heathen. I am Father Palomares."

I scoff. "Father. What a strange title for such a one as you."

Which glyph? Sitlali asks, anticipating my next move. *The sun?*

Their weapons are trained on me. Blinding light may not be the right option.

What's left? The bar with three lines curling away—

The wind, I realize with a start.

To blow them away?

Perhaps not. We call Tezcatlipoca the wind. Because he is invisible. And everywhere.

"That large shell you hold in your hands, boy," Palomares says, moving closer, his black robes swirling in the twilight air. "Cortés has sent word he wants it. I suspect it's the source of the light the Tlaxcaltecah say you wield to blind men. I doubt claims of such sorcery, but beware. These men will fire if you lift that conch or if a single ray of light begins to shine from within it."

The wind it is, Sitlali says. *On the count of three.*

One.

Two.

Three.

We press the glyph, and I drop to one knee, ready for anything. The world seems oddly out of focus, as if I've rubbed my eyes too hard upon awakening.

"What?" the priest exclaims. "Where did he go?"

The soldiers swing their weapons around, glaring at the gloom amid the trees.

As quietly as possible, I stand and walk between them.

Oh my God, Calizto: you're invisible!

I wait until I have gotten a hundred rods away before responding.

That was too close for comfort. But now we know something I feared.

A wave of dread comes from my beloved. *They're looking for you. They know what you have in your hands.*

Power.

What will you do? There is desperation flowering in her heart. *How can we make this work if they keep coming? You can't be on the run forever!*

As darkness thickens around me, I find a dense thicket of trees and ensconce myself within its depths. Sitlali's form settles in beside me.

All I need is you, I tell her. *If you're by my side, I can deal with any obstacle. I love you, Sitlali, more than anything. Will you—will you be mine, always? Joined with me before the cosmos itself, before gods and stars and swirling black void?*

I hear her sobbing. I'm afraid for a moment.

But in the midst of her tears, she gives a joyful response.

Yes, Calizto. A thousand times yes.

CHAPTER FORTY-SEVEN

Sitlali

July 16, 2019

The clatter of the breakfast tray as it hits the floor wakes me up.

"You need to eat, girl," snaps the guard.

I turn my head, not toward her, but to see if Calizto is up. He's walking along uneven terrain. Catching sight of my open eyes, he smiles at me.

Good morning, Sitlali.

Hey there, handsome. Last day till the beach?

Yes. By afternoon there will be sand, not rocks, beneath my aching feet. How are you feeling?

Weak. But okay.

The guard sighs heavily. "What are you smiling about? Crazy junkie!"

I turn my gaze upon her and lift my middle finger. "Fuck off. I don't have time for you."

The guard laughs. "Busy, are we?"

I press my fingertips against the bridge of my nose. The light is hurting my eyes, and I can't concentrate on what Calizto is saying. "Just shut up!"

The guard's face hardens. "I'll be back."

Walk with me, Sitlali. There's nothing for you in that cell. Let's leave these mountains together and behold the glittering sea of jade.

The guard closes the door, and I take the conch out. Calizto and I press the glyphs and fuse again. Content to be in each other's mind, we head east together. The path Calizto has chosen is easy. It slopes down slowly, giving a light spring to our every step. We go from mountainside to foothills, the forest giving way to bushy, grassy valleys. I relish the fresh air as it enters our lungs, the brisk touch of a brazen breeze brushing against our face.

By midday, I catch a whiff of the sea, a briny scent that tastes like oysters and mussels tangled in seaweed and tinged with gray sandy muck. As I daydream about burying our feet into that wet sand and letting the cold waves lap at our ankles and calves, I'm reminded of my last moment with my friends in Veracruz, of the feel of the conch in my hands when I pulled it out of its watery bed for the first time. But that was a lifetime ago. I am a whole other person now.

Now, I believe in the power of love to sustain us.

Even in our darkest hour.

No matter what happens, I tell Calizto, *I'm glad that I found this shell on the beach.*

As am I. It may sound terrible, but if our suffering was the price for our being brought together, then I'm glad I suffered.

A part of me hears the door to my cell bang open again; several people enter.

"See?" the female guard exclaims. "I'm telling you, she's high. Just look at those glazed eyes. And that stupid smile. She hasn't moved since I left."

"What do you suggest, Betty?" another guard asks.

Betty's voice is quiet, but firm. "We need to find her stash. Strip her down."

"A cavity search?" the other guard questions. "We've got to notify medical . . . She's got to be sent off-site for this."

"Fuck that! She already fooled the nurse with that negative urine test," Betty says. "I'm ending this now!"

What? I can feel Calizto's rage coursing through our body, right before one of the guards rips the conch out of my hands and I am pulled out of that other place where he and I are one and the same.

"You can't do this!" I scream. "It's illegal!"

Calizto feels my fear.

What are they doing?

Trying to put their hands on my body, I tell him, shame crawling over my skin, rising inside me like a swelling wave. *To search inside me, looking for the drugs they think I'm hiding.*

Part of me wants to throw them off. But no matter how much I fight and scream, nobody stops Betty from doing what she came to do. They begin to tear my clothes off. I close my eyes and pretend that what is going on is not happening to me.

I am no longer Sitlali Morales.

I am no longer my own self.

I am no longer human.

When it's over, and the guards are gone, I dress as quickly as possible. Tears are rolling down my face, and my knees are buckling as I tremble with rage and something else, something innocent, something sensitive that's died inside me.

And I grieve.

Sitlali, Calizto whispers from somewhere in the darkness of that darkest of moments. *Come back to me. Come back to me, beloved. Let me hold you in my heart.*

Trembling, I find the conch the guards have already forgotten about and let myself be in Calizto's consciousness again. There is no need to speak. Our thoughts are as one, so we just lie still and hold fast to the love in our hearts, until movement on a hilltop distracts us. We look up with our shared eyes to see a pair of Tlaxcaltecah scouts, who nod at each other and disappear down the farther slope.

Calizto!

I know. We need to get out of here. Now.

As we take off running, the wind carries us down a sloping path, and unexpectedly, from the nearby bushes and trees, a cloud of birds and butterflies bursts into the air. Startled, we stumble and stagger before we stop and stare. But there's something strange about the massive flock of colorful creatures that have taken flight, turning the landscape into a multicolored painting. We look more closely, and then I understand.

Calizto! They're spirits!

Yes. The ancestors, Calizto confirms.

The riot of colorful wings swirls through the air for a moment and then dives down to the earth, leveling off at the last moment to stream along a different path than the one we're on.

Transfixed, we follow.

The twisting, winding route pulls us southeast, across less even terrain, through the rocks and brambles.

But then Calizto's departed dead flutter their wings, take flight, and urge us forward again, leading us another way. We follow them because we know they are here to guide us in the right direction. As twilight thickens, however, the winged souls begin to fade. We stop on the crest of a hill overlooking the sea. Stars have begun to glitter above its roiling expanse.

In my time, my calf muscle spasms with a debilitating cramp that makes me cry out. I pull away from Calizto and come back into the present. I lift myself off the floor to sit up, rubbing my leg, trying to make the pain go away. Concerned, Calizto reaches out his long, lithe fingers and makes contact with mine.

The feeling is electric.

As our fingers interlace, he pulls me close and presses a kiss on my forehead.

"Oh, look at that," I whisper, as a soft glowing light calls our eyes up to the sky, and we witness the clouds separating and drifting apart. A bright, benefic light begins to descend on the world as they come apart. Its golden glow creeps across the waxing moon, casting a red flame over her face, creating a celestial crescent, and sending rosy rays of light across the gray of the midnight sky.

Standing beside me, Calizto wraps his arms around my waist.

"Beloved," he whispers against my flushed cheeks. His lips on mine are passion infused with warmth and light, a triumphant kiss that makes me melt. I wrap my arms around his neck and return his kiss with equal fervor. I've been longing for this for a whole month!

Calizto's hand leaves my waist, to sweep my hair back, away from my face so he might press kisses on my nose, my cheeks, my forehead, my temple. I bury my face into his neck and place a soft kiss there as we cling to each other.

"I missed you," I whisper, as he holds me tight against his chest. "So, so much!"

"I never want to be apart, ever again." His lips press sweet little kisses on mine, each one hungrier than the last.

The moon above is so radiant that I am afraid we might be discovered by his pursuers. So, I put my hand on his chest and push him away, just far enough so that I can look into his glistening eyes. "I think we should find a better place to hide. To rest. To . . ."

"Lie down?" The soft glimmer in Calizto's mischievous eyes makes me heat again.

I stand on my tippy-toes and plant a quick, playful kiss on his lips.

"Don't tease me!" I say, as I pull his hand off my hip and step back. I don't know why, but I am suddenly shy, which is strange, because I am sure that what he is insinuating is something we both want.

He is *my always.*

Created and brought to me by the Divine.

That is what the conch has done. I am sure of it.

As we make our way down the slope, we see where Calizto's ancestors have gone. Transformed, one by one, a myriad of ghostly apparitions step out of the tree line and look upon us. As we pass them by, they point us in the direction of the steep incline of a hill overlooking the beach.

Clinging to Calizto's hand as I walk beside him, I ask, "Why are they in human form?"

"The sun has set, Little Star," he explains. "Tonatiuh, who gives them wings, rests in darkness now, his flame rekindled by attendant spirits. And, perhaps, my ancestors wish to look with human eyes upon their son and the woman he loves."

I look at them carefully. Men, dressed in everything from maxtlatl loincloths like the one Calizto wears to cotton pants to modern suits. Women in clothing from different centuries, from colorful huipil and skirts to long, dark skirts and ruffled shirts.

"Wait," I whisper, "these aren't just your ancestors, Calizto. Some of them . . . some of them must be mine. How can they all be here at the same time?"

Calizto lifts his version of the conch to me. "Magic?"

"The goddess, no doubt!" I concur.

Our ancestors lift their arms up in the air, and the song of a thousand cicadas gives them voice, a cacophony of divine, delicate drums vibrating from under transparent wings and resonating around us like a magical moonlit chant.

We continue on the path, moving gingerly toward the hill's incline, unsure of where we are being led until we come to the mouth of a dark cave. An ancient couple with white hair and dark, weathered features lift the nightly veil, a transparent penumbra that allows the soft glow radiating from its depth to illuminate our way as we go deep into the cavern.

Inside, we see that everything has been readied for our arrival. A feast has been laid out beside a quiet fire that spits in a bed of rock. There are flowers everywhere. Petals of roses and hibiscus are strewn along the floor leading to a bed of straw with a soft-looking blanket cast upon it. The sight of it makes my cheeks warm, and I turn away, bumping into Calizto.

"What is this?" I ask him. "Why did they . . . ?"

Calizto stops. He lifts my hand to his lips and places a kiss over my knuckles. "They have come to celebrate our union—as is the custom."

"Our union—"

Calizto turns to face me. His dark, luminous eyes are suddenly hooded, eclipsed as the light of that golden moon. "Unless, of course, you have changed your mind about me, about us."

"No, of course not," I say, my voice strong. Steadfast. "You are the love of my life. My now and my always."

Calizto pulls me close and kisses me, a soft, lingering kiss that weakens my knees and makes every cell in my body vibrate. "As you are mine. You are *my* Sitlali. My guiding star.

"Beloved," he whispers, as he lifts one edge of his weather-beaten cape and holds it before me. "As my ancestors have done for centuries, may I tie my tilma to your garment as my promise to always stay by your side?"

Because tears are forming in my eyes and I can't find my voice, I nod. Calizto's fingers tremble slightly, and he fumbles a bit, as he knots his cape to the tail of my T-shirt. Then, because the antepasados are chirping again, as they look at us with love and joy in their luminous eyes, Calizto puts his arms around me and kisses me, a deep, unabashed kiss that lasts a lifetime because neither one of us wants to be the one to end it.

"I love you," I whisper when Calizto presses his forehead against mine and we open our eyes to look at each other. And that's when I realize it. "They're gone!"

Calizto looks around us. "So they are," he says.

"Should we eat?" I whisper.

But Calizto's lips are tracing small kisses along my jawline, licking hungrily as he goes, making me feel light-headed so that my body feels luxuriously languid.

"Perhaps, later," he whispers in my ear. "I have other appetites to satisfy."

"Me too."

As his hands roam down, to linger at my waist, I pull him close, wrap my arms around his neck, and caress the soft skin of his shoulders, tracing a long, thin scar, from some long-ago battle. I will ask him later what happened, but for now, I kiss it, tasting the saltiness there, and testing his strength with a tiny, teasing bite that makes him look up at me, surprised.

"Oh, you want to test your power?" he asks, and he dips down, puts his arms around my thighs, and lifts me up in the air so that my feet are off the ground.

I yelp, and he walks us over to the bed, smiling the whole way. And when he eases me down without letting me go, I put my hand on his chest and caress the softness of his skin, tracing my fingertips, like feathers, all the way down, past the flatness of his abdomen, until I find what I am looking for.

Gently, I tug at the flap of white cotton at the front of his loincloth. "So, how does this thing work?"

Calizto looks up at our shadows dancing on the wall of the cave and laughs, a hearty, sexy laugh that makes me tingle all over. "No need for haste, Little Star. The gods will make sure this night lasts long enough to let us explore everything we have in common."

In response, I let my fingers trace the maxtlatl until I find the knot. I tug at it, softly at first and then not so gently.

Calizto smiles as I pull the fold of cloth through the knot and his loincloth falls from around his waist, dropping in a pile that I kick off the straw bed.

A wave of passion comes over me as I stare at Calizto's tall, lean body. There is beauty there, but also power and strength. Calizto looks unabashed as he stands before me, waiting. And when I finally reach for him, he reaches under my shirt and traces his fingertips delicately up my spine. Then, laughing at the absurdity of modern clothing, he pulls me free of it, careful to keep the conch close to us.

His lips on my skin are tiny swirls of flame and ocean, burning and quelling at the same time, as he explores my neck and shoulders. I close my eyes as he leads me down onto the softness of that blanket, where we let our love consume us.

CHAPTER FORTY-EIGHT

Calizto

Day 13-Flint of the Year 3-House (July 17, 1521)

Morning sunlight slants in through the entrance to the cave. I lie beside my bride, letting the beauty of her naked form fill my eyes and heart. I whisper a prayer of thanksgiving to the gods who deemed me worthy of such a woman, strong and beautiful, wise and brave.

"Are you," she mutters drowsily, "staring at me right now?"

I give a soft laugh. "How could I not? I have but a few days to memorize every lovely curve of your body before the goddess slowly pulls you from my hands."

Shyly but with determination, she opens her eyes and looks back at me. "Then kiss me, Calizto, and—"

From outside the cave comes a sound I know too well.

The whinny of a Spanish horse. I spring from our marriage bed, wrapping my loincloth around me and grabbing the moon conch.

Sitlali follows my lead, dressing hurriedly. "I was really hoping we'd have another perfect day before this bullshit started again."

"As was I . . . beloved wife."

Sitlali smiles, radiant. In her time, the door to her cell creaks open.

"Wakey-wakey, crazy bitch. Got to take you to the infirmary. They want blood, not piss."

In my time, Father Palomares shouts from somewhere nearby.

"Come out, pagan!"

Premonition seizes my innards, twisting. The one outcome I have hoped to avoid looms inescapable.

This is the day I die.

Am I the one who shields Sitlali? Is she the one who is destined to wield the conch? To what end, I cannot guess. But it's not my place to guess. It never was. My duty is to get the trumpet to her. I need only survive till I have hurled it into the waves.

Our fleeting time together has been a gift. Though until now I believed it so, we were not brought together to love.

"Surrender the source of your power," Palomares demands, "or I'll pry it from your dead fingers."

Sitlali looks at me, eyes wide. "You have to run, Calizto."

I nod. "Yes. Right into my fate."

But as I say those words, they seem an echo of another phrase.

A verse.

The final one. It comes unbidden to my lips, and I sing it to a startled Sitlali.

At last, at the end of it all,
the heir with a clarion call
through time and wave and wall
will step into her fate,
opening . . .

"Opening *what?*" she asks, seizing my arm. "Calizto, *think*! I have to know."

I kiss her silent. "There's no time. But it seems to mean . . . you have a fate beyond the walls of that prison. I love you, Sitlali. I'll get this conch to the sea, no matter what. If I never behold your beautiful face in this life, I'll await you in the next."

Not waiting for an answer, I rush out of the cave entrance.

Thanks to the eye glyph, I can see my beloved in my mind as I run. The guards escort her out of her cell, past cages that contain other women and children. Her friends reach for her, crying out words I cannot hear. Bruises and blood mottle their bodies.

The baby is gone.

What?

Sitlali runs to the cage, thrusts her fingers through the gaps, clinging as the guards try to drag her away.

"What happened? Where's the baby? Where's Teresita?"

I finally glance over my shoulder. Hundreds of Tlaxcaltecah warriors swarm the hills behind me. At their vanguard come the Spaniards, several on horseback, including the priest, who spurs his steed hard as he pursues me.

I turn and keep running toward the last swells of land, more dunes than hills.

She's dead, Calizto! The baby girl I held in my arms, the one I rocked to sleep, she's dead. Gone. These monsters let her die!

Roiling with grief and rage, she lashes out at her guards. She is strong, my Sitlali. She breaks the nose of the woman who keeps humiliating her, the one who assaulted her, and slams a knee into the gut of another. But they have weapons, sticks like clubs they use to beat her down as they drag her away.

Howling inside, I crest the low bluff, and the vast ocean spreads out before me, jade green and sparkling. I've never seen so much water, though I've dreamed of the ever-flowing skirt of Mother Sea, twining itself around the world, swaddling us in her watery embrace.

At another time, I might stare for hours, but the enemy is on my heels. A glance tells me reinforcements have arrived from the south, converging from the Spanish city at the mouth of the Huitzilpan River.

Gripping the moon conch against my chest, I descend toward the beach, my feet slipping on the tricky sand.

I'm a child of the highland, born to live and die close to the sun. But she needs me. She must receive this sacred shell, this tenuous thread of magic that connects her heart to mine across expanses of space and time.

Sitlali is dumped into a chair beside a table in a different room. A guard throws her bag at her, and she hugs it to her heart.

The police are coming, Calizto. They're going to interrogate me. Charge me. For assaulting officers. They say they'll put me in the darkest hole they can find.

Be strong, my love. Think. There must be a way. There are two more glyphs. The rectangle. The crane.

Clinging to rock and root, I make my way down. A rod or so from the bottom, I let go and drop to the sand, resting for the briefest of moments.

Sitlali looks up at someone. Winces and rubs her arm.

The nurse just drew blood. For another test. I'll be alone until the police show up.

A breeze blows off the ocean, bringing a smell I've never known.

And a voice. Roaring soft like a shell placed to my ear.

Singing the final lines of the song.

At last, at the end of it all,
the heir with a clarion call
through time and wave and wall
will step into her fate,
opening the gate
to save her beloved's life

and put an end to their strife.
Though safe, the two will not just flee—
they will return to set the others free.

I was wrong, I realize, tears springing to my eyes.

Our love was always the reason. From the very beginning.

"I can save you!" Sitlali shouts, no longer bothering to dissemble in her time.

The rectangle, Sitlali. Perhaps it is—

"Yes, the gate! Press it, Calizto!"

I smash my thumb against the glyph as she does the same.

Nothing happens.

Movement catches my eye, and I glance up the strand.

A hundred Spanish soldiers are rushing at me, some mounted on horseback. At their head stands the priest, his eyes wide as he sees the conch in my hands.

There is no time to lose. I cannot fail her. She must find it.

Without it, she will despair.

Without it, she will not have helped me.

Both of us will be lost.

Both of us will die.

"Goddess, give me strength!" I cry as I burst into movement, my feet pounding the beach, driving me toward the sea.

Their harquebuses spit lead balls into the sand around me. An arrow grazes my stomach, leaving a long and bloody groove.

I do not stop. Ignoring enemy fire, I plunge into the foaming waves, the conch held high.

"Take it, Mother Sea! Take this sacred shell and place it in her hands!"

And with all my strength, I fling the pink spiral into the swells.

CHAPTER FORTY-NINE

Sitlali

July 17, 2019 *and* July 17, 1521

Through the will of heaven, the conch has remained intact, even after all the abuse and brutality I have endured. Guards and nurses having forgotten its existence, I pick it up and set it on the table. But I don't have to press any glyph to see my beloved.

A series of visions invades my senses. *Calizto, thrashing through shallow waves. His naked chest panting. His arms pumping. The conch flying through the air. Wind roaring. Rays of sun glinting off the surface of the water. Arrows flying through the air. The conch splashing into the ocean.*

Falling.

Disappearing.

Gone.

The moon conch in my time goes cold under my hands, and I feel the connection between Calizto and me sever. Trembling, I close my eyes and see it sink into the depth of a dark green watery grave. I weep as tiny bubbles of trapped air burst from its most intimate, secret space as if its last breath were leaving it. I inhale, pulling a desperate breath into my lungs, as if I am drowning too.

"Madres Santas," I pray, ignoring the blinking red light of the security camera, heedless of the danger. "Don't let this be the end of love. Point the way to bring Calizto home. Only you, Virgencita de Guadalupe, and you, Moon Goddess, can help us now. Whisper words of wisdom into my mind. Guide my hands, my heart, my soul."

I open my eyes and look down at the conch under my hands. And as I continue to pray, I press my fingers against the rectangle and crane glyphs. Nothing happens. Reverently, prayerfully, I trace my fingertips against its inner walls, feel its smoothness, and let my fingers explore those translucent folds. Feeling its silky smoothness, probing its secret depths, I realize its very shape echoes a woman's most intimate folds.

"What does it mean?" I ask.

As I shut my eyes tightly together, like a parade of images, one after another, every moon priestess who ever held this sacred conch appears before me. Each shows me part of what to do before disappearing, allowing for the next priestess to manifest. Transfixed, I watch their adorned heads tilt up, their shoulders roll back, and their chests expand before they put their lips to the sacred conch and blow.

Of course!

Of course!

This is a woman's tool, made for the moon priestess of Metztonalco in Tenochtitlan. Only a woman can fully possess it. Only a woman can wield its true power. The realization makes my body tremble.

I am the heir! To step into my fate, I must pass through time and wave and wall . . . *with a clarion call!*

I open my eyes, lift the conch up to my lips, roll back my shoulders, and inhale.

"I am Sitlali Morales, daughter of the Fifth Sun," I whisper. "I ask for your assistance, Coyolxauhqui. Help me save my beloved's life."

I am about to blow when the rectangle glyph on the conch lights up.

"The gate glyph!" I cry out. "Yes! Thank you!"

Then I put my fingertips upon the symbol, press down, and blow.

The deep, hollow ring sets the floor and walls to thrumming.

A glowing, sacred door appears suspended in the air before me.

Without wasting a moment, I put the conch into my bag, zip it, and throw its strap over my shoulders, securing it across my chest.

On the other side of the room, the knob of the physical door turns.

The police are here.

Looking up at the camera, I give my enemies a triumphant smile.

Then I step through the glowing door before they can stop me.

Instantly, I find myself in the ocean beside Calizto. He is struggling underwater. Arms and legs askew, his hair swirls around his head like dark seaweed, because he is fighting to stay afloat. Without hesitating, I throw one arm around his shoulders and neck, press him hard against my side, and kick, swimming toward shore even as I pull him along.

The mounted soldiers slow their steeds just yards away. Tlaxcaltecah swarm the dunes.

We stop in shallow waters, coughing, panting, pulling fresh air into our lungs.

"Tlazohtlé," Calizto whispers. "Beloved. You came back. But how?"

I lift my head and push my hair out of my eyes to look at him, but I don't have time to dawdle. Behind him, on the sand, archers prepare to loose their arrows.

I help Calizto stand.

"Put your hands on the conch, my love," I tell him as I unzip my bag and press the conch between us. "Like this. Here. It's the last glyph. The final destination."

"Home," Calizto whispers as the arrows leap from their bows, hissing in the wind like a murmuration of winged vipers.

We put our fingers together on the crane glyph. A new portal opens, a different, brighter door, more resplendent than the one before. Glowing, swirling, azure light, the color of the heavens, promises so much more than we have ever had, so much more than we could ever hope.

Hand in hand, we step through it.

EPILOGUE

The Ancestors and the Gods

Otherwhen. Elsewhere.

We watch as our chosen children step into the land we have prepared for them.

They stand in the shallows of the mist-shrouded lake, the water lapping gently at their waists. Fingers still entwined, they look around at the verdant forest that encircles them.

All is quiet, calm.

Waiting.

From our midst, Sitlali's grandmother steps forth, glimmering into visibility on the shore before them.

"Welcome, beloved children," she greets them. "We are so very proud that you have come this far."

"Abuela?" Sitlali asks. "You're speaking!"

The spirit nods. "Here, I have a voice. We all do."

"What is this place?" Sitlali asks.

"Ah, dear granddaughter," she replies. "For many years our people have whispered of this land. Tamoanchan, some called it. Others, Aztlan.

A place of peace and protection, prepared in ages past just for this moment. It's home, Sitlali. Home."

The spirit hovers before the couple, waiting.

We wait as well. All their ancestors. All their gods.

They must choose. It must come from their joined hearts.

"What do we do," Calizto asks Sitlali, "now that we're safe?"

And our beloved daughter Sitlali, our chosen priestess, lifts the conch, her voice resolute as she tells her young husband:

"We go back for the rest of them. The ones in cages in the US. The ones hiding in the rubble in Tenochtitlan. Ofirin. Enaben. Every broken, orphaned soul."

She takes Calizto's hand and lays it on the conch, whispering fiercely.

"We save them all. We bring them home."

ACKNOWLEDGMENTS

This book, perhaps more so than others I've worked on, exists because of the support and research of many other people. First and foremost, of course, is Guadalupe García McCall, who conceived the central idea of the book and approached me to collaborate with her. Gracias, carnala, for your trust and friendship, on this project and all the others to come! I couldn't have asked for a better literary partner.

My depiction of Calizto's life and culture was enriched by the work of fantastic researchers like David Carrasco, Camilla Townsend, Alfredo Federico López Austin, Caroline Dodds Pennock, Miguel León-Portilla, Matthew Restall, Eloise Quiñones Keber, Ross Hassig, and Michael E. Smith, some of whom were even kind enough to answer questions I had along the way. I should also recognize the three people who in different ways inspired me to study Nahuatl, setting me on the path to writing about pre-Invasion Mesoamerica: Francisco X. Alarcón, Mark Glazer, and Gloria Anzaldúa.

And as always, a writer is nothing without a team that stands shoulder-to-shoulder with them. For me, that means my wife, Angélica; my children—Loba, Charlene, Angelo; my children-in-law, Jesse and Rachel; my agents, Taylor Martindale Kean and Stefanie Von Borstel; and the editor of this book, Mary Kate Castellani, along with the rest of the amazing folks at Bloomsbury.

Tlazohcamati, ammochintin! Thanks to you all!

—DB

There are so many people who've been instrumental in making this book come to life. First, of course, is mi colega, mi amigo, mi hermano del alma, David Bowles, who was generous enough to agree to write this book with me and give Calizto his voice. I can think of nobody better to work with. Gracias, David, for going on this journey with me and making my work shine with your wisdom and powerful, lyrical prose! You are the best kind of human being, gente buena, and I am full of gratitude for your friendship!

Second, I'd like to thank my beloved husband, Jim, the hero warrior in my universe, who is always protecting me, nurturing my soul, urging me to believe in myself, and supporting this work I love so much. Thank you, beautiful dear boy, your love and support means everything to me. My heart will always belong to you!

Third, I'd like to thank my inner circle, my children, James, Steven, and Jason, their significant others, and the newest light in my life, my granddaughter, Juliana, for making me feel welcomed, protected, and loved every single day of my life. Also, my first familia, my brothers and sisters, the García clan, who make me feel chiflada with all their admiration of my creative works. I love you all to pieces. You are all stars in my universe!

Last, but not least, I'd like to thank my literary team, Andrea Cascardi, for being the best literary agent a simple girl from the border could ever have! Thank you, Andrea, for championing my work so enthusiastically and passionately! Also, our editor, Mary Kate Castellani, whose love and commitment to this book fills me with joy. Thank you for helping to make this book so beautiful! It's gorgeous and lovely because you loved it so!

From the first to the last, you are all blessings in my life!

—GGM

ELLA DIJO/ÉL DIJO
AN AUTHORS' NOTE

GUADALUPE: The idea for this story came to me many moons ago. It was late at night, and I was sitting on the couch watching movie credits roll by on the television because I had just finished watching *The Lake House* with Sandra Bullock and Keanu Reeves. I enjoyed the movie so much that I mused out loud, "Now, why can't someone write something like that, but for YA?"

My husband, who was standing nearby, overheard me and said, "Oh, if only there was a YA novelist in the room . . . maybe we could ask her." It was funny, but it wasn't, because I was wrestling with a different YA novel at the time, pulling that story out of my protagonist in bits and pieces. The idea of starting *another* novel was out of the question.

Nevertheless, I remained fascinated by the concept of star-crossed lovers separated by time and space. *What would it look like, for me to write a time-bending YA fantasy novel?* I asked myself. Suddenly, I had the characters, the settings, and the conflict! *She* (later Sitlali) would be a young Mexican woman fleeing the gangs in her small coastal town. And the only way she can save herself is by traveling to the United States to find her long-estranged father. *He* (later Calizto) would be a Nahua warrior, fighting to stay alive during the fall of Tenochtitlan. *He* would have to flee the city with the Spanish on his trail. And they would communicate through some ancient artifact she carries with her.

The story started unraveling in my head like a movie reel. They would connect and comfort each other, and help each other survive, even as they fall in love. Yes! I had it. But even as the story gained momentum in my imagination, I knew researching the Nahua, studying the culture and language, and building the narrative from historical facts would take me years. *If only you knew someone who could help you with all that*, a little voice inside me whispered. That's when I knew I had to reach out to my good friend David Bowles, the brilliant writer, translator, and teacher who knows everything I don't about the Aztec Empire! So, the next time I saw David at a conference I said, "Let's go get dinner. I have a literary proposition for you!"

DAVID: When Guadalupe first proposed the idea to me, I was excited. I had long admired her work, and the chance to collaborate on a project together really appealed to me. Add to that the fabulous idea she'd come up with—which fit perfectly with my interests in speculative fiction and pre-Invasion Mesoamerica—and you'll understand why I immediately said yes.

We spent some time brainstorming over the coming days. I had recently read an article about the discovery of an ornately carved marine conch once used as a trumpet in a Nahua city centuries ago. Something clicked. I suggested we use a sacred ceremonial mollusk shell as the tool that connects the protagonists across the centuries. Unlike in *The Lake House,* our characters would communicate verbally, which presented a dilemma—a young Mexica in Tenochtitlan in 1521 wouldn't normally know Spanish. And most modern Mexican teens don't know Nahuatl.

But some do. In fact, there are 1.5 million speakers of Nahuatl in Mexico and Central America today. So I also suggested that the modern-day protagonist be from a community where a variety of Nahuatl is spoken that is very similar to the Classical Nahuatl spoken in Tenochtitlan: Zongolica, Veracruz.

This choice solved some of the problems, but Guadalupe and I wanted the boy and girl to be able to do more than just hear each other's voices. There had to be a mechanism for bringing them together.

In Nahuatl, "conch" is "tecciztli." And the god who protects the moon is named "Tecciztecatl" (person from the place of the conches). So . . . what if the trumpet was once used by priestesses of the moon goddess? What if it's a . . . *moon conch*?

"Their connection reflects the phases of the moon," I told Guadalupe, excited at the revelation. "As the moon gets bigger, they start to see each other! And when it's full . . . they can touch."

After that, well, things started *really* falling into place.

For a while, at least.

GUADALUPE: For a while, to be sure. This sounds like it was all very easy, but it wasn't long before we both realized writing this novel in collaboration was going to take some serious commitment on both our parts. David and I had (at the time) full-time teaching careers. The first thing to slow us down was my taking a job across the country, at George Fox University, in Newberg, Oregon.

How would we talk about this, I wondered. *How would we get together for brainstorming sessions (and taquitos!) at local festivals and conferences if I lived in Oregon?* Not to mention the fact that we were both deeply invested and immersed in other projects. The second thing that slowed us down was the pandemic. But we were committed! So we pressed on . . . online. Thank goodness for technology, because David and I used Zoom to talk and make a plan of action. Then we used Google Docs to build a plot chart where we could work in tandem.

Of course, as it happens when you are writing a novel you really love, something magical occurred along the way. As the weeks and months went by, we took turns scrolling up and down that graphic organizer online, moving things around, thinking through the story, all the while sending each other DMs on Twitter to talk about it in real time. Soon, we were writing chapters, sending them back and forth through email. It was quite a system we had going—a magical system.

Of all the things this book means to both of us, I think there is one element that stands out for me: the way this book highlights our historical footprint on this continent. Both narratives speak to the challenges: the oppression, persecution, and genocide our community has endured. However, they also speak of perseverance: the grit, courage, and hope we carry within us, and how we as a community believe in our ability to change our stars. With this book we are claiming our destiny. It is ours and ours alone.

DAVID: There is certainly magic to this work, especially when centering community and ancestors. But there's also a lot of elbow grease. The two characters are from very particular places, and we had to get their cultural nuances right while also figuring them out as *individuals*. We knew who we needed them to be in order to craft this century-spanning story, but once you create a character and infuse them with the traits of a real human being, they take on a sort of life in your head, often contradicting your plans for them. "No," they say. "I wouldn't do *that*. I would do *this*."

We had two quite different settings—ancient and modern Mexico—and not only did we need to understand how the characters *within* those locales related to place, we also had to grasp how characters *not* from a given space (or time) would perceive it. What do trucks and the border wall look like to a sixteenth-century Mexica boy? What does a teen from modern times make of the canals and conflicts of Tenochtitlan?

Those complex decisions were made even tougher by two aspects of the story structure we chose: the phases of the moon—which dictate the protagonists' ability to interact—and the actual historical events during the siege of Tenochtitlan. Those considerations alter what can happen in a given chapter. You might think that such constraints take a writer's freedom away, but Guadalupe and I found much flexibility within those strictures . . . so much, in fact, that we wrote *thirty thousand words more* than we should have.

You know how it feels when you get an essay back from a teacher with lots of red marks and comments? Imagine getting hundreds of comments for a 400-page manuscript along with an editorial *letter* spelling out your strengths and weaknesses! That's the way professional writing works. But Guadalupe and I LOVE revision almost as much as we love planning and writing. So we created a complicated spreadsheet that took a look at our word count chapter by chapter. It helped us figure out where we needed to cut and by about how much. Trimming down your favorite fight scene or cool subplot isn't always easy, but when you keep the end goal of the book in mind, you find the courage to hack away at the weeds in your manuscript.

You see, what matters isn't our egos or the chance to show off our lyrical prose, et cetera. What we care about is the book that is now in your hands, speaking straight into your heart. What matters is *you,* dear readers.

We hope you come away with a better understanding of pre-Invasion Mexico and the lives of its very human and relatable peoples. Because this book is more than just a love story: it's a story of struggle and hope and thriving survival, both of the Nahuas of the colonial era and their descendants, including many Mexicans of the present. The oppression of the past is mirrored in our time as well, and we have tried to make those parallels clear.

GUADALUPE AND DAVID: As advocates of justice and equity, we couldn't help but notice the systems that imprison both Sitlali and Calizto are inhuman and wrong. As creatives, we wanted to illustrate how courage and love free them, because we can all agree on how noble, admirable, and universal those emotions are. As human beings, we try to emulate these positive energies in our own lives.

Perhaps you could try too.

Sure Shot and Other Poems «•»

Also by
Erica Funkhouser

Natural Affinities

Sure Shot

and Other Poems

ERICA FUNKHOUSER

Houghton Mifflin Company
BOSTON NEW YORK LONDON
1992

Library of Congress Cataloging-in-Publication Data
Funkhouser, Erica.
Sure shot and other poems / Erica Funkhouser.
p. cm.
ISBN 0-395-63750-3
I. Title. II. Title: Sure shot.
PS3556.U63S8 1992
811'.54—dc20 92-13262
CIP

Acknowledgments
The author wishes to thank the editors of the publications in which the following poems, some of them in earlier versions, first appeared: "Owl Pellet," in *The Atlantic Monthly;* "Apology," in *The New Yorker;* "Vagrancy," in *The Ohio Review;* "The Evening of the Stillborn Calf," in *Ploughshares;* "Apple Tree," "Cryogenics," "Grief," "Identification," "Tae Kwon Do," and "Valentine," in *Poetry;* "Lilies" and "Mayflies," in *Sojourner;* "Approach" and "Forgiveness," in *Stray Dog.*

"Owl Pellet" received the 1989 Consuelo Ford Award, and "Sure Shot" received the 1990 Gertrude B. Claytor Memorial Award, both from the Poetry Society of America.

PRINTED IN THE UNITED STATES OF AMERICA

BP 10 9 8 7 6 5 4 3 2 1

For Justin and Sophie

And out of what one sees and hears and out
Of what one feels, who could have thought to make
So many selves, so many sensuous worlds,
As if the air, the mid-day air, was swarming
With the metaphysical changes that occur,
Merely in living as and where we live.

Wallace Stevens, "Esthétique du Mal"

Contents

I.

« I »

Apology

You ask if my local shrubbery
might contain a nest —
last season's stopover
stitched to birch
or bittersweet.

I go out hunting
for the little disturbance
domestication creates,
the roadside nebulae
suspended from wintry limbs.
It's like looking for luck
in a field of clover —
either your eye adjusts
to expectation, fulfilled,
or you go home empty-handed.

It turns out many wild moments of hope
have been left behind
in the underbrush,
here constructed
from tenuous liaisons
of fur and broomstraw,
and here the result
of scavenged cigarette wrappers
delicately interwoven
with grapes.

Seeing them,
I cannot help
but touch them.
We have had conversations like this,

the rough monuments to love
catching us by surprise,
the frayed attachments
more beautiful than anything
they actually gave rise to.

They will not be detached
without unraveling.
I leave the nests, believing
you will accept
these words instead.

Sunflowers

From across the garden we hear
the *tick tick* like rain
as ripe seeds spatter the ground.
The cellist whose tenderness
slid from between her knees last night
grieves no more audibly,
nor the twice-divorced forty-year-old,
his daughters taken to another city.

Lovesick they are,
and tall enough to know better.
Bent to their stubborn devotions,
the sunflowers turn away from the sun
which all summer spurred them on,
bringing out whatever was in them
that most resembled itself.

After a season of outright mimicry
they stoop to stare wide-eyed
at the slight rise in the soil
from which they came.
This is where we drilled seed holes
and planted, where the root life
broke into groundlight and each stalk
grew thick as a spade handle.

The steady drop
of soft-shelled conclusions
reminds us of autumn bedrooms,
the windows thrown casually open.
What we taste is less sweet

than what we had expected,
so we let the flowerheads languish.
Soon the seed-eaters will come,
and the ones that remove
the last of the panicky worms.

We'll be left with the negative coronas.
Here an artful dawn was fashioned
from underlying darkness;
here the intricate attentions of desire
will be cultivated one last time
as we feed the seedless heads
to our winter fire.

Owl Pellet

I was crossing the field — that is all —
longing for nothing more than a color,
when I found the owl's pellet
coiled in the grass.
Beneath the glistening veil of mucus,
a mass of conflicting ingredients:
squirrel fur, rabbit hip,
feather of flicker and jay.
Further in, I came upon crow quills
splintered and wrapped into balls,
tidy parcels of polished bone,
a frog's spotted fingers.

It would almost be better to be young again,
the multiple longings
obscuring any need for detail,
but the ripening pellet
demands exploration:
pelt and stuffing enough to knit nothing,
remnant of mole tail, extruded ear,
the skull not yet skilled
at dodging or distance,
a pulsating grub embedded in beak.

It is never too late for rhapsody.
A kiss says nothing compared to this.
Joined hands? Sweat on the belly?
Lips, genitals — all of them edible.
Where inside does the owl assemble
these bundles of bone and fur?
How wide must she open her throat
to disgorge them?

Anyone can capture the fur standing on end
as small claws slip away from the glassy earth.
Anyone can feed on the instant of pleasure
that makes an animal sweet and defenseless.
No one but the owl makes use of every scrap,
licking beauty back into the coarse remains
before delivering them here so openly
at the feet of anyone crossing.

The Evening of the Stillborn Calf

FOR DANIELLE

Inseminator, hole-scrubber, midwife,
you ache from the scuffle and weight
of hauling the troubled cow into stanchions,
of thrusting your leek-long arms inside
to free the breech that fell
against your chest, a steaming new world
veined in fading latitudes.
Inside the dimly lit birth sac
lies the earth-colored calf already weaned
from earth's desires and routines.

From the eggshell hall
between your bedroom and your daughter's,
you hear the wretched birth-dirge of the cow.
You know her teats are huge.
She's gone back to sniff the grass
where the first specks of blood and fluid
dripped this afternoon.
It would have been her first.

Labor must have started earlier and stopped.
Did you misread the signs?
Tomorrow you will retrace the cow's steps
and your own powers of observation.
Tonight you go down to the beautifully
wrapped calf beneath the blossoming pear.
Shoveling against rock and root,
you make a good clean place
for the chestnut backbone, the folded legs,
the lathered valleys between the legs,
the glazed abdomen, the sable tail
coiled against the heifer rump,
the glistening ears, the silky nose,
the sealed lips ripening.

Ruth's Bronze Turkeys

She started with poults,
one hundred long-necked scrub brushes
hurrying into the corner
as if their heatlamp were lightning.

With the warm weather
she moved the birds outdoors.
When she gave them a water trough,
they drowned themselves one by one.
When she set up a tent for shade,
they fought for room on the ridgepole
and died of exposure.
The sight of her son's neon T-shirts
gave several of Ruth's turkeys
fatal heart attacks.

The story of her losses
passed from house to house.
We counted the bodies in the field
after a night of screeching tires;
the coyote crossed her yard
like a visiting dignitary.
Everyone talked about the experiment
with pink contact lenses for poultry.

Who can blame the farmer
for her gradual indifference?
During the last full moon
she watched the small flock freeze in place
like a grounded eclipse,
a panic-stricken disk of bronze
that barely breathed until dawn
took the hungry moon away.

Still, we call her outside tonight,
our friend and our neighbor,
to see the tarnished survivors
roosting in a low-slung
branch of the chestnut tree,
their feeble wings turned into capes
strong enough to complete
one significant journey.

We admire their green and gold plumes,
the blacks and burnt purples
a species of velveteen.
Their gaze is neither wild
nor tamed. Having lifted themselves
above expectation and folklore,
the last four turkeys meet us eye to eye,
refusing to be mocked.

Leeks

The washing is legendary —
at every turn the interlacing leaves
took in muck and grit,
sucking it all the way down
to where they were keeping white.

I hold them under running water,
run my fingers down as far as I can,
thinking of the friend I had as a child.
She had lost the use of her legs.
My sister and I would carry her
into the fields, into the woods.

We carried her over our shoulders,
her legs thudding against our backs,
or we carried her between us
like a rolled-up rug.
Sometimes all three of us
collapsed laughing.

Propped up in a canoe,
she looked like someone who could walk.
In the river shallows
we scrubbed her with duckweed and moss,
capped her toes with freshwater snails,
almost believing decoration
could undo disease.

We had known her when her legs still worked,
so we believed their pallor
was full of potential.
As I search the washwater
for today's succulent wicks,
my hands grow audacious and tender.

Lilies

Not days, not years,
these flowers mark
a less certain span.
The bulbs start up
months before opening;
by July they're heavy
with buds and tall enough
to shade me as I stake
the spikes too weak to carry
their own abundance.

They smell of clove
and yesterday's funeral
for a friend whose rare bloom
overtook her whole life.
I lift the white trumpets
and trace velvet streamers
back to the dark throat
of the trumpeter.

From the churchyard
we watched the sky fade
beneath the weight of noon.
The windmill on the island
never moved.
Fanning the heat from our faces,
we embraced briefly
as the bells emptied
their black pollen
into the sea.

Identification

The first long rain after your death,
I watch the mushrooms wedge their way
through running cedar,
the fallen needles of white pine,
forest duff of every hue and heft.
On the viscous caps ride
the squirrel's discarded hull,
shallow print of newt and grub.
Between the wavering scales
the final ochres of autumn take cover.
In the sponge beneath, the pinhole
where one worm has lodged its inquiry.

Boletes: the name you taught me in the forest.
We dusted the caps with great care
as if there were plenty of time
and no one at home hungry.
I will not pick these mushrooms.
They are the fruiting bodies
of everything I do not understand.
All around me, the delicate threads
of spawn lie undetected,
and somewhere in their center
the point where an airborne spore
came to rest, invisibly, to undertake
this naked colony.

Grief

I try to impose
the static beauty
of what remains,
like the one utensil
in an auctioned drawer,
upon the cluttered truth
of what is gone,
not even gone, but going.
I try to keep my mind at noon
at least as long
as noon lasts,
the length
of the firehouse whistle,
the full reverberation
from the forest,
the final couplet
spoken by the flicker
hammering for grubs
in fallen hemlock.

Valentine

You try to see without comparison,
you want me to try seeing
without comparing;
at the very least you want me to look
at what you have done
and not be reminded of anything.
I try. I am trying right now.
You know how we try to love,
how we try with those we love.
It's our inability to see what the other sees
that keeps you and me here in the first place.
I accept that.
I'm willing to refuse analogy,
refuse metaphor, refuse image.
Life is desire, that is all.
Open, fold, embrace, swallow.
Who's to say an invention of the heart
resembles anything at all?
In the dark corridors of the soul,
who's to guarantee a little light falls
on love, or that love is anything
small or large enough to land on?
Babies, physicists, hydroponic farmers,
men who paint portraits with tar and chalk,
women who weld or wear garter belts,
anyone who still uses a sextant:
there are lots of mysteries left.
Everyone I have met since I met you
defies explanation.
I have never been so soft and dumb
and curious. I used to have hard hands,
a hard mouth, but let me get back to you,
to your simple request:

look at me and be reminded of nothing.
Not stones, not flowers, not children.
If a single noun comes into your head
you're on the wrong track.
I am trying, believe me.
I am trying to unname the world,
at least your particular version.
Have you ever tried to write a poem
without referring to the visible?
Have you ever tried to eke out of abstraction
the little love cry that keeps a person alert?
It's possible, I believe it's possible.
That's why I'm here again today
at the border of detail and longing,
that's why I'm closing the gates
on nebulae, maggot, and silk.
I'm leaving them back there
charged and specific.
I'm closer to you
than I was in the last sentence,
but I'm not there yet, it's not over.
It's hard to abandon old habits.
You'll have to give me more, a bit more,
let me see something that reminds me
of nothing I know until now.

Why We Draw the Figure

I.

To begin at the poles,
never realizing.

To invent equators
at the waist.

To cross over
without ceremony.

Not to return
as we entered.

II.

To go far into the pocketbook.
Stacks of lipstick,
the partial memory
of lips on tissue.
A grocery list trailing
into the soft leather sky.

To discover sunglasses,
fractured pencils, coupons.
The scat left behind by cigarettes.
A tampon worn through its wrapper.
Silt of migrating coins.

To draw the torn photograph
and the bus ticket,
the fluted bottle of cologne,
the rabbit's foot, dyed purple,
the tinted bone within the fur.

III.

To return
to a childhood drawing,
the body a pair of pliers,

the circular head
attached directly
to two swift sticks,

pronged arms
thrust from each knee
to keep the head afloat,

the head itself
occupied
by two small caves.

IV.

To reach the smaller animals within,
the snub-nosed uprooters
of old fidelities,

ones that stalk
only dim intentions,
and ones so instinctively hungry

they both multiply and keep down
their own numbers
by preying on what falls
between the usual categories —
yours, mine, ours.

V.

To pay attention
as lovers pay their debts,
not in currency
but in kindness.

To prove we are good.
To go out into the night
with the darkest animals
and lift up the stones
that bury dream.

To relight the body
we rent for a lifetime
whose debt is never fully met.

The Story We Tell

The newly struck pheasant was still warm
when you carried him off the road, his emerald head
bobbing calmly. I brushed aside loosestrife
and you laid the bird down, straightening
the tailfeathers flecked with chestnut and jet.
In his eye's watery canal our faces floated wide as barges.
The argument we start whenever we are together in the car
stayed behind, we jumped out so quickly.

Dust from our digging falls over the pheasant.
All the time we have been here we have not mentioned
where we are going, how late we are, our fine leather shoes.
I admire the sweat as it runs under your collar.
You are scraping the earth with your housekeys
while I loosen a rock with my hairbrush.
For what happens next there is no precedent,
except that we have been together for years.

The burial stops. Without speaking, we agree
the dead at our feet will make a delicious meal.
You scuff over our initial grave scrapings
while I plump up the matted napweed and vetch.
The pheasant goes into a brown paper sack;
soon we are driving again, the details
of the bird's retrieval already assembled
into a story we will keep to ourselves.

Anniversary

Friends, I am thinking of your marriage
and how I want to be part of it,
how I want both of you individually
and what you have between you as well.
Love is nothing if not greedy.
I want to wake up beside the one
of you who sleeps later
and watch you investigate the texture
left by your husband's body in the sheets.
Of course he has been up for hours.
I will watch you put on your beautiful shirt
the color of planets while you tell me
that psychoanalysis is like black in a painting —
if it doesn't overwhelm whatever it touches
it can brighten the shadows.
As you speak, your hair and your hands unfurl;
you are a caryatid removing herself from the porch.
Now you will teach me the Yiddish words
for things I would never say
if there were not this whole language
devoted to provocative affection.
Together we will go downstairs and ask a fine man
if he wants to go for a walk after coffee.
You will be my husband, too, I'll tell him,
with your smoky eyes and your arms stretched out
after years of reaching for the good and the bad.

That sadness beautifully rimmed with defiance,
that commitment to grandeur, that blue-black laugh.
I'll gladly marry your obsession with condiments,
with suffering as it has been handed down to us
from Masaccio — good people struggling
to find their places against a background
of arches and barrel vaults.
I'll walk between the two of you in the Blue Hills
so I can hear you go over once again the marjoram
on the windowsill, the immediate need for justice,
the sureness of foxes, the pair of shoes
you went back to look at twice,
they were so soft and evenly stitched.
You never bought them. You buy almost nothing.
That's why I imagine myself fitting easily
between the commotion surrounding dinner
and the quiet chairs in which you read afterward.
Sometimes a simple declaration of love
is not enough. The love of one thing
or one person. When I tried to separate you
from each other, to choose,
I realized it will not work without both of you.
I must have you inside the caul of your marriage.
Don't worry, I will find a way in without breaking
or sacrificing any nuance or shadow.
I will be waiting at the top of the stairs.

Why I Did Not Bring the Roses

On the way to the roses
I decided not to give them away,
not this time, not in October,
when a new blossom stands for every kind of hope
as well as strength, longevity,
the madness and romance of vegetables.
Think what the roses have had to hold on to
in order to bloom this late in the season —
the selfishness, the hunger,
the perfume increasingly remote.
This is a cold climate.
Frost should have come by now,
but some conjunction of sunlight
and fortune has kept summer here.
The sugar maple stands completely still
inside green leaves, dropping nothing
onto the carpet of grass.
A whole field of rodents and raptors
watches out for the other
as if this were a night in midsummer.
Holes in the walls, in the dirt,
in the dark between branches —
something eager has come to each opening.
Just to see what is there.
Just to drink in the changes.
I made it to the fence beside the garden,
the chicken wire fence where I've trained
the white climbers to fall this way and that.
I watered them and mulched them,
picked off the earwigs and Japanese beetles.

I guided them a little with wire
now rusted into fiercely protective gestures.
I lifted the blossoms up toward my face,
introducing myself as I always do with flowers,
working my way around the white petals,
journeying down to the buttery center
where a confusion of holding and opening
guards the interior gold.
I couldn't clip the roses just now.
I couldn't untangle them from the white sky
and the serrated air where they grow.
I couldn't carry them into the house like rags
and go looking for somewhere to put them.

Mayflies

(Ephemeroptera)

During their brief hours
on the surface of the pond,
backs arched above every encounter,
the mayflies dip and skid
until the darker versions of themselves
are flung downstream
or laid against receptive webs of weed.
"Presiding over any place they live,"
the Greeks believed,
and they drank from mayfly streams
in search of inspiration,
even prophecy.
When a thing so small
receives so brief a span
we look and look again —
the golden filigree lending flight
to a living day,
the arched filaments of the tail
counterpoised.
I walk with a friend newly loved
and the earth's carapace expands.
Our children need our bodies less.
Unfolding from the pond,
they shake and dry themselves
in the temperate air.
We can live on any idea
as long as it will shed
as we grow older.
What to collect in these brief moments?
The biographies of private women,
a weather vocabulary, definitions
of *enough* and *swarm,* some proof
that lines are really restless points,
any working knowledge of the ephemeral.

Apple Tree

Well into its life, this spring
the apple tree divides into the half
that could pass as driftwood
and the blossoming half
whose wide, impulsive white
parachutes above the grass.

The flowers hold an apple in their future,
red or green, a certainty to aim for
amid the perfumed distractions.
At the back door, a woodpecker
insists on its meal.

The petals pass through the gate
of darkness, fall far from the tree.
The parent calls out, “I’m right here.”
The child thinks, “Nowhere to be seen.”

Bent as if to search for echoes
in the ground-flowering,
the hollow branches cast
narrow and narrower shadows.

When I walk by with my small daughter
she will not let our bodies touch
or “We’ll look like two sides of one thing
instead of two things.”

Crosswalk

As the light blinks DON'T,
I pull my daughter to the curb.
She's eye-level with a tapestry purse,
lithe swans and foxes
drinking from their own reflections.
The face above the handbag
is a warm morning moon
inquiring, "What's your favorite thing
in the world, little girl?"

My black velvet pocketbook.
What pocketbook?
She just learned to keep
her clothing on, I want to say;
we give her everything she needs;
she carries no valuables.
Why at age six
has she imagined she owns
a black velvet pocketbook?
I wish she had said
myself, my hamster, the rock in my yard.

I'll admit I once coveted
the sophisticated *click*
made by the bright clasp
as you remove your . . .
Your what?

That's why I never owned one.
I couldn't imagine what luxuries
to pack. Even worse,
I lacked all sense of timing.
At what point does the girl
arrest the evening
with her meaningful gold entry?

Is this something mothers teach?
Should the pocketbook have come
with ritual instruction,
the two of us
smoothing the black pelt,
easing the compact with its powdery mirror
in and out of the interior sleeve,
perfecting the angle
on a bright red lipstick?

The stoplight shifts to green;
the woman with the purse
is already crossing the street.
My daughter, eager with embellishments,
pulls me toward the fashionable stranger.
I keep my ring in it, I hear her say.
Shoelaces and pine needles.
Last night it saved me
when a moth came in my room.

Tae Kwon Do

This morning my son tests heaven and earth,
Chon Ji — the creation of the world
and the beginning of human history.
Forbidding prediction,
his arms fold and unfold
like tropical ferns
before his face
while his long white leg
with its pink heel
prepares to strike
the enemy chin.
The yell — EYES! or ICE! —
diminishes the empty *dojang*.

This is the boy who used to dress like a moth
before he'd enter any forest,
who listened for hoofstep
in order not to startle deer.
He taught us how a lizard's open mouth
can still the air.

Death hides in the world
so we disguise ourselves.
Now, as the boy faces a master
who wears the same loose uniform
and makes the same formal bow,
I see the enemy is anyone my son
believes he must prepare for.
His knuckles tighten with anticipation.
As he corrects his striking pose
to meet the skilled instructor,
his breath grows purposeful and sad.

Cryogenics

A memory moves from breathless waking
to the pelt of snow
across a windshield,
my father's smoke
in the upholstery.
Driving too fast over bridges,
one of us hums,

Mother, may I go and swim?
Yes, my darling daughter.
Hang your coat on yonder limb
But don't go near the water.

I wake up in a tent of oxygen.
On the other side, my father
clips holes in new cigars
but doesn't smoke them.
Behind him, a chart he calls
The Elements.
Their bold names:
calcium, iodine, molybdenum, neon.

"Oxygen is eight," he tells me.
"Just like you.
Why don't you memorize the chart?
The first is hydrogen,
an egg — one yolk, one shell."
The definitions follow
like prescriptions — proton, nucleus,
atomic number, valency.
The one in red is called uranium.
Unstable, overcrowded.
I have not yet seen the photographs
of ruined cities.

The boy beside me wears a hockey jacket,
Frank embroidered on the sleeve.
A schoolbus ran him over;
now his pee drips down a tube.
After the nurse empties his plastic bag,
I show Frank the element named Francium.

"What's an element?" he wonders.
"It's chemistry,
as small as you can go.
The science of how things change.
Rusty iron, moldy food, explosions."
I sound as if I know.
This is the way my father talks.
People believe him.
and retell his stories.

> *The common cormorant, or shag,*
> *Lays eggs inside a paper bag.*
> *The reason you will see, no doubt.*
> *It is to keep the lightning out.*

On the chart, a second alphabet.
Fe for iron, Ag — silver, Sn — tin,
the ones identified by alchemists
who melted lead in search of nobler metal,
a gold to make them wise
and young and well.
The doctors lay their cold coins
on our chests.
We name them
Titanium, Antimony, and Boron.

My tent comes down. Free breathing.
Outside, girls my age
skate downriver holding hands.
Frank teaches me his song,

First came the doctor
Then came the nurse
Then came the baby with the alligator purse.

My father brings us bubblegum cigars,
laboratory books, blue-red pencils
sharpened at both ends.
He sits between our beds.
"You ever heard of rare earth?
It's neither rare nor earth."
But Frank is very sleepy.
They take him for a second operation.

At night the hospital grows dark
beyond our Cyclops, the golden call light.
I hear Franky crying
and think of cormorants . . .

But what these unobservant birds
Have failed to notice is that herds
Of wandering bears may come with buns
And steal the bags to hold the crumbs.

"Francium, don't cry.
Look what the ocean does to shells.
That's salt.
It wrecks your cheeks."

I point my flashlight
at the periodic chart.
“Tears are mostly sodium and chloride.
You can change them into something better.”

Frank says the tears are stuck
above his collarbone.
“I got a pond down there.”
I press the call light
and tell Frank to freeze the pond.
“Skate your name in cursive on the ice.”

But Frank is shivering.
“Don’t make me laugh,” he cries.
“It hurts.
Tell me more about rare earth.”

“There’s no such thing.
My father made it up.
We’ll get more blankets.
Let’s play scissors-paper-stone:
one, two, three . . . shoot.”

The next morning Frank is gone.
Beyond his bed, platinum snowflakes
sift down like cinders,
are swept across the solid river.

Approach

Salesmen stop here for a good night's sleep,
Civil War buffs ask the way to Gettysburg;
everyone else was born in Hagerstown
or has taken the afternoon off to attend a funeral,
as I have: my father's father.

I was first sent here alone
as punishment for faking sick and skipping school
without embarrassment. I guess now I'd admit
I'd made the common discovery of childhood
that adults have nothing much to go on
but their own versions of the world,
nothing more definitive than that,
and in exchange they want obedience.

My own father still refuses any mention of God;
even Thoreau is too spiritual.
In the town where I grew up, the elementary schools
were named after transcendentalists;
Emerson's "Over-Soul" was required every year.
Still, my father taught us to worship facts.
The very words *cotyledon* and *feldspar* were enough
to bring him to his feet with praise.
He found them as beautiful as the names of goddesses,
but if they stood for something more he would not say.

My father's father, on the other hand,
spoke directly to God's own son.
In the yard after supper he and Jesus
were a pair of cardinals, Jesus the striking one,
and my grandfather a modest gray-pink

receptive to song and shame and hunger.
He was always pulling up a lawnchair for a neighbor
needing to dwell on things a moment longer.
This is Maryland.
Sadness is the regional distinction.

When my grandfather came to the airport to get me
that time I was sent alone to him,
he was already small with age,
his nose narrow and delicate, slightly chipped,
I imagined, as if he had been hoisted from ancient rubble.
Compared to his logical son, he asked so little.
His voice brought its own humidity;
listening, I'd grow drowsy and receptive.
But this time I was scared. The small prop plane
had jostled terribly; I'd cupped my head and realized
my own parents had sent me away knowing
death is final.

As the plane fell into pockets of empty air
I had imagined the fatal crash.
I would burn worse than eggwhites,
leaving behind only the coiled remains
of my stubborn resistance to long division,
the smell of the rotten terrarium
at the back of the classroom, the blue mold
climbing the sweaty mosses, Miss Kane's hair
frizzled at the edges as she leaned over me,
her breath of bacon against my cheek.

When the plane finally touched down,
my grandfather was waiting on the runway.
He drove straight through town,
never mentioning fourth grade,
right out to the new shopping center
for the grand opening of Woolworth's:
a blond oak floor, punch in bubblers,
departments labeled *Pets* and *Notions*.
I won a door prize, two goldfish in a plastic bag.
I knew enough to apologize beforehand
for the impracticality of living things,
their need for water and a steady home,
but my grandfather said, "Why not?"
and as the revolving door swept us out onto the sidewalk
we named the fish Archie and Veronica.

Before the funeral I walk my father to the racetrack
closed down years ago by Governor Agnew,
although my grandfather swore the thoroughbreds
had slowed down anyway because no one
could keep them interested in running.
My father tells me that the crushed stone
on the roofing shingles of the empty barns
was quarried from green basalt
in the Catoctin Mountains.
He's not well himself, but he's still working
the deep mine of cranial green
that has always fed him.

We remember how his father opened every story:
"I've got a little something about that myself."
Whether it was Scylla and Charybdis,
Abraham or his own Uncle R.J.,
he'd reach into any available past
and pull it down close like a branch of peaches.

When we stop at the red clay oval,
I can almost see the half-believing horses,
their muscles softened, their hooves gone heavy,
manes and tails barely lifted by the breeze.
When the breeze dies down
it takes their breathing with it.
One opal eye looks away from what the other recognizes,
and the introverted horses reach a standstill
while behind them the foothills run in place
with a velocity unknown to animals.

Forgiveness

This morning,
walking the dizzying aisles
with my father,
his small elbow
resting inside my own,
I recognize the change
immediately.

I could be cradling
a flat of parsley or carrying
a few bright leaves of mica.
Our years together and apart
have compressed into something frail
and transparent — forgiveness.

My father wants crackers,
but he can't remember
what kind he likes.
Shelves and shelves of bound wheat
close in on him.
I hold on until an answer
brings weight back to his body.

He frames his hands,
thumb to thumb, fingers upright,
like an old-fashioned film director.
"It's about the size of a box
of shotgun shells."

We laugh our identical laugh.
He could always bring
a black duck home for supper
more easily than he could sit
through any family meal.

I plucked those ducks
so bitterly —
the down beneath their feathers
sticking to my hands
in wet clumps
like something I had failed to save —

and yet here, in the market,
I recall instead the delicacy
of a single piece of down
as it breaks free to soar
above the empty vests and waders,
an ardent plumage caught
on the slightest gust of heat
or conversation.

We find the familiar biscuits,
and once again I am walking home
with a lucky hunter.
As I steer my father
across the parking lot,
we scan the horizon
with parallel devotion.

The marsh grass has turned silver.
The ducks are not far off.
A liver-colored dog,
her teeth bared with relish,
begs to be taken along.

Room Where I Work

The plaster above my desk
buckles toward me —
brow of disgruntled mentor,
cry of the unfed child.

Every time I open the window
it rides less well in its sash.
There are a finite number of openings.
I have no idea where I stand.

The wall works itself away from the ceiling.
Once when we pried open the corner
so many ants poured out
the carpenter cried, "Quick, put it back!
Fresh air makes them hungrier."
Now I listen as the ants inscribe themselves
into narrow chambers to breed.

Whoever taped these joints —
I'll admit I did a few myself —
had no understanding of joint compound,
no instinct for seamtape.
It looks as if my predecessors
were buried vertically
as punishment for a lifetime of naps.

The bookshelves are stable,
but the books pucker and fold,
making audible wisecracks.
Ash from the woodstove
has worked its way into the gloss.

The floor is cheap yellow pine,
mislaid originally, further distressed
by changes of habit and mind.
It moans when I move the furniture.

Still, there's a halting beauty
in the pale rosettes
that surround every nailhead.
Wherever the hammer
was distracted from its mark,
wooden petals
perpetually unfold.

Memorial Day at the Dump

Anyone can curate the new,
your sudsy babies,
your seedlings in vermiculite,
argues the guardian
of our dump's final days.
He makes his selection — spent bedsprings,
a blunt-nosed iron,
what's left of a quart of shellac.

Elsewhere in town, people tinker
with spinning reels,
wax the road salt from their pickups.
Girls skip down the sidewalk
in bubbly pink sweaters.
We've all got a story about the dump man —
mink he poached growing up,
the obscene playing cards in his wallet,
how he donated his short-wave equipment
to the indifferent Boy Scouts.

He was one of the first to go to Vietnam;
he still wears fatigues
and a Grateful Dead T-shirt.
Today it's the pastel skeleton in combat boots.
Call me your historian of exits,
your elegist of endings,
we hear from the makeshift altar
of shovel handles and shutters.

This installation will be his last.
The dump's been redefined a Transfer Station.
We don't know how to end a goddam thing,
he tells the loaded station wagons

as he flings a Zenith portable —
the straw cover punctured,
the interior destroyed —
into a frayed baby stroller.
Perfectly good spoons lie in the dirt.

Your overlord of so-long
is about to become the king of conchs,
he shouts at our rolled-up windows.
Drivers shift clumsily into reverse,
children murmur over plastic car toys.
I'm shipping out to nouveau paradise —
the real thing in southern Florida.
Got buddies down there from my old division.

Get someone else to decorate your graves,
he cries as he leaps the gunned exhaust
and swipes at the last rearview mirror.
Get someone else.

Cleaning the Kitchen

Tonight I give myself
to the wasted and spoiled,
the desiccated, the rancid,
the void of original value.
I honor the long wait
of pastry flour
overpowered by weevils,
the shiny husks
foaming to the surface,
the tiny gloved fingers
waving goodbye.
In the blackstrap molasses
the sheen of disaster
surrounds sweet-loving ants.
Their glossy black bodies
march eternally nowhere,
footsteps in tar.
Festering apricots,
rigid powders —
I pinch back the foil
to study their changes.
A sack of legumes
lies weightless,
a slept-out pillow,
the same dented beauty.
Each hollow bean
turns death-penny
to its own closed eye.
When I come to the thriving ruin
in the crabapple jelly —
temples, porches, arcades,
a blue-green reflecting pool! —
I understand that mold is the origin
of every beauty.

What monument to causes
natural or unnatural
speaks of anything greater than this?
In the larder, odd crusts
prepare to heave their last sigh.
Furtive turnips cultivate ferns
the color of exhaust.
I go all the way in
to saffron and carob.
Far in the corner
a flask of Tabasco
accomplishes a total reversal
of fortune: behind the ornamental label
abundant with slime
lies only eviscerated glass.
I throw it out with the others;
my idyll among losers is over.

Vagrancy

What I was hearing as I knelt there —
night gathered in my coats
and the high offices holding back dawn —
was my own name, *Louise,* the shelter
in the sound of it as my grown sons
hollered up from the cellar,
Come see the new burner, Ma.

I was bringing the old days back
to Government Center, hearing my name
on a distant evening in spring
when my husband and I got off work early
and ate heroes with the kids in the park.
Those were huge nights. We were still dancing
to Bessie Smith, never realizing
we wouldn't save a thing.

I was even younger than that,
eating coconut washboards in Scollay Square
in the days before seamless stockings.
I was memorizing my father's tattoo,
the skeleton beneath the parasol,
and telling everyone you can grow
tea roses in wet cement, you can buy
whatever you need with a nickel.

Listen, I knew this would happen.
When I looked up from the curb
and saw the two of them coming, I knew
I was headed for their smoky precinct,

everything that follows the apologies and paperwork.
They always send two when the news is bad.
We regret to inform you. Occupational hazard.
Missing in action. I've been through this before.
One minute you wave goodbye to someone you love
and the next minute strangers wearing gloves
will refuse to let go of your hands.

The Blue Ox

Okay, I turned blue —
that was long before Paul
stumbled on my frostbitten ears,
long before he and I got to invent
our colossal forms of affection.
It was one night
during the Winter of the Blue Snow
when a flurry of sapphire
tried to fool anything foolish enough
to be out walking believing in blue stars
into believing the sky had changed its mind
and wanted a life on earth.
A life with all the trappings
of tangibility.

Those flakes were freezing
and accumulated faster than ash.
That's how come I ended up in the drift,
just coming to terms with the bitterness of indigo
when a clumsy toe struck my ear.
His politeness brought me back from the dead —
"Excuse me" — those midwestern manners
and the deep ravines of his vowels.

An oversize death is not that different
from a regular one.
I was only a yearling
but I knew I was going fast.
I had started the long journey
to the end of my glacial eyes —
that's where I was headed
when Paul's apology
started ringing in my ears.

"Excuse me, excuse me."
Next thing I knew he was tugging at my ears.
I could tell this was the start of something big.
"Beautiful Babe," he cried,
as he carried me all the way home
and wrapped me in blankets.
He never set me down before dawn.
He sang until my tongue thawed out
and the blue-black of farewell
turned into the azure of welcome.

I butted his shoulders.
I licked the salt from his neck.
I worked my way up to his face.
There was nothing I did
that knocked him over.
So what if it took binoculars
to see from my head to my tail?
So what if there was room
for forty-two ax handles
and a plug of chewing tobacco
between my eyes?

The measuring was what made me decide.
The way he laid his ax across
the feathery blue down,
marking his place with that thumb
thick as a Douglas fir,
whispering each numeral
as if it were something special
I had done for him.
When he disappeared from sight
somewhere in the eddy above my nose,
I held my breath until I heard him again,
the counting sweeter than ever —
twenty-three, twenty-four, twenty-five.

« II »

Birdwoman

Fort Mandan, November 1804

When I have thought long enough
about eagles,
two specks of ash in the distance
soar into view.
Touch the fire on their wings.
Pluck a feather of gold.

Still holding the feather,
I stop thinking of birds
and give my thoughts to myself.
Lay them out in front of me
piece by piece like fine skins.
Place myself at the center.
What shall I make of all this?
How shall I carry it?

A squaw of fifteen,
I have earned many names.
Sacagawea, Birdwoman, *mon petit chou.*
I am all and none of these things —
a Shoshone living among the Minnetaree
who stole me from my people
when I was only a child,
a fullblood traded from brave to brave
'til they lost me to the Frenchman in a wager.
Two plum seeds determined my husband,
Toussaint Charbonneau —
fur on his knuckles
and fast-striking fists.

I could feel more affection for a bear,
but this much Charbonneau has done
(he knows how to use me):
he has bragged of his Indian wife
to the two white soldiers
looking for interpreters.
He told them, "My squaw is Lemhi Shoshone.
You will never cross the Rockies
without horses from her tribe.
Seulement ma femme can do your talking."

He stood me before them like a mule.
"A strong back. No trouble to feed.
As soon as the baby is born
she will be ready to travel."

The two soldiers stepped slowly forward,
their necks white as swans'.
They gave me their names —
Captain Meriwether Lewis, Captain William Clark.
Ugly on the tongue,
but the one called Lewis
is quiet enough to sneak up on magpies,
and the fox-red hair of Clark
sits beautifully under a headband of otter.

They asked for Sacagawea's help.
Would I walk with them to the Shining Mountains?
Would I speak to my people?
Would I do this for President Thomas Jefferson
who must obey his old dream
of reaching the Pacific, that far place
we call the Big Lake That Stinks?

They asked me to go with them
the way the wind asks a pony to gallop.
Only a stone would say no.
I pulled the fear up out of my stomach,
watched it leave notches on the jaybird's tail.
Sent my smile into the heart of the willow
so Charbonneau would believe I had agreed
out of honor for him.

If Sacagawea is to see her people again,
she will have to take these white men
where white men have never before walked.
They will leave heavy footprints
on the new grass of spring.
What shall I make of all this?
How shall I carry it?

As the eagles narrow their circle,
I return the gold tail quill.
Soon I will be walking the old roads
I have carried in my dreams
like a dance step from childhood.

I will see if any Shoshone have lived
to make a legend of the day
my mother and her sisters were killed
while downriver Sacagawea and her cousin
played among the bushes foolish as songbirds,
stuffing ourselves with berries,
letting our laughter flash its bright feathers
over every gossiping stream.

Fort Mandan, February 1805

Stitching and whittling,
I prepared for this child
as if it were a change in the weather.
A few squirrel blankets
for the cradleboard of cedar,
moccasins lined with fur.
I should have known better.
The baby came once to my dreams,
where it stayed hidden in foxskin.
Only the black mouth of the fox opened wide
to say, *I did not do this to myself.*
Tiny teeth glittered like knives.

Then came the night
of my longest captivity.
Deep into the buffalo robes beneath me
I drove my knees and my elbows.
Let it come, let it go, I begged
as Charbonneau prayed to his bearded God
and Lewis traveled the lodge in dumb circles
like the hands on his pocketwatch.

Finally the boatman Jessome gave me
his sticky finger to suck.
Très bien, encore, he whispered
as he dipped the finger once more
into a paste of snake rattle and water.
I broke through the bony confines,
headed straight for the dawn
at the tip of my backbone.

When I woke up, the baby was watching,
no bigger than a burrowing owl.
We call him Baptiste,
but I can hear the other names
he has given himself —
Ever-Thirsty, He Who Argues with Snakes,
Eyes That Work Day and Night.

When the captains look back and forth
between my boy and the buffalo calves
trapped on islands of ice in the river,
I tell them, *Where I go, Baptiste goes.*
His cry reaches no ears but my own.
We will never walk more slowly than white men.

Of that we are certain, says Lewis,
his fingers deep in the neck fur
of the handsome black dog
who sleeps at his side every night.

On the Missouri Between the Milk River and the River That Scolds All Others, May 1805

If the single quill of cloud in the sky
decided to come back to earth
it would find no place to land.
On both sides of the river
buffalo, antelope, and elk crowd together,
watching us work our way upstream.
The water is black with beaver.
We feast on the tail and the liver
until I forget I have ever been hungry.

When I show Clark the burrows beneath driftwood
where mice store their camas root for winter,
he fills up his satchel.
All the way back to camp
he sings to Baptiste.
When we come to an island of onions
he asks me to teach him to dig
without injuring the bulbs.

Only one thing Clark will not hear —
what the Shoshone know of black luck.
Black luck to take the mouse's last root,
I tell him, black luck
to kill a she-bear with cub.

It does no good to measure the bear
before cooking it, as Lewis does,
unfolding the ruler and counting out loud.
Five feet eleven inches at the breast,
three feet eleven around the neck.
It does no good to empty the stinking maw
and write down everything the bear herself has eaten.
Clark stands with respect while I speak,
but I can see his ears have fallen asleep.

For this reason I am not surprised
when the white pirogue capsizes,
Charbonneau at the helm.
As soon as I hear Cruzat the bowsman
calling my husband *cochon* and *vache marine,*
ordering him to steer or be shot,
I know the boat will not sink.
For the sake of his own life, Charbonneau
will obey another Frenchman.

I leave the crew bailing with kettles.
Hoist Baptiste high on my shoulders.
Leaning over the furious water,
I widen my arms like a fish weir
'til the rootless cargo has only one place to go.
Nearly all of the bundles come to me —
spirit level, compass and scope,
flour and pemmican,
even the precious tin boxes
holding the elk-bound fieldbook,
the red morocco journals.

I can already smell the pleasure
on Clark's fingers as he spreads the dry pages,
dips his pen in the shiny black ink,
barely dry himself before he takes up the story
of this evening's misfortunate squall.

After supper, Cruzat, my favorite Frenchman,
will play songs on his fiddle.
In front of the fire, all of the men
will dance in each other's arms
like trees grown a long time together.

On and off the river, we move as one people.
When one of us falters, the others take on more.
When one of us swells with laziness or pride,
the rest bare their teeth like coyotes.

The Cache at North Fork, June 1805

> "... the river is more rapid   we can hear the falls this morning verry distinctly.   our Indian woman sick & low spirited ..."
>
> William Clark, *Journal*

Heat passes through me, then chills.
I care less than a tent flap.
The baby at my breast stinks of weasel.
Clark's buffalo hump soup makes me spit.

Now Lewis is piercing my skin with a lancet
and I listen to the blood run into his cup.
Hear the bellow of the she-bear
who bleeds from the mouth
as she gives up her life to the hunter.

Drawn into the river of blood,
I ride to the bottom.
The riverbed is covered with blood-red footsteps,
some of them ancient, some of them fresh.

When I float to the surface I have become
the long black hair of my mother.
How I saw it that day on the shoals
where Running Deer and I were captured.
The satin in her braids shone like silver.
It was beautiful hair.
I had greased it that morning.

I am my mother's ghostpelt,
hacked off and dangling
from the belt of the Minnetaree warrior
who pulls me up from the river to his horse.
Where has he left her pride and her anger?
Where shall I go to find her?

One moment I was a gossiping girl,
mother of nothing but stories.
Anyone could see my body contained no secrets,
no matter how boastful my tongue.

Now between watery knees I must hold
the beautiful black hair of my mother.
I grow sick with the touch of it,
the braided black greasing my knees
all of the days and the nights
until the grinning Minnetaree
rides me home to his Knife River village.

Three Forks, July 1805

> "Our present camp is precisely on the spot that the Snake [Shoshone] Indians were encamped at the time the Minnetares of the Knife R. first came in sight of them five years since . . . O[u]r Indian woman was one of the female prisoners taken at that time; tho' I cannot discover that she shews any immotion of sorrow in recollecting this event, or of joy in being again restored to her native country; if she has enough to eat and a few trinkets to wear I beleive she would be perfectly content anywhere."
>
> Meriwether Lewis, *Journal*

Before the kingfisher wakes up
I hurry to the shoal
where Running Deer and I were captured.
There lie the berry bushes,
the sweet willow that failed to disguise us.
Sadly and happily nothing has changed.
The pain of that day
has disappeared from the river,
not even a thin white scar.

I unwrap Baptiste from his cradleboard
and release him in the shallows.
He crawls with his belly in the water
and drinks from the stream like a dog.

Soon I will learn who is alive
that remembers Sacagawea and welcomes her home.
I hide my face in my hands
so the clouds will not know
I am asking myself, *What is home?*

Land where I knew the greatest hunger,
where a handful of berries brought comfort
to the stomach shrunken by winter.
Land that taught me to walk, to watch,
to dig, and to listen.
To carry whatever my mother could not handle.
To eat only after the men had finished.

I douse my thoughts in the clear running water.
They float to the surface, polished
like the shell of a turtle,
to tell me what I already know:

at night when I wake up in the tent
with Baptiste, the two captains,
the black dog, and Charbonneau,
I feel I am among my own people.
Not one of them fullblood!

Now, as I bathe in the water of my childhood,
I rise like a stream in spring,
impatient for new destinations.
I scrape the white clay from the bank,
traverse fallen branches.
I am looking for the rivers
that do everything they can
to reach the Big Lake That Stinks.
Rivers where the sun lies down every night,
the lucky ones that carry the sun
back to the place from which it is possible
to rise up again in the morning.

By the time the baby and I are dry
I know what I will say to the captains.
I will tell them I have traveled far
in my thoughts, found room in my parfleche
for much I was never asked to carry.

Once, it was true, the only land
I could see myself entering was my old home
surrounded by mountains.
Now, without straining my eyes,
I see Sacagawea following many strange rivers
into the new world that has never heard of her
or any of the men in her party.

Lemhi River, August 1805

To show I walk in peace
I paint my cheeks vermilion.
Charbonneau is jealous of my new beauty.
Who am I courting?
When I do not build his fire quickly enough,
he beats me with a stick.
Only the arrival of Captain Clark
startles my husband into stopping.

My cheeks are still smarting
when I set eyes on my people.
Run forward sucking my fingers
to show I am Shoshone.
They suckle their own in return.
When we rub faces,
the elk grease polishing their cheeks
turns red from my own decoration.

All the years I have been away
disappear from my thoughts,
firesmoke in a strong mountain wind.
There is my cousin Running Deer, free again,
and my brother Cameahwait,
tall in the chief's cloak of otter.
Each one I embrace calls forth
a new-fledged Sacagawea.
Together we squeak like starlings in the grass.

As I walk back to camp among the people whose moccasins
are beaded with the same blue rose as my own,
I fight to keep my feet on the ground.

After many days of dancing and singing,
my brother gives two of his names to Clark,
Chief Red Hair and Chief Cameahwait,
these and a string of fine horses.
In return he seeks only guns
so the Shoshone may go back down to buffalo country
and hunt on even ground with the enemy.

All the men take off their moccasins
to show they will go barefoot forever
if they are not true to their promises.
The talking is long. Each word must fly
from Shoshone to Minnetaree to French and to English
without dropping its seed.
Then there is the long journey back.

At last everyone smokes and is happy —
a few furs and horses for guns.
A trade so simple
it might have been struck by women!
Quickly the canoes are buried,
the pack saddles cut and stitched.
Snow has already come to the mountains.
This morning Lewis found the ink
in his pen turned to ice.

Clark looks up from his packing.
For the first time since we started walking
he and Charbonneau agree on one matter —
Sacagawea and her baby will be safer
if they stay here with the Shoshone.
Running Deer has made a place for us in her hut.

I hold a council with Baptiste,
the one who will starve if I am stupid.
Speak up now, *demi-lune,* I warn him,
if you fear your mother lacks the strength
to carry her halfblood over the Bitterroots.
He crawls into my lap and falls asleep.

"We figured as much," says Lewis,
a smile working its way over his face.
And then Clark hands me the reins
of a fine spotted pony.
What do you think of this, Baptiste?
From now on, your mother's good feet,
like your own, will journey
without touching the ground.

Hunger Creek, the Bitterroot Mountains, September 1805

Hunger lies down with us at night.
Snow opens our eyes in the morning.
If a crow is foolish enough to stop by,
we shoot it for dinner.
Twice we have had to kill colts,

but I do not eat them,
not even the soup.
I turn my face from the fire
and suck on a tallow candle.

For many of the men
the pain in their gut is new.
They talk too much
about big feasts from the past.
I see their thoughts
slip away from their bodies
toward the smell of some far-off stew.

Sacagawea keeps her back to the fire,
tends to the fat in her mouth.
She puts the baby to her breast
and begs the bear fat to remember who she is.
Speaking slowly and kindly,
she keeps the attention
of the generous bear
with the oldest story she knows.

Running the Clearwater and the Snake, October 1805

Wherever the riverbanks draw close
to exchange their terrible secrets,
the river hurls us forward
into grinning gorges and boulders.
This is a trick I had never thought of —
moving in the same direction as water
is more trouble than moving against it.

I borrow the boldness of loons
and sit up as tall as I can,
the cradleboard high on my shoulders.
At the far end of every rapids,
the salmon fishers are camped,
their scaffolds covered with split-open fish.

Fishermen are never too busy to make war,
I remind Clark when he offers
to walk me around the worst water.
Only one thing keeps us from being seen
as a war party — that is Sacagawea.
Everyone knows women make a fine war prize,
and no warrior would set out for battle
with the burden of a woman in his boat.

Fort Clatsop, on the Columbia River, Christmas 1805

We have built a circle of cabins
where we await the warm weather
in which it is safe to start east.
It rains every day. The fleas keep us busy.
Still, we are planning a ceremony
with cannonfire and the exchange of small gifts.

I have prepared many tails of white weasel
for my friend William Clark,
who has offered to send Baptiste to school
when we return to Fort Mandan.
My son will never go to white school,
I tell William, but you have given his mother
another gift she will pass on to the boy.

When we were starving on Cape Disappointment
and you gathered the men together
to decide where we should camp for the winter,
you asked Sacagawea to speak her mind as well.
When she argued in favor of a place
with plenty of potatoes, you heard what she said.

You recorded her vote along with the others,
the votes of the hunters and boatmen,
the French engagés and the black man, Ben York.
You wrote the word *Janey*
in your red leather journal,
name like a wren's warm whistle,
name spoken only by you.

On the Beach near Tillamook, January 1806

Some of the salt-makers came home to the fort
talking about the big fish on the beach.
Many men wanted to see it. So did I.
I told William, *I have traveled a long way*
to see the Great Waters, to stand at their edge.
I will take it very hard
if you keep me from seeing this.

Like the pounding tail of a grouse
my words drummed the ground,
a new Sacagawea.

By the time we got to the place where the waves
had swept the big visitor ashore,
no meat was left.
Not one bite of flesh or of blubber.
None of the delicate oil.
Clark's anger was more white
than the rafters of whalebone.

For once I was not hungry.
Not in a hurry to get anywhere.
The sun that had been hiding for so long
played among the pebbles.
I let Baptiste wade in the yellow foam.
Put his nose in the water
so he would never forget its stink.

Then I lay down in the sand beside the sea creature
and saw I could do so twenty more times
and still not reach the end of its tail.
I invited myself into its belly.
Ai! To stand inside another animal
when you are neither dead nor waiting to be born.

I took the hands of Baptiste and showed him a dance.
He moved with the sun on his shoulders.
I left him with Charbonneau,
who was making big talk
to the pretty Killamuck guide.

I said goodbye for a while
and walked to the edge of the water.
There was no thought of crossing or following,
none of the business surrounding rivers.
I knew I would stay with the others
until it was time to walk back.

For today I had less on my mind than the plovers
running back and forth with the waves.
Beyond them the green-black water
showed us nothing but the top of her head.

Think of her people, I said to myself,
their wisdom and stature.
Nearly every stream I ever crossed
is looking for this water,
and now I am entering it myself —
Sacagawea, Birdwoman, Boat Launcher,
one of the braided waves,
one of the silver ribbons
riding the crest of the waves.

Fruitlands

> Summer 1843; Harvard, Massachusetts: "More people coming to live with us. I wish we could be together and no one else. I don't see who is to clothe and feed us all, when we are so poor now."
>
> Louisa May Alcott, age ten

All storms are sisters to the first
I fell in love with at Fruitlands —
the clouds silver-black and broody,
their companion wind
leveling our densest meadow.
I could not stay at home.
Utopias are dull as pewter.

I was a girl of ten
intent on private enterprise.
If thunderclaps could muster lightning,
this forager could scare up pleasures of her own
from Harvard's dark ravines.
I would haul in an apronful of blackberries,
see if the drop in pressure
had spawned inky caps.

I never heard my mother calling.
By the time I'd latched the gate,
she was an apparition.
For hours she and my older sister Anna
had been sweeping barley into Russia-linen sheets.

We worked against the teasing raindrops,
stretching every inch of hem and sleeve
to keep the gold grain dry.
My younger sisters, staked like goats,
whimpered between rows.

Smarting and bitten, we fell late
into bed that night.
Mother's weeping canceled out our own.
No matter how sharp the sting,
we must not exacerbate her burden.
Just this one grain left to carry us
through winter.

Father and his summery farmers
had refused to exploit brother ox
until they'd split their final spade tip.
Animal manure they had dismissed
as foul and contaminate
so wide aisles of barren earth
surrounded each row
of our vegetable congregation.

Where were Father and the other men?
Out walking the countryside,
peddling their lofty conversation,
the transcendental "newness,"
a nation's supremacy assured
by each soul's famished purity.

Even Mr. Emerson accused them
of testing their shoulders over-often
to see if wings had sprouted.

« • »

In New Eden, a daily routine
guaranteed denial of self.
We rose at five to bathe;
Father on the ladder
poured cold water through a sieve;
singing followed,
and a chaste breakfast.

Water and bread exclusively
at every meal,
one fruit or vegetable, most raw,
nearly always apples.

Tunics made of homespun linen
provided constant instruction:
no coat stolen from innocent sheep,
nor the freedom of black brethren
enslaved to cotton.
We were "consociate family";

new men at the table every morning
urged Father and Mother to give up more —
cocoa, working for hire, all ownership.
Perfection must be our one
sustenance and manufacture.
"Being in preference to doing."

If this we could achieve as family,
then surely a perfect society would follow.

« • »

As soon as Father listed the forbidden,
I was starving for the lozenge of its name.
Forbidden *idleness* and *lamp oil.*
Forbidden *milk.*

The daily battle to live off less
spawned appetites original to every hour.
Hunger for sheepskin. Hunger for ferns.
A strung bow and the skill
to stupefy a squirrel.

No waistbands, my parents and my teachers
ordered. No horse or carriage.
Be passenger to nothing but divinity.
The truest motion takes you nowhere
visible to others.

I gnawed at the crystalline perimeter
of Over-Soul and asked the questions
of an infidel: What is waiting there for me?
Will it ease my pain? Will it yield
a seed or two of comfort or of beauty?

« • »

A lesson from Utopia:

How gain love?
By gentleness.

What is gentleness?
Kindness, patience, and care
for other people's feelings.

Who has it?
Father and Anna.

Who means to have it?
Louisa if she can.

« • »

After breakfast Mother and I would flatten
cumbersome washing across broad rocks.
Father urged us to transcend all sensation.
"You are my two demons," he'd chide,
thin laugh accompanying.
Privately, I saw we were two angels
of the bottomless pit,
linked eternally in confidential chatter.

The sour apples poisoned Mother's teeth;
she grew squinty from mending by candlelight.
I expect the underworld is lit
with hand-dipped bayberry.
Behind her apron Mother whispered once,
"I am the one beast of burden
permitted in your Father's Eden."

« • »

Amid the acres of confusion,
Father's allies began to plant
extravagant fears:
his wife and children held him back
from absolute transcendence.
All must be rearranged
to prevent "domestic ambush"
or, more costly still,
his loss to habits of affection.

The more Mother claimed her daughters
as beloved territory,
the more Father dwelt on celibacy.
She refused his bread and he her company.

Ever larger in our lanky bodies,
Anna and I stole kitchen scraps
to feed the inner fires
we prayed would warm us.
Warm us but not consume us.

« • »

With the hoarfrost
we lost most of Father's
fellow visionaries,
even the prime minister of forgo,
Charles Lane, and his narcoleptic son,
whose half-sentence was enough
to put acrobats to sleep.

The whole conflagration of eccentrics
departed to more strict regimes.
Samuel Larned swore he'd lived one year
on naught but crackers and would again;
Samuel Bower required a nudist colony;
Isaac Hecker sought community
among men exclusively.

Poor Miss Page, who had come to help
with female chores and music,
was dismissed for treason:
constabulary fieldmice led Father
to her private hoard of cheddar.

« • »

Those several miles west of Concord,
winter's chill permanently
stationed at our doorstep,
words of my favorite woods-walker,
Henry Thoreau, began to tell their truth:
"Most of us cry better than we speak."

What eloquence I possessed
in barren November,
a poor girl drenched in tears.
What perfection of sentiment
flattened my narrow bed
when I heaved myself there,
speechless interpreter
of the family's consuming misery.

If I had dared to speak the truth
about the shrunken woodpile, the mulberries
undermining our stone foundation,
I would have been accused of disrespect.
Even illness was attributed to inner failure.

The day Anna fainted in the kitchen,
Father deprived himself of food as punishment
for his oldest child's unnatural appetite.

« • »

When to my journal I dared confide
the tenderest doubt,
Father scratched it out
with his superior orthography.
Mother treated the purloined testimony
as a necessary justice.

Chanticleer of honesty I longed to be
amid my distracted keepers.
Obliterator of obedience,
death knell to infernal
self-improvement.

« • »

At the Fruitlands of so little fruit
I sat up evenings with Mother
listening to her needle pester
coarse brown linen.

When my fingertips grew numb,
I'd bank the narrow fire,
inquiring once again why cats had been forbidden.

Utopia shall have no savage hunters,
no lappers of their own long fur,
no immutable howl.

Freedom to seize and to conquer,
I whispered to the embers.
Freedom to leap from the roof.

I loved her so I sat with her,
but I could not duplicate
her oath to duty.
In return for Mother's costly labor,
Father cultivated "genius,"
a questionable gift
even in a man who works for wages.

Publicly she bore his delicacy proudly,
while at home she borrowed from her family
to fund his dreams.
She blamed herself alone, we saw that.

What she required, however bitter,
from a husband, I swore from Fruitlands on
to fabricate myself.

« • »

My own infinity diminished
with December.
"Anna and I cried in bed,
and I prayed God
to keep us all together."

One memory yet rouses me:
feverish, ill-anchored,
Anna and I chafe
against the engorged darkness
of the sleeping attic.

Hunger's armies encircle us,
accomplishing night forays
into weakened dreams.
Waking to seize a ginger cake
from the oven of air,
we cry out simultaneously —
in our hands, nothing but sister flesh,
in our mouths, the mouse-brown Alcott hair.

« • »

The New Year at New Eden —
Father lay in bed refusing to eat,
his experiment a conspicuous failure.
While good-natured Anna
forced spearmint tea down Father's throat
to strengthen him for travel,
I lashed our few belongings
to a borrowed oxcart,
the bust of Socrates preserved
between a ladder and a hayrake.

Mother had rented rooms —
fifty cents a week
in the village of Still River.
At last our family alone and all together,
with neighbors to the left and right!
Thrill of the lamplit window,
the trampled path between kitchens.

We had no time to wrap the bundles
tenderly, to safeguard sentiment.
The cart was broad and long,
the huge ox stamped the ground impatiently.
We climbed aboard, plumes of ox breath
infiltrating scarf and cape.
The driver's whip instructed
all the hills to let us pass.

With what uncoiled anticipation
we drove toward everything abhorred by Father —
complacency of village, ordinary commerce,
inevitable afternoons of red meat
and sweetened tea among the perfumed matrons.

By the first thaw, his own Louisa
was selling doll clothes, a temporary industry
to get the family by until she fixed
on finer occupation.

I charged far less
than Father did for his vast enterprise,
but in my simple costumes —
you'll excuse the vanity —
my customers secured fresh linen,
a skillful smocking, the well-fed
rose or wren embroidered by a hand
whose rampant pulse
lent surplus satisfaction
to every stitch.

« • »

I hear that stormy child again this morning,
the final day of 1869,
as I pace my bedroom,
a woman of thirty-seven "quite used up"
after I "pay all the debts & make every one
as comfortable as I can."

The War Between the States
has silenced every visionary.
In exchange for my modest month of service
at the Union Hotel Hospital,
I will forever battle cramped limbs,
obligatory trembling.

Why must Louisa volunteer? —
I heard from every quarter.
Why? Because the war was just and new;
I lacked the better dresses
required by patriotic teas
and I loathed the mindless miles of bandages.
Besides, I longed to be a soldier!

I bought a crimson rigolette
and had my tooth filled;
I rode the train to Washington alone,
arriving just as the first of forty wagonloads
deposited their "sad freight"
from the defeat at Fredericksburg.

Nurse Louisa, who had never seen a wound.
A wound? She had never seen a man.
A slice of roasted pork still made her blush,
and here, in every corridor and ballroom,
lay the naked, mud-encrusted guests of death.
Layers of blood and filth washed aside,
only to reveal burnt and shredded flesh,
each man's divinity exposed to ridicule.

How quickly I became another patient,
flattened by the twin fevers
of typhus and pneumonia.
At night a Spanish roué in black velvet
perched at my transom cooing, "Lie still, my dear."
I obeyed each ravenous request.
Mornings I caught a glimpse of heaven —
everyone was nobly occupied and dismal.

When I finally awoke at home in Concord,
I had no voice, no hair, no equilibrium.
Heroic doses of calomel had purged
body and soul of war's disease
only to make room for the more sublime
poisoning of mercury.

When, at last, the crippled writing hand
had taught the left to do its work,
I sold my sketches from the hospital
for forty dollars —
enough to pay for Grandma's funeral.

«•»

I complete yet another lap
in my perpetual race
to outwit desperation.
Across the hall lies Mother,
her decline much eased
by my recent earnings from *Little Women.*
Already in its second printing, the fable
of childhood's victory "over selfishness and anger"
travels west on the new transcontinental railroad.

At home, duty's daughter
adheres to mop and poultice,
awaits the summons of her most beloved patient.
Just yesterday Father urged me
to interpret disappointment
as green manure for the spirit.

I can't. I won't.
There must be something more to tell
the village girls who wait outside
to view me like exotic fowl —
Miss Alcott, authoress.
Image of independence. Image of jam
resplendent upon toast.

I slip out through the garden
to avoid my own modest nod,
a begged-for autograph,
the spinster's wholesome aphorism.

« • »

Daughter of airborne principle
wed to an aching workhorse,
I pray I am the last little woman in America.
The profits I enter in my ledger
alleviate the burdens of everyone
except their author.

She swallowed her rebel nerve
and woke up weak and cowardly.
Fever of cleaning up after others.
Fever of miniature passions.

A whole mince pie still means more to me
than any city or philosophy.
The banquets original to the body
and the banquets original to the soul —
these I reserve for fictional heroines,
the women of whom I write
without signing the good name of Alcott.

Doctor, telegraph operator, suffragist:
they satisfy themselves without apology.
In their purses they carry speeches and daggers.
They stop each other in the street
to exchange dreams and addresses.
Imperfections abound, yet they go on talking.
Theirs is the vernacular of tomorrow.
Theirs is the transcendent feast.

Sure Shot

The only way to tell this life
is to squint away the details.
America is huge and all-consuming:
I've got little girls dressed up like me
in fringed skirts and holsters;
I've got kinetographs and headlines,
a name in history — Annie Oakley,
Maid of the Western Plains.

Everything on the periphery is waiting
hungry and cruel — call it wilderness,
call it fancy, call it signs of the times.
The West was dying and we brought it back.
We were legends almost before we began —
Buffalo Bill Cody, Pony Express rider,
and Chief Sitting Bull, who had defeated Custer
after receiving a vision of soldiers
falling upside down from the clouds.

In your own life, you're either a native
or a paying guest. Either way, restlessness
is the only sure way around memory.
Call it attention, call it avoidance,
after dark call it no sleep allowed.

Night after night I tossed new dimes
into the sky to make the sky disappear.
I'd watch the coin grow huge as a dinner plate
before I fired my hole through its center.
People were pleased I got what I aimed for.

They never reckoned I'd crawled inside
the ragged circumference,
splayed my Winchester across the hot ceiling
to guarantee the shot-up silver
came home to the dust.

« • »

At the age of eight, capable and healthy,
I was delivered by my mother
to the County Infirmary,
asylum of the bent and the broken,
the abandoned at birth.

I leave nothing out here.
We rode there together on a wagon, mute as eggs.
She did not say a widowed nurse
could not afford to keep her daughter;
she did not say my younger sisters suffered;
she did not say how far she planned to stretch
the weekly quarter she would be sent
in exchange for my hours
stitching pinafores and drawers.
She said only, "It won't be long,
Phoebe Anne Moses,"
and she would not kiss my lips.

I must have suspected. Why else
would I have packed in my new cloth bag
the single ruby button, the tawny stone
like a half-sad moon,

my sister Mary Jane's dented thimble,
and the hammer I'd stolen from the rifle?
My dead father's muzzle loader:
no one would fire it while I was gone.

« • »

While Mama had been traveling the district
nursing fevers, Mary Jane had taught me
to fire the garden clear of birds.
I was six and in it for the ritual and the noise.
I measured each load more carefully than flour,
welcomed the ache of learning in my shoulder.

Until you're strong, you're stuck
with ground creatures —
dumb squirrel or, if you're quiet, rabbit.
By the time I was seven I was hunting
in the waist-high grass.

You never saw such grass as licked me then,
kept me upright as I tried for quail,
letting my mind go plump and finicky
so I'd know ahead of time whether fear
would pull the birds up east or west.

What you learn from a moving target
is to stay ahead of it, to meet your bird
while it's still rising, just before
it finds the height of its climb.
Soon I was shooting dinner every night.

A year later I was lying in a row of cots
with nothing in my hands but the stolen hammer.
This is how I passed the night:
slowly, carefully, I took the rifle from the shelf
and cleaned the movable parts with oil
that brought my father back into the room.
I measured the load, showing him
the care the task deserved, and then I took him
outside into the grass that hid us
from every future except success.

We stood inside the audience of grass,
never speaking until my quail lit up,
and when I dropped it my father would say, "Fine,"
and I would load the gun again.

« • »

I've seen other children lose and find
themselves in the folds of their mother's skirt,
in the creases of a father's infrequent speech.
In the Darke County Infirmary
I had to ask myself: Against whose living form
will I take shape?

In my rifle I found the great all-returning pleasure
others find in place or family.
Wide-eyed is not for me.
I squint even in my dreams.
No, a made thing is what I chose to love:
butt, comb, trigger, guard, barrel.

« • »

Who came for me, a year later,
was not my mother but a new master,
the County Commissioner, a bank trustee.
He got me for fifty cents a week,
this man obese with socially progressive theories.
I would sleep upstairs beside the family;
I would learn to recite poetry and the presidents.

At nine I was impressed with the flowered wallpaper,
the damask roses indoors and out.
In my room there was the pier-glass mirror
where I first saw my whole body:
compact, quick, eyes as silver
as the air between the leaves of aspen.

Always the rifle of my dreams
stood by me in the mirror,
the well-worn grain easy against my palm,
the polished hammer my only heirloom.
During my hours off, I posed
and shot into the mirror's endless presence.

« • »

The first time I faltered on a sonnet
my master struck me on the mouth.
The second time he threw me off a wagon.
"You asked for that," he screamed
as my knees scraped the ground.
When the words to "She Walks in Beauty"
went muddy in my mouth,
he pressed my hand against a flame.

His son was watching. The next day
I was surrounded by boys
who forced me toward the open pants
of one whose meanness stiffened
like a turkey's neck. The son screamed,
"Lick it or we'll kill you."

My master moved me to the room behind the kitchen.
I found a grayness in the grease-stained walls
that preserved me for another year.
Then one night — I was going on eleven —
the dreamgun in my arms spoke up:
"Run home. It's now or never."

If I tell you I returned to the asylum,
I hope you can forgive me.
Looking forward, the mind
may see only the distant past.
So what if we ate boiled cabbage twice a day?
So what if the children moaned all night?
My treadle made a noise like wind in grass,
the white spools roosted at my side.
The infirmary was where my mother had left me,
where she would come looking when she could.

«·»

For my homecoming my mother chose
my sister Lydia's wedding day.
All I remember is the fit of the hammer
as I pressed it back into the muzzle loader
after all those years.

This is the real beginning, I told myself,
the part where fact meets fancy,
where every question I toss up
will have an angle of flight
I comprehend in plenty of time.

My body had a message of its own.
I was that age where surreptitious contours
make their way upward for all to see,
but I stayed far inside, a miner
obedient to the mineral glow
of priceless discovery.

« • »

On the day my husband and I met
I beat him at a shooting match.
Everyone in Cincinnati except Butler
knew I was a better shot.
For years I'd been sending quail
down to the finest restaurants.
Drawn and gutted, wrapped in swamp grass,
I sold the birds for twenty-five cents a brace.

Do you know how good it feels to win
when you're fifteen and already you've paid off
your mother's mortgage?
I remember my load — three drams powder,
one ounce number eight shot.
I was fifteen when Frank and I were married.
First thing he did was teach me how to read.

That's Butler — I've got nothing bad to say
about the man: way he holds my aces up,
lets me trim the edges without flinching,
way he rubs my shoulders with witch hazel.
No matter where we are, the guns are clean and oiled,
a pot of tea is warming on the spirit lamp.
When the show is over it's always Butler
lets me fold up like a spyglass in his arms.

« • »

The spring of 1885 we started to play with Cody.
He called his Wild West Show "genuine living history"
to irritate the circus men.
Genuine Sioux and Wichita,
genuine buffalo and cowboys.

Already the West was so far gone
Cody felt free to turn it into theater —
the Deadwood Stage, the Oregon Trail,
cattle drives and Indian massacres
staged in front of canvas buttes.

The thing is, people needed the Wild West.
In the big cities and in the skinniest backwaters,
people put their money down
and got what they came for.
They walked out of the show feeling lean and rugged.
They loped home singing a song.
No matter where they lay their heads that night,
they believed they were sleeping under stars.
Maybe a whiff of gunsmoke crossed their pillows.
Maybe they heard ponies nickering in the dark.

« • »

I could play to that audience.
We were telling a story that was already over.
Men who'd been scouts and squatters
in the territories were wearing
made-to-order fringe, arguing
over the trimwork on their saddles.

I whipped up my own disguises in the evening —
roses on my skirt, or buckskin knickers —
and Butler ironed them in the morning.
I ran through my routines 'til they were flawless,
imported smokeless powder from London,
and bought a gun chest big enough to carry
the Damascus and the Stevens,
a gold-plated Winchester,
the pearl-handled Smith and Wesson
I'd used to shoot the cigarette
from the mouth of the Crown Prince of Germany.

What else did I shoot? Flame from a candle,
apple from the head of a miniature poodle,
.22 through a spread of aces.
Why did I do it? I tell you,
to narrow my gaze over the plain open sight,
to spot what I was looking for
where I knew I would find it,
to bring it down like I do so well.

« • »

Sitting Bull came to the Wild West
straight out of prison,
villain of Little Big Horn.
First night he opened with us in Buffalo,
the crowd booed him and called him a bastard.
What they'd come for was make-believe,
not the medicine man of the Hunkpapa Sioux,
genuine braids, genuine pockmarks.

The Chief and I went riding every morning.
Just watching him taught me
how the parts of the horse come together
in a good rider's hands.
I learned to wear cream-colored doeskin,
to make a bonnet of white eagle plumes.
He adopted me and gave me the name
Little Sure Shot.
Listening to him inside his smoky tepee,
I believed in the country of our kinship.

By the winter of 1890,
the Chief had returned to his restless people
and the Wild West Show was quartered in Alsace.
All through Europe we'd been hearing about the Ghost
    Dances
stirring up hope among the Sioux and Paiute.
Maybe the dances would bring back the buffalo.
Maybe the plains would be given back
to the original hunters.
Maybe the fighting wasn't over.
This was the old-style talk that fired up Sitting Bull.

Of course the government grew nervous.
Their soldiers surrounded Pine Ridge and Rosebud,
ordered the arrest of Sitting Bull.
I learned all this in a letter from Cody —
a huckster, you might say, but he spoke the Chief's language;
he'd left us in Europe and wangled himself orders
to visit Sitting Bull's reservation.

He was there when the Chief walked out of his cabin
to saddle up the sure-footed gray
I'd seen him on every morning.
He was watching when the two Indian police,
Shave Head and Red Tomahawk,
shot the Chief before he'd fastened his bridle.

The minute Sitting Bull fell down, Cody wrote,
the horse kneeled like his master had taught him.
Kneeled and bowed and pawed the hard ground,
cued by the sound of the rifles.
You can fire at a thousand glass balls
and hit every one and still there will be a pain
that flies straight for the opening in your heart.

« • »

I began to ask myself,
What if there'd been no Wild West?
Where would I have gone with my shooting?
My whole act consisted of picking things out
of the sky. You don't so much sight them
as swing with them;
when it feels right
you pull and go on to the next.

Things I knew nothing about
were flowers coming up in the same bed
year after year, washing hung fresh on the line,
the comfort of a butcher who knows you by name.

Butler found us a house on a river,
but the whole thing was cursed from the start.
When the chimney wouldn't draw,
we took turns firing up the flue.
When the corn seed was planted,
the crows dropped in by the dozen.
We had a few good afternoons owning a house,
Butler and I, when we filled all the cornfields
with fresh-shot crow, but in the meantime
we'd let the watering go
and we lost the whole crop anyhow.

« • »

I'd rather do anything than live in a house.
When night came to me in a house of my own,
the shaky window I looked out of
showed me nothing but the night's heavy back
backing into me. No thanks.
In boarding houses, people are proud
of staying up all night,
proud to be peeling an orange
when you knock on their door close to dawn.

« • »

Hard as you look, you can't tell
where the new light will come from.
It's out there somewhere in the audience
like a pair of bright eyes among leaves.

I was thirty-six before my mother saw me perform.
In Picqua, Ohio, not far from my birthplace.
For nearly twenty years I'd been telling myself
she'd missed the show because she was Quaker
and the Wild West was show business.
No mention of her coming,
not so much as a wave when I spotted her
during the opening parade.

She sat through the whole performance
in that black Sunday dress,
lips dry as chalk, never a hint
of excitement or regret.
Afterward she came to my tent,
called me the name I had run from, Phoebe Anne,
saying it crisp enough to leave wrinkles.

"What do you think?" I asked,
knowing from the start it was wrong.
I can still see her spindly fingers
cautious on the flap of the tent
as if it were satin from Paris.

I look at her wondering who I am.
She looks at me wondering where I came from.
Why is there never someone who enters
at these moments to answer our questions?
I am sorry the West needed a child.
I am sorry the child needed a West.

She stood there forever without speaking.
A different daughter would have offered
camomile tea. In my own heart,
there was nothing but prairie and sagebrush
and a silhouette of myself poised to fire,
taller than anything in sight.

When at last she spoke,
she said, “Mighty fine tent.” That was it.
I knew what she meant, what she saw
in the canvas opaque as fine paper.
I knew how hard she was working
to narrow her glance.

« • »

Where are we tonight? The Imperial,
or the Royal, or the velvet-fringed stateroom
of the train racing from Charlotte to Danbury.
We have entered a new century:
a Rough Rider is president,
Cody has added Prussians to the show.
Cowboys and Indians don't sell
like they used to.

One stunt I'll never give up
is shooting behind my back with a mirror.
I can't tell you the pleasure it brings.
I use a hand mirror no larger
than the eye of a bull.
Trimmed in silver, it narrows down the choices
without preaching or applause.

With one hand I rest my rifle on my shoulder;
with the other I hold up the mirror
until it brings me the candles
set out on an old wagon wheel.

In my life — call it skill,
call it necessity — I have tried
to be as certain as that mirror.
One by one, the flames enter the glass
and I stop them.
I know where the next one will come from.
I have never missed yet.

Notes

Birdwoman

In October of 1803, the Emperor Napoleon sold the vast Louisiana Territory to the United States. Six months later the Voyage of Discovery, commissioned by President Thomas Jefferson, was under way. Its leaders, Meriwether Lewis and William Clark, then thirty and thirty-four years old respectively, were directed to search for the fastest and safest river route across the North American continent, the long-dreamed-of Northwest Passage to China.

In November of 1804, Lewis and Clark and their company, known as the Corps of Discovery, arrived at the Mandan Indian villages along the northern Missouri River in present-day North Dakota. There they met Toussaint Charbonneau, a French-Canadian who served as an interpreter for the local fur traders and Indians. One of Charbonneau's two wives was Sacagawea, a Shoshone girl of about fifteen who was at the time six months pregnant. Lewis and Clark knew they would need Shoshone horses to carry the expedition's baggage over the Rocky Mountains: the Shoshone were famous horsemen, and they were also the Indians living closest to the mountains. In part, at least, because Sacagawea was the only Shoshone-speaking person they had come across, Lewis and Clark hired her husband for the expedition, specifying that Charbonneau bring Sacagawea along with him. On February 11, 1805, Sacagawea gave birth to a son, Jean Baptiste; and on the following April 7, she, Charbonneau, and the baby set off with the Corps of Discovery.

The explorers left Fort Mandan in two pirogues and six small canoes. At the Rockies they abandoned their boats and traveled by horseback. Once the group had crossed the Bitterroot Mountains, near the border of what are now the states of Montana and Idaho, the horses were left in the care of a friendly band of Nez Percé Indians, and the company proceeded down the Snake and Columbia rivers in dugout canoes carved from large pine trees. By November they had reached the west coast.

Sacagawea, carrying her baby on her back, traveled with the Lewis and Clark expedition from April 7, 1805, until August 14, 1806, accompanying them all the way to the Pacific and back again to the Mandan villages.

Glossary

cache · from the French *cacher,* to hide; a hole dug out of the ground and used for storing or hiding provisions; anything hidden in such a place

camas · a small, sweet onion-like plant of the lily family that was an important food among many western tribes

cradleboard · a wooden frame carried on the mother's back and fitted with a laced-up animal skin in which the infant is securely bound

engagés · the French-Canadian watermen, boatmen, fur traders, and interpreters hired by Lewis and Clark

parfleche · a container for carrying things, typically made out of buffalo skin cut into a pattern and folded over, laced, and decorated

pemmican · a mixture of dried meat and berries mixed with fat and pounded into cakes for long-keeping

pirogue · a wooden boat forty to fifty feet long, twelve feet wide, pointed at the prow, square-sterned, which could be pulled, poled, rowed, or sailed

spirit level · a leveling instrument consisting of a sealed glass tube filled with alcohol that contains an air bubble which, when the tube lies exactly horizontal, lies in the center of the tube

tippet · a long, narrow strip of cloth or skin used as an ornamental collar. Cameahwait gave one to Lewis that was made from over one hundred rolls of white weasel, each about the size of a large quill, attached to a strip of dressed otter skin that hung down almost to the waist.

Fruitlands

Fruitlands is the name given by Bronson Alcott to the small farm in Harvard, Massachusetts, where he and his family moved in 1843. Louisa was then a girl of ten. Bronson and his English colleague Charles Lane hoped to found a utopian commune based on hoe cultivation, vegetarianism, the ideals of transcendentalism, and abstinence. The Alcotts moved to Fruitlands in June and stayed there through the following winter.

In the poem, Louisa May Alcott speaks from the vantage point of middle age. The year is 1869. *Little Women,* published the year before, is already in its second printing, making its author well known and financially secure for the first time in her life. (Its success so embittered Nathaniel Hawthorne that he predicted Louisa May Alcott would be just the first of many "female scribblers.") At thirty-seven, Alcott spends much of her time living at her parents' home in Concord so she can care for them and manage their affairs. Several times a year she moves back into Boston, where she takes a room in a boarding house and does most of her writing.

At the same time that Alcott was being hailed as a "genteel authoress," she was also selling — under various pseudonyms — lurid and sensational tales to a number of popular magazines. While *Little Women* was, for Alcott, sheer drudgery, these "earthquaky" stories of passionate abandon and violent revenge brought her no end of joy. In recent years, many of Alcott's pseudonymous stories have been discovered and reissued under her own name.

Sure Shot

Annie Oakley was born Phoebe Anne Moses on August 13, 1860, in the township of North Star outside of Greenville in Darke County, Ohio. Her father, Jacob Moses, died when she was five years old; her mother, Susan Wise Moses, struggled to support her seven children as a traveling nurse. *The Secret Life of Annie Oakley,* by Marcy Heidish, gives a good fictionalized account of Annie's childhood.

By her early teens, Oakley was working as a market hunter. At fifteen she and Frank Butler, another sharpshooter, were married. They toured the vaudeville circuits and traveled with various circuses until 1885, when they joined Buffalo Bill Cody's Wild West Show, where they remained for seventeen years.

Annie Oakley was a petite woman — five feet one inch tall and weighing about one hundred pounds. As "Sure Shot" opens, Oakley is forty-one years old. The year is 1901. She has been shooting for twenty-five years and is about to retire from the Wild West Show.